THE PRIMROSE THAT POISONED IVY

A Warren Vampires Novel

Daisy V. Eden

Copyright © 2024 Daisy V. Eden

All rights reserved

The characters and events portrayed in this book are fictitious. Any similarity to real persons, living or dead, is coincidental and not intended by the author.

No part of this book may be reproduced, or stored in a retrieval system, or transmitted in any form or by any means, electronic, mechanical, photocopying, recording, or otherwise, without express written permission of the author.

Cover design by: @jmccourt_art

To Charlie and Loz who read this first.

IMPORTANT NOTE

This novel may contain themes that some may find triggering. Please be mindful and consider before reading if these may trigger you: violence, gore and blood, profanity, mentions of rape and sexual abuse, mentions of dub/non con, explicit sex, kidnapping, mention of suicide, and death.

THE PRIMROSE
THAT POISONED
IVY

CHAPTER 1

The First Final Mistake

Angus

Angus had killed Isabella.

At least, that's what he thought she was called – he could hardly ever remember the name of his donors. In fact, he found it hard to remember many of the people in his life, especially those with little personality and eyes that had lost the blush and novelty of humanity. Not that she could have helped that. She had been *compelled* to have such traits after all, and Angus knew that his eyes held no such tarnish of human quality either, and that in the respect of lacking humanity, he and Isabella were more or less equals.

However, in the place in which they resided (or in her case, used to reside), they were not equals at all. Not really. Donors were never, ever, equal to clan members. They weren't equal in their lack of humanity, because donors were, after all, human – which was more than Angus could say for himself and his clan – and they were not equal in their evolutionary or predatory status either. In fact, Angus didn't think it right to compare them at all. It seemed unjust, and made poor Isabella seem rather pathetic.

Angus bent down next to the girl. She was young, with fair hair and skin pale. This was usually the general appearance of his donors, although her skin was paler now, taking on a pallor which was only ever possible in the dead, and perhaps the undead. Although it should have pained him to watch such a pretty thing lose life, his heartstrings, if he even had such things, didn't twinge for her at all.

I really shouldn't have bit her so hard.

That was his first thought, which led to another he had had many times before – that it might be better if donors weren't compelled to not feel pain, or anything unpleasant. Maybe it could have been avoided – the wasteful loss of blood – if only they could scream when you bit them too hard. This, although it seemed to be, wasn't a thought fabricated as a result of guilt for killing the young Isabella – Angus and his vampirism were not accustomed to such a feeling of guilt. The idea was merely for his own personal convenience as applying for a new donor was a most time consuming and annoying task which he did not wish to spend any more of his eternal lifetime fussing over.

Not only a selfish idea it was, but also an unrealistic one. Having uncompelled donors within the clan would, in the eyes of his father, be considered too much of a liability. If his father ever gave the final announcement to pass the law, the other members within the Warren would think it naïve, question the sanity of his father's leadership, and order a new clan leader to be appointed immediately. Angus knew he couldn't take away his father's rule over a bit of spilt blood, and this is why no mention of terminating compulsion over donors had ever escaped his lips at clan council meetings, or any other time for that matter.

But he also knew that if his father did allow it, even just for his own son, Angus wouldn't have killed five donors in the last twelve months. Now six.

He picked up the slight girl off the tiled floor like he had done with the five before that, and began to walk out of his room towards *the collection* which was located in the basement. Slight she may have been, but since she was now very much dead (again, how inconvenient), her body was heavier than it had been, her muscles no longer contracting to aid her posture. The prime example of dead weight, he thought.

He kept her body outstretched to prevent any blood touching his newly washed shirt. A trip to *the washers* would only prove to be another annoying inconvenience.

The collection was where any clan members went when they either needed a new donor or needed disposing of an old one. Angus had become, much to his intense aversion, a very frequent visitor to this part of the Warren. He shuddered to think what people must have thought of him. He never did like being in people's minds, and especially not negatively.

A donor was kept until their death, which was usually a ripe old age, or at least old for a human. The Warren was full of medical advances and had access to some of the most innovative and successful treatments available which meant that the humans received the highest level of care possible. Despite this, Angus's donors had not had the same longevity as some of their peers.

He took the stairs rapidly, his feet barely touching the plush red velvet carpet as he breezed past the polished brass hand rails before being confronted with large steel electric doors. They opened on his approach, allowing him to walk fluidly through them without slowing his pace. It was a room the size of a small warehouse that had no windows and was thus brightly illuminated by long, fluorescent lamps. Metal tables were sporadically placed around this room and double doors to the right hid *the pamper*, a space used to prepare new donors before they were introduced to their master or mistress. Overall, *the collection* wasn't pleasing to his senses. The lighting was too harsh for his hyper-sensitive eyes, bouncing chaotically off the shiny metal tables, and the smell was too sweet, like it was masking something unsavoury.

He walked into the centre of the main warehouse room,

towards a man with wiry, brown shoulder length hair tinged with silver and a beard of the same shade. His brows were thick and placed upon a sturdy, broad forehead. His translucent skin was flawlessly complexed and his eyes just a little too bright to be human.

"Angus, laddie? Is that you?" John asked. His question was colloquial and friendly, acceptable since he was in close relation to Angus's father, and yet it also held a slightly worried tone as it reached its end. This, Angus soon realised, was an unconscious response to the small donor in his arms.

"Jesus. That's, what, the fifth lass in a year, in't it? You on some sort of killing spree…? Becoming a ripper? Never used to be this bad you didn't." John wiped his palms on his upper thighs. It was a very human thing to do, often associated with sweaty palms, and since Angus knew that to be impossible in John's case, he came to the conclusion that the action was done out of nervousness.

"Sixth." Angus replied, in a Scottish accent which was softer, and less broad than John's, but which had more of a sharp annoyance in its tone. Angus didn't like to be shunned, even if it was by John. He placed the girl onto the steel table that was on his left. He lay her back against the hard surface and left her there for one of the other *collectors* to deal with. He didn't know exactly why he was getting so careless with his donors, but he knew that it was something he needed to change fast if he wanted to keep his reputation and respect. No one respected a ripper in the Warren. This wasn't like the highlands.

"I have no doubt that you will be able to find a replacement for me John, since you have not failed to do so before," he continued.

"Are you aff yer heid? I don't think I have good enough *gatherers* to find you another AB in this area, and I don't think I have ever been able to give you an AB negative if I remember correctly, which I know from your records is your chosen preference. Buggers are just too hard to find 'round here with how picky you are. I canny do it for yer Angus, laddie. Sorry."

Angus was perfectly aware about how constrained his donor description was. In the Warren, clan members were encouraged to write such a document in order to ensure they got the most out of their donor. This involved setting out guidelines about preferences that one seeks in such a being, such as sex, appearance, and of course, blood type. Angus had come to the conclusion that he preferred the taste of AB the best, or to be more specific, AB negative, which just happened to be the rarest of blood groups in the country. This, on top of his specific appearance, age, height and haematocrit preferences, made him one of the most disliked 'customers' at *the collection*. The discovery of blood types in the 1900s had made this process a little bit easier for the clan. Before, it was simply distinguished by varying aromas in the population which his kind gave their own names and markers – Angus believed that blood types would have been much more readily discovered if vampires had been involved. In fact, this could have been said about lots of advances in science, simply because of their heightened senses and thought processing.

Because yes, Angus and his fellow clan members were vampires. It was all very uninspired, really.

Angus mulled over his preferences for a few more moments. They had been written over fifty years ago, and although his preferences hadn't changed, his restraint definitely had. He willingly put this down to boredom. The Warren removed any excitement that his eternal life could give him: the hunt, the feed, the animalism.

It wasn't always like this. The Warren hadn't always existed, and Angus had certainly not always lived in the Warren. Six decades ago, Angus had roamed freely in Scotland, unrestrained by the vampire society he begrudgingly endured today. He was able to hunt, and allow his innate instincts to engulf him entirely in pleasure.

Feeding off a human wasn't just about the need for sustenance. Of course, when a vampire hadn't fed for long periods, this was the only need which required sating. However, when you simply 'could feed' rather than 'must feed', things could become more fun. You could seduce a human – a human who wasn't brainwashed to enjoy anything that they experienced. You could listen to their moans while feasting on their throat, drawing it out like a tantric experience.

You could have sex with your donor in the Warren. In fact, it was encouraged – hence why the preferences were not only inclusive of blood type. But the thing was, you could never *seduce* anyone in the Warren – because you can't seduce someone who doesn't have their own mind. It just simply isn't as enjoyable.

This is what Angus hated. And he hadn't had sex with his donors for years because of it. Now, that didn't mean that he hadn't been able to seek any form of sexual pleasure. The Warren wasn't just full of compliant little humans. There were hundreds of vampires too, some incredibly appealing to him, and he was more than aware that he had a degree of sway with females, and even some males too, if he ever decided to go that way. This was of course related to his physical appearance, but also his status. Being the Prince of the Warren did have some perks, even if they were less abundant than the downfalls.

He thought of a particular blonde that he was more than familiar with, and he felt his canines lengthen slightly. He would have to reach out to her, get his pleasure in the only way he knew how.

Because he was aware, now looking at the dead girl in front of him, that he was desperately, desperately bored.

At that moment, he brought himself out of his reverie and responded curtly to John. "Maybe you shouldn't be looking in this area anymore then," he said, running his index finger in small circles on the surface of the steel table next to him.

It was a risky suggestion. What Angus was asking of the *collector* was unheard of. There wasn't a single Southron who resided among them, and his father had an embedded hatred for them – a hatred which spanned over four centuries. If he agreed, Angus would assume that it was because he knew his son had been less than gentle with his recent donors and was therefore hoping he would give the Southron donor a gruesome death.

His father always had an ulterior motive. Everything had to benefit him.

John's brow furrowed deeply, highlighting the slight wrinkles in his translucent skin. He had the facial exterior of a man of around forty-five, but only an exterior it was, as it was a mere disguise for the 200-year-old vampire within it. "What? You mean look outside of Scotland? Get a Southron? Yer father wouldnae allow such a thing! I'd be fired! Oot of here before ye could say AB negative!"

"My father respects you, John. Is it not true that he believes you to be one of the greatest *collectors* we have ever had? He has said it countless times in leader meetings, I'm sure." Angus was also sure that after such flattery, if it had been possible, John would have blushed. He, as Angus well knew, was an admirer of compliments.

John was a loyal man, and one that Angus genuinely respected, which was a rarity in the Warren. He had known him from the second he had arrived all those years ago, being that John had been the person to introduce him to his first donor. However, Angus admitted to himself that he was not above manipulating the vampire in front of him to get what he wanted, no matter how much that respect seemed to stretch.

"Well, aye, you aren't the first to have mentioned it, and I do pride myself on that reputation." John began, unable to hide his pleasure. "But as I said Angus, I canny do it. And I certainly won't do it unless I have yer father's permission."

"Will you agree on the terms if I do get the permission you so greatly desire, *Collector*?" Angus said, the charm held within his previous compliments lost and replaced by patronisation. John took his time, considering such a proposition. He hadn't noticed the change in Angus's tone, and Angus was silently grateful, not wanting to come across as he knew he was.

"I canny imagine he would ever agree, but okay, Laddie. If you can get permission of your old man, I could give your crazy idea a go."

Angus had his father's permission within an hour, on the terms that the girl was taken from an area far from the Scottish border to prevent there being any association with The Warren. Angus didn't ponder on the lack of resistance from the king and instead he allowed himself to revel in the fact that John had organised some of his most skilled *gatherers* to make their way to the south of England later that day.

Gatherers were trained in the role of selecting donors from the outside world based on a clan members donor description. Just like any vampire, their senses were extremely attuned, but with extra training in olfaction, they were the perfect members of the Warren to seek out certain blood groups and such for members in the clan.

They had been given his strict donor description, which was not greeted with as much optimism as Angus would have liked, and were then sent on their way.

"And what is it that I will do, Laddie, if you kill this one too?" John asked as he watched his *gatherers* disappear out of the restrictions of the Warren.

"I do not know, John. I do not know," replied Angus. And he really didn't.

CHAPTER 2

Here Lies Beauty

Ivy

I finally walked on to my street. It had been a long day of shopping for household items, and I trudged up the steps to my apartment building door and unlocked it before ascending the stairs to my flat. The building was old and there was no lift. Some days I was thankful for the workout – nothing wrong with a little glute loving – but today the three flights felt like a really mean chore, and I was seriously wondering why I had chosen this place to start over.

After a failed relationship – one that I was happy to be out of I might add – I decided to haul up all my things and find a new city and a new life. This meant leaving my lab job and my long-term home in the north west and moving to the south east of England. I'd picked it because it was meant to be statistically sunnier and less wet than the rest of the country, but today the air was damp, making my hair feel like it sat just a little too far out of my head to be considered styled.

The break-up had also been pretty quick. I hadn't had the time to find myself a new job, so this month's rent was coming out of savings. I hoped it was the only month I would have to do it as I'd had some replies from companies I had sent my CV to and it looked like I had more than a couple of interviews on the cards.

I unlocked the door, transferring all my bags into one hand, the handles digging into my fingers like a torture device. The flat itself was small but bright. This was key for me – I was obsessed with natural light, even if it was the most unforgiving type of light to look at yourself in the mirror. Why did it have to make your pores appear so much bigger and why did it highlight every slightly stray eyebrow hair like a pariah?

Stepping inside, I dumped my bags on the floor and walked to the sofa where I slumped dramatically into a heap. It was Friday, but I didn't have that 'Friday Feeling' – in part because I was lacking in the job department, so it could have been any day of the week for me, but mostly it was because I had no friends in the area and wasn't one of those ballsy people who could just enter a pub and make friends.

Ahh, the trials of being an introverted extrovert.

I sent my mum a quick text to let her know the move went okay and I was settling in just fine. Me and my mother didn't do that thing. You know... the thing... where people... talk? We were more the *text-when-something's-wrong* type, or *check-in-to-make-sure-you're-not-dead* type. Unless it wasn't clear already, we weren't close. And since my dad lived in Australia with his new, younger version of my mum, I was lucky to get so much as a 'Happy Birthday' from him.

My sister was someone I had a lot of time for, however. When I looked at the people who made us, I really did wonder how she turned out to be such a good person. She was charitable, kind, selfless and beautiful. She was arty but mathematical – all things I was not. I liked to think I had values and morals, and that when push came to shove, I was inherently a good person. But my sister didn't need a push or a shove to be good, she just was. And best of all, I knew she had as much time for me as I did for her, because although I may not be quite as perfect, she knew I was one of the good ones.

She'd already messaged me and called me multiple times (she was a big fan of voice notes which exceeded five minutes – I was pretty sure everyone had someone like that in their life), asking for pictures of the place and giving me decoration tips. Currently the decoration consisted of a painting she had given me as a moving away present, and it had pride of place in the living area where people could see it. That was if I ever made a friend to bring over.

My friends were a little let down by me after I had gotten my boyfriend and decided that because he didn't pay them any attention, I wouldn't either.

Okay, maybe they were a *lot* let down by me.

Now I was single again, I couldn't quite bring myself to reach out to them. I was going to, *really,* I was. Just not quite yet.

Sometimes my inability to make friends scared me. I had been told I had a 'resting bitch face'. Now, I didn't exactly agree with that term. Why were women always meant to smile? Why were we always meant to be pleased and facially emotive in every situation? Was it such a crime to simply *be* without smiling? Saying someone had a resting bitch face was basically telling someone you didn't like their face in neutral, which was just absurd.

So, all in all, I was a friend-less, practically parentless twenty-four-year-old staying in on a Friday night in a new city with only my sister's painting for company.

I made myself some dinner, but after around an hour and a half of sitting by myself in silence (I still hadn't managed to sort out my TV or Wi-Fi), I decided I was quite fed up.

"Well, this just won't do," I said as I rose from the sofa and sighed dramatically. I decided that a run would do just the trick.

As a kid or a teenager, whenever I was feeling low or sad, my mum would always tell me about how I should go out and do some exercise because I needed the 'endorphins'. She may not have been the most reliable or comforting motherly figure, but that was one thing that I would always remember, and one thing I would agree with. In my eyes, endorphins were the true legal high. Speak to any person who runs for fun. They know what I mean.

I picked up my phone (no messages, obviously), clicked on the map app to explore the surrounding area, and noticed a park not too far from the apartment. To run it would be a nice 5k, so I dressed in running gear and headed out.

"Fuck. Bloody fuck," I swore as I clung to my twisted ankle on a back path in Clays Park. It felt mildly satisfying to swear as searing pain jabbed up my calf, and I couldn't help but feel it would do me better to keep swearing until the pain stopped rather than keep my mouth shut.

Turned out that I had managed to get a little lost on my run, and the 5k had ended up being closer to a 10k, which meant it was later than I would have liked. I had been running (foolishly) on the unlit paths deep within the park, and it had been on this unlit path that a large tree branch lay inconspicuously onto the concrete, making the girl running in the dark a very easy target.

I tried to put my weight onto my other foot and push my fatigued body off the floor with my hands. With little avail, I gave up, beginning to assess the situation. This was really bad. My ankle had already swollen to the size of a tennis ball, and I had no phone, no way of calling for help, and no way of running. My heart began to beat hard, harder than it had done when I'd been running, and I could feel the carotid artery on the side of my neck pulse vigorously with each plundering contraction, trying to get as much oxygen to my brain as possible so that it could think harder and come up with some sort of solution.

Clays Park was a perfectly safe park. In the day.

Fuck.

It was then that I heard it. It wasn't particularly

noticeable, and I doubt that I would have heard it if my senses hadn't had been heightened by the adrenaline coursing through my veins. But I *could* hear it, and it was close. It sounded like an animal, sniffing out its prey. And yet the sniffs were not short and brusque like that of an animal in haste – like an animal which feared a missed opportunity. No. These were long, deep inhales of a predator that already knew it had won, and was simply enjoying the stalk.

"Hello?" I called to the dark, hoping that my voice would startle the animal and send it in another direction. I watched as my breath turned into wispy clouds in front of my face and hoped that it would not be the last breaths I ever took.

I was being cradled in someone's arms. It was not a warm embrace, but a cold, iron-tight grip similar to what I could only imagine to be a metal claw. We weren't still either, but moving at impossible speeds through some baron land blurred with shades of lilac.

What an odd thing to be doing once you die. Surely death would involve something more pleasant, like an endless nap.

I couldn't remember exactly what had happened after I had heard the noises, but whatever it was had knocked me out cold because there was no way in hell I would have voluntarily allowed someone to carry me in this way.

In another world, it could have been deemed romantic, like a groom carrying his new bride over a threshold. That is, if the bride was semi-conscious.

And the groom was running at full pelt.

So not romantic at all, really.

I attempted to concentrate more attentively. My body ached, like I had been dumped into open water with battering rapids or had spent the last few hours as a human punching bag. If it weren't for the strong arms around me, my head would have been lolling backward, my neck unable to hold its weight. However, despite their necessity, I couldn't say I particularly appreciated their support. The arms were cold and hard, lacking the give that one's arms usually have when another was being held by them.

I felt the fresh air on my cheeks. It wasn't southern air. It was crisper, not smothered in pollution and humidity. It was soothing, washing like waves over my humming skin, but cold. And I *was* cold. So *very, very cold.*

The wind lashed. It wasn't a still breeze like those in southern England, but more of a brusque gust associated with the coast, or the high north.

And that's when it all clicked. I wasn't dead. I was in Scotland.

Years ago, when my Mum and Dad actually spoke to each other, my family would drive up to Scotland for two weeks each summer. Looking back on those days, they held a certain charm. The heather on the hills and the lack of mobile signal promised peacefulness and the loss of worries from one's bustling life. But at the time, with my Mum complaining about the cold (despite it being midsummer), and my sister complaining about her inability to stay in constant contact with her needy, good-for-nothing boyfriend, it didn't seem to live up to those expectations.

It was these memories which seemed to flood back to me in my semi-conscious state. I remembered the cold air. I remembered the lilac shades of heather. I remembered the wind as it whipped my long, dark hair around my small head like ribbons tied to a fan. I remembered Scotland.

We descended into an open plane of land located in between two large hills. My mind hummed as it slowly began to regain some of its precious consciousness, allowing me little by little to take my surroundings into a deeper focus. This was limited, however, by the inhuman rapid speed at which we were travelling. It was like being in a car, except lacking the comfort and absence of wind.

Wild heather, which was so commonly associated with the beautiful land in the North, covered the land. It was much more densely distributed on the slopes of the two hills before thinning as it merged into the flatter ground. In the flat, the heather lay alongside thick brushes of green shrubbery and grass. As we approached it, I narrowed in on its contents. I was able to pick out spear thistle – a plant with a similar colouring to heather and one that could easily be mistaken as such. As a general area of land, it was overgrown, the tallest of the vegetation able to reach close to the knees of the individual who held me so coldly. It was clear that we were in an area which was little travelled and little noticed, which was not good for me. Not at all.

We began to approach a shrubbery with what appeared to be purposeful direction, each member of my kidnapping shifting their direction directly towards it with speed and finite agility. I noted that all their movements could be likened to that of a panther. However, I also noted that they moved with a grace that not even a feline predator could emulate. Again, not good for me.

It appeared that the specific shrubbery that the individuals approached (there were four of them, including my very own iron vice), was an opening to another place, and in a flash we were inside a relatively dark corridor with an iron door at its end. The door opened on our approach, and I was carried into a large room with metal tables. It was clean and sterile, and the air held a smell that burned the inside of my nose as I inhaled. *Bleach?*

I was placed on the cool, smooth surface of one of the tables, back flat and legs out, staring up at the rows and rows of clinical strip lighting. I tried to focus on anything but the negatives, siphoning my thoughts to the feeling of all the surfaces of my body which touched the table, and those which didn't – the backs of my ankles and knees, my lower back and back of my neck. But no matter what I did, my feet just wouldn't drop out the way they should have done when lying down and relaxed – it was as if my hip muscles were clinging on to dear life, refusing to give in. It may have also been because my ankle was throbbing from the likely sprain or break that I had endured in the park.

My fists clenched. My only means at resistance.

I turned my head, taking in the large room, trying to distract my escalating thoughts. I had a habit of overthinking everything, and this was certainly no exception to that very inconvenient rule.

As I observed the other tables, I noticed other people were lying on them also. They were all stock still.

Suddenly, someone was fussing around my arms and hands, tapping here and there. I felt a sharp pinch in my right hand and winced.

What was that?

But I didn't get a chance to think much more about it, because the strip lighting became black, and my mind became nothing.

When I became conscious once again, I felt heavier – mentally, physically – although I couldn't pinpoint why. My body was sending signals about something, but when they reached my brain, they had nothing to connect to, the messages becoming confused, the union between the two broken, like wires cut clean.

I squeezed my eyes shut, irritated by the light above me. It was like I was hungover. Perhaps I was, or hallucinating.

Please, please be that.

I moved my sprained right ankle in curiosity. It seemed better, but restricted. Perhaps it had been bandaged up. I didn't have the energy to look. This wasn't the time to check if I could do a crunch.

Something firm slid underneath my back, lifting me up off the firm metal table. The same man from before began to carry me towards a smaller door which looked considerably narrower than the first. I was placed onto a chair covered in clean, black leather. It faced a plain mirror about the size of an A2 page. It was polished to perfection which only seemed to highlight my *imperfections* – sullen eyes from tiredness, blotchy skin from the elements of the highlands, and hair windswept like nothing I had ever seen.

My escort swivelled the leather chair toward him and leant his hands onto the arm rests. He towered over my slight body with ease.

He was blonde. It was a rather dull blonde however, with oil that slicked it back from his forehead further dampening any suspect of golden tones. A straight, pointed nose was in the centre of a large, angular face with deep set brown eyes the shade of maple syrup and lips thin and wry over unusually white, gleaming teeth. He was also pale, almost cyanotic.

His features, harsh and distinct, induced a fear in me that I had been suppressing. I suddenly felt the delayed response of my heart to the adrenaline in my blood.

His lips twitched ever so slightly, so little an expression that if we hadn't been so close, I would never have noticed. I was clearly missing a private joke or was simply a very amusing character. Either way, the response annoyed me. I hated being mocked, and being mocked by my kidnapper sure seemed to light an ever-increasing flame in my gut.

Don't laugh at me, arsehole.

I was smart enough to realise that this was not the time to voice my displeasure, so I remained tight lipped, clutching my hands together in my lap with a force I could only hope would diffuse some of the anger. While I did this, Mr Oily Blonde leaned closer to me, maple eyes locked purposefully onto my black ones. I flinched ever so slightly from the proximity.

"You do not know how you got here," he began, in a Scottish accent.

So I was right, then.

He spoke softly as if he were speaking to a frightened child, but with an intensity I could not explain. "You do not remember the incident in the park, or the trip to the Warren. It's all very blurry. You are content to be here. You are *so* content that you won't ever consider trying to escape. This is your home now." And with that he left without a goodbye, leaving me stranded in the white room alone in the leather chair, unable to voice my objection.

I had a feeling that whoever the blonde man was, he

had an unrealistic perception of his persuasive ability. The sterile confinements of the room had not felt like home at all. My home had windows and plants, and the walls were painted with colour, unlike the pigment-less wall ahead of me. Also, within two seconds of him leaving, I had already briefly devised one escape plan, if not two. However, my thoughts were interrupted by another male walking through into the room of mirrors causing my measly plans to be lost as quickly as I had conjured them up.

This man was older than the blonde, maybe in his forties rather than twenties. He had a thick beard which covered the chalky pallor of his jaw.

As the bearded man entered, he did so with a grace that didn't at all match his external person. It looked like it was fit for labour rather than the royal ballet. Odd. I wondered if he also held unusual speed like the others I had met. And then came my first conspiracy theory – perhaps my captors were all on a new drug and I was their next guinea pig. That would certainly fit in with the clinical decoration of the rooms.

I sat patiently, unwilling to say anything, fearing that it would compromise my safety. I had come to the conclusion that if I appeared compliant like the blonde man expected me to be, they (whoever they were), would drop their guard enough to allow me the degree of slack I required to escape.

The bearded man began to pull out various scissors, brushes and combs from a side cabinet next to my mirror. A brief and unwelcome image of Sweeney Todd skittered though my mind and I felt my stomach flip and my mouth dry immediately.

He brought his hands up to the nape of my neck and gathered my long hair gently in his cool grasp before pulling it behind me so that it all flowed down the chair back. Such a delicate motion that it could almost be interpreted as affectionate, but I wasn't naive enough to believe that to be the case.

He then began to gently run a paddle brush through my hair, making quick work of the tangles as he did so, without summoning any real pain. This man was a hair marvel, even if he was liaising with kidnappers. It seemed that talent was always wasted on people who didn't deserve it. Similar to when boys had really long eyelashes.

I found myself staring at the man, eyeing him in the mirror. I noticed that with every stroke the brush took through my hair, my anxiety ebbed just a little bit further away from me. I shut my eyes, revelling in the feeling.

When there no longer seemed to be anything touching my hair, my eyes flung open. The reflection of the mirror showed that it had been tended elegantly with a curling wand to create flowing waves around me. I looked perfectly put together, like a machine-made toy. All that was missing was the cardboard box and plastic front.

This wasn't how I was used to looking. I wasn't one for spending much time on my day-to-day appearance. You'd be lucky to see me drag a brush through my hair before it was placed in a low bun at the nape of my neck, and nothing could beat minimal makeup – mascara and blusher could go a long way. At least that's what I liked to tell myself. But when I looked straight ahead, makeup had been applied to my face in a manner that was a little heavy handed. Don't get me wrong, if I needed to make an effort, I would rise to the occasion. But this smoky eyed girl in front of me looked ridiculous.

When I was in high school, I would coat my lashes in swathes of mascara and line my eyes with black kohl. If it was a special event – say one of the boys was having a house party to celebrate their birthday – that aforementioned kohl eyeliner would have been smudged in what I thought was a tasteful smoky fashion around my eyes. I was twenty-two before I realised that smoky eyes, whether kohl eyeliner was used or not, did not suit me one bit. It's a shame I didn't get to mention this to the MUA before they made a sinful mistake.

At that moment, I was sure that whoever I was being dressed up for was going to be very disappointed.

But I didn't have the heart to care.

CHAPTER 3

The Glass Box

Angus

Angus was summoned at about noon two days after the *gatherers* were sent to the south. It was an awkward time of day for him. His muscles ached and his eyes were irritated from the sun despite it being a cloudy summers day in the highlands.

He had meant to be sleeping, he knew it. And yet he couldn't. The knowledge that his donor had arrived had kept him from slumber. He had been quite fed up of feeding out of cold blood bags and had missed the touch of a warm female neck against his lips. Not only this, at the precise moment he had been called, he had been sitting in the library (it was always dark in the library), in the middle of a book that bored him deeply and didn't have the strength to read any further, despite its recommendation from his good friend, Sorcha.

He glided down the empty halls and took the stairs as brusquely as he had done two days previously when he had been dropping off Isabella's body. This time, however, he did so with more optimism than the last. Angus, if he didn't know any better, might have even deemed himself excited. A live donor was always better than a dead one, after all. But him and excitement in the Warren didn't come hand in hand. It had ceased to years ago.

The doors of *the collection* opened, and he stepped into the warehouse. Two *gatherers* that Angus recognised came to meet him and guided him into *the pamper*. There in the centre was a large glass case which stretched around two metres tall and one and a half metres wide. Inside the case was a girl standing upright, and a long, large tube which travelled out the case to the wall.

Oxygen, Angus realised. He became all of a sudden quite pitiful for the human species, who were so dependent on the simple phenomenon of two atoms joined at the hip. This was shunned away almost immediately by the realisation that he was also dependent on something equally as measly – on the fragile human themselves, and the blood that surged through their arteries.

"What is her name?" he asked the *gatherers*, who were looking at him with an expression which could only be likened to those seeking approval. The taller one with blonde hair answered his question.

"Ivy, sir. Her name is Ivy."

Ivy was not at all what Angus was used to in a donor. She had lengthy, dark hair the shade of coffee beans, slightly tanned skin, and eyes like pools of obsidian black gemstones.

No, this was an unjust description, he decided. As he unconsciously edged towards the case, he noticed her hair had shades of russet blended in with the coffee, and her eyes were outlined with obsidian black as he had previously observed, but filled with obsidian mahogany.

Yes, much more just.

She looked like an untouched china doll wrapped in a plastic box, ready to be opened and ruined by the careless hands of a monster. He couldn't help but think that this was to be some sort of foreboding.

Despite his astute observation of her, Angus knew it shouldn't have been misconstrued as fascination. If anything, it was more related to disappointment. She was not what he was expecting. And not what he had wanted.

Where was the flowing long hair of spun gold that he craved? The colour which reminded him of the sun he missed so dearly. Where was her translucent beauty? The kind that made veins more visible in the neck.

"Why is she in a glass cabinet?" He dragged himself out of his spinning thoughts. It hadn't gone past his attention that this was not the way that a donor would usually be presented to their master. There was normally no glass, or any barrier for that matter. "And why is she a brunette? I don't recall that being one of my preferences," he added bitterly.

In response to his questions, the blonde *gatherer* once again answered but this time with what seemed like hesitation.

"New protocol, sir," he cleared his throat before continuing. "And the hair choice is because we felt she suited some of your other preferences to a higher degree than another with lighter hair. Does she suit your tastes?" By this, Angus knew he was asking if he found her attractive. If he said no, she would be released, compelled to forget, and then replaced until a donor was found that was more suited to him, such as a blonde.

Angus toyed with the idea of rejecting her. He imagined telling the *gatherers* of his disappointment and sending her away. He thought of the time this would incur. He was exasperated with waiting and fussing any longer.

"Aye, she'll do," he chipped, his annoyance clear in the unconscious colloquial Scottish slip of the tongue. "All things sorted for her disappearance?"

"Yes, sir. She is in minimal contact with her parents so they shouldn't notice her missing, but the sister has been compelled to not get suspicious." The *gatherer* nodded towards the glass cabinet before continuing. "She was in between jobs and new to the area so no friends or boyfriend. I doubt she'll be missed."

"Good. Great." Angus nodded. "Send her to my quarters."

"Very well, sir. Oh... but, sir–" he called out as Angus turned his back. "I have been ordered by John that I disclose some information with you before I do."

"And what is that, *Gatherer*?"

"The reason she is in the glass case is not new protocol." Angus's eyes narrowed at this comment. He did not like being lied to.

"Go on."

"You see, sir, Ivy is a rather special case in that she is AB negative. We thought it in your best interest that you were not aware of this as it could have clouded your judgement, and so we put her in glass to prevent her scent from escaping."

Angus looked back at the girl. Of course she was AB negative. It would have been wrong for her not to have been somehow.

When he responded, he kept his exterior cool. "Very well. Tell John I appreciate his efforts." And with that, he left.

Angus was in his room waiting for the girl called Ivy to enter. He felt as if he had been waiting an age for her, their brief meeting earlier in the day an almost foggy memory.

He sat ramrod straight at his mahogany desk which faced the door, head neither tilted right nor left but instead entirely central. He played unconsciously with a pen as he sat, rolling it skilfully through the deft fingers of his right hand. As he stared at the wood of the desk, he couldn't ignore the similarity it had with the girl's long hair – the shades of light and dark imitating it almost exactly. He suddenly dropped the pen, annoyed at himself for being so adolescent. She was simply like any other donor he had ever had (his donor description made sure of that), except for the minor difference in hair and eye colour. However, Angus thought that the girl called Ivy wasn't at all like the rest. He didn't know what made him think that way. He didn't particularly find her attractive, and yet here he was, thinking about her hair.

Interesting, and slightly irritating, he thought.

He quickly came to the conclusion that it was in fact the novelty of brunette hair, rather than the girl who possessed it, which intrigued him. She certainly wasn't bonnier than any of the other donors he had had. In fact, he had noticed a rather visible scar on the left side of the skin of her chin. She was spoiled already. And she hadn't suited the makeup the *collector* had applied to her eyes – it was much too heavy.

Perhaps all the fuss was because he knew she would smell like dreams wrapped in desire.

AB negative blood was rare because of genetics, of course. The owner had to have a parent with the A blood type and another with the B blood type. Neither parents could hold the rhesus positive gene, either. Well, that was the case in simple genetics, anyway. But this alone, despite its reduced possibility as a combination, would still account for millions of AB negative humans, more than enough to allow a donor to fit Angus's description exactly. But AB negative was considered to be even rarer because of a disease which previously targeted this specific blood group. Something to do with antibodies. Angus had read up on it, but his brain had given up the information, likely favouring it for something else entirely.

The disease wiped out so many that they were a mere speck in the population. Of course, as more years passed, the amount of AB negative had increased. After all, all that's needed is more A and B negative humans to procreate. But it was still rare, and Angus knew that all too well. That was a fact he certainly hadn't relinquished.

Angus had tasted one AB negative in his vampire life. It was around sixty years prior, before the Warren, before there were restrictions on his vampirism and before his blood lust was remedied through the draining of brainless humans.

He had been working in a bar in Glasgow. Loud, drunken humans were such easy targets, making a bar the perfect place to feed inconspicuously. Angus could satisfy severe cravings without it looking any more than simple human attraction. Her name was not something he could remember. In fact, Angus couldn't even seem to remember what the young woman had looked like. All he could remember was the taste. Rich, smooth, spiced. Bliss. The perfect concoction to ensure the demise of the owner.

That was the first and last time he had tasted it, and it had left it's mark. He had killed that girl on that night simply because he didn't have the self-control, or more likely the compassion, to stop. Being many decades passed, Angus liked to think that his restraint would be a little more admirable this time, even if his compassion was unchanging. His head told him this was not at all a thought worth thinking, unless he was keen on plainly lying to himself.

He picked up the human's file – the one that had been handed to him by the light-haired *gatherer*. It was rather thin in comparison to the ones he had previously been given for other donors, and he wondered if that made her more or less remarkable.

Opening to the page with the information he sought, he read.

> **Name:** Ivy Crest
> **Date of Human Birthing:** 3rd February
> **Age:** 24
> **Blood Type:** AB Negative. Clear of disease.
> **Haematocrit:** avg. 46%. range 44–48%
> **Eye Colour:** Brown
> **Hair Colour:** Brown
> **Skin Colour:** Light Olive
> **Weight:** 60kg
> **Height:** 167cm
> **Body Type:** Mesomorph
> **Sexuality:** Heterosexual
> **Social Affairs:** Tied up

His eyes flicked to the haematocrit, and if it were possible, his skin might have pricked with goose-flesh. The *perfect* percentage. The *perfect* range. He was salivating at the thought, and his fangs elongated, subtly pushing his upper lip out.

He heard the footsteps long before the knock on his door came, and he smelt her even before that. Her scent was like freshly cut grass and hot bread out the oven all rolled into one. These smells Angus cherished from his human years and were engraved onto his vampire brain even centuries on. For her to smell as good – if not better – than those memories was like nothing he could have imagined. The anticipation he felt was tangible, and he had the sudden desire to freeze the moment and savour it. His fists clenched tightly, and he engaged the muscles of his lower limbs so that they were encased in an anatomical vice. This kind of control would be needed initially, and he knew without it, he might already have been out his bedroom door, carrying her in himself.

He closed his mouth, conscious that his canines were making him look predatory. Despite his nature, he didn't wish to be that version of himself for the brunette at that moment.

The knock came as expected, and Angus gruffly responded with a reply which encouraged the vampire to enter.

It was John who brought her to him, and the *collector* walked into Angus's room with a toothless smile on his face. To a human eye, or perhaps even to a vampire who didn't know John as well as Angus did, it might have appeared that he had no emotion on his face at all. However, Angus knew this wasn't the case. John wanted to bask in this win – he knew it.

The woman named Ivy trailed in after the *collector*. He took her in for a second time, his head a little clearer since he had since overcome the shock of her. She looked the same as he had remembered, perhaps a little more refined. But no, he had been right. She was nothing special. He was making a fuss over nothing. She was wearing an outfit which he would have thought was more fit for the gym than anything else, and although it hugged her soft curves, it wasn't anything to fawn over. Nothing was on show. He couldn't even see the slither of her midsection or the top of her breasts.

When he looked to her face, Angus half expected her eyes to be cast down modestly or perhaps observing plainly. However, the girl's eyes were vigilant and appeared to take in her entire surroundings with an eagerness he couldn't quite understand. It was unusual, he thought. Very unusual indeed. He would remember that.

"Here you go, Gus." Angus flinched at his unfavourable nickname involuntarily. "She's all here for you," John announced.

In that moment, Ivy's eyes snapped to his and he felt a jolt right in his stomach. A literal gut feeling.

Can she see me, really see me? Is she truely in there? Is her soul seeking my soul?

Eugh, he felt sick at the thought. *Don't be ridiculous.*

Angus flicked his eyes to John, who he noticed was eagerly waiting for a response. "Yes, thank you, John. I hope the *gatherers* sent over my gratitude?"

John nodded.

"Well, if that's all, I suppose you should be getting back to work." Angus assumed, raising his eyebrows towards the *collector* in encouragement. He wanted to be alone with the girl called Ivy, or more so, the blood she possessed. Her scent could have been attached to anyone in that moment and he wouldn't have cared in the slightest. It engulfed his quarters as if it was displacing the other air molecules that had been there before she had entered, taking precedence. He was shocked, and rather proud that he had been able to take in her physical appearance when her aroma was as captivating as it was. Even his fangs had retreated.

"Yes, yes." John cleared his throat and looked towards the ground in embarrassment at the dismissal. Angus watched in mild amusement. John, he believed, was one of the most human vampires he had ever met. "But, Laddie, I just need to ask of you one thing, okay?"

Angus nodded to him to continue.

"Please, don't kill this one."

CHAPTER 4

Meet Cutes

Ivy

I didn't like the way the man was looking at me.

I couldn't tell whether it was admiration in his eyes, distaste, or pure animalistic hunger. In all honesty, it didn't matter what he was thinking. The simple fact that he was looking at me at all made me mentally flinch.

John (I knew his name now), told him not to kill me. Why would he want to do that? What normal human person would kidnap someone they have never met to then kill them? On second thought, that was too heavily reliant on the person in question actually being normal, and I was well aware that there was nothing normal about my current state of affairs. Nothing at all.

When I had been in the glass box, the man with the slicked-back hair had mentioned my parents. These people knew about my sister, my unemployment and even my marital status. He'd said I had no friends. He'd said I wouldn't be missed.

I wasn't sure what about that specifically had upset me the most – the fact that no one would be able to come and save me, or that fact that they wouldn't want to in the first place.

To stop myself from spiralling, I allowed my eyes to take the room in some more.

It was large – not really a room at all. When entering the quarters, it opened into a space which was wider than it was long. Straight ahead, opposite the door, was a large wooden desk in a deep wood, and behind it was an office chair which sat slightly askew. To the right of the desk was another chair, a bit like an armchair, which had a steel blue jumper resting along its back. To the left quite a way away, was a large and neatly made bed which was sat back into a depression in the wall. Small side tables were on each side of it; a well-loved book sat on the table on the right. To the left of the bed was what appeared to be a spacious bathroom with a slate grey and white colour scheme. The wall opposing the foot of the bed was an open doorway which was filled with clothes – mostly female from what I could see. The floor was carpeted with a thick, beige carpet and under the bed, extending past its extremities, was a patterned rug.

There were no windows as such, but the light which emitted from the light fixtures above had an unusual day-like quality to them. The light bounced off the large, arched mirror on the wall next to the door.

I wondered what time it was. I peeked down at my left arm, noting that my watch had been removed and then felt in my pockets. I also didn't have my phone. I then looked at the walls, searching for a clock, but there wasn't one. And there wasn't one on either of the bedside tables, either.

And a clock wasn't the only thing missing. I'd immediately noticed the lack of security or restraining devices. The front door had a lock, but it was lockable from the inside which meant that I would be able to leave as I wished. There were no other rooms to put me in except the bathroom – the rest of the space was made up of open doorways and all those also appeared lockable from the inside. There was no sign of any means to keep me here, and John hadn't even bothered restraining me on the way from the glass box to the room, almost as if he didn't have the slightest reason to believe I would try and run or fight. My ankle had fully healed (much to my surprise), wrapped in some form of dressing, and I couldn't help but think that it would have surely benefited my captors to have kept me decrepit. Why not keep me hobbling, unable to run? At least that would have hindered my escape. The only time I had ever felt even mildly restricted was when I was in the glass case, but the man with the slick hair made it clear this was due to my scent and blood type rather than anything else.

On reflection, what an odd thing to mention – my blood type. I didn't even know what my blood type was. Not until today, at least. It wasn't something that the NHS thought was important enough to let you know. But here it seemed like the most important piece of information. Perhaps I was going to be used as a lab rat, and my blood type was the type they needed to do it. Oh God! Was that disease which affected AB negative back in circulation? Why hadn't that been on the news? Was it classified information?

Suddenly, I was washed with a wave of nausea, my feet faltering slightly beneath me.

I'm going to die.

A cool, firm grip encased my left arm and my eyes flew upwards to meet the person who it belonged to. His eyes were blue. If it had been my sister, she would have been able to articulate the colour of them more beautifully, perhaps saying his eyes were a steel blue with flecks of moss green running through them. But I was not my sister, so they were simply just blue. His hair appeared brown but in certain lights, it was more a shade of tawny, and I expected that was a product of this Celtic background. His nose and lips were thin, and he had the beginnings of a beard which ran onto his neck. His skin was the same as John's. The same as them all. Not in shade – I'd seen people with all skin colours here – but the same in quality. Firm, translucent, icy. This man was pale also, but the characteristics that he shared with all the other members of this group made it paler. Unlike John who appeared to be in his forties, he was in his late twenties, perhaps early thirties. Overall, he was sculptured and fascinating to look at. Good-looking seemed unfair and I could feel myself sinking slowly, into an unknown abyss...

My mind snapped suddenly to focus back to the grip on my arm, the hairs on my upper limbs rising, sickened at the contact. I couldn't bear his hand on me, even if it was meant to be one of concern or kindness. It was still like a vice, and it made me want to shrink away inwardly in disgust. I clenched every single muscle I could muster my mind to communicate with, fighting all my instincts that were demanding I pull away from the clinical touch.

I needed to appear content. The lack of guards, the lack of confinement I was under, it meant something. It meant that I was supposed to act normal, not as if every bone in my body was screaming at me to run, to escape, to fight. But why would they so blatantly expect this from someone? How could these people expect a victim of kidnap to be pleased enough with the situation to not contest it? Stockholm syndrome didn't happen that quickly, surely?

His hand loosened from my arm suddenly, as if he was correcting himself, and then released it completely.

"I'm Angus," he said, his eyes crinkling slightly as he did so, as if he was reaching his hand into a pool of water and was unsure of the temperature. I continued to stare blankly at him, and in response to my *lack* of response, he continued. "These are my quarters, and they are yours now, too. You may leave as you wish, but you are always to return here by night. Ten-thirty at the latest. I am to be your master. Is that understood?" I nodded in response, my eyes darting slightly to my left as I did so, my brain mulling over the term he had just used.

'Master' could mean a multitude of things, but in this situation, I was more concerned with what the term 'master' suggested *I* was meant to be. Was I to be a servant? A slave? Had I been dragged into some sort of sex trafficking ring?

As I processed an endless stream of eventualities, my

body hummed with a barely suppressed fear. The last tendrils of suppression stemmed from a conscious need to keep up the facade. The facade that this was home. The facade that I felt safe. The facade that I didn't want to run.

My eyes flicked back to Angus's to find him staring at me inquisitively. He was puzzled, I was sure of it. Maybe I hadn't been acting right. Should I have been saying more? Should I have been on my knees or curtseying to my master? The thought made me nauseous, and I was poignantly aware that that was the second time I'd felt so since entering the room.

"Your heart rate is elevated," Angus stated, curiously. His eyebrows pinched, and his eyes sharpened. "Is that normal for you? Do you suffer from tachycardia?"

My ears twitched at the medical term. Perhaps he really was a doctor as I predicted, wanting to use my blood for his crazy experiments. But how did he know my heart was pumping like a steam train at full pelt? My hand flew instinctively to the pulse point at the side of my neck, and I watched as his eyes moved as quickly as my extremity. Perhaps quicker.

Angus became fixated. His tongue ever so gently poked out of his parted lips to press on his right canine, and his eyes became a pool of liquid black rather than liquid blue as the pupil engulfed his iris, greedy to see more. He appeared to be a man possessed, but as soon as it materialised, it disappeared, and I was left wondering whether I had imagined it entirely.

I cleared my throat, pulled my shoulders back ever so slightly so as to not seem timid, but all the same not appear confrontational or aggressive. Angus's response seemed to suggest I struck the right balance, as his eyes softened slightly.

That's it Ivy. You can do this.

"Yes, that's correct. Tachycardia. Runs in my family." I took a risk at the end and dressed my face in a closed-lipped smile. If it paid off or not, I wasn't sure, but it didn't cause him to suspect me enough to say anything. I tipped myself an imaginary top hat.

You're a real natural, truly.

I didn't suffer from tachycardia – a condition which caused a high heart rate when resting – and I sure as hell wasn't in any way aware of whether or not it ran in my family. I felt that knowing such things required a degree of closeness that I simply didn't have the luxury of sharing. That degree of closeness being of course, talking. At all.

"Are you medicated for it?" he asked, abruptly. If I had been surer of myself, I would have almost said that he was irritated at the thought. "I can't smell any medications in your blood." Angus's nostrils flared slightly, and his face took on a mask which was close to that of an animal seeking out prey. It was haunting, but my mind couldn't ignore that it held an endearing, fantastical quality.

It was then that it happened – me being dragged back through a mental time portal, my mind trying to remember something important, something absolutely critical.

I arrived at the room with the mirrors and salon chairs. The man with the oily blonde hair was there again, and he was using the same voice he always had – the soft, hushed one. The one that felt like insects on my skin. He was telling me that I won't feel any pain when it happened. I won't feel *anything.* I won't run. I won't fight. I won't scream. I'll do nothing when the man who I will call 'master' will drain my body of blood.

I didn't know what my face looked like to Angus when I realised that he, and likely everyone else in this place, were vampires. I could only hope that the previous barely suppressed fear was still just that.

It became in that moment absolutely imperative that I did as I was asked. It was more important than I had initially given weight to – my previous behaviour now seeming reckless.

My knowledge of mythical creatures such as the vampire were vast, but the important term was *mythical.* What I knew about the real thing was less immense, as I didn't think there was any literature I had ever read that believed the notion that vampires were anything but fiction, and I certainly hadn't entertained the idea myself, either. Stephanie Myer didn't prepare me for this.

If there was any literature on the 'real vampire', I assumed it would likely be in this place, but I doubted I would ever be able to get my hands on it. I didn't think asking Angus if I could browse the library for facts about vampires – facts I would then try and use to overpower him – would go down too well. I didn't even know if there *was* a library. However, Angus had said I could leave the quarters whenever I wanted as long as I came back. That meant I could explore, and although I may have been clutching at straws, I had a feeling that was important. As I had noticed, there were no precautions in this quarter, or any other part of the place, that had had means to restrain or lock up a victim, which meant that they were sure it would never be needed.

It was mind control. It had to be. What was the word they had used? Compelled? Was that the term they used to describe mind control? I swear I'd heard it before somewhere. Was it here? Or was it on a TV show?

Suddenly, a memory of someone mentioning that my sister had been *compelled* to not get suspicious came to the front of my mind. They had also said that my parents didn't talk to me, that I had no friends, and that I had no job to turn up to. They were right, I really wouldn't be missed. I had no one I could rely on. No one was going to report me missing. The one person who would have had been weeded out, no longer a threat. This was something I was going to have to get out of myself. It was this, or the realisation that I was going to have to die trying. I hated how cliche that was.

So, this brought me back to my original point – it was absolutely crucial that I did as they said so as to not arouse their suspicions. Because for some reason, their mind control didn't seem to work on me. At least, not as well as they thought. Perhaps it was my unloving childhood – maybe it had primed my brain to be more resilient. I shook that idea off almost instantly. No way was I giving my trash mother and absent father the credit for this one. No, this was just one of those things. One of those glitches in the universe. A glitch that's sole purpose was to keep the balance. To prevent one species from creating some sort of a monopoly over the others. This was the world fighting back one tiny mutated DNA code at a time.

I had to use it to my advantage. This meant attempting to convince these creatures that I was under their spell long enough to allow me to find a way out. It would require practice. From what I had seen of the place called 'The Warren' (that's what oily blonde had called it), it was large. This meant there had to be a ton of other humans like myself here, and since the place was likely unknown to the world, it was fair to assume that these humans were not lucky enough to have some sort of mind control buffer like I was. I would need to find these people and study them – emulate their character and the way they spoke to others, especially their masters or mistresses. And get really good at it, fast. I would have to make sure that I concentrated when I was talked to, picking up on when the vampires were attempting compulsion, ensuring my mind was sharp enough to evade it. They had got me once, in that weird salon room, but it hadn't lasted long, and I was adamant that it wouldn't happen again. It *couldn't* happen again.

"Are you hungry?" Angus asked, pulling me out of my head and back into the room. His eyes crinkled again when I looked up to them, skirting around their outline, rather than looking directly into them. "You've gone all peely-wally all of a sudden and your blood glucose has taken a hit," he said, very matter of fact, but there was a hint of something in his words. It was worry. I knew it was not for my welfare, but it was still there. He was worried about *something.*

"Sit," he demanded bluntly, gesturing to the bed located through the open doorway.

I did as I was told and walked over to the large bed, sitting myself on the side, feet firmly planted on the carpet, hands clasped. I felt his eyes on me the entire time as I walked, and my shoulders slumped inwardly, away from those eyes.

He approached me with what appeared to be caution, before sitting to the right of me, hand out, palm upward in an offering gesture. "May I have your wrist?" he asked, before giving a sideways glance and adding, "Please." You could tell it had been an afterthought – the pleasantry. He seemed uncomfortable with the word, as if his mouth rarely had to shape it.

I outstretched my right arm and placed it into his hand. I tried not to flinch at the shock of his cool and stone-smooth skin. It was so unusual – nothing like normal human touch – and if I hadn't known any better, I would have thought myself in the presence of a God.

He flipped my arm over smoothly so that my wrist was exposed, and paused briefly, taking what I assumed was a highly unnecessary breath, before placing his fingers on my wrist pulse point. He held them there for a while and I became acutely aware of my blood coursing around my body. *Thump. Thump. Thump.*

Feeling my own pulse had always made me feel lightheaded. I also had an aversion to feeling other people's pulses, but my own pulse was worse somehow. It was the same with getting my blood pressure taken. They always told me my blood pressure was low and I'd likely live forever because of it, not knowing that this was a product of my light-headedness, not from a glorious cardiovascular system.

Angus's eyes were closed as he concentrated. His eyelashes fanned out, thick and dark, lightly dusting his violet-tinted lower lids. He then opened them to stare at my wrist, tracing his index finger over one of the veins there. He hummed briefly, and I could feel it within myself, a deep low rumble.

He dropped my arm, placing it back in my lap, before placing his hands on either side of my outer thighs to allow him to twist my body towards his slightly. My feet were no longer fully grounded, and I could feel myself become more and more uncomfortable as Angus forced himself further into my personal space.

He looked me square in the eyes, and I had to use all of my willpower to not look away. Someone who felt safe no matter the circumstance wouldn't look away, so *I* couldn't look away.

Angus brushed my long hair behind my shoulders, skimming my neck with his fingertips as he did so, and gently ran his thumbs under my eyes, examining them. I was exhausted. I didn't know what day it was, or the time, and he was right – I was very hungry, my blood sugar likely low. I decided to tell him this, because it was the truth, but also because I wanted him to take his icy hands off my face at once.

"I *am* hungry. Can I have something to eat, please?" I felt like Oliver Twist. The only thing missing was the, 'sir'.

Angus appeared almost surprised, blinking once, twice, before nodding and taking his hands away from my face. He looked ashamed, and a little frustrated. *Odd.*

"Of course. It's just gone six-thirty anyway, so the canteen will be ready for you. I'll take you there."

I nodded my agreement. It was also good to get the time, even if I didn't know the day.

"Would you like to change your clothes before you go?"

I looked down at myself. I was wearing gym leggings and a zip-up running jacket – the clothes I had left my house in. A wave of longing washed over me, and I felt a lump begin to form in my throat. At that moment, I would have given just about anything to go back home, sleep in my own bed and eat on my own dining table. But the realisation was that I would probably never see that place again, and if I ever did, I would likely find myself so changed that I wouldn't think of it as mine anymore.

"No. I'm fine," I said as I shook my head. But I didn't know if I was shaking it at the question, or simply using it as a small act of defiance against my dire situation.

Angus escorted me towards the canteen. He kept his distance, but I could tell he was very aware of me, as if there was some sort of gravitational pull from myself to him.

The thought made me sick.

◆ ◆ ◆

The Warren was a mixture of both old and new. Some areas were highly clinical and modern, while others were cosier and appeared to be modelled off a large scale cottage. Despite the stark contrast, all of it was opulent. There was money here, that was certain.

We passed the odd person in the halls as we walked – some human and some not. I noticed, having observed now a few members, that vampires had a certain look about them, so I was able to distinguish them from the others.

The people we passed were very respectful towards Angus, nodding their heads as they walked, and a few women gave him large, flattering smiles.

We were approaching somewhere which seemed to emit a low-level hum, and as we got closer, the hallway widened towards wide-open steel doors. Beyond the doors were tens of long wooden tables and benches filled with people – humans. They talked happily; some were laughing or smiling widely, their ages ranging from what I assumed was eighteen up to late sixties or even seventies. It was an entire civilisation. There were hundreds of them.

The scale of the wrongdoing hit me like a freight train. This was on a magnitude I couldn't comprehend. An entire underground community built upon deceit and mental coercion, blanketed by a shroud of fake happiness. Surely these people weren't *actually happy* here? It was all just a farce.

Along the far wall there was a classic style canteen where a small queue was forming. There was a large analogue wall clock telling the time as six fifty-eight. The height of dinner.

I began to walk towards the queue, intending to join it, but Angus caught my upper arm, pulling me towards him.

"Don't worry about the line there." He nodded towards it. "I'll take you to the front. They won't mind." He kept his hand on my arm, guiding me towards the front of the line.

I could feel the people watching me, but I was surprised to find that they weren't looking at me like I would have expected them to look at someone who was queue jumping. Instead, they were smiling fondly.

God, this was awful. I hated being the centre of attention.

We reached the front of the line and Angus addressed one of the severs.

"Callie, this is Ivy." He nodded towards me, smiling openly to the human woman behind the hot food counter. His teeth were pearly white, but no sharper than a human's, and I wondered if that was something that changed when he needed to... eat.

Eugh.

The woman had dark skin (which looked slightly flushed now after the attention from Angus), and dark hair which was covered with a hair net. Her skin was flawless, but I assumed that she was around forty-five.

Angus was still holding onto my arm, his cold hand tangible even through the sleeve of my top, and I peered down at it as subtly as I could muster. He didn't turn to me, but it was as if he knew my thoughts because it was only a second later that he released me.

"Evening, sir," Callie smiled, and did a semi curtsey-bow before turning to me. "And evenin' to you, young lady. Please to meet ye." Her Scottish accent was stronger than Angus's and more on par with John's. "If we knew you'd be coming to the canteen with your donor, sir, we would have cleared a wee table for ye," she said, looking slightly embarrassed.

"Not to worry, I'm not staying. My donor is malnourished. I need you to give her something filling but healthy to get her strength up," he stated, bluntly.

Callie flushed harder and nodded, shouting orders to some other servers before handing me a tray holding a plate of meat pie, mash and veg. I couldn't deny that it looked like exactly what I needed. There was also a large glass of water.

"I'm going to leave you here with the others. Find a

table, and I want to hear from Callie that you ate all the food on that plate, and the water. You look ill, and I can't have a donor who is ill."

At that, he turned on his toes and walked out the doors at the other end of the large room, followed by the eyes of many sitting humans in the cafeteria. He was clearly an important member of the Warren. I didn't know if that was because he was one of the vampires. Looking around it didn't look like the vampires frequented the cafeteria. It hit me then that it would be rather pointless to, considering their diet wasn't meat pie and veg. I shuddered at the thought.

I briefly mulled over the term 'donor'. Just like 'master,' it didn't sit well with me. The idea of donating anything to the man was horrifying.

Pushing the thought away, I scanned the room, picking a table with a space for me to join. Sitting next to a guy with dark hair and tanned skin, I smiled at the group with as much vigour as I could muster, trying to return at least fifty percent of the enthusiasm that they were giving to me.

"I'm Ivy," I announced. "It's nice to meet you all."

"We know," exhilarated the girl at the end of the table. She had bleach-blonde hair and a soft Edinburgh accent. "Everyone's heard about you! And *we* are all very excited to meet *you*. Welcome to the Warren." She smiled broadly at me. "We wanna hear everything! What is he like?" she asked.

"Yeah, tell us all. We're dying to know what he's like. I've heard so many rumours... I need confirmation!" The man next to me chipped in, before adding "I'm Andy, by the way. And that's Heather." He pointed to the blonde who was now waving at me. I smiled back at her, weakly. "Cutsie accent you've got there too, wee one," he added.

"An English person in the Warren is certainly a first," Heather said, nodding thoughtfully. "I wonder who green-lighted that."

At the same time, I heard a muttered, "She's not even *blonde*," coming from the girl next to Heather, but I ignored it.

"Are you asking about Angus?" I asked, responding to the earlier questions.

"Wait," Andy turned to me, placing his hand on my arm, a look of shock on his face. "He lets you call him Angus?" I looked at all the others on the table – two more in total. There was another woman who was also blonde, but less so, and a man with coffee skin and close-cut hair.

"My master *never* lets me call him by his name!" The other blonde whispered, but it was still pretty loud.

"Nor does mine. It's master or nothing." Andy added, looking at me in disbelief.

"Yeah, my mistress would give me a stern talking to if I ever called her–" The guy who wasn't Andy dipped his head and dropped his voice to a small whisper, "Margot."

"I'm almost certain Izzy couldn't call him Angus." Heather mused, but her tone went up at the end, like she was asking for confirmation from the rest of the group.

"Nope," said the other blonde. "It was master to her. Maybe she called him Angus and that's why he went crazy and bit her too hard." She giggled playfully, and the rest joined in, laughing too.

I felt sick, and wondered that if I was going to survive in this place, I was likely going to need some anti-emetics.

'Izzy' must have been the name of my predecessor. And she was dead. And they blamed her. And they were laughing about it.

I picked at my food, shovelling a little into my mouth. I couldn't taste anything. It was like eating dirt.

"Oh, my mistake," I chuckled, feigning ease, and friendliness. "He doesn't let me call him that, obviously." Point one: call him master, or sir, *always*.

The man with the short hair laughed with me. "Yeah, what a silly question, Andy."

"Oh, *I'm sorry*, Duke. Sorry I ever asked a question over here." Andy raised his hands, palms face forward in mock surrender.

"Will you guys stop. I want to ask our new friend Ivy about the prince," said Heather, a look of disapproval directed at her peers.

"I'm sorry, did you say 'the prince'?" I asked, my brown furrowing in confusion.

"OHMYGOSH," exclaimed the other blonde, slapping the girl called Heather on the arm to get her attention. She was loud enough this time that a few people at some other tables turned around in interest. She had the decency to appear embarrassed, and then added in a harsh whisper, "she doesn't *know*."

I looked at the four people at the table, the same look of confusion on my face.

"Your master is the *Prince* of the Warren, my friend," Andy stated, patting me on the back in sympathy. "Do you really think that just anyone can skip the food queue? No wee one, they cannot." They all chuckled at that.

"Yeah, you walking in here *WITH THE PRINCE* and skipping the queue like that was *EVE-RY-THING*," said the other blonde. You could almost see the excitable energy that buzzed off her. She was overflowing with it.

"Sass, will you *please* stop yelling every five seconds, kind regards, every God damn person in this place." Andy retorted back to the blonde who I now knew was known to them as 'Sass'. Perhaps it was short for Saskia.

She rolled her eyes at Andy and mouthed a less-than sincere 'sorry'.

"So, what? I'm like a princess?" I joked, trying to be in-keeping with their laid-back energy. But inside I wanted to scream.

"I'd say you are the closest a donor is ever going to get to being a princess," noted Duke. "The prince doesn't actually have a sister, so technically yeah, you are the princess."

"Yeah, if the princess was to sit with all the shitty peasants," added Andy.

"And eat the same bland food as said peasants," piped up Heather.

Andy slapped Heather on the arm. They all seemed to do that a lot to eachother. "The food is *not* bland and you know it. Callie and her team are angels."

"Ermm excuse me Mr Rude, my job is important in the

Warren too, you know. People need their hair cut. It's a basic human right!" she exclaimed. I felt her statement ironic, considering that her free will was not her own and that she was unable to exercise the most basic human right of them all.

"My job's important too," added Duke.

"Oh, purrleeaasee, Duke. Everyone hates you. You are a tooth-pulling devil," Sass interjected, giving Duke serious evil eyes.

"Normal people just call me a dentist, Sass," he replied, rolling his eyes before forking a bit of pie into his mouth.

"Duke, if you think for one second that poor old Sass over here is normal, you are going to get the shock of your life." Andy then turned to me and added, "Duke's the newest member of the group – apart from you, obviously. He's straight, and therefore nowhere near as cool as me, but he'll do." He ended his introduction with a nod and a wink.

"What do you do?" I asked Andy.

"Moi?" he asked flamboyantly, pointing to himself in mock surprise. "I, Princess Ivy, am a humble doctor."

"I don't think the word 'humble' and 'doctor' have ever been in the same sentence together," said Heather, rolling her eyes.

"Not unless the sentence is: 'that doctor is *not* humble,'" muttered Duke.

Andy gave him a stern look and then turned back to me with a sweet smile. "If that prince of yours ever gives you an STI, you know I'm here for you girl." He gave me a smirk and they all laughed again.

"Oh my gosh! You just must must MUST tell me what the sex is like!" demanded Sass, her voice creeping louder with each word. Andy was right, this girl needed a volume button. Her eyes were expectant and wide as she waited, her hands grasped in front of her face as if she was about to explode at the mere thought of the answer.

Andy tutted. "Lord, Sass, give the girl time to settle in! I doubt she's had the time to taste any of that tall drink of water. I mean, look at her. Not a single bite mark. She's a vamp virgin – in all senses of the word – aren't you, Princess?"

Heather spoke up before I could voice any reply. "Ohhh I remember my first time," she reflected, fondly, and her eyes seemed to drift past me, to some unknown spot in the canteen. "It was the best night of my life. I swear to God."

I focused on Heather, taking in her entire person. She wore a v-neck jumper and what appeared to be fitted jeans. Her blonde hair was expertly blown out, lavishly pooling around her shoulders and exposed chest. Her face was perfectly perfect, but distinctly human, with just a lick of mascara and bronzer to compliment her natural beauty.

And her neck was covered in bite marks.

I turned to Andy, whose right wrist had clearly been bitten, perhaps not recently, and then Duke, whose neck had also been feasted on. Sass had no visible bite marks, but I wasn't naive enough to think that meant she didn't have any. She'd have some, and I willed my brain not to ponder on where they might be. The term 'donor' suddenly became very self-explanatory.

"No one cares about your soppy romantic vamp sexcapades, Heather," Andy said, dismissing her comment. He turned back to me. "Heather is in love with her master. It's kinda pathetic."

"It is not pathetic, Andy. Hey, Duke, tell him!" Heather defended, reaching over Sass to nudge Duke on the arm.

Andy held up a hand in front of Duke's face to block his reply. "No, Duke, I'm begging you to please not tell me about your vamp love. It makes me physically sick."

"You know, for someone who is meant to care for the vulnerable and sick, you really can be an arsehole," Duke said, shaking his head at his friend.

"No, Duke, I *like* arse holes. You are getting confused."

Heather hit him then, and he grabbed the injured arm in mock horror.

"You deserved that," she declared. "Not everyone wants to talk about arse holes at dinner."

"In my defence, Duke was the one who brought up arse holes. I just made it more interesting," Andy replied, shrugging.

"You are heartless," Heather hissed.

"Incorrect my little loved-up friend." He shook a long finger at her. "Me and my master just have an understanding. And that said understanding doesn't involve love," he shrugged, clearly feeling he had justified himself. "We get on just fine otherwise," he added, winking at me. He sure did like to wink.

"Apparently that understanding is about each other's arse holes," muttered Sass.

Now it was her turn to get a thump from Heather. "Seriously." She pointed to everyone on the table, looking very stern. "Enough about arse holes. Next person who mentions any hole whatsoever will have a dead arm for three days because I am *not* holding back on my next arm attack, got it?"

They all nodded, Andy snickering slightly, but agreeing with muttered apology.

I felt oddly conflicted. These people were friends, and good ones too, it appeared. They laughed with each other, called each other out on their flaws, and simply enjoyed each other's company. Here they were, talking humorously about each other's love lives without a care in the world. They weren't scared. They weren't in pain. They didn't miss their old life. I was suddenly whole-heartedly and completely jealous of them.

I stopped my thoughts in their tracks. I couldn't be jealous of them. They didn't belong to themselves anymore. Fundamentally, they were unchanged. You could tell that each of their personalities shone through – that Andy was the controversial one, Heather the mum of the group, Duke the laid back straight talker and Sass the one with uncontainable excitement. But their lack of self-preservation was haunting. They had been taken from their homes without their permission and were being used as human blood bags, *again*, without their permission. Some of them were even deluded enough to think that they were in love. It was madness. And I *couldn't* be jealous of that.

"So, do you like your masters and mistresses?" I asked. I needed more information. How did they perceive the creatures that bit them daily?

I was faced with four confused faces. They all then looked at each other in unison and laughed.

"Of course we do," chuckled Sass. "They are amazing! And the Warren is home."

"Don't you miss your real homes, though?" I asked, subtlety probing.

"What do you mean?" Duke said, squinting at me slightly, not understanding the question.

"Well, you haven't always lived here. Surely you miss your homes, your families? Friends?"

Andy laughed, as did Heather, while Duke and Sass smirked.

"Of course not! Why would we miss our past lives when these lives are so damn amazing!" Sass buzzed.

"Yeah, I wouldn't trade this for anything!" added Heather. "I can't say I ever think about my family. And I have friends here." She gestured around herself, smiling.

"Second that. This, and my mistress, is all I need," Duke nodded. Andy rolled his eyes at that, clearly still revolted by Duke's affection towards his vampire.

I nodded back, mute.

"Gotta say, pal, I could never imagine being anywhere else," confirmed Andy.

And there it was, the truth behind the facade. On face value, they were the most content and happy beings, in the prime of their life, enjoying dinner with people they genuinely enjoyed the company of. But underneath that, they were unable to suffer loss, unable to miss previous pleasures, unable to truly live. I was suddenly bombarded with a deep need to right this. Yes, the people were happy, but they were not happy on their own free will. They were souls trapped within mindless body-suits.

In order to right this, I needed to survive. And that meant I needed to pay attention and write extensive mental notes.

So far, it appeared I was meant to act as if this life was

amazing. That I was lucky. That this was a gift. It also seemed you were allowed to build a 'normal' relationship with your master or mistress, romantic or not. I assumed you could act as you were, and that if that behaviour was somehow deemed to cross some arbitrary line, it would be compelled out of you. As long as I stuck to the compulsion I was believed to be under, I was safe. This meant I wasn't to appear fearful, I was meant to let Angus bite me, and I was supposed to convince him that I either liked it, or didn't hate it.

If only it was easy to execute as it was to think.

CHAPTER 5

The Test

Angus

Angus arrived back to his quarters in an oddly irritable mood. He was irritable, he believed, because he had a hunch about the girl with the dark, dark eyes. Her behaviour had been the most unusual. Hadn't the *gatherer* compelled her to feel relaxed? She had been stiff as a board and had even had a funny turn near the end. When she had nearly collapsed, he had instinctively reached out for her, and her face had contorted slightly, as if in pain. That bothered him. Initially, because he was annoyed that he was concerned about whether or not he was causing her pain, but more because she shouldn't have felt any pain at his hand anyway. Also, he didn't want a feeble donor. There had been no mention of any health conditions when she had been presented to him, and yet her heart raced constantly. It was horrendously distracting. So much so that he hadn't been able to stop himself from touching her, like some human teenage boy unable to control his impulses.

Sitting her down and feeling the hum of her blood under her skin's surface had sent waves of anticipatory pleasure through his body – pleasure he hadn't felt in what felt like years. And yet, despite all of that, he hadn't fed on her.

Angus had never, not once, deprived himself the simple pleasure of feeding whenever he so desired. But today, with the girl, he felt a weird feeling right in his chest which had stopped him. He couldn't quite place the feeling, but he knew he had felt it before, perhaps in a past life. It was strong enough to lead him to the hospital wing where he compelled the medic at the blood transfusion centre to give him another bag of AB.

She had smelt like nothing he could remember. Every single string of DNA in his body had been screaming at him to allow his fangs to elongate fully so that he could pierce the soft, delicate flesh of her neck. But the girl had just looked too pale, and so, for a reason unknown to him, he had suppressed all those urges.

Her eyes had appeared sad, but it hadn't escaped him that they also appeared worryingly vigilant. He had noticed her take little sideway glances now and again, almost, Angus thought, as if she were trying to find a way out. But surely that couldn't be the case? A compelled donor wouldn't act in such a way. So why was she acting the way she was? Why wasn't she acting like the brainwashed, content little donor she was meant to be? And most importantly, why did Angus like that?

But it didn't matter if he liked it or not. If for some reason Ivy was not susceptible to compulsion, she was a threat. Although he had mused about it before, when faced with the possibility of a non-compelled donor in his quarters, he suddenly realised the immensity of the possible consequences. He needed to ensure she was under the Warren's spell. If not, it could lead to a disaster.

At that moment, Angus decided he would test out his theory. He would attempt to compel her that evening when she came back from the canteen. He would ask her to do something she wouldn't otherwise do, and surely if she didn't do it, or appeared even the slightest bit conflicted, he would know for sure. And if it were true by some anomaly that she was indeed resistant to compulsion, he would have to kill her.

How feckin' inconvenient.

She arrived back into Angus's room looking healthier in colour. He had heard from Callie that she had eaten all the food that was given to her, if slowly, and finished the water. Her heart still raced a little, he noted, but it was more muted than before, and he was grateful for it. It was so very, very distracting.

She stood just in front of the door she had closed behind her and smiled warmly at him. Angus was sitting at his desk, going over some finances (yes, even the Warren had to think about money), but all numbers flew out of his head the second she smiled like that. The smile lifted her face in such a way that complimented all her features perfectly, and Angus was taken aback by the vision of it. It wasn't that he was dumbfounded by her beauty (he'd already established that she wasn't his type), he was just surprised at the emotion. It looked almost sincere. More sincere than the smile of a human who had been compelled to be happy, anyway. And that was important to him for some reason.

He cleared his throat before asking, "How was dinner? You look much better after it."

Why was he asking her that? What did it matter whether his donor enjoyed dinner? He couldn't think of a time previous to this when he had ever cared about such a menial thing. And yet, he was asking.

She stepped further into the room, taking a seat on the armchair which sat facing slightly towards his desk, and settled there, like it was her own chair in her own home. Angus found this pleasing for more reasons that he could fathom, but mainly because it meant that the compulsion was more likely to have worked. This meant he wouldn't have to kill her. He really didn't want to have to do that.

"Lovely." She nodded fondly. "Cassie makes a mean pie. I feel like a new person." She ended her reply with another smile, and Angus had to look away for a brief second to compose himself. Also, her accent had shocked him again. The soft English flowed through the room, holding none of the harshness of his glaswegian one.

His opinion on the English was rather muted. He didn't hold such a hatred for them as his father did (it was still a shock that the king had allowed a donor from anywhere but Scotland to enter the Warren), and yet he wasn't a massive fan of them either. After all, it was in his blood to dislike them. That hadn't stopped him joining the Black Watch, but he knew that that was more related to his relationship with his father than his relationship with the Southrons. Call it a personal rebellion.

"You look it," he said, looking up again with what he hoped was just enough interest. "Cassie does know her way around the kitchen. You'll go to the canteen for breakfast, lunch and dinner. My orders. You need to have consistent sustenance. I can't have you feeling ill like earlier." He didn't want her missing meals. He needed her for his own meals, for God's sake.

She nodded her agreement. "Absolutely. Anything you say, Master."

Angus's eyes snapped up at her words. She had called him *master.* He didn't know why that bothered him so much – it was standard for a donor to address him in that way. But why was his stomach in knots? And why did he say the words that next came out of his mouth?

"Call me Angus," he demanded.

Her eyebrows shot up for a brief second and if he wasn't who he was, he likely would have missed it, but his heightened senses caught the expression of surprise with ease.

"Of course, Angus." She nodded, curtly.

He regretted it immediately – letting her call him by his name. It wasn't because he didn't like it. It was actually oddly warm and comforting. But what was nice about it was also why it was a problem. Angus didn't want Ivy to make him feel warm. He didn't want her to make him feel anything. Having a person in your life that made you feel good meant you were vulnerable, and Angus couldn't afford such luxuries. He was much safer if he felt miserable.

He stood up, picking up his desk chair, hands on each of the arms, and walked towards her, placing it next to the armchair she sat in. He sat down so they were about one foot apart, where he could smell the glorious scent of her, and for the first few moments, allowed himself the pleasure of letting it wash over him.

"Are you alright, Angus?" Ivy asked.

Angus realised at that moment he had closed his eyes, clearly high on her aroma. He opened them slowly, pinning hers with his.

"Do you like it here, Ivy?"

She squinted ever so slightly before responding in a clear, cheerful tone. "Of course I do. It's like being home."

Satisfied, Angus continued his compulsion investigation. "Do you like *me*?"

"I can't say I know you very well, but I would say that I do, yes." Her eyes twitched to her right ever so slightly, and he almost missed it. *Almost.*

"And how would you feel if I put my mouth here?" He reached out then, tentatively, and placed his index finger up against her carotid artery. Her heart remained fast, but it didn't increase in speed. She did however get her next breath caught in her throat, before sighing it out. It washed over him like an ocean wave, and he had to use all his self-restraint to not inhale it deeply.

Her breath was paralysing to him, and at the same time, the most powerful stimulant. He felt the muscles in his predatory body coil, and he had to use everything in him to stop himself from tightening his hand around her neck and dragging her to his mouth. The effort it took him to do so would have made him breathless, if air was something that he craved. But it turned out all he really craved was her blood. He would have to make sure she didn't do that again if he wanted to keep her alive.

"I think I would like that." She nodded in reply to his question, although her voice had quietened slightly.

"What if I bit you here?" he added, this time slightly encasing her neck in his hand, his voice a little gruff.

"I think I would like that, also," she said, eyes still locked on his.

Angus dropped his hand, feeling conflicted. On one hand, he was thrilled at the prospect that it appeared she was susceptible to compulsion. It made his so-called life much easier. But on the other hand, he was washed with disappointment. How much he would love to have her uncompelled. How much fun it would be.

He knew he could remove the compulsion and then compel her once more after he had had his way with her, but this again took away any pleasure in it. And Angus had a distinct need to gain pleasure from the girl in front of him. He realised that her simply existing in his presence – to act as a food source – wasn't enough. He wanted to feel the rush of trying to seduce a woman, even a brunette one, and the glory when he won the task. He wanted her to pant deliciously under his mouth and mean it.

But he couldn't have such pleasure. Instead, he needed to confirm the compulsion was working. He needed to make her do something she wouldn't normally do, without thought, without hesitation – the ultimate test.

He leaned in, reducing the distance between them even more, filling his personal space with her, only her, and said, "Kiss me."

Ivy didn't hesitate. She closed the gap between them and pressed her lips onto his. Angus, a little surprised, opened his mouth, his tongue tracing her lower lip. She tasted like a fresh meadow, and he found himself raising his hand to the nape of her neck, drawing her closer to deepen the kiss.

Suddenly, he felt as if he were human again, needing breath – in and out – except she was the breath he needed.

He broke the kiss with a start, snapping his face away from hers.

When he focused on her again, her eyes were wide with shock and her lips beautifully puffy from his assault. Angus was suddenly deeply embarrassed – embarrassed at how much he craved her and how her response had simply been fabricated from a lie. It made him feel somewhat hollow. Even more than usual.

"I'm sorry," he said, shaking his head as if doing so would make his thoughts clear. "I just got carried away."

She smiled at him sweetly and shrugged her shoulders. "It's okay. I thought that was nice."

He chuckled, but more to mock himself. "Nice." He nodded, left wanting. He looked up at her then with regret in his eyes. "I wish you could feel more than nice, and I wish that it could be you – the *real* you – that felt it."

He stood then, taking one final look at her, before leaving his quarters and heading back down to the hospital wing for another cold blood bag.

CHAPTER 6

A Fascination

Ivy

I sat in the chair, static, mind reeling, for what seemed like a lifetime.

I thought about all the possible reasons he had kissed me. I wondered about whether he did it with every donor, as if to test the water and the possible chemistry. I wondered if it was because he had simply wanted to do it.

No. It was clear that Angus had been testing *something*, but it wasn't our chemistry. He had been testing *me*. All those questions in quick succession – the questions that seemed to line up with what I was meant to have been compelled to feel. I had raised his suspicions with my actions earlier and he had to try out his theory. His words at the end, the ones he said before he walked out, were an indication that I had passed that test. I couldn't decide if that made me lucky or not.

When he asked me to kiss him, my brain had been on auto-pilot. The kiss still lingered on my lips. His had been firm, yet soft. Cold, yet warm. And I had hated it. I had the same horrible feeling you would get when you were sleeping, and a fly would land on your lip – that feeling. The feeling that would make you bat your lip for the next few minutes because it felt that horrible. That's how I felt. And yet what he had said at the end was oddly beautiful. That he wished I could feel more than nice, as if he was hinting that he wished his theory had been right – that I couldn't be compelled.

He had apologised to me, as if he had felt some sort of distaste for his actions. Surely if he was a monster, he wouldn't have felt that way.

My head pounded at the possibility that Angus was actually a human within a vampire casing, slowly trying to bring himself to the surface without quite knowing how. But those thoughts very quickly dissipated like fog after dawn. I wasn't going all Stockholm syndrome on the guy. After all, I was really trying desperately to reduce the clichés in my life. So I stuffed all the hunches I felt about the vampire with the blue eyes, and instead focused on not acting like a person trying to find an escape route 24/7.

◆ ◆ ◆

The next two weeks were much the same as the first day. I got into a mundane rhythm: waking up, going to the cafeteria for breakfast, reading a book from Angus's small collection, lunch, perhaps a walk around the Warren, before dinner and more reading until it was time to sleep.

I didn't see Angus much. In fact, it was almost as if he went out of this way to avoid me completely. There had been no physical contact since the kiss we had shared, and he seemed to make a conscious effort to come to bed after I had fallen asleep and leave before I had woken.

I'd never actually ever seen him sleep and wondered if in fact he even needed to. Sleep, after all, had the purpose of aiding the function of *living* things. It seemed odd in that case to assume he ever came to bed. Maybe he didn't. I had to admit that I was grateful for that. The thought of sharing a bed with Angus made my stomach turn.

Our brief encounters came when he would sit at his desk to work, me on the bed reading silently, oddly content in each other's company. He hadn't once attempted to feed off me and I was beginning to think he never would. This I was also grateful for, but there was also a part of me that found it infuriating. If I wasn't going to be used as a walking blood bag by the guy, it was surely a total waste for me to be here. Why couldn't he send me back? Why did I have to stay here, living the most unfulfilled life, while he ignored me?

By week three, I was beginning to get antsy. It was surely only a matter of time before he had to give in and feed. I didn't know much about a vampire's reality, but it was justified to assume that they needed to feed at least once in a month.

At dinner that evening, the need for information consumed me.

"How often do your vamps feed on you?" I asked my canteen friends, trying desperately to air a disposition of nonchalance.

'Vamp' was a term used a lot by the group, so I had decided to incorporate it into my own vocabulary. Calling them 'masters' and 'mistresses' all the time was kind of a tongue twister, and although I couldn't totally put my guard down, the cafeteria – and just being around them – was the only time I ever really got to be even a smidgen of my former self.

Sass piped up first. "I'd say..." she paused, pursing her lips and rolling her eyes to her head. "Probably every other day?"

"Yeah, around about that," nodded Duke, halfway chewing on some steak. "Depends on the day."

"Definitely depends week to week for us," said Heather. She said the word 'us' in such a way that I was almost struck by the familiarity and adoration in it. "Depends how much we wanna get it on...if you know what I mean." She winked at me, and I shuddered.

"Jesus Christ! *Of course* she knows what you mean, Heather. Everyone and their mum knows what 'getting it on' means," poked Andy, rolling his eyes dramatically.

"Sooorrrryyy," drawled Heather, clearly offended. "She's still a newbie. I'm just trying to keep it light."

"Yeah, to be fair, Andy, I really don't want to know the in's and out's of Heather's sex life," said Duke.

"In and out could probably sum up Heather's sex life."

Heather hit Andy on the arm for that, hard. He chuckled, raising his hands and said, "I deserved that."

"So, they need to feed a few times per week then?" I probed.

Duke shrugged, "I guess so. I don't know the exact frequency, but I remember my mistress being away for four days and after that she went pretty crazy when she saw me again. If you know what I mean..." He winked at Heather mockingly. She stuck her tongue out at him and scowled, but laughed in the end when Duke returned the gesture.

"Why you asking anyway? Is the prince tryna jump your bones more often than you can handle? Have you got carpet burn?" Andy asked in mock sympathy and they all laughed, even Heather, who tried to hide it behind her hair. I laughed too, joining in on the supposed banter.

"Just curious is all. Like Heather said, I'm a newbie. But I'm also an information hunter, I just love to be in the know." I forked a piece of carbonara pasta, twirling it around before forcing it into my mouth.

So, not only would Angus expect my blood, he would expect my body, too. And I would have to pretend that I enjoyed it. *Fan-fucking-tastic.*

"But in all seriousness Ivy, do you feel like you can't handle it? 'Cos I'll take him off your hands for a couple of days if you like?" asked Sass, definite hope etched onto her child-like face.

"Sass?! What is wrong with you?!" exclaimed Heather, her face horror stricken.

"What?! So a woman can't like sex now?! It's the 21st century, Heather, be a feminist already."

"Amen sister," said Andy.

"That is SO not what I meant Sass. I just meant you can't ask Ivy if you can have a slice of the prince. Number one, it's not up to you. Number two, I've heard you get more than enough cake from your master as it is so I'm surprised you would even have the time between eating and oh, I don't know, *breathing,* and stuff. And number three, who's to say the prince would want you. He's got so much power that I'm pretty sure he could get the pick on anyone's donor and they would just have to hand them over, no questions asked."

"She's got a point there, Sass," agreed Duke. "I think the prince would have already asked for you if it was ever going to happen."

Sass's shoulder's sagged, and she sighed heavily. "A girl can dream…"

"You know," started Andy, "there was a time when the king took one of the other vamp's donors. Do you remember that, Heather?"

"Yeah, actually. Caused a bit of a storm but the vamp did have to just hand her over. Think she is still his donor, you know."

I sat at the table, listening to their conversation, constantly absorbing information. It was possible that Angus had commandeered another donor and was using them for all his needs, nutritional or otherwise. I was thankful to whoever the person was as it meant my neck wasn't on the chopping board (pardon the pun), but there was still that feeling of undeniable injustice. I didn't need to be here. I was a placeholder.

I continued to sit and finish off my pasta, nodding and laughing at the right moments, responding to questions when they were directed my way. Although I was eating, my stomach felt hollow. To be confined to this existence was so cruel. At least if I was compelled, I could at least believe I was happy and I could enjoy these moments of eating good food with friends. Instead, I was constantly on edge. Constantly worried about being found out, constantly stressing over Angus and his intentions, constantly fighting an internal struggle.

I worried about whether Angus would be at his desk when I walked in from dinner. I worried that he would ask me to kiss him again. I worried that he would ask me to do more than kiss him. I was in a constant condition of fight or flight – heart rate never at full rest, mind never fully at ease.

"You look awfully miserable, do you know that?" Heather whispered in my ear as we walked out the cafeteria doors.

I snapped my eyes to hers, alert. "I'm sorry, I didn't realise."

"Don't apologise. I can't say I have that feeling often, nor do any of the gang, but there is this one girl who comes to the salon, and you are reminding me of her right now. I sometimes take her to the spa after work and she always says she feels much better."

"There's a spa here?" I asked, surprise leaching into my tone.

"Yeah, it's on the floor below. There's a sauna, jacuzzi and all the trimmings. How about you grab your swim things and a towel, and we head over there now?" Heather had the warmest smile on her face, like an angel, and I couldn't say no to her. In fact, I didn't want to say no. It sounded perfect.

I smiled warmly back at her before replying, "I'd love that. Thanks, Heather."

"Not a problem. I'll meet you back here in fifteen to twenty minutes? Then we can walk together to the spa. Don't want you getting lost, Newbie." She bumped her left hip against my right one, before walking away, waving behind her.

I walked back to Angus's quarters, still troubled by the lack of security in this place. If I knew how, I could get out of here relatively easily. No one was here to guard me. I was free – in that sense of the word. In all the other senses, I was anything but. I tried not to linger on that fact.

Expecting an empty room, I walked in using the key he had given me. I was surprised to see Angus sitting on the bed, legs crossed casually at the ankles, bare footed, reading a book. His eyes locked onto mine, pinning me in place.

"Good evening, Ivy." His voice was incredibly smooth, like velvet. It was almost smothering.

"Evening, Angus," I nodded, smiling slightly, but not with full power. I didn't want to attract his attention. We were doing so well with the avoiding thing, and I really didn't want that to change.

I'm a coward. Sue me. Kinda happens when your life is on the line.

"What will be occupying your time tonight?" He cocked his head to his left, appearing intrigued, and smirked ever so slightly.

"I think I'm going to head over to the spa. Heather is joining me."

"Heather? The blonde?"

"She is blonde, yes," I said, matter-of-fact.

He nodded curtly in response, taking his eyes off mine and frowning slightly. "You aren't blonde," he muttered.

I remembered what Sass had said when I had first met her. She had also commented on my lack of blonde hair, and the man who introduced me to Angus while I was in the glass cabinet thing had mentioned that my hair didn't fit Angus's preference of lighter hair. There was a running theme here...

I frowned at him in confusion. "No, I'm not blonde. But I've heard that people with different hair colours can in fact interact, and perhaps even get along sometimes, you know." I blurted out the words without any real thought, and then regretted it instantly. That was too sarcastic. I shouldn't have said that, not in front of Angus. I was aware that in the cafeteria, donors were allowed to let loose, but I'd seen other interactions, and they weren't like that with their vamps. It was politeness, meekness, worship. Not snide, sarcastic comments.

Shit.

He looked up at me again and smiled broadly. I was suddenly taken aback. Jesus, he was *stunning.* His eyes sparkled, the crease of them somehow allowing more light into the spheres, his cheek bones were pulled up and out, creating deep, muscular lines down the side of his face, highlighting his shapely, strong jaw lined with stubble.

"Is that right?" he asked, humour slightly lacing his

roughened voice. "Well, you have educated me greatly tonight. I am quite in debt to you." With that, he closed the book he had in his hand – an old hard back it seemed – and placed it lovingly on to his bedside table. Uncrossing his ankles, he landed his feet lightly onto the soft rug next to the bed and began to stalk towards me.

The word stalk wasn't used lightly. His feet padded along the floor like the decisive prowl of a wolf, taking the exact path to reach its prey. It was completely efficient, ensuring he moved without expending unnecessary energy. I stayed planted, unwilling to move from fear. I was the rabbit in the headlights.

Please don't bite me.

Angus surprised me by standing opposite me, toe-to-toe, before raising his hand to my face in a gentle caress. "You look like you need a visit to the spa. Your eyes look tired." He ran his thumb under my left eye. "And you are holding tension in your shoulders." His hand travelled down the side of my neck, squeezing gently when it reached my trap, before releasing.

His eyes then flashed with something, and he asked, seemingly casually: "what will you wear?"

"I was just going to have a look in my wardrobe to see if I had any swimming things."

The quarters had been stocked with clothing when I had arrived, all my size conveniently, for all occasions. I had a walk-in wardrobe but rarely wore anything but leggings and oversized jumpers. Comfort beat fashion any day in my opinion. And you couldn't blame me considering that most of my daily brain function was channelled towards figuring out how to survive in this place, rather than what I was going to wear that morning.

"I'll pick you something if you'd like?" he asked, raising his eyebrows in expectation.

I didn't want him to pick me anything. I didn't like the idea of him going through the options, thinking about how my body would look in each one, and picking the one which he believed would be most pleasing to his eyes. But I couldn't say no, because a nice, compliant donor wouldn't do that.

"Of course, Angus."

He stepped into my wardrobe, perusing the area which obviously held swimwear. I saw him pick up a bikini with what looked like very little material attached to it, and winced. He turned towards me, frowned slightly, before putting it back down. I let out the breath I didn't realise I was holding and allowed my shoulders to sag in relief.

He came out holding a very practical swimsuit, still frowning to himself. His fist balled around the material as if it offended him."This. You'll wear this."

I couldn't understand his reaction. Perhaps the thought of me in a skimpy bikini actually repulsed him. I mean, it *would* explain why he didn't feed on me. Maybe I really wasn't to his tastes – pun intended. Maybe I was just a little too plump around the thighs, and a little too flat in the chest.

The thought upset me. No one ever wanted to feel undesirable, even by their vampire kidnapper.

Pushing away my vain thoughts, I nodded in agreement. "It's perfect," I said, before taking it from his tight grasp.

Just as I was about to turn away from him to pack a bag, I felt him grab my wrist, spinning me back towards him.

"It's really just you and the blonde going tonight, isn't it?" His eyes were sharp, light cascading into them from an internal source, and I was able to recognise it as an attempt at compulsion. I made the conscious effort to glaze my own eyes over, playing the role of little-miss-compliant-donor.

She was my least favourite role of them all.

"Yes, just me and the blonde." I had an urge to point out that her name was Heather, that she was a *person*, but I knew that wouldn't go down well, so I replied using the words as he had used them.

He shrugged, holding my wrist for a little longer than necessary, stroking the veins with his thumb before walking back to the bed, picking up his book and crossing his ankles once again, as if the last ten minutes never happened.

I got together a gym bag, packing a towel and flip flops before leaving the quarters without a single word more to my master.

◆ ◆ ◆

I sunk my shoulders beneath the warm bubbles of the jacuzzi and let out a sigh. It dragged out, burning through my lungs and my trachea, willing that I be healed of my chronic emotional burden.

Heather sat on the other side of the jacuzzi, eyes closed, and lips turned up slightly at the corners, hinting at her blissful state of calm. I tried to do the same, breathing in and out through my nose with my eyes closed, trying to remember that one piece of meditation I had learnt at the single yoga class I'd attended two years ago. Unsurprisingly, I hadn't quite managed to get the knack for it. Turns out that meditation and mindfulness was actually really fucking hard. It wasn't just sitting with your eyes closed muttering 'namaste' and 'om'. It actually required a load of dedication, motivation and brain power, which were all things I seemed to lack.

"You are doing that thing," murmured Heather, eyes still shut. I tried to look inward, wondering what she meant, but came up blank.

"What thing?" I questioned, a frown forming in between my eyebrows.

"That thinking thing you do," she explained.

"Is that a bad thing?" I asked, confused.

Her eyes blinked open and she squinted. "Considering that it always makes your eyebrows pinch in that way, I'm going to say yes, it *is* a bad thing. Frown lines are a woman's worst enemy." She smiled light heartedly at the end, letting me know that she was joking, but I had a sense that Heather was the type of person to limit frowning for the simple reason that it would make her less attractive. I didn't mean that in a spiteful way, and I certainly didn't think less of her because of it. Heather was just someone who was proud of her appearance. I had never seen her with a hair out of place, or an eyelash that wasn't curled. She was pristine. A pageant queen.

"No, but in all seriousness," she continued, "I don't think I've ever seen someone brood as much as you do on a day-to-day basis. What's happening in that pretty brunette head of yours?"

I was surprised at her use of the word 'pretty'. Heather was stunning – so much so that the thought of her thinking of me in such a way was startling.

"It's mostly a lot of empty space."

"I don't think that you could have told a bigger lie than that single sentence," she quipped, tilting her head to the side, as if doing so she would suddenly be able to read my thoughts. "Do you and the prince get along okay?" she asked.

"Define 'okay'," I replied dubiously.

She laughed, rolling her eyes. "Do you like each other?"

"I think he's okay."

"Define 'okay'," her eyes pinned mine, using my own words against me, and we both laughed together. It was nice. Her laugh made me laugh and vice versa. It made me feel a little lighter, even if I hadn't actually gotten anything off my chest.

"I just mean it's neither here nor there," I shrugged. I couldn't tell her that he actually semi-repulsed me, or that there was a part of me that thought he was insanely human.

Or a part of me that thought he was beautiful.

"What's feeding like? I noticed that you don't have any visible bite marks. He obviously very private…?" Her tone was such that I knew she was probing.

I mulled over the risks and benefits of telling Heather the truth of the situation. If I told her that he hadn't tried to feed on me, there could be possible repercussions. He could lash out, feed on me, or worse – kill me. I could be like poor Izzy, or like the other girls that John had alluded to the other week. But he hadn't compelled me to not say anything. And if I didn't tell her, the only part of this existence that I enjoyed – the relationship with canteen friends – was futile. How could I have friends that I couldn't even tell simple things to? This wasn't me telling her that I couldn't be compelled. This wasn't me telling her the truth about the Warren, about how she was living in a dream world – a world where everything seemed perfect, when in reality it was anything but. This was just me telling a friend that my vamp master hadn't nibbled on me yet.

Nothing, really.

"I wouldn't know," I began, treading lightly, gauging her response. She didn't say anything, so I continued. "He hasn't fed on me yet."

Her eyes widened suddenly; her mouth opened. "You're kidding," she gasped.

"No," I shook my head in emphasis. "I'm not kidding. It's never happened."

"So, no sex?!"

"No sex," I replied, shaking my head again. The two really must come hand in hand.

"Well, I am honestly shocked." I shrugged in an 'it's no big deal' kind of way. "I can't even begin to unbox this right now, Ivy. It's way too much for me and my chakras."

"I'm sorry, your what?"

"My chakras. You know, my energy centres." She waved her hands around in a gesture.

"I really don't."

"Never mind. I can't explain Hinduism to you as well as deal with the bomb you've dropped on me right now. You are asking too much of me." She sighed, pushing her hair away from her face with her damp hands before appearing to re-centre herself.

"There is no reasonable explanation for your master not to feed on you. It literally goes against anything and everything that we, and they, *are*. It's why we all love being here. No wonder you are so miserable!" She breathed out, chuffed at her investigative skills. If only she knew that this was in no way the reason I was miserable.

Poor Heather.

"You should come to the salon tomorrow! I'll do your hair all nice. It might build your confidence a bit so you can face the prince. Maybe he'll see you in a different way?"

I sighed, sad that my attempt at confiding had ended up being so fruitless. It somehow made me feel more alone. But I didn't want to offend her – after all, she was being nice – so I agreed to meet her in the salon the next day for what she described as a 'pamper day like no other.'

We sat in the jacuzzi for a little longer until the skin of my fingertips reminded me of dried fruit. Heading to the dressing rooms, I showered all the chlorine off my body, washed my hair, and just stood under the stream of hot water for what seemed like a lifetime.

My thoughts turned to the idea of freedom. Over the last three weeks, the shock of being in the Warren had almost paralysed me – so much so that I had entered some sort of Groundhog Day. I felt disappointed in myself. I wanted, no, I *needed* to try and escape. But could I leave my friends? Could I live with myself knowing that I was free and they weren't? I could imagine myself entering some sort of shame spiral and my heart got immensely heavy. I realised suddenly how insignificant I was. How useless I was. This mental glitch of mine – the one that meant I wasn't able to be compelled – it was wasted on me. I was powerless to help anyone.

I stepped out of the shower and towelled my body, dressed and dried my hair with the styling tools hanging on the walls. My face looked hollow and lifeless. I realised I hadn't actually looked at myself in the mirror in days, and to see myself so starkly unhappy was depressing. I practised smiling, tightening my facial muscles to bring about the characteristic upturned mouth and squinting eyes, but I just ended up looking so much worse as a result.

I huffed dramatically at myself. *You are pathetic. You need to try harder.*

There were never meaner words spoken than the words we said to ourselves in our own minds.

I collected all my things from the locker I placed them in earlier, determined to be more useful to myself than I was currently being. More useful to everyone.

I scraped my hair back into a ponytail and began to leave the spa. I walked through a corridor that ended at a junction which went either left or right. A sign straight ahead said one was the exit and the other was the gym. I headed towards the gym, not only to assess the facilities – I was sure they would be to highest of standards – but also to get my bearings on the size and layout of the Warren. If I wanted to escape, I was likely going to have to play the long game, biding my time. It was apparent that the first part of that game was sussing out everything about this damn prison.

The spa was, to my knowledge, on the floor below the main floor of the Warren. *The collection* (a term I'd picked up), and the salon room were what I was certain was the lowermost floor. From what I could remember when I had been taken here, the Warren was entirely underground. However, the areas above this appeared to have natural light. The canteen, for example, had what I assumed was a large south-facing window near the ceiling, spanning across one entire wall. I would have to give it a closer look. Perhaps they used mirrors to direct the light inwards.

That made me start thinking about the vampire body clock. From what I was aware of, we were running a day to night schedule. That meant that the vampires were either sleeping in the night the same as would be normal to humans, or hardly sleeping at all like I'd thought before. But why adhere to a human schedule in the first place? Weren't they allergic to the sun?

God, I was in way over my head.

I continued along the corridor until I reached the gym reception. A human man stood behind the desk and when he caught sight of me, began to smile enthusiastically. He was small but broad, with muscles for days. His skin was tanned, and he looked Mediterranean.

"Good evening," he beamed. "I'm Ronan. Are you here for an evening gym session?"

I winced. I couldn't think of anything worse.

"No, actually," I shook my head. "I'm relatively new

here and I just wanted a tour of the place, suss out your facilities, you know?"

"I certainly do know!" He smiled even more broadly. It made me feel kind of uncomfortable. Even before the Warren, I was never really a fan of overly enthusiastic people. "You just wait here... um, what was your name sorry?"

"Ivy," I said. Ronan flushed.

"Oh, *the* Ivy?" he asked expectantly, eyebrows raised.

"I don't know what that means," I stated, knowing that I looked dead behind the eyes, but not able to bring myself to life. The resting bitch face was likely in full swing.

"You are Prince Angus's donor! *The* Ivy."

"Okay, you can stop calling me that," I chuckle half-heartedly. "It's *just* Ivy."

"Okay, *just* Ivy. I would be more than happy to personally take you around. It would be my absolute pleasure! Just wait right there, okay?" He gestured to the area I was currently standing.

He returned, bringing out a woman in tight gym wear and a face full of makeup. She was tanned (although it was likely from a bottle), and her hair was a deep chestnut which complimented her light blue eyes perfectly.

"Okay, Freyja. You know how to man the desk, right?" Freyja looked very uninterested in what Ronan was saying, her eyes pinned to my face like a laser from a sniper rifle.

"Who is this?" she asked, sourly.

"This, is *the* –. I mean, *just* Ivy." He presented me with a flourish, and I was suddenly washed with embarrassment. Did they all really see me as some sort of vamp royalty?

"Eughhh," she rolled her eyes dramatically. "*This* is who everyone is talking about? *Seriously*?" Ah, so it seems they didn't *all* see me as royal then. "She is literally *so damn plain*." I half expected her to stamp her foot in defiance at the end, but she just continued her scowling instead.

"Oh my gosh! I'm so sorry for her behaviour!" Ronan said, shocked. He turned back to Freyja with slits for eyes, rivalling her own, actually. "We are going to have a chat about this later. But in the meantime, just man the desk and squeeze out the tiny ounce of politeness you have hidden under that seven-inch-thick layer of foundation, got it?"

Freyja gasped, but nodded, turning her head to the computer and typing on the keys. She muttered something about 'hating uggos dressed as VIPs'. I suddenly felt grateful for the over-enthusiastic Ronan. He just saved me from my first jealous bitch war.

"Thanks for that," I mentioned as we began to walk through the double doors towards the main gym area.

He shrugged off my thanks, smiling. "Not at all! I would have done it for anyone. Freyja can be a real snidey cow sometimes, but she certainly can't talk to you like that! It's just not moral." He shook his head, as if he was violently offended by her behaviour. I didn't blame him – she was a lot to take. "She doesn't actually work here. Her master just sometimes gets her to come down and help out when he wants some space."

I wondered why she was the way she was. She had looked uncomfortable, not physically, but... in some other way. I couldn't pin point it. But there was one thing I was certain about: I was going to stay far away from Freyja.

Ronan led me towards the girl's locker room but also showed me a unisex locker room, too. They were all very similar to the spa. He then took me to the swimming pool.

"It's regulation olympic size," he nodded towards it. Within it there were multiple lanes but in some lanes the people in the pool were going considerably faster than others. "That's the vamp's side of the pool there," he pointed to the side furthest from the door, "and this is the human side."

There were a couple of humans doing lengths. I was suddenly jealous at that moment of their ability to float, to feel completely supported by the water, and just let go.

"Do you like to swim?" Ronan asked, curiously.

"I don't know," I shrugged. "I've never really thought about it. I *can* swim. It does look oddly peaceful though, as if they are in some sort of moving meditation."

"Ahhh, if it's moving meditation you like, I know just

the place." He gently took hold of my arm and led me towards a corridor with doors on either side. Each room appeared to have some sort of class – one appeared to be circuits while another looked like aerobics mixed with weight lifting. The final room was candle lit and looked cosy. The people in the class – humans only – were doing Yoga.

"Ummm," I started, "I tried Yoga once and I just don't think it's for me."

"Well, why don't you give it another go? Mel, the instructor for this class, she's a real gem. We are lucky to have her."

"Okay, sure. I'll look at the timetable."

"Brilliant! The timetable for classes is split into human and vampire classes. We feel it works better to separate due to the differences in physical ability. We have human and vamp PTs also. The main gym can be used by humans and vampires at any time and is open twenty-four hours a day. Our main gym room also has a boxing ring. I'll show it to you now – we might have some takers in the ring tonight."

We headed over to the main gym. Ronan opened the doors and in the centre stood a large boxing ring. Within the ring, two males sparred. It was obvious they were vampires. They moved in a way that any human, no matter how athletic, could only dream to emulate. I was almost taken aback by the beauty of it. I'd never thought boxing could be such a thing, but they managed to make it so. I realised then that I hadn't actually spent much of my time in the Warren in the presence of vampires. Me and Angus rarely saw each other, and the canteen was for humans only. Watching them now, I became transfixed. Their movements were sometimes smooth and crisp and then would suddenly become a blur, my eyes struggling to keep up with the speed of them. Before I realised it, I was walking towards them, my legs unable to control themselves.

As I got closer, the sparring stopped. The male vampires were laughing with each other. Both their faces were bloody, as were their hands as they wore no gloves. One of the men was very heavily built, with thick, carved muscles from head to toe. He was glossy from sweat and his dark skin almost appeared to shimmer. The other man was his opposite. He was taller, and leaner, but still muscled. His hair was floppy and wet, and he had a bloody smile. They went to their corners, wiping their faces and hands clean. In doing so they looked almost healed of all their wounds.

Both were beautiful.

Both were terrifying.

The taller of the two men caught my eye, turning his head towards me slightly. He smiled in such a way that the left side of his lip turned up into a smirk. "Hello." He nodded, eyes glimmering. We continued to stare at each other before he shook his head in disbelief and muttered, "Well, aren't you fascinating."

I blinked many times over, relieving myself from his eyes. I turned to Ronan, who had come to join me closer to the ring. "I think I've seen enough now, thank you." He told me it was no bother and escorted me out the gym.

As I walked away, I had a feeling of eyes boring into the back of my head the whole time.

CHAPTER 7

Sorcha

Angus

Angus sat on his bed, unable to concentrate. He would usually go to the library, but he had been spending more time in his quarters than he could ever remember. In his cool hands he held his favourite book. After the disappointment of the novel he had been given as a recommendation from Sorcha, he needed something that he knew wouldn't let him down. However, even with it in front of him, he struggled to read the carefully crafted words as his eyes ran over the pages.

You're being ridiculous.

If he had ever been in this restless state before, he would have indulged in his donor or taken himself out of his quarters to go and find one of the female vampires to pass the time. He knew a good few of them which would be thrilled to have his attention again; he was well aware that over the last few weeks it had been uncharacteristically absent. But this somehow did not interest him. In fact, nothing interested him. Nothing at all.

At that moment, he heard movement in the corridor and his excitement piqued. This was short lived, however, when he heard the knock at his door.

"Angus, it's me." It was Sorcha.

Sorcha was Angus's closest and most valued friend. She was tall, with fiery red hair which he believed was a product of her equally fiery personality. He had met her while she worked in a pub in Glasgow around sixty years prior. Her accent was strongly glaswegian, and her use of Scottish slang was unmatched.

She had been human then – when he had first me her – and an attractive one at that. But that's not why he took an instant liking to her. If anyone caused any shit in the bar, she was sending them out on their arses, tail between their legs. Her banter with the men was charming, but she also wasn't afraid to call people out on their misdemeanours – even Angus's – and she had a fiercely strong moral compass. She had known about his vampirism, but unlike others, had been acutely aware of the burden of the curse, and never once glamorised it, appreciative of the sanctity of humanity. She never once begged to be turned, and instead occasionally pitied Angus, which he found amusingly charming. But above all, she was immensely loyal. Her undying loyalty to him was something that couldn't, and hadn't to this day, been matched. He had never once compelled her. She had been perfect the way she was.

One cold, winter night, Angus had been out at another bar in town, feeding. Sorcha was at the pub she worked, alone, putting up Christmas decorations for the upcoming festivities. It was that night that the pub got broken into and Sorcha, being the person she was, had attempted to fight them all off, desperate to get justice. She couldn't have done the normal thing – the self-preservation thing – and just given them the money. She had to fight. And although that was what Angus loved about her, it was her biggest fault, and she paid for it that night.

On his walk home, he was around one mile away from the pub when he had smelt her blood. Her blood wasn't particularly appealing to him, but he knew it distinctly and began to run at full pelt, not caring if anyone saw him glide with speed no human could ever dream of.

When he arrived, Sorcha lay in the centre of the main room, a large shard of glass protruding grotesquely from her stomach, moving only with her delayed, laboured breath. At that moment, Angus made a decision that was probably the most selfish of his entire existence. At the time, he hadn't seen it that way. He believed that he was saving her life. If only he had known that she believed he was taking it.

They didn't talk for some years after her palingenesis. Sorcha had felt robbed of her life and robbed of the plans she had made. They only really began their friendship again when they both entered the Warren, and that was a slow, tentative process. Now, they were closer than they ever had been, but that didn't mean that Angus wanted to open the door to her.

"Angus, ye wee shite. I know you're in there. I can hear the wee cogs in yer brain turning! If ye dinnae let me in, I'll batter this door doon!" Sorcha was angry. It didn't take a genius to figure that out.

He had no doubt in his mind that she would indeed fling the door off its hinges if he refused her entrance. She was *strong*. And not just *vampire* strong. She was *red-haired-female-in-a-rage* strong.

He stood from the bed and walked to the door with reluctance, peeling it away from the frame. Sorcha stood tall opposite him just inches from the threshold, arms folded aggressively in front of her chest, red hair cascading over them.

She strode in, pushing Angus with her broad shoulder as she passed, orientating herself next to his desk. "Sit," she commanded, pointing to the chair just opposite her, directing the scene for her interrogation.

"I'd rather stand," he responded, in what could only be described as a sulk.

"Do *not* start with me, Laddie. Sit down, or I'll drag ye to that chair by yer hair."

"Must you always say such sweet things to me, Sorcha? You gonnae gie me a skelpit lug, too?" he asked, walking towards the chair in question, sitting with a sigh. He briefly let his mind wander to the fact that he was sitting on the same chair Ivy had when she had kissed him, but quickly brushed the thought away.

"I know what you've been up to." She frowned, her eyes slitted, as if she was trying to compel him to confess to something.

"I've not been up to a hell of a lot, so I'm surprised that this has caused you to fling yourself in here like a tornado," he replied, stony faced.

"Oh, don't try that with me. Callum told me, Angus. Callum told me aboot the blood bags."

Angus flinched slightly at her words, before replying. "What could he possibly have had to say?"

"That you are compelling the poor wee medics in the hospital wing for blood bags. Ye do know that they dinnae donate the AB stuff to feed yer blood lust. The humans need it," she said, disapproval cloaking her words like a shroud. She always was a softy for the mortals.

"It's not really any of his business," he snapped.

"Ye haver! It is one hundred percent Callum's business! He oversees the human blood bag donations!"

"They aren't donations. We compel them to do it."

"Okay, aye. He oversees the blood bag input and output. Happy?"

"Not in the slightest," he muttered.

Sorcha observed his face carefully. "What? So yer depressed now, is that right? So much so that you're needing more blood than yer donor can provide?" Her voice was increasing in octane with each question, and Angus had to raise his hand in a gesture to lower her volume.

"I'm not drinking from my donor." He tried to say it nonchalantly, but he knew there was no way to mask the absurdity of his actions.

"Why the hell not?" she asked, pure confusion on her pale, freckled face.

Angus shrugged a response. Not even because he didn't want to answer, but because he didn't really understand the reasoning himself.

"Jaysus, Angus. I know she's a brunette and all, but do ye really have to be so picky? I've seen her, she's bonny enough."

"Feck sake, Sorcha. It's not because of her damn hair!" And it really wasn't. He may not know the exact reasoning, but he knew that it certainly wasn't because she wasn't blonde.

"Well, what the feck do I know? It's mad for ye not to feed from her! Why choose a blood bag over her neck? Eejit." She began to pace, puzzled.

"Don't say feck."

"You started it."

"Well, don't continue it," he snapped. A friend she was, but Angus also saw Sorcha as a little sister, and his spine twitched whenever she swore, or came close to it.

"Fine." She stopped pacing. "It's ridiculous though. I'm half in the mind to demand ye feed from her."

"You can't judge me. You've never had a supposedly conventional relationship with your donors," Angus retorted.

"Oh, come onnn," she drawled, arms flying up in frustration. "You know why I dinnae sleep with donors."

"Yes, yes." Angus nodded, rolling his eyes. "Your love for Callum is enough."

"Aye, that. But also the whole sleeping with someone who hasn't really consented doesn't sit well with me," she added.

Angus's head snapped up at that. He wasn't sure before, and had always related it to being less pleasurable, but he suddenly realised the reason for that – Sorcha had described it perfectly.

"Right. I suppose that's how I feel about it," he replied, staring off into the distance, as if not concentrating on the physical world helped to concentrate his mind. "And maybe even how I feel about the blood thing."

"What do ye mean?" Sorcha frowned at him, but her voice was soft, so he felt comfortable enough to answer.

"Well, just like the humans don't have the ability to consent to have sex with us, they don't exactly have the ability to consent to be bitten."

Sorcha let the concept roll around in her head for a few seconds before replying with a frown. "I have to say, I've never thought of it like that."

"Nor had I until recently."

"Until the donor called Ivy?"

"Yes, I guess so."

Sorcha walked over to Angus's desk chair and slumped into it with a sigh. It was a very human action, and Angus felt suddenly nostalgic. She pushed her long legs out, rocking back in the chair and crossed her arms. "What's different about this one?" she asked. "Apart from her hair, obviously." She was so used to Angus picking blondes that Ivy's hair colour probably bounced around in her head a lot, unable to find somewhere to land.

"I couldn't really tell you…" He trailed off, rubbing his face with his hands for inspiration.

"Okay, well what do I tell Callum about the blood?"

"Tell him I'm working on it, but not to expect changes any time soon."

She nodded in response, perhaps finally understanding his thought process, and, reluctantly, accepting it.

"When do I get to meet her?" She wagged her eyebrows, acting as if Ivy was his new mysterious girlfriend that she was dying to meet.

"If I got any say in the matter, it would be never," he jested, smirking. "But I'm assuming the ball."

"Eugh, why so protective of her?"

"I'm not protective of her," he bristled, "I just think you like to meddle, and I'm not interested in dealing with that at the moment." He stood up from the chair he was sitting on and began walking to the door Sorcha had stormed through a few minutes prior. "Please leave. I'm reading."

Sorcha rolled her eyes before standing. She walked up to him, patted him on the shoulder in pity and said "Sure ye are friend, sure ye are," before leaving without another word, her chuckle resonating in the hallway.

Angus walked back to his side of the bed, but didn't bother picking up his book again – he didn't need to lie to himself anymore today. Instead, he thought about Callum's face when Sorcha told him about his new found feeding habits, and flinched slightly. Although it was shameful, he was lucky it was Callum rather than a vampire who was less in favour of Angus who controlled the so-called 'blood bag donations'. Callum would keep his secret. He was almost as loyal as Sorcha herself.

Callum was Sorcha's long-term partner. They had met, from what she had told him, around two years after her palingenesis.

Before Callum, Sorcha struggled with her vampirism. Her knowledge of his lifestyle had tainted it for her, and unlike any other new vampire, she didn't revel in her new found speed, strength and beauty. Instead, she entered self-loathing, and at one point even attempted to starve herself – a vampire suicide.

The thing was, vampires were awful at starving themselves. Although not human, each vampire did hold some of their humanity, carrying it with them to this new life. However, with each day a vampire didn't feed, their humanity – what was left of it – leached further away, to the point when if one hadn't fed in say, one month, nothing within them could stop their need to feed. That's what had happened to Sorcha. She had starved herself for five weeks straight, her humanity a tiny memory inside her. On passing a road accident, the smell of blood consumed her with a hunger that even she couldn't fight, and she gorged herself on all the victims until she swelled with blood. Callum, already a vampire, had found her in a remote forest, trying to tear out her own tongue, her own limbs off. She never had tried to starve herself again, nor tear herself apart. For all those years, Angus had thought that *he* was the one who had saved her, when really it had been Callum. Angus knew that Callum loved Sorcha so much that if she asked him to end her 'life', he would honour her decision and rip her heart out himself.

A vampire could only die from having their heart ripped out. It was ironic, considering that they were a species considered to be heartless, but it was the one thing they needed to stay 'alive'. They couldn't be decapitated – many had tried and failed – and they were completely fire resistant. A stake to the heart was an inconvenience, but once it was out, the healing process would resolve any injuries incurred.

Angus pondered over what it would be like to have someone as devoted to him as Callum was to Sorcha. He found it hard to understand – he had never experienced such emotion in his human life, which made it even more difficult to understand it in his vampire one.

He felt, for what he thought was the millionth time in his existence, bitterness towards the Warren. The place was so restrictive that it was fair to predict that he would never find such a connection. He didn't know why this bothered him – it never had before. He decided, as he did with most things, that it was best not to overthink it.

He heard movement in the corridor again. The door opened with a click of a key and a smell he would have previously killed for.

Ivy's head popped around the door, and she closed and locked it behind her smoothly. When she turned to face him, her face was a little flushed, perhaps from the heat from the jacuzzi. She smiled at him meekly, and he returned the smile, disappointed.

"It's rather late, no?" he asked.

Her eyes widened suddenly, darting to the clock on the wall which read ten-oh-five. He didn't know why, but he'd put it up after she had arrived. He'd had a feeling, although no concrete evidence, that she liked to know the time, and he thought it courteous to place a clock there so she could see it.

"I'm sorry, Angus. I didn't think you would mind." She blushed, and Angus had to look away.

"I don't particularly," he answered.

"Okay, I'm glad." She nodded, before pulling things out of her gym gear into the washing basket. He could smell chlorine, and it made his nose sting. It irritated him that it masked her scent almost completely.

"If you go back, just remember to take that swimming

cossie." He gestured to the one in her hand, about to be dropped into the basket, and she nodded back in answer.

She continued organising her things. She then walked into her walk-in wardrobe and took out a set of pyjamas before heading into the bathroom, locking it behind her.

He tried not to listen, but he couldn't help but hear her removing her clothes, the sound of fabric running against her skin, the unclasping of a bra. He imagined how smooth her skin would feel to the fabric.

He realised that he had no other choice but to leave then, so he put on a pair of shoes and walked out his quarters, leaving her alone to get to sleep. He would return when she was sleeping and the temptation to do anything was less.

CHAPTER 8

The Truth

Ivy

Over the last couple of weeks, I had been making a map of the Warren. Initially, it had been a map in my head, but the extent of it was too big, and I'd had to transfer it to paper that I'd taken from Angus's desk. I kept this map on my person at all times, apart from showering, but Angus was rarely around when I showered so I wasn't concerned about that.

I had mapped the entire basement floor which included: the entrance I was brought through when I first arrived, the place with the steel tables where they seemed to swap and collect donors, the salon room, and another place where clothes were washed and dried. There was also a locked room which I couldn't enter, so on the map it was just a blank space with *UNKNOWN* written in the centre.

The floor above this was the gym and the spa as I had known, but also the hospital which was run mostly by humans, with some vampires scattered about as well – this was where Andy worked. That was all that level entailed and from what I was aware of. There was no means to exit anywhere on it. Above that was the level with the cafeteria but also I had found an 'outside' courtyard area. It had grassy patches and trees with large windows which let in sunlight. On closer inspection, there did indeed appear to be mirrors behind the glass, reflecting the light from outside into the room. It was peaceful, with a central pond that water gently ran into from a fountain. It had become my new favourite place.

Also, this floor had all other amenities such as salons, dentists, shops – it was a bit like a mall. Off this floor was a wing which appeared to hold the living quarters. This was where me and Angus stayed, although it appeared that our quarters were considerably bigger than the rest. The perks of being a royal.

On first impression, this didn't give me a lot of options for escape, and I had to admit that even if I was able to escape somehow, once I was out, I would struggle to find somewhere safe to stay. We were in the middle of nowhere. It would be next to impossible. Luckily, we were in the height of summer which not only gave me more daylight hours, but also a warmer climate. I also had some degree of understanding about the security in the Warren. From what I could see, there were no security cameras. Wardenesque vampires patrolled the opening on the basement floor twenty-four-seven, but I was sure that this was more to keep people out, than keep them in. Having said that, some vampires were clearly not the happiest living here, and I had a feeling that Angus included himself in that group. He always seemed very uninterested. In me. In everything.

No wardens patrolled the halls. These were 'free' zones. I used that term lightly. There was a degree of surveillance in the cafeteria, this was an 'amber' zone. I was aware Callie and her staff reported back to people about their (mainly my), behaviour, but it wasn't always open. It appeared to run between seven am until ten am, twelve pm until two pm and then five pm until 8.30pm. This meant in the evenings, the cafeteria was empty. I sometimes used this time to gather resources. I had obtained a few non-perishable items from the large pantry behind the open kitchen, and kept them in my wardrobe, a place I knew

Angus rarely frequented and never snooped. I'd also obtained a knife. Likely a futile weapon, but still better than nothing.

I kept my head down for days on end, me and Angus rarely even exchanging a few words. He still hadn't fed from me, and if possible, paid even less attention to me than he had done before. The trip to Heather's salon had made very little difference to his interest and aside from a slight comment about the smell of my hair, he said nothing more about it.

I wondered what Angus did with his days. He never seemed to be around except when he worked at his desk. I thought about him roaming the halls, being ogled at by the women of the Warren as he passed. I wondered if he smiled at them or if he ignored them entirely like he did with me. For some reason, I wanted to know the answer.

I realised then that my childhood was always going to affect my life. My parents not giving me any particular attention meant that I craved it from others. Angus ignoring me did something to my psychology. It was like being a kid again, being ignored by people that were meant to love you unconditionally, and desperately wanting it to be otherwise.

The thing was, I didn't particularly like Angus. He was cold and bossy. He was the prince of a community which thrived on mind control, binding people to a life they never consented to. And yet, I didn't want to be the only donor he ignored. It just seemed to confirm something. Something my parents must have seen. Something that I didn't want to believe was there.

So, despite desperately trying to avoid my fate as a walking blood bag, I wanted *something* from him. And I really hated myself for it.

I thought about Heather and her master. She was in love with him, but was he in love with her? Surely not. And if he wasn't in love with her, how could she possibly think that he was? Was he compelling her to believe they were some sort of romantic power couple? I didn't know why I was unable to believe that. Of course a vampire could compel a human in that way. They would compel them any way they needed to in order to provide themselves with a favourable outcome. Because they *weren't human.* I needed to remember that.

As a society, we always talked about 'humanity' and how it makes us good people. Caring simply because a human can relate to another human – because it was in their humanity to simply *care.* Vampires weren't human. Therefore, they couldn't have humanity. And therefore, in simple terms, they couldn't care.

But there were humans who exist who were said to lack humanity. If someone were to do something heinous, a terrible crime, it was considered to be out of a lack of humanity. But did this really mean they lacked the fundamental components of a human? People liked to detach themselves from people who did bad things. We liked to think we had nothing in common with them. So we deprive them of humanity. It makes us feel better.

I wondered if that was what I was doing with vampires. It was easier for me to deprive them of their once human emotions than to consider the possibility that they still remained. Because if they still remained, why were they able to still live in the Warren and do the things they did to humans?

My mind was conflicted. In some way, I really wanted Angus to be unfeeling, and in others, perhaps more so, I wanted him to feel it all.

◆ ◆ ◆

One evening, after dinner, I was having a shower to wash off the day. I had spent my afternoon in the courtyard, reading on a bench, smelling some of the flowers, watching the water move like black and white ribbon in the wind, and to my surprise, I had become slightly muddy. Heather had pointed out a stain on my cheek at dinner, rolling her eyes saying, "The prince isn't going to sleep with you if you look like that, Newbie." I'd laughed, but I'd also felt a little unsettled at the comment, which was my usual reaction whenever someone mentioned Angus carrying out any donor-related tasks on me.

The thought of Angus wanting to sleep with me was a difficult thing for my mind to process. On one hand – the hand in my mind which was entirely female and heterosexual – it was entirely desirable. Angus, at the end of the day, was undeniably attractive. He had a look in his eyes that was domineering and in the real world – a world I lived in not so long ago – I would have lapped that up, even if it were just for one night. I would have been stupid not to.

But in *this* world, those domineering eyes didn't suggest he could take control in the bedroom. It suggested he could take control of your life. That your life would literally be in his hands. One wrong move, and it would be game over. And that knowledge meant that the other hand in my mind, the hand which recoiled at the thought of Angus taking me to bed, won every time.

I began to take off my clothes absentmindedly, letting the reminisce of the thought sit for a while, swirling slightly.

When it finally ebbed away, I allowed my mind to stress over another detail. I was aware that I had been at the Warren nearly two months (Angus kept a wall calendar and crossed off each day as it went), and had not had a period once.

My heart had begun to race even more than normal, and I began to sift through the bathroom cupboards wearing only my underwear, trying to find any sanitary products. When I had no luck in the bathroom, I moved into my walk-in-wardrobe, and also came up blank. Everything else that I had ever needed since I had 'moved in' had been available to me without the need to ask. The people involved in the preparation of the room and my hospitality had left no stone unturned. So why hadn't they considered that women have monthly cycles?

After ten minutes, I decided that this room wouldn't have the answers, and began to strip fully before I showered. Angus, as usual, wasn't in the room, so I left all my clothes on the bed before entering the bathroom and locking the door behind me habitually. I let the hot water fry off any of the worrying thoughts about immaculate conception, or even worse, successful compulsion, and washed my body and hair systematically.

I was nearly finished when I heard a sharp banging on the door. I jumped, in complete shock at the obtrusive sound, placing my hand over my chest to keep my heart inside it.

"Ivy, get oot of the shower, right noo!" Angus's voice was stern and decidedly more Scottish than normal, teetering towards violent. My mind reeled with possibilities.

Reluctantly, I switched off the water. "Yes, Angus," I responded.

I briefly dried myself and put on a pair of knickers and my silk dressing gown, before shaking my wet hair out and opening the door.

On the other side, Angus stood, clutching a piece of paper in his hand. My heart dropped; it was my map. In my panic, I hadn't brought it with me into the bathroom and instead had abandoned it with the clothes I had recklessly left on the bed.

Why was he going through my clothes?!

"Care to explain this?" he asked, holding the map up. His eyes were filled with rage, and he appeared so much bigger than normal, as if the anger within him couldn't be contained and was pulsing itself out of him like a force field.

I tried to be as honest as I could. Someone once told me that if you were going to lie, you needed to keep as close to the truth as possible, only altering the absolutely necessary pieces of information. "It's a map I drew of the Warren," I explained.

"I can see that my wee bonny brunette, but why have you drawn it?" I flinched at his nickname for me. Is that who I was to him? His 'wee bonny brunette'?

"I like to draw maps. I like information." Again, not

necessarily a lie. *Keep going, Ivy.*

"And what," he flattened the map in front of my face so I could see it more clearly, and pointed to the bottom right corner, "is this?" He was pointing to the key code – the 'red', 'amber' and 'free' zones.

Fuck, I'm done for.

I breathed in a full breath, blowing it back out directly into his face, making the map rattle slightly as I did so. It was all over.

Angus responded to my breath by stiffening slightly. Then suddenly, all the anger dissipated from his body and his shoulders slumped. He turned, dropped the map onto the bed, ran his hand through his hair before turning back towards me, now two metres away.

"I knew it." His eyes locked onto mine, and he squinted slightly, as if this could help him see me clearer. "You can't be compelled. Fuck!"

I began to unconsciously pick at my nails – they made a *snap* sound every time and it filled the room. I shrugged, as if to say, *you got me.*

He let out a sound that was half way between a chuckle and a huff, running both hands through his hair this time. Suddenly his eyes lit up. "But you kissed me!" he exclaimed in disbelief.

I pushed the thought of his lips on mine out of my mind with a sharp shove. "I had to," I replied, again shrugging. I felt myself waiting for the penny to properly drop in his head. I waited for him to end my life. I had mulled over this so many times over the last few weeks. How would he do it? There were so many options: bleed me dry, snap my neck, paper knife through the heart, against my neck. What would he choose?

"That's where you're wrong," he muttered, and I could have sworn that he had a smirk on his face. "You're the only human in this place who has a choice." I realised his smirk was disbelief. He couldn't quite fathom what was happening.

I piped up then, his last sentence raising my blood pressure to a simmer. "Oh, yes, I'm sorry, *Master,*" I dragged the word out cynically. "I *did* have a choice. The choice was be *kissed by you* or be *killed by you.*" Angus came up short, stunned by my outburst. His eyes narrowed. "Please, do tell how anyone was meant to make that so-called *choice*?" My eyes narrowed right back at him.

"I can't deny, I wanted to kill you," he admitted, deadpan. I stared at him, waiting for an explanation. "If I'd found out on that night that you weren't compellable, I would have had to have killed you." I could have sworn I saw him flinch.

"Well, now you know!" I exclaimed, erratically. I was at the stage where I was aware my life was about to end, so I might as well just let it all out. "Kill me, Angus! Because this life I'm living isn't worth much to me anyway! You don't even speak to me, and on bad days, won't even look at me! The people here are victims of kidnap and mind control. They don't have their own minds! It's sick, and every other bad horrible thing I can think of! And don't even get me started on the blood thing! How is it that the sole purpose of me being here is to be fed on, and apparently, I'm not even good enough to be used for that!" My hands were flailing all around the side of me, my gestures trying to dissipate some of the pent-up energy. I didn't think I had been particularly offended by him not feeding off me, but apparently, I had been, and this made me hate myself.

Angus was perfectly still, listening to my rant. He seemed almost in shock, as if he was unable to comprehend that I had that many words and feelings all crammed inside of me. He stepped closer to me then, just by a single step, but he was tall, so this brought us considerably closer together. I tried with everything in me to stay put.

This is it.

"So that's what you want? For me to bite you?" His lips slid up into a snarl and his eyes became predatory. He rushed to me, picking me up by the waist and flinging me against a wall on the opposite side of the room. We stopped with a *thump.* My feet were planted firmly on the floor, but his broad, cool hands were still wrapped firmly around my middle, as if he thought I needed support. He ran his hands up my sides, over my dressing gown, skimming the sides of my breasts, and I flinched. But it was not for the reason I thought. His hands continued their path upwards until they encased my head, my wet hair clinging to my skin, and he stared firmly into my eyes. His gaze then travelled towards my nose, lips and then my neck, where he allowed himself to explore every detail. He was enjoying himself, and I could tell. I was breathing heavily into his face, and it seemed to only spur him on more.

"Your neck is incredibly distracting," he murmured. "I hate that you always wear those baggy jumpers that slide off your shoulders." He moved in closer, rubbing his nose up and down the side of the collum, inhaling deeply. "If it were up to me, you'd be in polo necks all year round. But I have to say, this robe is quite a feast for my eyes" My breath hitched, and he noticed. "Hmmmm, make that sound again," he hummed.

"No," I said in defiance, trying to free my head, but being completely unsuccessful. He chuckled then, pulling his head back to look at me.

"Your resistance is only making this more fun for me, you have no idea," he smiled, his sharp teeth close to my face like a threat. "Would you scream if I bit you my wee bonny brunette? Or would you moan?" He was back at my throat again, tilting my neck to the right with his hand, allowing himself better access. I could hear the wet sound his mouth made when it opened slightly, his lips peeling away, and my body stiffened in pure, concentrated fear. But he didn't do as I expected him to. Instead, his tongue began to run along my neck, taking the same path his nose had before, tasting the skin and collecting the droplets of water that had begun to run down it. His lips then closed slightly, and his licks turned to little nips and kisses. It wasn't threatening and my head lolled to the opposite side as I found myself giving into his touch. He tilted my head to the other side, and began his pursuit again, balancing the two sides out.

"Your heart rate is always a little fast, but now it's going mad." He pressed his fingers to my pulse point, a little like he did on the first day we met, but this time his eyes were full of hunger. He slid his hand further down my neck, over the space where my collar bones met, and then towards my heart. I tried not to concentrate on the fact this was also where my breasts were, but this was made even more impossible when he moved in, bringing his mouth next to my ear to whisper: "do I make your heart race?" His breath so close to my ear made me stiffen again in defiance.

"Oh, come now, wee bonny brunette, let go," he cooed. When I didn't, he released me, stepping a couple of inches away from me. I found myself half relieved, and to my disgust, half disappointed. He chuckled slightly, clearly seeing these emotions flash across my face. "I won't kill you tonight, Ivy. Actually, I think I'll keep you." He looked up to the ceiling in disbelief, smiling. "And as for the feeding, I think I can persuade you," he added, his eyes back on mine now.

"I don't want you to persuade me." I was breathing heavily, and I could see Angus watching my chest in interest. I suddenly remembered my robe, and quickly adjusted it, pulling it closer around my body.

"Fair enough," he shrugged.

"And you're *keeping* me? What does that mean?"

"Well, it just happens that I have been looking for someone just like you. So, I'm going to keep you."

"Someone like me?" I asked in confusion.

"Yes." He nodded. "Someone free."

CHAPTER 9

The Ball

Ivy

I had just woken up when Angus made an announcement.

"You have to attend a ball tonight."

After his realisation that I couldn't be compelled, he let me get properly dressed into pyjamas, allowing me some privacy. When I emerged from the bathroom again, he was lounging on his side of the bed, looking unusually happy with himself. He was very attractive when he thought things were going his way, and I had had a sudden need to make sure he always felt like that, so I could continue to be in awe of the way it made him look.

He had patted the space next to him. "Why don't you get in bed. It's been a day of revelations, and I'm sure you are tired. I know I am."

This sounded like Angus was being considerate and caring. But I knew better. This was a command. Me getting into bed was only to benefit him, not me. And yet he was playing the role very well. A little *too well*.

"I didn't know that vampires could get tired," I had replied. He rolled in his eyes in response.

"We do," he confirmed. "But we don't sleep as much as

humans. And this is rather an odd time of day for me to be tired, I admit." I had stepped closer to the bed with a degree of suspicion, and this made him chuckle. "I'm not going to pounce on you again tonight, Ivy. That instinct is sated in me. For now."

"Why are you being like this with me?"

"Like what?" he had asked, raising his eyebrow.

"Nice." *Flirty.* I crossed my arms over my chest as I replied and his eyes had darted down to them quickly, before rising to meet my face again.

"I don't recall ever not being nice to you."

"You aren't *not nice*," I had started nervously. "But you aren't exactly *nice* either."

"I'm not known for niceties I have to say, my wee bonny brunette."

No shit, Sherlock.

"Do you have to call me that?" I sighed as I got under the duvet and arranged my pillow until it felt comfortable under my neck.

"I don't, but It's a term of endearment, I assure you."

"I thought that you were more into blondes," I had replied, sharply. Heather had confirmed my suspicions one lunch time.

"I thought so, too," he mused before standing and taking off his black t-shirt. I had felt rude staring, but for some reason I felt he had taken something off me that night, and that somehow if I stared at him I would be able to get it back.

His body was as expected – sculpted and expertly crafted. It appeared that whenever he was not in the quarters, he was in the gym. He was heavily scarred though, and I made a note of that, ensuring that one day, perhaps when I was confident enough to, I would ask him about them.

He undid the top button of his jeans and then the zip before sliding them down a pair of muscled thighs and calves.

"Stop staring, pervert." He had chuckled, and I had turned away, closing my eyes tightly in an attempt to rid myself of embarrassment. I had then felt him get into bed and whisper, "Goodnight, the girl called Ivy." And that had been the end of it.

I didn't know if he had actually slept because the second my eyes had shut, I had been gone to the world. But he wasn't next to me when I had woken up the next morning.

Since that night, Angus had been a lot chattier with me. It wasn't as if we were friends, but he didn't ignore me, and we had some degree of easy conversation which flowed throughout the day. He hadn't come nearly as close to seducing me as before, but he was less careful with physical contact, sometimes touching me during a conversation. The other day he had picked an eyelash off my cheek and stared at the dark fleck on his finger with interest, before brushing it onto the floor.

I turned my head to the side, eyes squinting from the light he had turned on. The lights replicated natural light, so it felt like the waking rays of the morning sun. "A what?" I asked, still squinting. He lay next to me, fully clothed and on top of the duvet, his hands behind his head in a relaxed manner.

"A ball," he replied, smirking ever so slightly, before frowning and removing a piece of hair away from my eyes.

"For what possible reason?" I knew that I sounded like a bratty child, but I couldn't help it. I brushed away at my face, his touch lingering there.

"We hold an annual summer ball in the Warren. It's tradition. It's not exactly mandatory to attend but–" I saw my opportunity and cut him off.

"Not mandatory. Fabulous. I shall stay here."

Angus scowled, shaking his head in frustration. "As I was *going* to say, it's not mandatory to attend, but since you are *my* donor, it most certainly *is* mandatory."

"Can't you just say I'm sick?" I asked.

"I cannot."

I let out a heavy sigh and pushed myself up in bed, propping the pillow behind my back in support. I turned to face him, concern etched all over my face. "Angus, I don't think I can attend a ball with vampires. It's hard enough to convince the humans that I'm compelled, let alone hundreds of vamps."

"Don't worry your wee head about that. I'll make sure you pass with flying colours," he said, attempting to reassure me.

"And how exactly will you do that?"

"In my cruel, wicked ways, of course," he smirked.

I could feel my face contort into shock, and he laughed out loud, throwing his head back slightly. It was a sight to behold.

Do that again.

"I'm kidding. Trust me. Just be polite, hold your tongue whenever you feel a sarcastic comment is on the tip of it, and smile. People will be distracted so much by that smile that they won't ask questions."

I rolled my eyes at his flattery. He had been making remarks like that for the last few days, and I still hadn't figured out the best response. Assuming it was sarcasm was the best defence I currently had in my arsenal.

British people were really shit at taking compliments.

"And no eye rolling," he added, admonishing me.

"If you think a few smiles and pleasantries is enough to convince them, you are clearly not thinking about this hard enough," I huffed.

"It worked on me." He shrugged.

I winced. "I think that says more about *you* than it does about my ability to be convincing," I commented, and regretted it immediately. *Too honest, Ivy.*

He turned to face me more, his body almost square to mine. He had dropped his arms to the side of his body. His eyes locked on mine, blue to brown, and I took in a sudden breath, surprised by his intensity. At the sound, his eyes travelled to my lips. I watched as his tongue darted out in the way it had the first time we had been in the room alone together, pressing onto his right canine tooth. *What does that mean?*

His stare continued down, caressing my neck, my collarbone, and I found myself crossing my arms across my chest, suddenly acutely aware that I was only wearing a pyjama vest. The intensity soon became unbearable, and I made a desperate attempt to break the spell between us.

"So why do I need to attend again?"

The sound of my voice snapped him out of his thoughts, and his tongue quickly retracted back into his mouth with a delicious sound. He swallowed, rubbing his hand down his face, an expression there which I couldn't quite place. I couldn't help but think it was his reaction whenever he wanted to snap my head off. I had learnt that he hated it when I asked him loads of questions. But when he'd finished, he seemed more centred.

"You're *my* donor. And I'm the prince," he said, finally.

"Yes, but *I* am not a prince," I retorted.

"No, but you are as close to a princess as they come in this place."

I thought back to what Duke said at the first dinner I had had at the Warren. He had warned me about this without me even really knowing it.

"So, what? I'm just supposed to look pretty on your arm?"

"Is that what you think princesses do?" he asked, the question loaded.

"I can't say I know what princesses do," I replied, mind wandering.

"Well, I guess that means you get to make up the rules then, doesn't it?" I looked at him sternly in response.

"I don't think I can act compelled and make up the rules at the same time. I feel they contradict themselves, surely?"

"Maybe you are right," he shrugged, his lip turning up ever so slightly at the corners. "I'm excited to see what you come up with."

I groaned, flinging my head against the pillow behind me, covering my face with my hands. He chuckled almost silently, before getting off the bed and walking to his desk, some papers there taking some of his attention.

"John will be here to get you dressed for the event at around five."

"Well, if that's the case, and I absolutely have to come,

can I make a request?" I asked. Angus's eyebrows flung upward in surprise, and he gave me a look of question.

This was the first time I had ever actually asked him for anything. I was usually too scared to. He had a fantastic ability of saying the word 'no'. He was also a rather selfish being, only really doing things which were for his benefit, and not if they only benefitted someone else.

"You may, although considering that you are meant to be my compellable subordinate, it will have to be me who makes this request, so please make it passable," he said, his eyes now narrowing, hand no longer holding the pages with interest.

"Am I no longer a subordinate?" I asked, in a tone that I shamefully recognised as hope.

"No, you are still my subordinate," he said, with a deep frown, dropping the papers completely, and turning towards the bed. "It's the compellable part we struggle with."

I thought about how Angus still hadn't fed from me and couldn't help but believe that he didn't really understand what I was to him at all, and I certainly didn't have the courage to ask. After all, he was volatile and could turn on me at any instant. I was one wrong word away from being the new Izzy. I decided to ignore his last response and focus on my request.

"I don't want him to put as much makeup on me this time," I stated.

Angus's head cocked to the side, as if the motion placed his brain in a better position to remember something, before re-centring.

"I have to say, I agree."

"Really?" I asked, sitting up a little more in bed, surprised.

"Yes. That stuff he put on you for our introduction was…" His eyes tipped to the ceiling, as if a dictionary was pinned on it and he was looking for inspiration. "…distracting."

I frowned. "Distracting from what, exactly?"

"From you. Something a little lighter is something I

would be happy to request," he said, nodding, going back to his papers once more.

But I wasn't done. For some reason, his acknowledgement that I didn't look my best in the glass case frustrated me, as did the knowledge that he was only giving me a choice because it benefitted *him also*, not just me. Perhaps if I had asked for heavier makeup, he would have refused, simply because he would think me less appealing.

"The makeup on *my face* distracted *you* from *me*." My voice sounded slightly whiny, and I hated myself for it.

"Perhaps distracting wasn't the right word," he sighed out, clearly frustrated that I wouldn't let him concentrate on his work.

"Perhaps," I muttered.

"Enough!" he shouted, startling me. I could feel my eyes widen, taking in the situation, hedging my bets on violence. "You'll attend the ball and that's the end of it. Go do something now. Stop asking questions. The dress you will wear is hanging in your wardrobe whenever you have the time to see it. But now, I'm done talking to you, subordinate." He sat in his chair, not looking at me again.

I couldn't decide what was worse, being called his 'subordinate' or his 'wee bonny brunette'. I worried that the one I was fonder of would say too much about how I felt about him, and I wasn't able to confront that. Not yet.

His reaction had confirmed something that made my heart feel heavy. Angus didn't really *care* about me. He didn't care about my choices or my wills. He said he had wanted someone free, but he meant free on *his terms.* And on *my terms*, that wasn't free at all.

◆ ◆ ◆

Angus had left by the time I had come out of the shower. I put on my trusty leggings and baggy jumper that hung over the chair near his desk, feeling secure in the familiarity of it. It was the one part of home I could cling on to.

I headed to the canteen, the buzz palpable. I'd missed breakfast, so it was lunchtime. Everyone seemed to be talking about the summer ball. It didn't escape my notice that they hadn't mentioned this once prior to that afternoon, and yet they spoke about the ball as if they had been waiting for it for months.

Heather was practically vibrating with excitement, her voice nearly reaching the octaves of Sass's, which was quite a difficult feat. Andy was excited for the eye candy, even though he was distinctly aware he couldn't do anything with said eye candy. When I asked him why that was, he found it difficult to fathom any words, and I was suddenly sucked back into reality. He didn't know *why* he couldn't, he just *couldn't*.

Sass was rather muted about the whole event, stating that she hated to dance and found the dresses uncomfortable. When I asked her why she didn't ask to not attend, considering it wasn't mandatory, she stuttered. Her eyes narrowed, as if she was thinking really hard, and I could almost see her brain fizz in frustration. She didn't know.

Duke didn't know why he hadn't asked to change the suit he had been assigned – he hated it. Heather didn't know why she had to dance with one of her donor's vampire friends, just that she had to.

Although I was aware of the compulsion that surrounded and clouded their minds, I had never quite seen my friends in this way. Often, their compulsion made them happier and more content with their entire existence. This compulsion, however, seemed to pain their subconscious. It was as if there was a tiny part of their brains which were rebelling, willing them to fight the control – to push – and just before they got to the point of release, the compulsion would latch back onto that rebellion, snatching it right back to the beginning.

I found the entire exchange painful, and left earlier than I would usually, blaming the need to prepare for the evening.

On the way back to Angus's quarters, I detoured

towards the courtyard rather than returning straight away. I sat amongst the trees and listened to the water running into the pond. It was rather empty. People seemed to be more concerned with getting ready than anything else. I allowed myself to think about the summers in Scotland with my family. The walks in the hills, close to little streams and rivers which filled the crisp air with a hushed melody. The cold, fresh wind which would sometimes knock the air out of your lungs. The feeling of damp ground under your feet, and the smell it would invite into your nostrils. I allowed my senses to be engulfed with memories, entering into some sort of meditative trance. It was almost blissful. *Almost.* But an unwelcome feeling took away the unadulterated sense of calm – the feeling of someone's trained and sharp eyes on me. It was like a target had been placed on my back, but every time I looked around, I saw no one there.

When I finally felt more centred, I took the walk back through the corridors and halls. Again, it was all pretty deserted. When I opened the door, I found Angus was once again at his desk. He seemed engrossed, scrawling bullet points down on a page bound within a diary or some sort of organiser.

I couldn't quite believe it, but it seemed that he hadn't even noticed me come into the room. Normally, whenever I had returned back from the canteen, it was almost as if he had known I would arrive even before I had. But today, now, he was concentrating so entirely that he seemed to have completely overseen my return.

I cleared my throat. Angus's eyes found mine and within the same motion he flipped his left hand to shut the book. He clutched it with both hands, opened the desk drawer on his right, placed the book within it and locked it, all without taking his eyes off me. *What are you hiding?*

"Are you okay?" I asked, eyebrows raising in what I hoped was speculation.

"Of course," he said, leaning back in his chair and placing both hands behind his head, feigning nonchalance. I didn't buy it.

"Fine," I replied, pushing him no further.

His eyes followed me around the room as I moved and carried out small errands – tidying the bathroom, placing dirty clothes in the washing basket, brushing the knots out of my hair. He said nothing.

I walked to my wardrobe and stopped when I saw the dress. It was floor length, as would be expected with a ball dress. It was made from a heavy, silky satin material and I ran my hand over the edges, pinching it between my fingers in awe. It had dropped shoulders with a draped neckline which then appeared to cinch into the waist before flowing out again towards the tail, and the colour was the deepest navy blue I had ever seen.

Next to the dress was a set of lingerie. This pleased me considerably less than the dress itself, and I could feel my face contorting at the sight of it. The strapless corset was black and lacy with suspender fasteners at the bottom. Stockings were draped gracefully next to it and a pair of underwear also.

Angus was suddenly at the entrance of the wardrobe, leaning casually against the frame.

"Your heart rate has increased," he stated, folding his arms across his chest, scanning me from toe to crown. "What's up with ye?"

Him talking about my heart rate brought me back to the night when he had me against the wall. I shuddered, and regretfully admitted to myself it was out of pleasure. As if rejecting my unwanted thoughts, I stood tall, rolling my shoulder blades down my back. "I want to dress myself." I could feel the stern frown forming on my face.

"Why, exactly?" Angus's eyebrow raised at his question, and I could have sworn that there was a slight smile playing on his lips.

"Because, I don't want John to see me in that." My head nodded to my left, towards the offensive lingerie. My skin was becoming hot, and I felt a rare blush form above my collarbone.

"Hmmm…" Angus rubbed his chin with his hand, contemplating what I saw as a completely reasonable request. "John won't be happy with that," his eyes glimmered.

"Please. I don't ask for much. But I really need you to respect this." I tried to level my eyes with his, trying with all my might to come across as his equal. I knew that Angus didn't see me that way. And sometimes, he certainly didn't make me feel that way either. But after the conversation earlier, I had a need in my chest to try and gain more ground with him. For my own sanity. I wasn't used to being told what I could and couldn't do. I actually thought it to be a very dysfunctional trait in any type of relationship, and I felt that if I had that belief, I had to stick by it.

I was allowed to be intimidated by Angus. I was allowed to not ask questions in case he responded badly. He was a predator after all, and I was the prey. But I couldn't cower forever, because then I would probably end up losing everything that made me *me.* And I wouldn't let him do that to me. He could never have that power.

In response, his expression changed, suddenly becoming pensive. His eyes shifted over my face, searching, reading. He finally nodded, eyes still locked with mine, and the breath I had been holding blew out of me in relief.

I watched then as Angus stiffened slightly, clenching his fists at his side, before releasing them. I noticed it as odd, wondering what could have possibly caused him to react in such a way. Angus did this sometimes. We would be having a conversation, or perhaps we wouldn't even be engaging, and I would simply catch his eye, and his muscles would instantly stiffen like a predatory cat ready to pounce on an unsuspecting gazelle. Except, to me, it didn't actually seem predatory. It almost appeared defensive, as if he was protecting himself from something. In those moments, I wished I could read his thoughts, wishing they were written on the pages of a diary. I would lose myself in those pages, fascinated.

"I'll tell him I wish to dress you. He'll take it badly, but I'll insist on it. But don't worry, I won't *actually* insist on it.

Not with you." He turned before I could thank him, sitting back at his desk.

Not with you.

He unlocked the drawer on his right, took the book out and wrote one single line there, before closing it and locking it right back up as it was before.

◆ ◆ ◆

John arrived at five sharp and got me ready as per all of 'Angus's' requests. I was allowed to put the undergarments and dress on myself, although John did have to pull the zip up when I couldn't reach any further. He didn't comment on the fact that Angus hadn't been there considering he had requested to dress me, which I was grateful for.

He did my makeup more conservative, with an eyeliner wing instead of overly blended eyeshadow, but he did put on a red lip, which I wasn't mad at. My hair was waved slightly and placed in a low bun at the nape of my neck, some tendrils framing my face. Finally, I was instructed to put on the heels which were left (simple black heeled sandals), and wait on the chair opposite Angus's desk until he arrived. He had compelled me to do that which frustrated me no end. Why would anyone need to be compelled to put shoes on? I wasn't a petulant child.

It wasn't long until Angus returned. He had left to allow John to have full creative control over the situation. His hair was slightly more styled than usual, pushed off his face, but still with some of the un-did quality it usually had. He had clean-shaven in the morning, but now there was a slight shadow to his jaw.

He wore a kilt. I found myself eyeing up the bare skin of his legs. The kilt was made out of a green and purple tartan. Where the two colours overlapped they created a navy blue colour that almost matched my dress. His top half was clad in a classic shirt, waistcoat and suit jacket. A bow tie was expertly done, not even the slightest bit askew, and I began to imagine him standing in front of a mirror, using his long, strong fingers to tie it deftly. A bag hung off his hips.

"It's called a sporran," Angus said, gesturing to the bag I was staring at. "Are you ready?" he asked, scanning me with his eyes, his face giving nothing away.

I felt the question was ridiculous. Would I ever be ready to attend a large-scale event with 'people' who wanted to kill me, and certainly *would* kill me if they knew the truth? *No, Angus. No, I am not ready, you idiot.*

"In one sense of the word, yes." I nodded, standing up from the chair, brushing down my dress so it sat right. I ignored his overt gazes and picked up the small bag that John had prepared for me. It was cream, and it matched my nails. I had to say, John had taste.

Inside the bag he had left me with a tub of face powder, a small vial of perfume (one that smelt of nothing to me, I might add), and of course, my statement red lipstick.

"Okay, let's go." He held out his left arm for me, and I reluctantly linked mine in his. However, as we began to walk towards the ball room (which was apparently in the canteen – a feat I found unbelievable), I was thankful for the support of his arm.

"Just remember, you love being here. Smile. Laugh. And perhaps maybe even enjoy it a little," he snickered slightly, nudging me sideways. I liked this version of Angus. He was almost fun to be around. It very nearly made me forget about his outburst that morning. But not quite.

He had the unflinching ability to flit between characters – the stern master and the playful friend. Perhaps he has borderline personality disorder? I made a mental note to look into that.

Unfortunately, I didn't have access to any mobile devices in the Warren. We weren't given mobile phones (for obvious reasons), and access to a computer was limited. There were some in the hospital that I was aware of, I'd asked Andy once, but these were only connected to a medical server and medical records. Google was off the cards.

"And what happens if I'm rubbish at all these things?" I asked, voice shaking slightly.

His head turned towards me, watching my profile. "Then we'll retire." He rested his other hand over my forearm where it sat linked with his.

"Really?" I swung my head around to face him, shocked.

"Really. I don't need people getting suspicious of you. It would be an awful headache, and I don't have the time for it," he said, blankly.

Of course, silly of me to think it would have been for any other reason than a 'headache'.

We approached the canteen double doors. Two vampires stood on either side. Both were tall and broad, and they were wearing suits, but not tuxes. Some form of earpieces sat in their right ears. They opened the doors for us, nodding formally to Angus before we passed.

"Your Highness," they said in unison.

The doors opened to the canteen, and we stepped inside. Except it wasn't the canteen, not as I knew it. The long bench-like seating had been removed and instead there were tens of round tables, dressed in glorious and expensive white tablecloths. The chairs were all ornate. They had plush, velvet cushions supported by beautiful carved wood with hand-crafted details around the upper part of the legs and backs. The tables themselves were decorated with deep-red primrose centrepieces. I flinched at the colour; it resembled something that made my stomach turn.

Dragging my eyes away from them, I turned towards the left of the room where there was a cleared area for a dance floor and some instruments – mainly strings – on a slightly raised stage. On the far wall was a long straight table with chairs only on one side, facing towards the inner room. At the centre of the table stood the grandest of chairs, with a high back.

Angus noticed my gaze and answered my internal questions. "That's the king's chair. My father's." He shrugged as if the second part was an afterthought, one that he wasn't keen on. "It's his throne which is usually in the boardroom in the basement. They bring it in here every year for the ball."

I nodded, my head ticking with fresh information. It filled in a gap in my understanding of the Warren. The unknown room in the basement was the boardroom. I wanted to ask Angus what was done in the boardroom, but decided those sorts of questions were best asked in private. If anyone overheard my questions, they would know my secret.

"The chair on his left is for his donor."

"No queen?" I asked, trying to sound sympathetic.

"No," he responded, not elaborating further.

"Who sits on his right?" He squeezed my arm with the hand that before had been resting gently upon it, and I let out a little huff in pain.

He turned to me, frowning. "Sorry, did I hurt you?" He pulled back fully, inspecting my arm, where a slight flush had begun to appear in the shape of finger marks. He began slowly tracing the marks with his fingertips, frowning deeply. His fingers lightly prodded, and then began to caress. I looked up to his eyes. He appeared to be in some sort of trance.

"Angus, stop. People are staring." I said, smiling up at him in hope to disguise my anxiety. He said nothing, linking my arm in his once more before taking me to the long table with the throne.

"I sit on his right," he said, staring at the chair in what appeared to be despair. "And you'll sit on the right of me."

I nodded, letting him know I understood, and that I wouldn't make a fuss. I could tell a lot was coming up for Angus at that moment. I almost felt bad for earlier when I had made it about me, not thinking about how this event affected him.

Then I got pissy at myself. Why the hell should I care what Angus was feeling?! He had abducted me. I owed him nothing, physically or emotionally.

"More people are entering now. We will have to stand in front of this table and people will greet us one at a time when the king arrives," he explained.

As if on cue, the doors opened with a magnificent gesture, and a man looking no more than ten years older than Angus stepped in, a petite dark-haired, dark-skinned female at his side. She was stunning, in the human sense of the word.

Angus flinched beside me, and his right hand once again took a firmer grip on my forearm, but not as firm as last time, and I was able to tolerate it.

The man was tall, like Angus, with a head full of rusty-brown hair and a gruff beard. I wasn't close, but I didn't have to be to know that his eyes would be the same shade of blue as the vampire who stood next to me, arm entwined as if it were some sort of physical support.

The king walked with a gait which assumed both authority and grace. He didn't wear a crown as I expected, but something attached onto the lapel of his jacket caught my eye as he continued towards the high table. It glinted, throwing the light from the ceiling chandelier into every direction.

He smiled, nodding at people who caught his eye as he passed tables, before locking eyes with his son. His smile only waivered slightly, but it was subtle, and the look he gave after suggested he thought he had got away with it. I attempted to pull my right arm through the loop of Angus's left, but he grunted and shook his head.

The king approached us, ignoring others he passed. When he was around three feet away, he stopped, as did the dark-haired woman. She smiled brightly at me, and I did my best smile back.

A single primrose broach was attached to the king's lapel. It was red. My eyes darted to the flowers on the tables.

"Angus, son," the king nodded, now with a slightly stern look around his blue eyes. He was wearing a red tartan kilt, very similar shade to the colour of the flowers and the brooch. In fact, the majority of the male vampires were wearing the same or similar tartan. Angus's stood out like a sore thumb in comparison.

"Father," Angus replied, bowing slightly at the neck. I silently cursed him at that moment. He hadn't told me what to do when I met the king. I thought quickly on my feet, remembering the way the door guards had greeted Angus when we had entered.

"Your Highness," I bowed a little deeper than Angus, hoping this was considered a mark of respect. The king's eyes turned towards mine, narrowing slightly, before becoming bright.

"Quite lovely! Even for an English woman," he beamed, but there was something cut sharp behind his cool eyes. "This must be your new donor... Ivy, is it?" I noted how he didn't direct his response to me. This was, I realised, probably not a bad thing. The less attention on me, the better.

The fact he knew my name, however, didn't sit well with me.

"Correct," Angus nodded, straightening slightly, his right hand loosening, and then gripping again. It was close to being affectionate, if that was possible.

"She's quite something, and she smells positively mouth-watering. No wonder you wanted to search outside Scotland. Bonny, for sure. What a gem!" His voice became more Scottish the more he raised his voice. "Anyway, enough of this nonsense! We must prepare for the greeting. Get yourself in place." He raised his hands, gesturing them around as if to organise us into position.

Another vampire also approached the table. He was greeted fondly by the king before standing next to the king's donor in silence. Once again, Angus noted my curiosity. He tapped me gently on my arm with his index finger and began to trace out letters on my bare skin, spelling something out. *A-D-V-I-S-O-R*.

I nodded. This was the king's confidant, the vampire he went to for advice. His Thomas More or his Thomas Cromwell.

Hadn't they both ended up dead?

People began to arrange themselves in such a way to greet us, and I repeated a mantra in my head over and over: *smile, laugh, be happy.* It momentarily made me remember a little *live, laugh, laugh* plaque my sister had bought me for my new home as an ironic present, and my heart dropped a little.

The first vampire who approached was an old gentleman with stark white hair and dark eyes. On his arm was another vampire. No donor. She was taller than he was, with slick blonde hair tightly contained within a hair tie high on her head. It swished elegantly when she moved.

They both shook the advisor's hand, saying pleasantries before addressing the king.

"Ahhh, Lachlan. How lovely for you to have joined us for this glorious evening. And to see your lovely wife, too! Alianna, it is my pleasure." They both bowed, and then Lachlan did something quite disturbing. I watched on, the whole movement slowing down in my brain as if it were a movie. He leaned in to the king's donor and pressed his lips onto the right side of her neck, before moving to the left. Alianna did the same. My stomach flipped and I felt my heart rate increase. *Will they do that to me?*

I was suddenly distracted by Angus's fingertips once again on my arm. *Y-E-S.*

Fuck.

He immediately noted my anxiety, most likely due to the increase in heart rate, and began to draw lazy circles on my arm. His fingertip was cool, and smooth. It was stark next to my overheated skin. The sensation was remarkable in that it was able to distract me from the upcoming assault, and instead soothe me into a sense of semi-calm.

I looked up to him, jumping slightly when I realised he had been staring at me. I smiled genuinely up at him, my lips still together, and he responded with a nod. Almost like a *'you're welcome'*.

Lachlan and Alianna approached Angus, smiling broadly and complimenting him on his lovely donor. He responded just as pleasantly, being equally flattering about Alianna's obvious beauty.

The compliments towards me seemed like absentminded pleasantries and they left a slight bitter taste in my mouth.

Don't lie.

Lachlan smiled slightly at me before leaning in and

pressing his cool lips to my neck, directly over my pulse point. Angus squeezed my arm – gently this time – in reassurance. I let him kiss the other side of my neck and then let Alianna do the exact same thing.

I endured this countless times over, from every vampire that walked past. Each time I became a little more numb to it. That was, at least, until one vampire presented himself and his donor to the king.

I recognised him instantly. He had the same floppy hair he had had when I had seen him the first time, if less wet, and his eyes still glimmered with mischief. It was the beautiful vampire from the boxing ring. He was also wearing the same tartan as Angus.

"Anthony," the king began. "Always a pleasure. And this lovely donor you bring each time is such a treat, a feast for the eyes!" He clasped his hands together in excitement, smiling broadly, his canines elongated in the subtlest of ways.

"She's bonny enough," he shrugged. "But certainly not the bonniest," he stated, and then turned his head to his left, locking eyes with me, before turning his lips up into a seductive smirk. He pinned my eyes into place, and I became paralysed. But this wasn't mind control, he wasn't compelling me. He was just fascinating – just as he said I was to him. And I couldn't look away.

Anthony and his donor were dismissed from the king's attention, and he strolled over to us, still smirking at me.

"Prince," he smiled at Angus, drawing his eyes away from me. "Looking dashing as ever."

"Stop with the jesting, Anthony. It's getting old," Angus replied, scowling slightly.

"Oh, but we have such fun, do we not, Prince? Why not jest back, for old time's sake?"

"Because we are not in the old times anymore, Anthony," Angus bit, before sighing. "But I have to say it is nice to see you, it's been a while."

I watched the encounter. Anthony and Angus appeared to be acquaintances, although I made the observation that it wasn't quite a friendship.

"It has, Prince, it has. But nae bother. I'll see you around soon enough, I'm quite sure of it." He once again turned towards me, the smirk returning.

I waited in anticipation. The vampire walked closer until he stood right in front of me, toe-to-toe. His eyes travelled around my face, occasionally appearing to find something they liked, smiling slightly.

"Hello, again," he murmured. I stood staring, refusing to blink, refusing to speak.

"Fascinating as always." He leaned in then, taking his time with it, enjoying every second of the pursuit. His breath tickled the right side of my neck, and my breath hitched in my throat. I could almost hear his smile before he landed his lips on my neck. He then moved to the older side, this time, his tongue snuck out from his soft lips too and I audibly gasped.

A low growl vibrated next to me and Anthony's head snapped up at the sound of it. "Apologies, Your Highness," he smiled, having the good grace to look slightly embarrassed. He nodded once more to Angus, before turning and walking away. He did not look back at me.

I suddenly had the urge to check my little bag next to me, a feeling coming over me in waves. Inside was still my powder and lipstick, but the perfume was nowhere to be seen, and I was almost certain that Anthony had been the one to take it.

CHAPTER 10

Suspects and Seduction

Ivy

I stood near the top table for what seemed like hours. I saw all my canteen friends pass, each with their respective donors. Andy's donor was a medium built, medium height middle-aged Scot. He was polite, if not a little boring, and I almost certainly saw him looking Angus up and down with eager fantasy. His kisses on my neck were uninterested and sloppy. Andy winked at me as he passed, and I smiled back, genuinely.

Sass's master was young and tall but slightly on the larger side. His eyes were interested but his face was not interesting to look at – no more than any other vampire's. Sass smiled weakly at me, and my heart bled for her as she passed, head not quite as high as it usually was.

Heather was in much better spirits, smiling broadly at everyone she passed and even gently squeezing my hand as she passed with her master. Her master rolled his eyes at her, but it was almost fondly, before frowning and pulling her along. He had been broad and tall and classically handsome – someone out of a 1950's movie.

Finally, Duke walked past, all professional and to the letter. His mistress was stern looking, tall and broad with long, wild mousy hair. She was polite, but cold. I wondered what they were all like together behind closed doors. It worried me, which meant I had to let it go, for now.

Freyja had passed by with her master, also. She looked miserable, her face that of complete disinterest and yet her eyes were spitting venom. Mainly in my direction. She looked up adoringly at Angus, but when she was left wanting, appeared entirely irritated by it. Her master was older and stout. She had seemed very uncomfortable to be next to him. Her eyes had locked on mine, and she had reluctantly curtseyed, wincing as she did. She then flipped her glossy hair over her shoulder and sashayed off.

A red-headed woman with a dark-skinned vampire took my attention as she appeared to know Angus very well. They hugged, and he kissed her on the cheek affectionately. She smiled at me warmly, holding my hands in hers as she kissed me on the neck. As she did so, Angus seemed to give her a look. She rolled her eyes as something more seemed to pass between them, took a final look at me, and then walked on.

The line finally ended, and I could relax my shoulders and let out the breath I had been holding.

At that moment, Angus grabbed me a little more firmly by the arm, directing me out of the ballroom. The door guards nodded to him on the way out and he nodded back.

When we had found a place away from prying ears and eyes, he spun to face me, eyes bright but stern. His lips were pressed together as if they were holding him together or holding all the tension in his body.

"What was that, Ivy?" he hissed.

"What?" I asked, a little stunned by his behaviour.

"Whatever was going on with you and Anthony! What was it?"

"Nothing! He–" I abruptly stopped myself, embarrassed of the words that were about to escape my mouth. I looked around, making sure we were alone. "He licked my neck."

"He what!?" Angus visibly shook, enraged at the revelation. "That fucker. I'm gonna kill the wee bastard." His hands fisted into balls and then released, before he ran them both aggressively through his hair, making it stick out of place.

His expression was full of internal conflict. I could almost see his mild flitting between one version of retaliation versus the other, neither sitting well with him for some reason.

"You can't do that. And you shouldn't," I soothed, being the voice of reason. "He's just teasing. And I can tell you two have a history. He's just trying to get a rise out of you. The best thing would be to leave him be. He knows you don't appreciate his flirtation. You *growled* at him for Christ sake!"

"I should have done a lot more than growl," he huffed. "He can't just touch you like that. I'm the–" He broke off his sentence, and shook his head, closing his eyes. "You're right, I'm letting it go. But please, be wary of him. He's a high society vampire here and he's bored. That makes him dangerous. I used to know him well, but now, he could be anyone."

It was odd to think of Angus warning me about dangerous vampires. I thought about Izzy and fought my desire to flinch. Instead, I told him I would be careful before fixing his hair for him. He hummed as I ran my hands through his scalp, and I stopped at the sound, frightened of the familiarity of it.

We stepped back into the room and it was as if we had never left. People were chatting and laughing. We kept to the side of the room, out of the throng of people and chatter. A few wait staff were walking around the room, holding trays of silver goblets. I watched them walking around the room as vampires picked goblets off the tray. One waiter began to approach us.

"Don't take one of these. You won't like it," he said, as he took a goblet off the tray. He grabbed the waiter by the arm – a vampire – who turned around in response. "Please may you get an alcoholic beverage for my donor."

The waiter's eyebrows rose before frowning slightly. "I'm sorry, Your Highness, but you know that donors aren't allowed intoxicating drinks at the ball. Or ever, actually."

"I'm sure you could break the rules, just this once," he said, lips turned up in a seductive smile. "For me," he added, touching her arm.

She smiled broadly and nodded. "Of course, Your Highness, just this once." She bowed, smiling, and it was as if a silent exchange had happened. As if she knew she would get something in return. I shuddered at the thought of what that might be.

"You can only have one of these, so savour it. If you have more, you won't be alert enough to act compelled, but also the vampires will smell it in your system. Take it slow. If you sink it, you'll regret it later, trust me," he warned.

"Okay, I'll savour it. Thank you."

The waiter came back quickly and before I knew it, I had a glass of gin and tonic in my hand.

"It looks like a lemonade. They won't suspect unless they take a massive interest in the smell of your drink. But with you next to it I can't imagine that would be the case," he said, matter-of-factly. I wondered if it were a compliment or an insult, but then stopped myself, thinking myself weak to wonder about anything of the sort.

We stood in silence for a few more moments, both simply observing the events unfolding in front of us. I took small, slow sips on my drink, monitoring how each one made me feel, ensuring I didn't become tipsy, as if I was back in a lab somewhere, completing the most precise titration.

After a few more minutes, a female vampire approached us. She wore a floor length silver silk dress with thin spaghetti straps and a draped cowl neckline. The material skimmed over her perfect figure, and I gulped, intimidated by her beauty. She was fair skinned. She was blonde.

I tried to place her but couldn't remember her place in the line. She was probably about the time that I had stopped paying attention.

"Angus," she purred, resting her hand over his outer shoulder. She smiled, her teeth perfectly white and straight. I subconsciously began to run my tongue over the front of my own as if doing so would align them better or make them more appealing.

"Skye," Angus returned, a tight-lipped smile on his face.

"How have you been?" She didn't wait for an answer. "I've been waiting on your call, but it just hasn't come. I started to think that maybe you were no longer interested? But then I thought that that couldn't be right. I mean, especially when you look at your donor!" She scoffed, her face crinkling with humour. Her hand then began a leisurely path form Angus's shoulder down towards his hand. She grabbed it in hers. "She's brunette!" she laughed, throwing her blonde, pretty head back.

Angus snatched his hand away from her.

"I'm aware of her hair colour," he snapped. He said it in such a way that made me think he found the mention of it very irritating.

He's probably disappointed by it.

"Then why haven't you asked for me? Are you playing hard to get?" She squinted her eyes in a playful, flirty manner. Angus's eyes remained irritated.

"I haven't had the desire to." Another snap.

Her face scrunched, but she still managed to look stunning. It annoyed me, but I was also intrigued. Her face was clearly human, and yet at the exact same time, it was anything but. I wondered about the many possible faces of a vampire – a vampire in hunt – and pondered if the reality was more 'a little snarly with long teeth' versus 'grotesque and decaying with the jaw of a snake'. We were taking Vampire Diaries vs Buffy. I peered up at Angus. Surely it was the first?

"Why the devil not?" Skye's annoyance was visible around her. The thought of Angus not being interested in her was clearly unimaginable to her. It was to me, too.

"You just don't interest me like you used to. I'm bored of it. I'm bored of you."

I flinched at that. Angus was being very cold, and even though I didn't particularly like Skye, he could have let her down more gently.

"You can't be saying that you prefer *this* undesirable creature to *me*?" Her voice was almost a squeal.

I immediately retracted my sympathy for her, flinching for another reason entirely. I already felt inadequate in the beauty department, and I didn't need one of Angus's ex's reminding of me of the validity of those thoughts.

"Who said it was her that was sating my desires?" Angus replied, his face one of complete boredom and disinterest.

I stood there, silently, trying not to let the conversation hurt. But it did hurt, and I felt my eyes stinging. I hated myself for that. I hated myself for a lot of things, actually.

"I need to go to the bathroom," I announced, handing Angus my drink without looking at him. He didn't get the time to nod. I was already walking away.

I walked into the bathroom and entered one of the cubicles. As I sat down, I placed my head in my hands. No tears came, and I silently congratulated myself.

I sat there for a few more minutes, passing the time by reapplying my lipstick, using the mirror which was on the back of the door. I blotted off the excess and placed the tissue in my bag. Then I heard a voice that I recognised, and winced.

"She's just so damn plain. I saw her, standing all high and mighty next to the prince, and it honestly made me feel sick, girls," Freyja snarled. Her voice was cruel, but it was also laced with something else that I couldn't place. She continued. "The fact I had to walk past her and say nothing made me want to vomit. I wish that I had vomited and that it had gone all over her gross dress. You know, it might have improved it." There were some giggles and Freyja continued. "I really can't see what the prince sees in her. He must be into uggos." More giggles.

I was suddenly sucked back to high school. The chatter was just like that. Bitchy, nasty, trash talk. The kind that came from jealousy and insecurity. I sat there in the cubicle and came very close to feeling sorry for Freyja. Her master was an unattractive man with a large belly and a bald patch, and he obviously hadn't compelled her to find him attractive. I found that odd. Perhaps he liked her resistance. The thought made me feel nauseous. Out-right refusal wasn't sexy. Any man who thought it was, was the kind of man that needed to be in jail.

But that didn't give Freyja the right to act the way she did and say the things she said. It was just God damn *mean.*

"Don't worry Freyja. He'll kill her soon enough, so we won't have to." This came from another girl, but I didn't recognise the voice. I was glad. I hoped I never encountered her in person, whoever she was.

"Why do you always have to be so violent?" Freyja asked, her voice irritated. "I said I wanted to vomit on her dress, not kill her, Jesus."

There was more laughter, then the sound of high heels on tile and the room went silent. I unlocked the door, washed my hands and powdered my nose before walking out of the door looking for Angus.

He was waiting right near the entrance of the ladies bathroom, back towards the wall, and grabbed my forearm, pulling me back to him before I passed him. He dragged me down a corridor, similar to what he had done earlier.

"You took your time," he said, mouth a thin line.

"Sorry, just didn't feel like being in the vicinity of someone you used to fuck while she outwardly called me ugly," I snapped.

"She said *undesirable*, not ugly," he stated, eyes darting away from mine. He frowned into the distance.

"Oh, I'm sorry, Your Highness. That makes me feel much better to know you see me as *just* undesirable."

"It wasn't me who used that word." His eyes were back on mine, and he looked very stern.

"Well, you hardly corrected her!"

"Why does that bother you, exactly?" He tilted his head to the side, his lips tilting up the tiniest amount. It wasn't a smile, but I noticed it, whatever it was.

"It's not nice to be deemed undesirable."

"I agree," Angus nodded. "But if the comment were

made about me by someone I didn't approve of, I can't say I would let it bother me."

I scoffed. "Says the man who has probably never been called undesirable in his entire life."

"Existence." Angus corrected, a mutter under his breath. "All I'm saying is, your response to all this can only mean one thing." I raised my eyebrows up at him in a *'go on, then'* gesture. "That you want me to find you desirable."

I reared back from him, creating enough space between us that he had let go of my arm. I watched as his face took on interest. He was enjoying himself.

"Your ego never ceases to surprise me," I deflected.

"Trust me when I say that it is *me* who is the surprised one tonight, not you."

"You're being very cryptic," I said, disapproval lacing my words.

He shrugged, saying nothing more about it, and I rolled my eyes at him. He provided another lingering look in my direction, before linking my arm in his and directing me back to the ballroom.

We sat at the top table, and he mentioned that dinner would be served in due course. I decided to fill the time with a question, still a little embarrassed about the conversation in the corridor.

"Do you know a girl called Freyja? She's a donor," I asked.

"You know, I don't really remember donors. I've been known to forget the name of even my own from time to time." I frowned at him, but he ignored me and continued. "But I *have* heard of her. Apparently, she's a real shrew. I'd avoid her like the plague. Can't for the life of me understand why you wouldn't compel that trait right out of her. But hey, each to their own," he shrugged, taking a sip from his goblet.

"I overheard her talking about me in the toilets. She called me plain and said she wished she could have vomited all over my dress. Then she and her friends all laughed when one of them said you were going to kill me soon anyway."

Angus visibly recoiled from my words, flinching. "Wee bitch. What a thing to say." He slowly shook his head from one side to the other in what looked like sadness. "I'll talk to Baron, get her in line."

"Is Baron her master?" I asked.

"Yes."

"I don't trust him," I said. In response, Angus raised his eyebrows in question. I shrugged. "I just wonder why he hasn't compelled her to find him attractive. I understand that in principle, even if she is compelled, it's still wrong, but at least she wouldn't have to endure… *it*," I said, sadness engulfing my face.

Angus frowned further, clearly thinking about what I had said. "Perhaps he doesn't take her to bed, so he doesn't need to," he replied.

I turned to face Baron. He was sitting at a table and Freyja was next to him. His hands weren't visible above the table, and Freyja was making a face that made my stomach twist.

"I have a feeling that is not the case. And the truth is a hell of a lot darker than that."

"You have an ill-trusting mind, my wee bonny brunette." There it was again, that nickname.

"Not long ago you were asking me to have such a mind."

"I never said it was a bad thing." He turned towards me more, staring. "Perhaps it is why you cannot be compelled. Your mind isn't trusting enough."

I rolled my eyes. "So, the theories begin."

"Don't roll your eyes. A compelled donor wouldn't do that in front of their master, Ivy. It's too human."

"Donors *are* human," I stated.

Angus raised his eyebrows at that, but didn't look at me, his eyes watching the room. "Not in the ways which matter. Look, just don't do it. It could compromise us both."

I had the decency to bow my head. "Sorry. I just got too comfortable."

Angus's back straightened, and he ran his hands

down his thighs. It was a very human thing to do, and I wondered what it meant. "It's fine. Just don't do it again. And I'll look into Baron. If he's being an arse, he wouldn't be the first, but I do agree with you, it's sadistic, and not the fun, mutually enjoyable kind. I'll sort it."

I thanked him, trying my best not to focus on his BDSM comment. But my mind locked on to it, unwilling to let it go. *What's he into? Does he do that with his vampire girlfriends, like Skye? Will he do it later this evening with her?*

Shut up, shut up!

The food arrived shortly after. For the humans, it was a lavish three-course meal. For the vampires, it was a variety of different goblets. When I looked over at Angus as he sipped one, he gave me a face as if to say *'don't ask'*, so I didn't.

When the meal ended, I was the fullest I had been in ages. That triggered a question I simply had to ask. "How long have I been here, Angus?"

Angus stopped mid sip, placing his goblet down before finishing his gulp. His Adam's apple bobbed as he swallowed the red liquid, and he licked his lips. "About two months, why?"

"I'm curious." I clasped my hands together tightly, willing myself to ask the next question.

"I can see you need to ask me something else, so can you just do it before my immortality runs out?" he asked, sarcastically.

I huffed. "Why haven't I had a period?" I asked it quietly, only really moving my lips, knowing he would understand.

Angus nearly choked on... air? His eyes widened to the largest I had ever seen them and then began to dart around the room. Everyone was otherwise engaged, no one was going to care about my lack of a menstrual cycle. "I–. Well, I–" He was visibly rejecting the words before they left his mouth. I could see that the conversation was physically painful for him to endure, and this almost made me smug. Angus was squeamish.

"I can tell you want to answer me, so can you do it

before my *mortality* runs out, please," I asked, sickly sweet. He rolled his eyes at that.

His voice was very quiet as to not attract attention. "You have the implant. There, in your arm." He pointed to my left arm. I raised my right hand towards his, pushing on the same spot, and felt a thin firm line there. I winced.

"I never had the implant," I responded, still fascinated by the firmness underneath my skin.

"They inserted it in you when you arrived. They would have knocked you out to do it. It's not a compulsion thing." His voice was still soft to make sure we weren't overheard.

I thought about when I arrived and how I'd passed out on the metal table. *Those fuckers.*

"But...*why?!*" I exclaimed in a hushed tone, trying to be more subtle than Sass. "That's GBH!"

"I suppose it is, yes. In human law."

"And I *am* human."

"I know that, Ivy."

"But...*why?*" I repeated.

"Trust me," he started, "It's for your own good."

"Sorry, but I'm really struggling to see how that is right now, Angus." I snarled his name, the frown on my forehead feeling like it was going to crack my skull open.

Angus pulled me to stand and took me over to a corner where we were unlikely to be overheard, his hand grabbing my arm. To other people it might look like I had stepped out of line, and he was about to compel the shit out of me.

"Will you *stop flapping* and let me explain!" He released me from his grip. "Think about it, Brunette. You getting a period every month would be a disaster."

"Still not seeing it," I replied, fuming, shifting my eyes to make sure we weren't drawing any attention. Apart from the occasional glance, it didn't seem like it.

"You live with literally *hundreds* of vampires. Vampires have a certain diet... a very heightened sense of smell..."

"Oh my God!" I gasped, slapping my hands over my mouth in horror. I turned away from him then, face redder than I had ever felt it. "I think I'm going to be sick."

"Please don't do that," he said, wincing. "You *did* ask."

"I wish I hadn't."

"So do I." He bristled, and began the lazy circles on my arm again. I focused on them, letting myself be transported to a tranquil place – a place where my vampire master didn't want to literally eat me when I was due on. *Eugh.*

"Maybe if you have any more questions about it, you should ask me in private," he said, eyes lingering on the oblivious crowd.

"I doubt I'll want to know any more, but yes, I agree."

"Finally, you agree with me. It's a new feeling, I like it," he smirked.

"Are you joking with me?" I asked, smiling back at him.

"I think I just might be." His eyes sparkled, and my breath began to increase. "Does that bother you?"

We were suddenly interrupted by a familiar voice.

"Sorry to interrupt, Your Highness, but may I have this dance with your lovely donor?" Around us, the strings had begun, and people were in hold, whirling around the dancefloor, vampires and humans alike. We hadn't even noticed, and that made me feel warm somehow. Anthony stood waiting for a response.

"It would be up to Ivy, but I allow it," responded Angus, a slight clipped tone to his voice. He didn't want to allow it at all. I looked at him, giving him a look that I hoped conveyed that I was proud of him for not snapping Anthony's head off.

"It would be my pleasure," I replied. Anthony's lips tipped up on one side, his crooked smile giving his face a playful edge. He held out the crook of his right arm, and I placed my left there in the same hold I had been in with Angus a mere couple of hours before.

Angus took one final look at me before returning to his seat.

"You are quite flushed, Miss Ivy," Anthony commented, sneaking a glance at me from the side as we walked towards the dancefloor. "Do I intrigue you?"

"You licked my neck," I stated, not giving anything away. We reached the edge of the dancefloor, and Anthony took me into his arms in a gentle caress.

"I did do that, yes." He nodded, unashamedly. "Would I be so off the mark if I said that I think you liked it?" The smirk was back. He really was quite dazzling.

"I was surprised you would be so brazen, if I'm honest. Surely, it's quite a ballsy thing to do to the prince's donor, in front of the prince himself," I said, coolly.

"Ballsy, you say?" He chucked, his hand coming to land softly on the small of my back, bringing me closer to him. "What can I say?" he murmured, bringing his lips closer to my ear. "I couldn't help myself."

My breath hitched, and I internally kicked myself at the involuntary response. *Get a grip, Ivy!* He pulled back then, expression suddenly serious, frowning.

"There it is, that intake of breath." He brought his right hand to cup my face, brushing his thumb over my lips softly. "I heard it the first day I saw you. It's fascinating." I didn't reply, scared of the response I would give. We continued to sway to the music, which was slower now. "Your eyes are bright when I look in them. They see things. I'm enthralled by it. Explain that to me, Ivy," he asked, his hand lowering now and moving to the back of my neck, tilting my head so I had to meet his gaze. I could see the compulsion a mile off, and I was suddenly on high alert. Turned out my weakness to compulsion was not paying attention. But I knew the cues now, and it only took a little will power to stop it being able to take hold.

"There's nothing to explain," I said blandly, keeping my eyes on his, unblinking. I could feel Angus's eyes on me from across the room and prayed he wouldn't come over. "I'm just like every other donor here." His eyes released mine and he frowned, disappointed. I felt deja vu encase me. He had the same look Angus had when he had thought I was just a plain, boring, compellable donor.

"Very well, Miss Ivy." He released my body, bowing in front of me, once again kissing me on either side of my neck (no tongue this time), before leaving me on the dance floor.

I wasn't alone for long, Angus's arm snaking around

my waist in seconds, pulling me into another dance. "He's suspicious." He frowned, brushing a stray hair away from my face. It must have been annoying him. "And he's wiped some of your lipstick off," he added, muttering. "And how much I liked it, too," he mused. "I'd prefer if you stayed away from him from now on. I'm not convinced he would put you in harm's way, but I can't risk that."

"I think he's just a flirt," I commented, my heart still pacing slightly from the encounter.

"Yes, he does make you blush. It makes your skin go this glorious colour and you look so…alive." He took in a big breath and blew it out in my face. The smell of it was like a potent version of the aroma which emanated from his body, and I felt myself subconsciously close my eyes and lean into him ever so slightly.

"You occasionally go that colour with me." He raised his eyebrows, smirking.

Angus's smirk was different to Anthony's in the sense that you knew it was rare. Angus didn't give his smirk to just anyone, and it was a gift for it to be bestowed upon you. When he did it, his blue eyes crinkled ever so slightly, as if he was hiding a secret, and his eyebrows slanted on one side.

"You are sometimes a flirt," I commented, a little embarrassed. I turned my head to the side, attempting to feign disinterest, watching the other guests as they danced.

"Am I? Could you be so kind and give me an example?" He brought his left hand to my bun at the nape of my neck and gave it a firm squeeze before tracing what I assumed was his index finger down the length of my upper spine until he reached the top of my dress. He then splayed his hand out, continuing his path until he stopped at the very base of my back. It was intimate, and I clenched my teeth together to stop my body shivering.

"You're flirting with me now," I stated, staring at him with a face which I hoped said *'I know what you are doing, buddy'*.

"How, exactly?" he asked.

"The smirking flirty eyes and the touchy hands!" I whisper-exclaimed, frowning.

"No, this is dancing, Ivy. I'm sorry if you don't like it but I think we need to keep up appearances." He moved his right hand to the crease of my hip. He began to run his thumb up and down it, and I knew he could feel the lingerie I was wearing underneath my dress. "Did you like it when Anthony licked your neck?" he asked, and I knew the blush was going to come back. I tried to tell my brain to constrict all my arteries but there was no success, and the heat began to build again in my face. Angus continued, so I didn't have to answer. "It's just you made that lovely noise again. The same noise I made you make the other night when I had you against the wall." He wasn't looking at me when he said this, instead looking over my right shoulder absentmindedly.

"This is another fine example of flirting, Angus. Saying that I make lovely noises when you try to *seduce me*, is flirting."

"Does it bother you?" His eyes drew back to mine, and he held them there without emotion on his face.

I sucked in a breath. Angus suddenly released my hip and placed his palm flat in front of my face. "Don't blow that breath out of your mouth. Not this close. Don't." He was stern, his face suddenly sharp, holding all the emotion he was lacking seconds earlier. My eyes widened, and I gently released the breath through my nose in increments, cultivating all manner of control to do it, although I had no idea why it was necessary.

"Thank you," he whispered. "I've had enough. I think we should leave."

We left at once, saying goodbye to no one, and headed towards his quarters. We entered the room in silence, and Angus sat at his desk, head in his hands.

"Have I done something wrong?" I asked, ashamed that I was asking like some sort of needy child seeking approval and forgiveness.

Angus scoffed and dragged his hands through his hair in exasperation before placing them under his chin, using them as a little shelf to hold his head up. "Not exactly."

"Then what's wrong?" I questioned, hands on my hips. Angus's eyes travelled to where they sat. He shook his head and pulled open the drawer to his right, took out the little book again, wrote a couple of lines, before placing it back. It was infuriating to watch.

"Why do you always write in that thing? What is it?" I pushed, snapping the words out of my mouth.

Angus ignored my question and answered the one I had asked before. "There is nothing wrong. There is something different."

"I don't understand," I retorted.

"And you don't need to," he replied, staring firmly at me.

"I would like to."

"That sounds like *your* problem, not *mine*, Brunette."

"Not wee and bonny anymore?" I snarled, my words venomous.

"That *bothers* you, doesn't it?" he claimed, leaning back in his chair lazily. The power had shifted back to him. He could tell and he was enjoying it. "That nickname bothers you, but you can't pinpoint why. Fascinating."

Fascinating.

"You know," I began, turning on my heels to enter the bathroom. "What *bothers me* is how overused that word is around me!" I slammed the door as I entered the bathroom, locking it behind me as loudly as I could. I stood in front of the mirror and began pulling the pins out of my hair a little too aggressively, releasing the bun. I then contorted my right hand to try undo my dress, attempting with all my might to get a hold of the little navy zip which would unleash me from it, but to no avail. I fumed in annoyance, unaware as to where all this anger arose from.

I didn't want to ask, but I knew I had to.

"Angus!" I yelled, rolling my eyes at myself for my incompetence. I placed either hand on the edges of the sink, frustrated.

"What's wrong?" I heard his reply through the door, but he sounded close.

"I need help with my dress."

"Well, unlock the door and I'll help you with whatever."

I reluctantly turned to face the door, took a deep breath and slid the lock to the right. The door handle bent as Angus opened it, and I stood out of the way as it swung inward. I stayed static as Angus entered, the room suddenly feeling tiny with the two of us in it, even though it was massive. This had never happened before. It had never been just me and him alone in it. The lights suddenly seemed too bright, and I felt like I wanted to shrink into the corner, away from everything I was feeling.

"What's wrong with the dress?" He stared at me, looking completely uninterested. For some reason, this annoyed me further. How could he have been flirting with me so much no more than twenty minutes ago, and now be stood there looking like he had never been more bored to be in my presence.

"I can't unzip the fucker," I snapped. My mood was foul, but I couldn't help it. Venom just seemed to drip off my tongue. Emotional outbursts were kind of my thing. I was able to hold emotions in for ages, caging them up like an animal, but sometimes they just got a little too strong for their trainer, and the result was catastrophic.

"Why is the dress a fucker?" he smirked, clearly amused by my foul mouth.

"Stop with the smirking and just unzip me." I was on a roll.

"You know, if I was in my right mind, I'd be doing something to you right now which ensured you would never snap at me like that again." His eyebrows were raised high, but the smirk remained. "But luckily for you, I'm not in my right mind tonight."

He raised his finger, twirling it in a motion which signalled I should spin around so my back was to his front. I did as he asked, no sarcastic comment in tow.

He first began to run his hands deftly through my hair, untangling it. "I liked the updo..." he muttered, "but the smell which comes off your hair when it's down, and the way the light hits it, is in my eyes entirely superior."

His hand gathered my long hair and moved it so that it

hung over my left shoulder. I watched his reflection as he did it. His eyes were fixed on the back of my neck, and he briefly stroked his fingers down it tenderly. He continued his pursuit down my spine with one finger, slowly running it over each individual vertebrae, almost as if he was counting them, checking if I was truly human.

His fingers finally reached the zip I had been complaining so much about. He looked up then, meeting my eyes in the mirror, almost asking my permission. I nodded slightly, and he picked up on it instantly. He began to slowly pull the zip down the length of my back, and I felt the slight cool air hit my skin as he did. With each second, the lingerie underneath the dress became more and more visible and the tension in the bathroom reached an unbearable intensity. I closed my eyes to reduce the feeling. I couldn't watch him watch me any longer.

A few seconds later, I felt the dress begin to slip down my arms, and I knew he had pulled the zip completely free. I shifted my arms side to side to free myself of it and it fell to the floor, pooling at my feet.

"Open your eyes," he whispered, gruffly. I did as he asked, slowly, allowing my eyes to adjust to the light again. He was still standing behind me, but the look in his eyes had intensified tenfold and he wasn't staring at my face anymore, not even my neck. He was staring at my body.

I held the side of the sink again, this time for some support. I could feel my legs shaking.

"I'm so glad John didn't see you in this. If he had, I think I would have had to have kill him," he said, frowning, as if confused. "I'll leave you to finish getting undressed. I'm going to run a quick errand. You can go to sleep without me."

And with that he left the bathroom, and left me standing in it, completely dazed and confused.

CHAPTER 11

First Taste

Ivy

The days after the ball passed slowly. Angus's errand that he so desperately had to rush off to that night seemed to span for over a week, leaving me quite bored. I would return back from dinner and, unlike normal, his desk chair would be empty, and the quarters completely silent. When he was at his desk, he would still continue to make notes in that little notepad of his. The notes were often made after a stern look my way which was highly frustrating. One day, I would read those little scrawlings of his.

On the sixth day after the ball, I was close to pulling out my own hair. It was then that I confronted Angus one evening.

"I would like to get a job," I announced, standing by him as he busied himself at his desk.

"For what possible reason?" he asked, not even making the small effort of turning his head slightly to look at me.

"I'm bored. And everyone else has a job, so why can't I?"

"Because you are my donor," he stated.

"What's that supposed to mean?" I asked, frowning.

"I've told you this before," he sighed, sounding

exasperated. Finally, he looked up at me. "You're the equivalent of a princess here. Well, a human princess, which I suppose holds less weight, but still." He ran his hands through his hair, looking down again. "My donors have never worked."

"Well, I would like to." I placed my hands on my hips, demanding attention.

Angus's eyes turned to my hips, and I saw his right hand twitch slightly, almost as if he was subconsciously reaching for the drawer that held his little notepad. "And how, exactly," he began, raising his eyes to mine again, "will I swing that, Ivy?"

I flinched slightly at the sound of my name on his lips. He hardly ever called me just by my name. It was usually an all-singing, all-dancing nickname.

"I'm sure you will think of something," I shrugged.

His lips tilted up slightly, almost in a flirty manner. "You are very demanding tonight. What gave you this courage?"

"Boredom," I replied, deadpan.

He laughed melodically, and I found myself swept up in his happiness, smiling broadly at him as I watched the emotions fill his handsome face. He hadn't shaved in a few days and his stubble was starting to turn more into a beard. I started to wonder what that would feel like between my inner thighs–

What the fuck? Stop, brain. Stop.

"You're blushing again. What did I do?" he asked, staring.

"Nothing. I just want a job," I deflected, but Angus didn't look convinced. He didn't push it, though

"Fine, I'll look into it, Little Miss Demanding." There the nicknames were again. "But if you are so bored, why don't you treat yourself tomorrow? Go to that blonde human's salon and–"

"Her name is Heather, Angus." I interrupted, annoyed he had forgotten it already. She was a person, and he needed to know that, not just a blonde.

"Yes, yes." He nodded. "Heather. Go to Heather's salon

and get a treatment. A blowdry, maybe?"

"I'll do that if you promise to help me get a job."

"I said I would." His eyes became stern, scolding. I could feel tension radiating off his body in waves. "Don't question me, I don't appreciate it." The way he said it made me stand slightly taller.

"Sorry, sir." It came out of my mouth without permission – an involuntary response to his authoritarian demeanour. Angus's breath hitched. It was the most glorious, sensual sound. I felt my thighs clench together.

Seriously! Stop it!

There was a part of me, however, that celebrated that moment – that little intake of his breath. I thought about the times Angus had enlightened such a response in me, and I was elated to finally be on the scoreboard.

"What's your trade?" Angus said, interrupting my thoughts.

"Sorry?" I asked, unsure what we had been talking about before. My mind was all hazy.

"What job do you want? What skills do you have?"

"Oh!" I exclaimed, realisation dawning. "Well, I'm a biomedical scientist. So perhaps something lab based? Or in the hospital?"

He nodded. "I'll see what I can do."

After that, he looked up and it appeared to be a look of dismissal. I got the message and decided to put on some gym gear and take up the offer of trying out some new gym classes. Yoga it was.

Angus was scribbling in his book before I could even leave the room.

◆ ◆ ◆

The class was oddly challenging. Turned out that Yoga wasn't just about stretching and breathing really loudly. We held poses for what felt like an age, and I could feel my quads screaming at me. Sweat beaded from my forehead and I could see the teacher giving me looks of sympathy.
Poor thing, she doesn't know what she's got herself into.

I left the studio feeling oddly invigorated, rather than sleepy as I had expected. However, I was also very relaxed. It was a heady concoction of feelings, so much so that I booked myself onto the next available class. Who knew, I could become a Yogi. *Eugh*, I hated that term.

When I returned, I made the pledge to shave my legs. I'd noticed little spiky hairs peeking out the bottom of my leggings when I was in downward facing dog which was a little distracting. It wasn't as if I didn't have the time to shave them. And although I was a big advocate for keeping body hair if it made you feel comfortable, I thought shaving them would at least pass some time and reduce the deafening boredom.

I ignored Angus when I returned, doing the same as he did to me. I walked straight into the bathroom, closing the door. I stripped down to my underwear and began to fill the sink with some water. Yes, I was a sink shaver. Sue me. Doing it in the shower always washed away the shaving foam before you'd even gotten around to touching it with a razor. Complete waste if you asked me.

I foamed up my legs with some shaving cream that I found in the cupboard and picked a fresh razor from the pack. I started with my right leg, running the razor in upward strokes, rinsing it after each one. When the right leg was smooth, I did the same with the left.

On the last stroke of my left leg, the razor caught slightly, just above the knee. A stinging sensation filled the area, before a thin crimson line began to run down the length of my shin. The cut was the classic depiction of what often occurred when skin fell victim to a razor, all bark with no bite, looking a lot worse than what it actually was. The red colour against my skin was stark.

It was only after a couple of seconds that the weight of the situation dawned on me. But the vampire who now stood behind me, having broken the lock on the bathroom door, a murderous look on his face, made it blindingly obvious.

Fuck.

◆ ◆ ◆

Angus

Angus had nearly finished with the paperwork he was dealing with when the smell hit his nostrils. The assault took him back entirely, and he dropped the pen he had been holding, it striking the desk with a clatter.

The smell was an intensified version of the one which emanated off her lovely skin and hair. It was as if the smell had been collected and distilled to make it into its most potent form. The smell from her body was the *eau de toilette*. The smell from her blood was the *parfum*.

His head suddenly went into a frenzy. All he could think about was her blood, his mouth filling up with her blood, his throat wet with her blood. He needed nothing more in his entire existence than to completely devour her.

Without any real thought, Angus's body rose smoothly from his desk chair. He moved with inhuman speed to the piece of wood which separated him from his greatest desire, and forced it open, uncaring if she was hit by it.

She stood there, wearing matching black, lacy underwear. Angus didn't notice that, though. He was staring at her left leg. The leg glimmered in the light, bouncing reflections back into his eyes. The smooth skin was beautifully decorated in red. That one, stunning, glorious, delicious red line. That was all he could see – all he *wanted* to see.

He stepped forward and picked the thing up – the thing with the leg. It was warm to touch, so very warm. Much warmer than him.

He propped it up on the side where the sink sat and dropped in worship to that single leg.

Something was being said. He could tell from the ringing in his ears. He could also, somewhere in the back of his mind, feel something clawing at his shoulders. He found this highly irritating and decided to look up.

His eyes were met with very, very dark ones. They were filled with anguish, and Angus focused on them for a second. He recognized those eyes. They belonged to something, *someone.* He blinked his own eyes many times, willing himself to concentrate and forget the red line. Somehow, his body knew this was an important thing to do, an absolutely imperative action.

It was a girl who held the eyes. She was rather pretty, and he knew her. Although, he wished he knew her more. Her eyes relaxed slightly, perhaps in response to his face. That made him relax also, and he unclasped his hands from her leg and sat on the floor in front of her, staring into her eyes like he was the most religious man, and she was his deity.

"Angus?" she whispered, her voice barely audible, even to him. "Are you back?"

He knew what she meant. He had gone away, and the monster within him had claimed his mind and his limbs. But he was back now. And he wouldn't let the monster hurt her, even if he wanted to. Because he really couldn't be the vampire that killed another donor. He just couldn't.

He pushed himself backwards, sliding along the floor, and closed the door so his back was flush against it. He planted his feet on the ground and bent his knees so he could rest his arms on them.

He continued to watch the red line, some blood now dripping onto the floor tiles. But he looked at it with a clarity which he hadn't had a few seconds ago. He still wanted her blood in his mouth, but he could control it. Just.

He cleared his throat. "I'm sorry about that."

She let out a long breath and Angus's fists clenched. "It's okay," she signed out, her shoulders sagging slightly.

"I really want to taste your blood, you know," Angus admitted, candidly.

"I know," she breathed. "Maybe you should just do it."

"What?!" His head snapped up, eyes angry. "Why would

you say that?!"

"I don't know. I–" She stopped herself, blushing slightly. "You are going to have to sooner or later." She shrugged. "And to be honest I'd rather you did it without having to bite me first." Her eyes were wide.

Angus's mind whirled. On the one hand, he was desperate to say yes. It seemed that it was all he had ever wanted – to taste her. But on the other hand, he was worried. What if the monster came back again? What if it hurt her? She'd feel it, and he wouldn't be able to take it away. And she would hate him. And he couldn't bear the thought of her hating him. He really couldn't. And that thought irritated him entirely, because he didn't understand the reason for it.

"You don't really understand what you are saying. It's not as simple as you might think, *mo leannan*." He shook his head, frustrated. "Me and you and your blood are not a good combination, trust me." The Gaelic term floated in the air, unwavering.

"Is it the AB negative thing?" He looked at her confused, so she continued. "I heard that vampire talk about my blood being AB negative, you know, when I was in that glass cabinet?" He nodded that he remembered. "So? Is that why you don't want to? Because it's a weird blood group or something?" She was frowning, and if he was right, looked slightly offended.

He chuckled dryly, amused that she thought her blood group was *less* appealing to him. "Not exactly." He would tell her at some point, he swore he would. Just not now. It seemed a little too cliché to say out loud at the moment. "It's more just the fact that I haven't fed from a human in months. I would be worried that my self-control would be lax and well... I don't want to kill you."

"Did you want to kill the others?" she asked, her voice quiet as if she knew the question she was asking was on a sensitive subject.

Angus hadn't told Ivy about the other donors, and he was surprised that she knew. It was likely the other residents would had mentioned it, the gossipers.

"No... and... yes," he drew out, trying to be honest. "I didn't go into the feed intending to kill any of my donors, if that's what you mean. But once I started feeding... at that moment, I wanted to kill them, yes."

Ivy's eyes shifted in thought before she spoke. "I think you should give yourself more credit," she said resolutely. "I mean, you were literally so close to losing it just then, and you didn't. You brought yourself right off the ledge. You *do* have self-control."

"Perhaps. But that's credit where credit is due. Who knows what will happen if I actually *taste* you." He hadn't realised it, but their conversation had taken his mind off the smell of blood in the room. Now, his focus was right back to it, and his nostrils flared.

"Look, can you just do it? I'm *asking* you to *please* taste my blood. Like I said, it makes me feel better knowing you aren't going to have to break skin. For me, this is a controlled environment, and I feel oddly safe. The alternative is you sinking your teeth into my flesh, and I'm sorry, but that is just not something I can even comprehend being okay with," she admitted, her eyes looking slightly frantic. Angus could hear that her heart rate had picked up. He noticed this made the blood from her leg pool out marginally faster, which pleased him.

Angus thought about the proposal. She *was* right. Without biting her flesh, he would likely be able to have more control over the situation. The bite was an additional means of gaining control. It made a vampire more power hungry. And hungrier in general. But mostly, he just really wanted her blood in his mouth.

"Okay," he said.

Her eyes widened more – if that was even possible – and she took a deep breath in.

"Breathe that out now, okay? Don't do it when I'm close to you," he demanded, and she abided, even if she did look slightly confused, her breath gliding slowly out of parted lips. He wished she would breathe through her nose.

At that, he stood and slowly walked towards her. He took her head in his hands, cradling it. His thumb lightly brushed over her lips. They were so smooth, almost like glass, without the coolness.

"I think you are brave," he said, not letting her reply before he dropped to his knees again in front of her leg. He picked it up, much more carefully he assumed than he had done previously, and dipped his head slightly until it was dropped close to her ankle where the last trace of her blood was. He let out a long breath, readying himself, before releasing his tongue and running it up her leg. She made little sounds as he did it, but he tried to ignore them. They were dangerous and could easily convince him to make bad choices.

His hands continued to snake up her leg as his mouth followed, leaving a wet trail of saliva as he did. When he reached the source of the blood, he swirled his tongue around it a couple of times, allowing it to explode in delight. The taste of her was like nothing else, and he was revelling in it.

But, to his delight, he was in control.

He peeked upwards to look at her. Her head was lolled back slightly, eyes closed, and lips parted. He watched for a second at her chest rising and falling, her breasts stretching the fabric of her bra deliciously.

He dipped his head once more, wondering if he could try his luck. He left the cut above her knee and instead began running his tongue further up her leg, where no blood was present. He lifted her leg slightly, allowing better access to her inner thigh. She didn't protest, eyes still closed. He raised his left hand and grabbed her waist, sliding her closer to his mouth, allowing him better access to her. Again, no protests. He couldn't believe it. He gently licked higher, the smell of her intoxicating, before gently sucking on some skin high up on her inner thigh. He just wanted to hear her moan, that was all, and he wasn't disappointed. The sound escaped from between her open lips just as if he was expertly playing an instrument.

He stood so he could look fully at her face. Her eyes were still closed, and he almost felt like he was intruding on some sort of private moment. But he didn't feel like being a gentleman, so instead of looking away, he continued to stare greedily.

Her skin was slightly flushed, and her chest was still having to take over-exerted breaths. There was a slight sheen of sweat in the dip in between her collarbone, and Angus had to stop himself from running his tongue over that, too.

He decided at that moment that he had been wrong. Ivy was in fact a very attractive woman, and he could understand how she might intrigue a man. When he'd seen her in the bathroom after the ball, in her under garments, he had been unable to keep his eyes off her. At the time, he thought it was due to simply how much flesh she had on show and how this made her so much more vulnerable to his possible attack – if he had chosen to do it – but on reflection, he realised it was because she simply looked stunning.

Angus believed that it was her *blood* that intrigued him more than anything else, but he could still appreciate her beauty, or acknowledge it, at the very least. And there was also nothing wrong with enjoying watching her relish his touch. It was an ego boost he had been craving after years of donors without their own mind. At least he knew he still had some sort of skill in pleasing a woman. Yes, he had pleased many female vampires, but it was something entirely different to please a mortal. He didn't know why that was, he just knew it to be true.

Her eyes slowly opened dreamily, and she blinked multiple times, adjusting to the bathroom lights.

"Are you done?" she asked, looking almost sleepy.

"Yes," he whispered.

"How was it?" she asked, tilting her head to the side in question.

Angus's brain strung together a multitude of lewd responses, but he decided on something more proper in the presence of a lady. "Delicious," he smirked, showing teeth.

She laughed, and his skin prickled. "I'm glad." She yawned loudly, and Angus turned his head away to avoid the breath which would likely ensue.

Unwilling to break the spell with words, he picked her up, holding her close to his chest and placed her on the bed, tucking her under the duvet. She slept peacefully, and Angus watched her all night, unable to leave her.

He would deal with the broken bathroom door tomorrow.

CHAPTER 12

Confessions

Ivy

It was a Monday. I knew that because I'd checked Angus's calendar. It also happened to be the first day of my new job. The job was indeed to be working in the medical labs in the hospital, but it wasn't to test samples from patients as I had expected. Instead, I was to be working on the testing of a new drug.

I woke up earlier than normal – work beginning at eight-thirty sharp – but ended up getting to breakfast around the normal time, perhaps just looking a little more presentable.

"Woah!" exclaimed Andy as I approached the benches the gang were sitting on in the cafeteria. "What happened to Little Miss Activewear?" His eyebrows were raised so high they almost appeared to get lost in his hairline.

"Haven't you heard?" I said, doing a little twirl in my pencil skirt and blouse. "I'm a working woman now."

I was feeling oddly cheery, and I couldn't help a little smile in Andy's direction. For one day, I just wanted to feel even the slightest bit normal. I didn't want to be the woman whose brain didn't work like everyone else's or the woman who had a constant grey cloud hanging over her. I just wanted to be Ivy, the scientist.

"You know, I did hear that," Heather pursed her lips, raising her spoon towards me in thought. She was eating fruit and oats – very Heather. Andy had a fry up with all the greasy, salty trimmings. It seemed that doctors were always the worst at taking their own advice.

"Yep, that's it!" Heather's eyes lit up suddenly. "Sophie told me."

"Who's Sophie?" I asked curiously, sitting next to Andy as I usually did, the other three opposite us.

"Oh no! That's not the sad one, is it?" Sass asked, turning towards Heather (who was sitting next to her), with her hands over her chest in what appeared to be over-exaggerated sympathy. However, I knew Sass better than that. Her sympathy was entirely visceral and heartfelt. It was what I liked about her.

Heather nodded yes, her mouth full of oats. She was too polite to ever speak with her mouth full. If any of us ever dared to do it, we were sure to get her signature arm thump before we could get even a full word out. Oddly violent, our Heather.

"Define 'sad'," Duke enquired. He leaned into the table, his elbows resting on it, and placed his head on his hands, listening intently. Perhaps this was his concerned *'tell me about your agonising toothache'* face. It seemed sincere enough.

Heather shrugged. "She just gets a little low, is all. Nothing a spa session can't fix." I remembered Heather had mentioned someone who she took to the spa when she was sad. I wondered if she was speaking about the same girl.

"I don't get it." It was Andy's turn to enquire now, a piece of square sausage an inch away from his mouth. A square sausage was exactly what it sounded like. It was like a burger, so it didn't have the normal sausage casing, except it was square, and made of pork. Scottish. Yeah, I hadn't known it had existed, either.

"She works in the lab that Ivy is starting work in. She sometimes comes to the salon, and she just looks…" Heather thought, her eyes searching upwards for the right word. "...deflated."

"What could possibly be causing her to deflate?" Sass began, eyes sad. "We live *here*. Happiness is *guaranteed*."

"Amen, sister." Andy nodded to his friend in agreement, and she smiled back at him.

I felt very sympathetic for Sophie, whoever she was. I knew the feeling of deflation very well.

"Some people just aren't as lucky as others, I guess," said, Duke. He picked up his spoon again to eat his cereal (low sugar shreddies because, come on, he was a dentist), clearly finished with the conversation.

It was an odd thing for Duke to say, I thought. He was normally an entirely compassionate person, often putting Andy in his place when he said something vulgar or insensitive. But his comment was void of all that, and I couldn't help but notice the abnormality in it.

"Is that really how you feel, Duke?" I asked, not realising I was going to say it until his name had left my mouth.

He looked up to me, dark eyes confused. He had a very kind face and was awfully courteous. I would have loved to have met him in the real world. I couldn't help but picture him with a kind, warm family who he cherished dearly. My heart sunk a little.

"How I feel about what?"

"Do you really just think that Sophie is 'unlucky' and that's why she sometimes gets sad?"

"I think it is an unlucky thing to be sad," he replied, almost coldly.

"Would you not agree that in order to feel true happiness, you also have to be able to feel true sadness?"

Duke's eyes squinted slightly as he processed my words. He had an expression of deep thought, and you could see the muscle in his jaw tick with concentration. And then I saw it – right in the depths of his eyes. Duke *did* believe in what I said, he just didn't *know it* anymore. It was suddenly undoubtedly clear to me that Duke was someone who had suffered great loss, and that that loss had been taken away from him. *Compelled* from him.

When someone experiences a loss, the immediate

response is to wish that the feeling it creates is taken away. But then, over time, and this may be *a lot* of time, they realise that the feeling it left originated from a feeling of joy. One wouldn't feel loss if the thing or person that was lost didn't, at some point, provide them with joy. And therefore, to take away the sense of loss, would also take away the sense of joy. Similar to the idea that you cannot have happiness without sadness, you cannot have joy without loss.

Perhaps Duke was right. Some people were luckier than others. But to me, Sophie was the lucky one, not Duke.

"Jesus, Ivy!" Andy interrupted my thoughts, rolling his eyes. "It's not even nine am! E*nough* with the heavy."

Everyone laughed. Everyone but me. And everyone but the trapped soul in Duke's eyes.

◆ ◆ ◆

After breakfast was finished, I headed back to the quarters to pick up my work bag. Angus was sitting at his desk, looking pensive. He held a pen in his right hand and rolled it masterfully between his deft fingers. I'd seen him do this countless times. I wondered if it was a nervous habit, or perhaps something he did to help him concentrate. The pen flowed seamlessly, running like water between his smooth, pale fingers. It was hypnotising to watch.

I didn't think very highly of Angus – at least that's what my conscious mind told itself. He was involved – and if his father was the king, I assumed *heavily involved* – in a system which emersed itself in abduction, brain washing, sexual trafficking and abuse. But when he sat at his desk like that, looking almost human mar the too-paleness of his skin, I could almost forgive myself for finding him beautiful.

"Number crunching?" I asked, lightly. This was us now – light banter while skirting around the obvious encounter of the other night.

He hummed, low in his throat. "Hmmm, something like that." His eyes then raised to meet mine, intense as ever. "Nice skirt," he added, although his face had a frown covering it.

"What's wrong with it?" I countered, hands on my hips.

"Nothing at all. I said it was nice."

"Your frown says otherwise."

His lips twitched slightly, his brows suddenly freed from the constraints of the muscles in his forehead.

"It's on the tight side," he added, finally, looking back at his papers.

"You know, I had an ex who used to tell me what to wear, and I want you to know right now that I no longer take that shit from anyone." I stood firm, my eyes boring down on him.

What I had told him was indeed true. I wasn't spinning a lie to elicit his guilt, because I had a feeling that Angus was brought up in a time where sexism and control of women were common-place. Also, the feeling of guilt didn't seem like his forte.

That reminded me, I would have to ask him how old he was. *Maybe another time... way in the future.*

He looked back up to me, interested. "Is that what I am then, a potential ex? Does that mean you're mine?" His lips were even more amused now, and I caught a slight glimmer of his canines.

"Don't be ridiculous!" I deflected, spinning on my heels to grab my bag.

"I did suck on your inner thighs the other night. Do other people do that to you as well?" he baited. I could almost hear his smirk getting wider and wider. Classic Angus enjoying his games.

I spun around, alarmed by his admission. "In all honesty, I didn't know other people were *allowed* to suck on my inner thighs. But since you brought it up, perhaps I'll go and find Anthony." It was a low blow. A blow which landed perfectly on target. A knockout.

I went to walk out the door – it was getting closer to half eight and I wanted to make sure I was a little early to ensure I gave a good impression – but Angus had other ideas. He was suddenly in front of me, a smirk no longer on his face.

I jumped back, in shock. He rarely demonstrated his speed to me, so when he did, I was always left off balance.

"Is that what you want? Anthony in your bed?" he asked, eyes demanding an answer. I could tell he was close to using compulsion, so I channelled all the energy I could muster to ensure that I wasn't in danger of it.

"I don't have a bed," I replied, obtusely.

Angus's nostrils flared and he rolled his eyes. "Don't start with technicalities, Ivy. Either you want him, or you don't."

"Why would it matter either way?" I challenged, locking out my body, getting ready for battle.

"It just does."

"Why?"

"Because." His eyes shifted, losing contact with mine briefly, and my shoulders sagged in relief.

"Clearly we both aren't in the mood to answer questions today," I began, "and I need to go to work, so I don't have time to argue about who gets to have their head between my legs." I shoved past him and left the room knowing exactly what he was going to take out of his desk drawer the second he regained his sanity.

◆ ◆ ◆

I walked towards the hospital where I met a woman who introduced me to the lab. She handed me a lab coat and a name badge with a fob attached to it which allowed me access to varying areas. She told me working hours (eight thirty until twelve-thirty and two until four), before introducing me to my team.

The team was made up of eight individuals, including myself. Our job was to test a new drug for the correct components, and if correct, allow it to be processed and packaged.

There were four men and three other women. One of

the women was called Sophie.

Sophie was petite, maybe around five-foot-two. She had large, round eyes that reminded me of Bambi, and a slightly wide upturned nose. I would guess she was around my age, if not a little older. Her lips were plump, and her skin was smooth – the colour of cinnamon. Her eyes were green, and her hair was curled around her face in a loose afro. The combination of her features was startling, and I felt very plain next to her.

Plain. Just like Freyja had said.

She smiled at me, although it didn't really touch her eyes, and I suddenly felt like I was looking in a mirror. *Deflated.*

Her introduction was polite, but her eyes shifted in all directions, as if she found it difficult to make eye contact. For some reason, I didn't think that was the issue at all, but I couldn't pinpoint the real reason for it either.

I settled at my desk and began to work after a quick demo. It was relatively similar to what I had been doing previously, so although I started slow, familiarising myself with the new equipment, I quickly picked up speed.

At lunch, I was sat on a bench alone, not able to see my friends, when a tray dropped in front of my eyes, cinnamon hands holding its edges tightly.

"I know," Sophie said, matter of fact, unboxing the tuna sandwich in front of her.

"Sorry?" I asked. And I truly was, because I had literally no idea what she was on about.

"About you." She nodded towards me, just in case the word 'you' didn't translate correctly in my brain.

"You mean that I'm the prince's donor?" I guessed, raising my eyebrows. "Yeah, I mean, I know it's not normal for his donors to work but it keeps me busy." I shrugged nervously, taken aback with the woman who sat in front of me now. She was miles away from the shy little Bambi in the lab.

"No." She shook her head and her hair bounced slightly. "I mean that you can't be compelled."

I felt my eyes widen. My heart raced and my mind

whirled. The words hung in the air for what felt like an eternity.

"I don't understand," I replied. And I truly didn't.

"I've been watching you. In the cafeteria and in the courtyard. You got here and I saw something in you that I see in myself. I've never had that before. And I've been here for four years." She took a bite from her sandwich, chewed and then swallowed before continuing. "Your eyes shift. You are curious. And sometimes, you are sad. And it's not the confused sadness like you see on some donors. It's a sadness that only comes with clarity."

I sat unmoving, watching her eat, unable to say anything.

She finally finished her sandwich and looked up to me, her eyes greener than before. Her face then suddenly became engulfed in the most glorious of smiles – one that was lit from within. *That* was what happiness looked like.

"Ivy," she said, eyes beaming, "welcome to the club."

"Wait," I started. "There's a 'club'?" My voice was hushed, but excitement was heavily lacing my words.

Sophie laughed musically. It was nice to watch someone find something genuinely amusing, despite all of this. Even if it was at my expense. "No, no. Unless a club can be made up of one person," she frowned, considering it, before shaking her head. "Now two people." She gestured towards the both of us, now holding an apple.

I watched her for a moment, eyeing her as she took large bites out of the fruit, crunching loudly. Her eyes darted around the canteen in an animated fashion. She had a bite mark on her neck.

"You let him bite you then? Your master?" I asked, curious. She turned her eyes back to mine – this time they held slightly less animation – and then absentmindedly touched the side of her neck where the wound was.

"Don't really have a choice. He can be a real bastard." She looked down at her hands, rolling the apple around, before placing it on the table, no longer hungry. "You know, if I could, I'd kill that man." Her eyes snapped up suddenly. "Can I even really call him that? A *man*. He's more of a parasite. My own personal parasite. A *leech*." She visibly shook, her body shivering at the thought of him.

"Who is he?"

She winced. "Garrett." When I didn't show any signs of recognition, she continued. "The king's advisor. He would have sat on the table with you at the ball. You can't miss him really. He radiates sleazeball." She shuddered.

I remembered him now. He had had very dark hair, made darker by the oil he used to push it off his face. He was handsome, in an older-gentleman sort of way, but his eyes had been beady and untrustworthy, like what I assumed all advisors' eyes would be like – always looking for a chance to gain more power, even if that meant betraying the person they currently served. *Bastard* seemed about right.

"That must be awful, having to pretend you don't feel anything when he does that to you. I'm sorry."

"Why are you apologising?" she asked, genuinely surprised. "Surely you have to endure the exact same thing?"

I liked Sophie. I truly did. But I hadn't known her long enough to be completely candid. So I didn't tell her that Angus knew about me. And I didn't tell her that I still hadn't been fed from. Even if I had trusted her completely, it seemed cruel to mention it somehow.

"Sure, sorry for apologising." I looked down, ashamed of my lie of omission. "So, how would you kill him then, if you could?" I asked light heartedly, changing the subject.

She seemed to like the way the conversation was going because she grinned wickedly. "The only way you can," she smiled, a hint of amusement in her tone. She clearly enjoyed the idea of pretending to kill Garrett. Perhaps it gave her a sense of control in a world where she had no control at all.

I remembered when I was in sixth form studying psychology. I read a study about stress in the workplace and how employees who had less control within their job suffered more from stress than those who had more job control. I wondered if this was transferrable here –

that Sophie's *deflation* was in some ways related to lack of control she had over her own life.

"I would rip his heart out," she said, nonchalantly, taking a sip from a bottle of fresh orange juice.

I laughed, finding the image ridiculous. "How could you possibly do that?"

"You'll know when I figure that out," she said. "Because Garrett will have one less heart. And I'll have an extra one. In a jar."

I laughed again, smiling widely at her. "Surely a stake would be easier?" I said in between laughs.

"See, that is where you are wrong. Stakes don't kill vampires. Vampires also don't burn. Holy water is a God damn myth, and don't even get me started on garlic or silver." She rolled her eyes.

"Apologies for the ignorance… but what about cutting off their head?" I probed, interested now

"Another impossibility. Their heads are stuck on with Gorilla Glue or something… impervious to decapitation. It's all very inconvenient."

"I can imagine," I muttered. "Where did you learn all of this?"

"I'd love to say that it was by trial and error through my multiple vampire-slaying escapades, but that would be false." I laughed again. Sophie was witty. I wondered when the last time she was able to be like this with someone. All that wit must have been bursting to come out. "I've picked things up over the years. Vampire's spill all their secrets when they think the ears around them can't listen." She shrugged again.

"Arrogant arseholes," I added. She looked up at me, smiling broadly.

"Too damn right. That arrogance will be the death of them. They don't even know it, but the resistance has doubled its numbers today already!"

"They would be shaking in their boots if they knew." I nodded, chuckling as I took a bite out of my own sandwich, finally able to concentrate on eating.

Sophie was easy to be around. The girl in the lab was

quiet and polite. This girl was smart, funny and bolshy. I loved her.

"Speaking of the resistance, what is our game plan?" I asked.

"Game plan?" Sophie asked in return, her brows furrowing deeply. Her eyes darted to each of mine, reflecting the cogs in her mind spinning.

"You know... aren't we going to try and get out of here somehow?" My heart raced. *Finally*, someone I could confide in and bounce ideas off. Ideas which would help me to get back to my little apartment. To my job seeking. To my sister.

The happiness was squashed when Sophie began to laugh, flinging her head back.

"Are you joking? There is no way in hell we are getting out of here." Her eyes glittered, but not with a positive emotion. Instead, she looked unhinged, as if the only way she was able to handle the idea of staying here forever was to become a little unstable. I understood that, and it upset me. "There are hundreds of vampires in this place," she continued. "All of them incredibly strong. All of them incredibly fast. The odds aren't even close to being in our favour. I don't even bother fancying the thought of escaping anymore. It's like waiting for a bus that's never going to come. In the rain. With eighty mile an hour wind. And you don't have a coat." She twisted her spine to her right until it made a pop and then spun in the other direction, popping that side too.

"What if we had vampires to help us?" I suggested.

"And what if I told you I could fly." She rolled her eyes. "They don't care about us. And even if there was one that did, that's not enough. A single moral vampire isn't enough against the hundreds of immoral ones."

I mulled that over. It was sour in my mouth. She was right. Except if the *right* vampire was on our side – a vampire with a degree of sway – could that be enough? I saved that thought for later.

"Well, let's leave that for now. I'm just happy you exist!" I beamed. "Being able to speak about the craziness around me is refreshing. I love my friends here, but I can't speak to them about things honestly. And I'm a big believer that you can't truly be friends with someone if you can't be honest with them."

She raised her eyebrows in thought. "No, I guess you can't. Not really. Who are your friends here?"

"Umm...so there's Andy. He's a doctor. Then Duke the dentist. Heather – you know Heather?" Sophie nodded yes. "Yeah, Heather and Sass." I realised I didn't actually know what Sass did. I'd have to ask another time. "Who are your friends?" I asked in return.

"I don't have any," she replied, no emotion on her face. It was almost chilling.

"What? None?" I couldn't hide the surprise in my voice.

"I mean, I *did*," she said. "But after a year or so, I couldn't look at them in the same way. Over time they just became more and more like characters in this bizarre life I was living, rather than people of their own. I watched each of them change subtly, with each thing they potentially did wrong with their masters or mistresses. I watched them forget things they used to know, or used to *be*. It just became more painful to have them in my life than not have them in my life. It became easier to keep people at arm's length."

Her eyes were fixed on the wall behind me, obviously remembering things vividly in her mind, no longer taking in the present moment.

"Well, you won't have to do that with me," I reassured her, reaching for her hand and squeezing it gently.

She blinked a few times, re-focusing her eyes back to the here and now, and smiled. "Thanks. You have no idea how much that's going to help my sleep patterns. You may be better than zopiclone."

"Glad I could be of assistance." I chuckled, letting go of her hands. "How would you feel about sitting with my friends at dinner tonight?"

She twisted her lips as she mulled over my proposition. "I suppose I could be a walking poster child for the 'happy donor' and put a smile on my face for the occasion."

"Good, because I think they are exactly what you need. They are *my* zopiclone."

We both finished our lunches in silence, happy to not have to keep up any pretences. Although, from what I had observed of Sophie's behaviour in the lab, she seemed to be long past keeping up pretences anymore. People knew she was odd, and yet she hadn't been found out. Or if she had, no one cared, but I thought that unlikely.

We left the canteen, and I told her that I wanted to head to the courtyard before starting work again since we still had over half an hour left of lunch. She declined my invite to join her, saying how she wanted to be alone for a while. It seemed that the interaction with me had wiped her out, which didn't surprise me considering she had likely not had any meaningful or real interactions in, well, years.

I walked through the hallways with a purpose and entered the expanse that was the courtyard. It was sunny outside, and the light reflected inwards, creating an almost hazy and ethereal atmosphere. Light bounced off the water and the leaves on the trees. I felt a sudden sense of deep calm.

Making my way over to my favourite bench, I sat silently, trying to cultivate some of the meditation techniques that I learnt in the Yoga practices I had gone to. I didn't want my mind to whirl with the conversation with Sophie – it was too much for my mind this afternoon. I would ponder on it later.

Unfortunately, it wasn't long before my peaceful mindset was interrupted. I felt a light presence to the right of me. It was an odd sensation. There was no heat emanating from the presence like there would have been if a person had sat next to me, and yet when I opened my eyes, the presence was distinctly person-shaped.

"Hello again, Miss Ivy." Anthony's voice was smooth honey running over gravel.

I turned to face him slightly, my knees knocking over to the right. "Anthony," I nodded, politely. I only briefly touched his eyes with mine.

"You looked so peaceful," he said, a slightly playful

smirk on his lips.

"Then why did you interrupt me?" I quipped, not able to hide my annoyance. Anthony was difficult to engage with. His tone and flirty manner meant I was unable to have full restraint of my words – the sweet, happy, innocent donor act evaporating completely. This made Anthony dangerous. Perhaps Angus had been right.

His smirk widened, becoming charmingly lopsided. He chuffed, running a hand though his floppy hair, staring at me. "It seems I cannot help myself." He shrugged, looking slightly ashamed. But clearly it was not enough to change his habits. "What have you done with this beautiful day?"

"May I ask you why you are making small talk with me?" I huffed, now giving him my full attention, very much out of my meditative, relaxed state. "Do you not have anything better to do?"

"It appears I do not. So, humour me, wouldn't you?" He cocked his head to the side, anticipating my response. He looked excited to hear what I would say.

"I was working in the medical labs," I said.

"Working?" Anthony asked, puzzlement etched all over his handsome, boyish face. "Why?"

"Because I want to," I replied, bluntly. I was fed up with vampires asking me that.

"Fascinating," he muttered, turning away from me and rubbing his chin with his hand in thought.

"You are easily fascinated," I said.

"Is that so?" he probed. "Perhaps you are right. There isn't much to do around here."

"So, you decided to disturb me?" I snapped.

Anthony laughed, his eyes crinkling with humour as his face took on a beauty that was immeasurable to a human. "And I'm glad I did. I could listen to your little snappy retorts all day. They are more refreshing than anything to me."

"That's sad for you," I muttered.

"I'm happy enough, don't you worry," he smiled, his eyes tracing my face in curiosity. "Perhaps happier now," he added, as an afterthought. After a silence, he spoke again. "I have a confession," he admitted, looking almost sheepish, but not quite.

"Please, share. I'm sure it will thrill me."

He laughed again, this time throwing his head back ever so slightly before staring again in complete disbelief. I wished he would stop staring.

"As you wish, Miss Ivy." He turned further to his left, reaching a hand up towards me. He gently pinched a piece of hair which framed my face, and began to twirl it deftly around his fingers. "When your hair moves, it releases this amazingly potent smell. I can't place the smell, I just know that it's distinctly *your* smell, and that I simply cannot get enough of it." He released my hair then, placing his hand into the front pocket of his black jeans, pulling something out of it.

"Do you recognise this?" he asked, eyes locked on mine. I concentrated hard, knowing that compulsion was always on the cards. Looking down, a small vial was sitting in the middle of his large, pale palm. It was the small perfume vial I had taken to the ball – the one which had gone missing.

"Yes," I gulped. "It's my perfume vial."

He took it from his palm, holding it now in between his index finger and thumb. "Do you know what it smells like?" he asked, tilting the liquid this way and that. It was almost empty.

"I never got a chance to use it because *someone* stole it from me," I said, irritated. It was to elicit guilt, though, because I *had* smelt it. And I obviously didn't have strong enough olfactory nerves because it smelt of nothing.

He ignored my dig and instead sprayed a couple of puffs of the perfume onto his left wrist, holding it up to his nose and inhaling deeply. His eyes closed, and he smiled slightly, the points of his canines slightly elongated.

He then presented his wrist to my face, gesturing for me to smell it. I leaned in, inhaling the scent, smelling… absolutely nothing… again.

I wrinkled my nose. "I can't smell anything." This only made him smile.

"That's because this little vial contains *your* distinct fragrance," he smirked.

"I don't understand," I frowned. I felt like I was saying that a lot today.

"There's none more potent a perfume to a vampire than a human's natural smell. Obviously, we all have our tastes, but what better perfume than just a heightened version of the lovely smell you already have."

"It's almost empty," I said.

"Ahhh, yes." Anthony nodded, looking slightly embarrassed. "I'm an addict," he admitted, smirking up at me. He reached for my hair again, bringing it up to his nose and inhaling deeply. His sigh after was erotic, and I had to pull back.

He stood suddenly, stepping away from the bench to face me. "Well, that's enough confessions for one day. Perhaps next time I'll convince you to confess something to me."

He turned on his heel and walked away, shoulders broad and legs long with what appeared to be a slight animation to his steps.

I sat on the bench, watching after him, noticing that he had kept the vial and slipped it into the pocket of his jeans once again.

CHAPTER 13

Honest Conversations

Angus

"Ahh, just the prince I was looking for."

Angus had been passing through a hallway on the way to the blood donation wing of the hospital when Anthony addressed him. He hadn't fed all day, and his throat was becoming tight.

Ivy's work attire that morning had left him feeling wound up – he needed something to take the edge off. He just wished that it didn't have to come from a bag.

Well, it didn't *have* to. This was Angus's choice. A choice which still confused him daily. He wondered how long he could keep it up, stealing the blood bags like this. Sorcha was already well aware, so perhaps it wasn't long before the rumour spread.

Angus could just imagine it. *The prince?! Drinking from blood bags?! What a pathetic excuse for an immortal!*

But Angus's thirst was not to be quenched as he would have liked. Instead, he had to deal with the irritating vampire in front of him.

"How can I help you today, Anthony?" he asked, straining slightly, teeth clenching. Anthony had never particularly bothered him. In fact, Angus once thought of

Anthony as a friend, and perhaps even more than that. He had, after all–

No. Don't think of it.

Angus pictured his fist contacting Anthony's sharp jaw with enough force to dislodge it out of joint. He smirked at the thought in pleasure.

Anthony swaggered towards him, smirking also, although Angus doubted it was out of a desire for violence. He probably didn't want to know what the reason for it was.

"I was hoping we could have a chat." He stopped in front of him, eyes twinkling.

"What is it you wish to discuss?" asked Angus, frowning.

"Can we perhaps go to your quarters? I have a feeling you'll want to speak in private."

"Stop toying with me, Anthony," Angus snapped. He didn't have time for this cryptic 'banter'.

"I am not toying, Prince," Anthony began. "I genuinely believe you'll agree with me once I bring up the topic I wish to discuss."

Angus sighed loudly, his exasperation palpable. "Fine." He turned on his heel, gesturing to the vampire to follow him.

When they entered his quarters, Angus assumed his usual position at his desk. He asked Anthony to sit on the chair opposite. He saw that to be Ivy's chair. He didn't know why, he just did. He didn't like Anthony sitting in it, but he turned the heat down on that emotion and composed himself.

"Spit it out, Anthony."

Anthony crossed his right ankle over his left knee in a relaxed manner, clasping his hands together in his lap. The simple nonchalance of the action triggered within Angus an irritation unmatched.

Was this creature out to vex me?

"It's about Ivy," Anthony announced, rather bluntly, in a way that didn't at all match his relaxed demeanour. Angus stiffened at the sound of her name on the other vampire's lips. He hated the way it rolled off Anthony's tongue. It sounded almost possessive. He recognised the tone perfectly – it was the exact same tone he used to speak her name as well, although he rarely said it out loud.

"What about my donor?" Angus had to use all of his metal control to not over articulate the word 'my'.

Anthony shrugged, eyes darting away from Angus's. "She's fascinating," he mentioned.

"She doesn't like that word."

"Yes, I've noticed that," Anthony nodded, thoughtfully.

"I don't see why she should concern you. She isn't yours." There. He'd done it. Claimed her as *his.* He would have done it with any donor. He was possessive in that way. He thought of what Ivy's face would look like if she ever heard him claiming her like that, smiling slightly at the picture.

Anthony's eyes once again met Angus's. His head cocked to the side. "I have a feeling that she isn't *anyone's.* She's rather independent, no?"

"I can't say I've noticed," Angus lied. He pushed back into the chair, moving his body in some way to distract himself from the feelings he was experiencing. He couldn't place them, but he knew they weren't pleasant.

"If that's the case," Anthony began, "then you are at a disadvantage, Prince. And I would even say sorely missing out." He smirked, appearing to remember something pleasant. "Do you compel her to be like that? Do you like a challenge? Is it a new kink of yours?"

"I compel only what I need to compel," Angus replied, not really answering the questions.

Anthony chuckled at Angus's frigidness. "I'm not kink shaming here, Prince. Just interested."

"*Why* are you interested? Why are you *really* here?"

"I guess I wanted to know if you saw what I saw. And what you thought about it." He shrugged. "But it appears you do not see, or if you do, you won't admit it. You always were very proud."

"Pride has nothing to do with it."

"Or everything, Mr Darcy," Anthony chuckled. "Anyway,

enough of the jesting. I'm here to say that I want Miss Ivy and, being the gentleman I am, I'm letting you know of that fact. But I'm not asking your permission, Prince. Let's be clear on that."

Angus's body vibrated with anger. His throat was even drier now than it was before, the energy needed to keep his emotions in check draining his last reserves. Was Anthony saying that he wanted to *pursue* Ivy?! His blood boiled.

"You have a lot of nerve saying that to me." Angus's voice was brittle like porcelain.

"What can I say? I've always been the one with nerve in this friendship," Anthony wagged his brows, goading.

"You are a piece of work. Ivy isn't a toy you can play with at your will."

"Is she not?" Anthony looked surprised, but his eyes showed something else, as if what Angus said irritated him. "Isn't that what donors are for?"

"You have your *own donor* for such things," he replied, gritting his teeth with full strength. He could feel the muscles in his cheeks screaming, desperate for oxygen that his poor blood reserves couldn't provide. His arteries felt scratchy – like they were lined with sandpaper.

"But she isn't Ivy," Anthony stated, bluntly.

"She is *mine*." Angus stood to his full height. If he was a snake, he would be spitting venom.

Anthony also stood, but in a less aggressive manner. "I think I'll let her decide on that. No compulsion, just her," he proposed.

"What are you saying?"

"I'm saying I think we should let her choose who she 'belongs' to. And that we should let her do that without compulsion. I propose we both agree to not coerce her mind into making a decision, and instead let the *real* Ivy decide what, or who, she wants."

"How can you be sure I won't cheat and compel her anyway?" Angus asked, bristling. Of course, he knew that was an impossibility, but he wanted to verbally joust Anthony into backing out of the absurd proposal.

"Ahh, simple really," Anthony grinned. "It has

everything to do with that pride of yours I mentioned earlier"

◆ ◆ ◆

Once Anthony had left the room, Angus was finally able to head to the blood bank and grab some blood. He drank it greedily despite it having no real appeal on his tongue. It was cold, and a little too thick to be considered savoury.

As he finished the bag at his desk, he also reflected on the conversation he had had with the infuriating vampire. He knew he had the ability to completely block Anthony's advances – he was a prince after all – and yet he understood where he was coming from. He understood that Ivy and her free will were important. To take away Anthony's advances would in some way take away Ivy's ability to make a choice. He realised, reluctantly, that he wasn't able to do that. Not about this.

It was also – although he really would never admit it to anyone but himself – about his pride.

With Ivy not being compelled, things were suddenly exciting. He was in a real-life love triangle, and he wanted to *win*. He wanted to be more charming than Anthony. He wanted to be more attractive than Anthony. He wanted to seduce Ivy better than Anthony. It was all about beating Anthony, he told himself. Nothing to do with the brunette.

Suddenly, Angus felt very pathetic. But he didn't have time to dwell on the emotion, as Ivy entered the quarters, back from work. He hid the blood bag in his top right drawer, next to his notebook.

She looked a little bit more unkempt than she had that morning. Her hair was a little tangled and her clothes slightly crumpled. She brushed her hair away from her face unconsciously, and then brought her hand up to her eye, rubbing it. In doing so, the makeup she was wearing smudged a little, making her look tired. She placed her bag on the floor, sat on her side of the bed and took off her shoes, flexing her feet when they were free from the pumps, pressing her thumb pads into what he assumed were sore spots. Humans were so fragile.

"Want me to do that?" he asked, not even realising he was going to offer before the words came out of his mouth.

Ivy turned her head towards him, frowning. "Do what?"

He nodded towards her feet where her hands were wrapped. "Give you a foot massage." He felt his lips twitch slightly, trying not to smile at her surprised face. "I've got strong fingers." He raised his hands to her, wriggling the digits in demonstration, smirking *charmingly.*

Oh, had he really just done that? Was he *flirting?* It was shameless. He would have blushed if it were possible.

"I've not had a shower yet." Her nose scrunched ever so slightly. He couldn't help but smile at the way it made her face looks a little childish, like a toddler. Not that Angus had been in presence of a toddler in decades, but still.

"So?" he asked. He liked watching her squirm.
Sadist.

She sat taller. He watched the challenge flit through her eyes. *Game on*, they said.

"Fine, since you offered. Where do you want me?" she asked, grabbing a hair tie from her nightstand and running her hands through the strands to place it in a flowing high ponytail.

Angus wanted her everywhere. On the bed, in the shower, over his desk. In the chair he sat on. But he didn't think that was what she meant. Ever since he'd seen her in that damn underwear after the ball, he had turned into a horny adolescent. He needed to reign it in. Horns were for devils, not vampires.

"Stay there. I'll come to you. Swing your legs onto the bed though." He stood, walking into the bathroom and picked up some massage oil from one of the cabinets. He had never used it before, but had eyed it a time or two.

When he walked back into the room, she was where he had directed. He frowned, looking at her feet. "You'll need to take them off." He nodded to her tights.

They were the kind of tights that made a man excited. The ones which were really sheer, yet still black. You could see her legs through them, but they were covered enough to remain alluring. The dark contours accentuated her legs – they were athletic and shapely. How had he never noticed that?

She began to pick at her nails, making that snap sound again. He frowned at her, and she stopped, looking embarrassed. "Can't you just do it through the tights?"

"I can't put oil on your tights. It would ruin them." And he *really* didn't want to ruin them.

"Then don't use oil," she said, getting slightly irate. He found it amusing but kept a straight face.

"That would be a sub-optimal experience for all parties."

"*All parties?*" Her eyebrows raised. "What? You have a foot fetish?"

Angus laughed, shaking his head. "Definitely not."

"Then tights on it is," she declared stubbornly.

"Oh, so if I had told you that I did indeed have a foot fetish, you would have taken the tights off for me?"

Ivy visibly shuddered with irritation. He loved it. "That is *not* what I meant."

"I'm only joking," Angus smiled, shrugging. "But, honestly, take off the tights. It will be worth it, I promise."

She frowned again. It was her favourite expression.

Something changed in her and she finally stood up. "Are you going to turn around?" she snapped.

"Why would I do that? I'm going to see you without them on in a second anyway."

She turned her head to the side slightly, a slight blush creeping up her neck. "It's the process of taking off the tights that's the issue."

"Stop over thinking this. It's a wee foot rub."

She let out a long, exasperated sigh, defeated. She turned slightly, so she was at a slight angle to Angus rather than standing straight in front of him. She bent, sliding her hands underneath her pencil skirt (that damn skirt!), and hooked her thumbs above the top of her tights.

She was wearing tiny pants, he noticed. *Of course* he noticed.

She dragged her hands downwards, pulling the thin

material along with them. He was surprised the material didn't rip under the force – she was rushing things, but in Angus's mind, the whole motion was far from rushed. His heightened senses made sure of that.

He slowed everything down, missing nothing.

As the tights progressed to her middle thigh, she had to bend a little further down, causing her arse to become more visible.

Tiny knickers. Tiny purple knickers. Thong.

As she got to the shins, her legs straightened slightly so her arse was more in the air. Her hair fell forwards around her face, and she subconsciously shifted her head slightly to move it out the way. When she reached near her ankles, she sat back down for some reason and pulled the tights off each of her feet separately. In doing so, her legs had to open slightly. Finally, she shimmied the skirt back down her thighs to a more acceptable length before repositioning herself back on the bed.

This was all completed in a matter of seconds. Ivy thought he saw nothing. But Angus had seen *everything*.

"Done," she said, her face stony and expressionless. Well, that's what she was trying to convey. But Angus saw the truth. He could see her pulse point in her neck – it was working double time – and the sound filled his ears like the beat of a song. His new *favourite* song, he decided.

He sat near the foot of the bed, near where her feet were. Her toenails were painted a deep rose colour, and it brought out the tanned accents in her skin. Ivy wasn't exactly dark in skin tone. In fact, she looked rather pale – ghostly against her dark hair and eyes. But when he looked closely, she had slight golden undertones to her skin, making the veins under the surface appear green in colour.

On her right ankle, she had a little tattoo. Again, this was not something he had noticed before. It was of a small tree, no colour, just outlined with subtle shading. He couldn't place the tree itself, but it appeared large and regal despite the small size of the image, with tiny leaves that held a fragility. It suited her – powerful and yet dainty all at once.

Angus opened the cap on the massage oil, dripped some into the centre of his palm and began to rub his hands together. He wanted them to be warm to her, like a human's hands. He didn't know why.

He grabbed her right ankle, lifting it slightly, then stopped. "I'm going to grab a towel."

He went into the bathroom and picked up a fresh hand towel. When he sat on the bed again, he cocked one of his legs up so it was on the bed, slightly bent it, and placed the towel over it. He picked her ankle up again and placed it onto his leg, around where his knee was.

"I don't want to get oil on my trousers," he explained, although she hadn't asked. He could feel the heat off her, even through two layers of material.

Angus began on her right foot, spreading the oil on the sole and instep and then up towards her ankle. He was tempted to spread it to her calf, but he didn't think that very gentlemanly of him considering it was only meant to be a foot massage – the ankle was enough of a diversion from the brief. The word *gentleman* reminded him of Anthony, and he had to resist the urge to squeeze tighter in annoyance.

He began with light pressure, not really focusing on any specific points, just warming up her muscles and familiarising her skin to his touch. She didn't seem phased by his cool hands. In fact, her heart rate had dropped slightly, and she had shifted on the bed so she was more comfortable, resting her head back against her pillow, neck exposed.

He tried not to look, he *really* did. But it was just *there*.

Her neck was just a neck. But it belonged to *her* which seemed to make it more delicious.

No! He couldn't afford to think about those things. He needed to *win*. So, he teared his eyes away from her and focused on her feet.

After a couple of minutes, he began to focus on the sole, around about the point where he had noticed her putting pressure before. He placed both his hands around her foot, thumbs towards her sole and fingers around the instep, and started with slightly firm pressure, particularly around a spot on the ball. Ivy sighed delightfully and Angus felt like a dog being given praise. He repeated the same motion, desperate to hear the same sound escape from the back of her throat.

"Why are you doing this?" she asked, a mumble from her lips. It was quiet, almost as if she hadn't really meant him to hear it. But Angus's hearing was acute enough that it was clear to him.

A vampire had many heightened senses. His ears were sharper than a human's – the venom of the vampire transition causing a mass increase in the number of synapses which attached to the cochlear nerve. It also made the tympanic membrane more pliable, allowing even small vibration in the air the ability to move it. The dilator pupillary muscles of their eyes were stronger, allowing the pupil to open wider for broader vision, and the sphincter pupillary muscles were more abundant, allowing their eyes to hone in to the tiniest of details – their pupils able to become pin-point in nature. This, however, had its restrictions. Vampires were irritated by bright sunlight as a result of their anatomical differences. Their avoidance of certain environments fuelled the 'allergic to the sun' myth. It was simply an annoyance – nothing that a good pair of sunglasses couldn't remedy. But prolonged exposure became draining to them, so it was often that vampires preferred overcast days, or night.

Touch was an unusual vampire sense. He wasn't entirely sure the difference between his and a human's. He was aware that texture was more vibrant to experience, but he assumed the differences mainly lay with the experience of pain. It was possible for vampires to feel pain, but it was at a much higher threshold than a human. He remembered blurred memories from his human years – stubbing a toe on the bed, slicing a finger on something sharp – and how this used to light up his pain response immensely. Now, pain was only really possible at the hands of another vampire – someone with as much, or more, strength than him.

Smell and taste weren't really senses he wanted his mind to linger on in that moment. He didn't need to think about Ivy's blood when he was this close to her.

He didn't answer her. Instead, he focused on the task at hand, trying to keep his aforementioned senses in check. He decided to ask her some questions. The best way to win against Anthony was to get to know her, surely.

"What does the tree mean?" he asked, running his finger over the outline of the tattoo on her ankle.

She lazily opened her eyes, meeting his, before looking down to where his finger was tracing. She squinted slightly, before turning her head away.

"Just thought it was a cute design. Isn't that why anyone gets a tattoo?"

Angus studied her. Although her face was turned away, he *knew* she was frowning. He would bet his immortal life on it.

"I believe that's why *most* people get a tattoo," he offered. "But I have a hunch that's not why you got it."

She turned back towards him. He was right. There was that frown. "What makes you say that?"

He shrugged, eyes piercing hers. "Like I said, it's a hunch."

"I didn't know vampire's got hunches. How very human of you," she sneered, deflecting. Angus ignored her. It surprised him that she obviously thought calling him human would offend him.

"Can you at least tell me what kind of tree it is?" Not very personal, but he just wanted to keep her talking.

"A silver birch tree."

"Right." He let that sit there, in the air. He hoped that his silence would encourage her to explain. At first, he thought it was the last she would speak of it, but a couple of minutes passed, and she finally divulged.

"It's going to sound really silly to you," she started, turning her head away from him.

"Try me," he urged.

She took a deep breath, a really high, upper-chest breath, her lower abdomen hardly moving at all. She was anxious. Humans who breathed with their chest and not their abdomen had dysfunctional breath patterns often related to a stressful lifestyle. He had learnt that once.

"There was a tree in our front garden back home. It was a silver birch tree. I used to sit under it when I was a kid. I remember it was really small when we first moved in, almost like the previous owners had just planted it. But that tree grew with me. As I got taller, so did the tree. Which of course makes sense, doesn't it." She chucked slightly, running her hand through her ponytail, swishing it over her shoulder. "But it wasn't just that. I felt like the tree was a reflection of me – of my life. Whenever I was going through a good time in my life, the tree would thrive, growing several feet, and its leaves would be this gorgeous healthy shade of green. But whenever things were tough, the tree suffered. It would just look like…" She paused, looking for inspiration – the *right* words. "It had receded into itself."

Angus had stopped touching her feet and she pulled her legs towards herself, reflecting her words. She began to touch her tattoo subconsciously.

"Anyway, one day my parents chopped down that tree. *My* tree. And I just felt such a sense of…loss." She sighed heavily. "It was as if they had removed a part of me. So, I guess the tattoo was to get a part of me back. The bit they took."

"I have a tattoo." Angus admitted, meeting her eyes gently. Her eyebrows raised slightly in response.

"Where?"

"On my inner bicep," he replied.

"What's it of?"

"My mother's name. She passed away," Angus explained briefly, not wanting to expand further. But Ivy had other ideas.

"How did she pass?" she asked, sympathy in her eyes. He hated that look.

"Blood loss." His reply was blunt and sharp at the same time. Ivy's head tilted slightly.

"Vampires?"

"Vampire."

"Someone you knew?"

"Someone I *know*." He frowned. "Someone I wish I didn't"

Ivy sat still. Her eyes continued to search his face, looking for answers. After a minute or so, she seemed to find what she was looking for.

"It was your father, wasn't it?" she whispered, as if she was worried she would frighten an animal or small child if she spoke any louder. Angus's eyes snapped up and he was suddenly transported to that first day he had met her. *You can see into my soul. I'm sure of it.*

"Exactly right," he said. And suddenly, he just wanted to tell her the story. A story that even Sorcha hadn't heard. "I was fifteen when it happened." Angus could see a question in her eyes, so he answered it. "I'm thirty-one now. For eternity. Obviously, the years since I've turned have been many but…" She nodded her understanding but said nothing, waiting intently on the storyteller. "My father had just turned. He was turned by request – he paid someone to become a vampire. We were wealthy and influential. He could afford the price for immortality, so he did it. Always was a power-hungry bastard." Angus's face was firm, more stony than usual, as he continued. "He wanted us to be an immortal family. Me, him, my brother and my mother." Angus felt Ivy shift, so gave her the information she wanted. "My brother passed of natural causes. He got small pox."

She nodded.

"Anyway, my mother detested the idea. How could he have spent our money on something so immoral? She was a religious woman, and in her eyes, what my father has done went beyond sin. She out-right refused to be turned, unable to put her soul and the soul of her sons in jeopardy. He tried to convince her, tried showing her the benefits of vampirism – how he would have the strength of tens of men and run as fast as lightning. How he could heal with immaculate speed. How we'd never have to fear. But my mother rejected his proposal and left him, taking me and my brother with her. He found us. I remember him bursting into our modest housing. Rage – his rage was literally tangible. I remember it vividly. He said he was going to compel her to like the idea, and she just broke down. The rest was a bit of a blur, mainly because I think my father tried to compel the memory from me. But basically, she took a knife to her heart and…" He stopped, composing himself. "Anyway, the blood drove him crazy, and he drained her of it. Her heart didn't even get a chance to stop beating before he mauled her. It was awful. And I've never forgiven him. Needless to say, he got me in the end." He shrugged, helplessly, shoulders sagging. "Found me hiding out in Canada. Nova Scotia. Turned me himself. His final fuck you to my mother, I always assumed. He's got my soul forever and me and my brother and mother can never be reunited."

"What a fucking bastard." Ivy spoke, her eyes a little glassy.

And then Angus did a thing he never thought he'd do after telling that story. He laughed. "Yes, he really is."

"No wonder you hate him. I mean, *I* hate him, for God's sake!"

"One day, I will kill him," he declared, unblinking. "He owes me a heart."

"By the sounds of it, he owes you more than one," she replied. He nodded solemnly.

"How did he get you to live in the Warren?" she asked after a beat.

"He didn't," he replied. "I chose to live in the Warren."

"For what possible reason?!"

Angus shrugged. "Gain his trust. Get closer to him. Kill him. You know, the usual."

"How's that working out for you?" she asked, and he sensed sarcasm in her voice.

"Not well, actually."

"You don't say," she muttered.

CHAPTER 14

Unlikely Allies

Ivy

It was that Sunday when I bumped into Freyja. Well, I say bumped into, it was more that I came across her in the courtyard, crying.

I had been sitting on my favourite bench when the sobbing hit my ears. In search for them, I stood, walking towards the sound. It was then when I saw her, hugging her knees. She sat under a tree out of sight, but not, as she maybe didn't realise, out of earshot.

Her face was ridden of her usual thickly applied make-up, and I reluctantly allowed myself to accept that she was actually rather beautiful. It was a shame she was such a rip-roaring bitch. I considered leaving, pretending that I had never seen her, but then I remembered that her master was that creepy Baron dude, and I thought better of it. Perhaps he'd done something really depraved and she'd a breakdown.

I approached her slowly, taking my time so as not to frighten her. Right at that moment, she might as well have been a tiny defenceless animal. She looked that vulnerable.

She finally heard my approach and whipped her head up. Her swollen eyes hardened and shrunk in size as they became slits. I nearly flinched.

"What do you want, bitch?" she snapped, wiping the back of her hand aggressively against her cheeks as if doing so would make her suddenly look like she hadn't been crying. *Good luck with that.*

I ignored her insult and proceeded with caution. I mean, last time I had seen her (or heard her), she had been laughing at my expense.

"I wanted to see if you were okay," I answered softly, taking a step forward.

"Do I *look* okay?" she snarled, her face contorted into something sinister.

"No. In all honesty, you look like crap."

"Takes one to know one."

"You know... I'm trying to be nice. Why don't we try having that in common instead? It seems like a less terrible affliction," I replied with a sharpness in my voice that I couldn't quite squash. She really was a piece of work.

"I don't feel like being nice right now."

"Do you ever?" I asked, genuinely curious.

Her eyes softened ever so slightly, a very subtle change, and her lips tilted up the tiniest amount. Her tears had stopped. "Touche."

"You want to talk about it?"

"Not with you." More snapping, like a Jack Russell Terrier.

"Well, I hate to break it to you, Freyja, but it looks like I'm the only one you've got."

"I'll find someone to talk to about it later, you snidey cow."

"Takes one to know one," I muttered.

She scoffed. "Why don't you go run off back to your prince, Little Miss Perfect?"

"Why don't you run off to Baron?" Freyja visibly stiffened. Her body took on an inhuman quality. *Bingo.* "Did he hurt you?" I pressed, moving closer to her.

"I don't know what you mean." Her face was strained. She was frowning strongly, and her eyes were shifting away from my face, drifting towards the abyss – the eyes of someone who had been compelled. Then they flicked back to mine. "I mean, I *do* know what you mean, but I don't know how to answer that question."

I walked further towards her and sat opposite her bent legs, slightly off centre, crossing my legs in front of me and resting my weight on my hands behind my back. "Did he... do something you didn't like?" I asked, trying to find a loophole in the compulsion.

"I don't know." She rested her chin on her hands which were being propped up by her elbows on her knees. It was a rather relaxed position compared to the one she had been in a couple of minutes ago, and I took that as gaining her trust.

The thing was, I didn't like Freyja. But, hey, my humanity was showing, because at the end of the day, if I had to choose between Baron and Freyja, I'd pick Freyja every time. Us humans had to stick together. Especially when we were against a sexually-harassing, blood-sucking sadist.

"Look, I saw Baron with you at the ball," Freyja's eyes widened as I continued. "I think I know what's going on. Freyja, did he–"

"You know, my name isn't actually Freyja," she interrupted, matter-of-factly.

My face took on what I could only assume would be one of complete confusion. "Now I'm the one who doesn't know what *you* mean," I said, intrigued.

"It's Jane." She turned her head to the side, looking away from me. "Boring, I know."

"Why did you change it?"

"Because I could. Especially here. You can be whoever you want to be." If only she knew how wrong she was.

"So, you chose to be 'Freyja the Bitch'?"

She smiled, a slyness taking over her face. "No. I was always a bitch. Freyja is just a kick-arse Norse Goddess."

"I know who she is. She's the Goddess of beauty. But she was also supposed to be loving and caring and kind."

"Yeah," she scoffed, "I've always been a fan of irony. Apart from the beauty part. That bit we have in common."

"You aren't wearing any makeup today," I commented, the words coming out my mouth before I could stop them.

"I don't really like wearing makeup," she admitted, blankly.

"No? Then why are you always caked in the stuff?"

She scowled at my blunt question. "Baron likes me to. I personally think it makes me look like a trashy hoe bag but what can you do?" She shrugged, smiling weakly.

"You don't like Baron much, do you?"

"What gave me away?" She smirked, eyes twinkling slightly. "But no. Not in the slightest. Don't ask me why. I wouldn't be able to tell you."

"Why wouldn't you be able to?" I probed.

"My brain physically won't let me," she said, deflated. She reached a hand up to her eyes and rubbed them in frustration. "You know what fucking sucks?" she asked, rhetorically. "That every damn human in this place *loves* their master or mistress. It's as if they were specially picked for compatibility. But me? I *hate* Baron. And you know what's worse? I think Baron *likes* that I hate him." As she spoke, her eyes were trained down to her fingernails, the ones on her right picking at the ones on her left.

"Don't you ever think that it's so very convenient that every donor is so content in this place?" I uttered, cocking my head to the side.

"All the time." She nodded. "But nothing ever comes of those thoughts. It's like I can't get past them."

"Do you ever think about *why* you can't get past them? Why you can't tell me what Baron does? Why you wear makeup even though you hate it?"

"Yeahhh...," she drawled. "What are you getting at?"

I came to a crossroads. One fork was a road towards abandoning the conversation and leaving Freyja to be the bitch that she was so proud of being. The other was the road to telling her about compulsion.

While we were talking, something had hit me. Baron had made a big mistake. By making Freyja hate him (or more likely not compelling her to like him), he had allowed her mind to fuel itself. By hating him, she had no real loyalty. Yes, he could *compel* her loyalty, but for some reason, her hate for him was stronger. She couldn't tell anyone about his abuse, she couldn't physically retaliate, but she could *emotionally retaliate*, and that was exactly what her mind was doing. Her hate for him was her strength. Her hate for him was her free will. Because Baron hadn't compelled that. Baron had no control over Freyja's hate. And that meant Baron's control over her was fragile.

I realised at that moment that Freyja could be just like me and Sophie – with a little help, obviously. But could we trust her?

Finally, I shrugged. "Just food for thought." *Coward.* "Why did you tell me all that stuff? Don't you hate me?" I asked.

"Beats me." She shrugged, sniffing slightly. "But if you tell *anyone* about this, I'll cut you." Her words were sharp, but they didn't match her face. "And this *really* doesn't mean we're friends. I'm not friends with royal-wanna-be uggos."

I began to stand up. "Don't worry, this uggo won't spill the beans about you being an ugly crier with a boring name." I walk away, hearing her chuckling behind me as I go.

"Touche again, bitch," she muttered.

◆ ◆ ◆

It was Monday afternoon when I mentioned my interaction with Freyja to Sophie.

"So, she was just... crying?"

"Yep. Under a tree," I said, nodding, shovelling some pasta salad into my mouth. It was lunch time, and we were both having a well-deserved break after working hard in the labs. We were working on some concoction that was tricky to sequence. It almost made me regret asking for the job.

"Do you think that *maybe* she's finally realised that she's a complete bitch face and had the mental breakdown we all saw coming her way at, like, one hundred miles per hour?" Sophie asked, eyes wide and innocent, but I could see the humour within them. She was perfectly aware of Freyja's reputation, stating that she had also not been immune to her torment when she first arrived. Turns out, Freyja had been here a *really* long time.

"I wish that was the case, I really do. But no. She seems pretty happy with her bitch status," I said. "She didn't actually say what had made her cry, but I am almost certain it was Baron."

"Who the hell is Baron?" she questioned, her nose scrunching up.

"Her slimey donor."

"Should fit her perfectly then," she muttered under her breath "But no, I knew who he was, I just wanted to hear how you described him. Slimey donor I give... a six out of ten." I raised my brows up at her. "What?" she asked, not a hint of shame on her face. "Greasy, overweight cockroach – eight out of ten. Toe-curling arse rag – nine out of ten. Ugly mother fucker – ten out of ten."

"Seriously? *'Ugly mother fucker'* gets a ten?"

She shrugged, nibbling on her sandwich. "It's a classic." I couldn't deny that. It was like calling someone a son of a bitch. Just a classic insult which rolled off the tongue.

"I think he's sexually abusing her," I stated, eyes suddenly serious.

Sophie cocked her head to the side, her eyes also sharpening. Her sandwich was lifted up to her lips as if she was about to take another bite, but her lips remained pressed together instead. "I don't mean to be a total bubble burster here, Ivy, but I'm pretty sure every vampire sexually abuses their donor." Sophie's eyes were sad, and I suddenly felt awful.

"I mean... yeah... I know that," I said, shoulders slumping. "But this is different."

"How?" she asked, intrigue in her eyes.

"Well with you... and me," I added, still not able to admit that Angus knew about me. Was I trying to protect him? *Don't think about it.* "They at least think they are doing it in a semi-kind way. Like, they think we are compelled to enjoy it so... we shouldn't know any different. Right?"

Sophie winched, but then finally nodded. "Right."

"But with Freyja, her donor hasn't even tried to compel her to like him. If anything, he's done the opposite. Actually, I don't think compulsion was needed. The hate and distaste she has for him is all hers."

"What are you getting at, friend?" I had a feeling that she knew, but she just wanted me to spell it out for her.

"I think Slimey Baron like's her... resistance. He gets a kick of having control over her and knowing that she doesn't want to be with him. I think he's a rapist."

"Okay. Number one, 'Slimey Baron' is my new favourite nick-name and we will be calling him that from now on. Number two, what a *fucking bastard*."

"I *know*," I replied, glad that she was on the same page as I was. "But I think he's made an error–"

"No shit, Sherlock!" she blurted. "I'd say being a rapist is a pretty big error too," she said, hands gesticulating around her head.

I grabbed her hands, encouraging her to bring them back down to the table, worried she was attracting people's attention. "Would you stop that, Soph?!" I hissed.

"Sorry," she muttered, looking a little ashamed.

"As I was *saying*. Other than the obvious error of being a rapist, Baron has also made another error." Sophie raised her right index finger, rotating it around the air as if to say – *'which is...?'*. "By allowing Freyja to have her feelings of hate for him, he's made her less pliable. She sees things the other donors don't. She's aware of the abnormality of the Warren. She knows that her brain isn't in complete control. And I think with a little nudge, we could bring her over to our side." I could feel that my face held a hopeful expression, and I allowed myself to revel in it, if only just for a few seconds.

"Let me get this straight," said Sophie, her eyes closed and her head shaking from side to side as if she was trying to rearrange the words I had just spoken so they made more sense to her. "You want to tell *Freyja* – 'Queen of all

Bitches' – about compulsion?"

"Correct." I nodded, once.

"You're mad," she said, deadpan.

"Probably." I started. "But aren't we all a bit mad in this place? In some way or another?"

"Probably," she replied, mirroring me. I smiled. "I'm not going to be able to convince you that this is a bad idea, am I?" she said, almost disappointed.

"Unlikely."

She was about to say something more, but I put my hand up to stop her. "Why don't you talk to her yourself, see what you think?"

Sophie rolled her eyes, and then focused them back on mine, before letting out a huff. "*Finnne.*" She dragged out the word. "But she'll have to be a fabulous new shiny version of the bitch troll we all know before I even *think* about saying yes. And let's just say I'm not hopeful, friend."

When she said it like that, I wasn't that hopeful either.

CHAPTER 15

The Council

Angus

He had been called to a council meeting.
Angus hated council meetings. There were many reasons for this, but they mostly revolved around the fact that it involved spending time with his father.

His father was aware that Angus disliked him. Whether he knew that that dislike was actually nearly four centuries of burning hot rage, Angus didn't know. And didn't care.

The request had come from John, of course. It seemed that John wasn't only considered to be a collector of donors, but also that of vampires as well. Odd, though, that he wasn't actually considered to be a council member. He was only in the meetings if there were issues with *the collection*. And this was rare. Most likely because it was John himself was in charge of it.

Council meetings were held around once every couple of months, but more frequently if there were pressing matters to discuss. The Council was made up of vampires that his father deemed trustworthy and politically minded. Angus, on the other hand, thought they were all *lavvy heids.*

Sometimes the true Scot in him slipped out, and it was mostly when he was thinking about how he could insult the council members.

Angus hunched over his desk, looking at his watch in distaste. Surely time could just be kind and stop ticking, or perhaps speed up so it was past the time for the meeting to be over. He was an immortal being, for God's sake. He really wasn't asking for a lot.

But unfortunately, he didn't get his wishes, and soon it was forty-eight seconds before the meeting began.

He got up off his chair and slung a jumper over his T-shirt. It wasn't cold, and even if it was, Angus wouldn't likely have felt it, but he didn't want his father to see his tattoo. No, that was just for his eyes only. His father wasn't allowed to look at his mother ever again, no matter what shape or form, not as long as Angus existed.

He left his quarters and descended to the basement floor to the boardroom. The boardroom was a large room with high ceilings. At the far end facing out there was a chair, raised on an upper level, similar to that of a throne with chairs on either side of a less flamboyant decoration. The walls were lined with chairs all on higher levels than ones below them, arranged like amphitheatre seats. They curled around the throne, facing towards it in all directions. In the centre of the room there was another raised area. It was circular, the curve of the seats around it following the line of it. The lighting was dark, no sunlight being able to enter, and there was a blue wash to the room, as if someone had draped a cool filter over it in post-production, like it was in a film.

Its design was old, which confused Angus considering that, relatively, the Warren was fairly new. It was as if his father wanted to portray a longer reign than he had actually served. The bastard was always controlled by power.

The room itself was only really used for council meetings and trials – the latter much rarer than the former. Angus couldn't recall the last time a trial took place. If a human stepped out of line, they were punished accordingly by their master or mistress, and this was often behind closed doors. A vampire trial was unheard of. There was nothing a vampire could do that was deemed depraved enough to need a trial.

Angus suddenly felt grateful for that. His behaviour in the six months before Ivy had arrived could have easily been deemed as reckless and damaging. But nothing was ever said about it. It felt slightly unjust. Angus had a rather strong feeling that he had managed to get away with something quite wrong, but he let his mind release that thought quickly. Angus didn't want to think about things that could lead to the feeling of guilt. He never felt guilt, ever. And he didn't want to. Feelings of guilt and vampires didn't mix. They were like oil and water. A guilty vampire wasn't a stable vampire. Sorcha was a prime example of this – her response to killing the victims of the road traffic accident the evidence.

Angus couldn't afford to be unstable. He didn't have the energy for it.

"Ahh Angus, son. Cutting it fine again, I see." His father addressed him as he arrived with seconds to spare, showing no signs of apology on his face.

That was one of the perks of vampirism – speed. He was able to leave his quarters just before the time he needed to be present. There was never really such a thing as being rushed for time.

"I would say better late than never, but I have to say I would have preferred the 'never'," Garrett snickered, talking to the vampire next to him but knowing full well that Angus could hear him as if he were speaking directly into his own ear. As he often did, Angus ignored Garrett entirely. *Haud yer weesht.*

"Father," Angus nodded respectfully, even though he felt no such respect. He settled himself in one of the seats which faced the throne his father was approaching.

The king sat, his dark clothes contrasting against the white marble chair. He was in all black. It suited everything about him, Angus thought.

Following Angus, the remaining council also seated sporadically around the room, keeping generally to the seats closest to the throne.

The council consisted of himself, the king, Garrett, a gentleman called Fraser who was one of his father's oldest allies, and the final vampire whose name Angus always forgot. He stuck to Garrett like glue and as a result, Angus had no time for him.

There were no women on the council. Angus used to think this was a shame merely because the council meetings were exceedingly dry, and an attractive female face would have made them decidedly more interesting. But on reflection, that was not the right way to look at it.

Sorcha was one of the most fierce and intelligent vampires he knew. She would have been a valuable addition to the council, attractive or not. He valued her opinions, and she had an uncanny way of being able to see situations from the perspective of all parties. This was a trait he struggled with completely. His empathy as a vampire seemed even less than what it had been as a human. His decision to turn Sorcha after her attack was a prime example of this. Had he perhaps been able to see things more from another's point of view, he would never have made such a selfish decision, and she would be at peace.

But women were not allowed to be on the council. Their empathy was deemed to be an unfavourable trait indeed. Apparently, emotions clouded judgement. Angus now found that to be a rather odd thing to suggest.

When someone was considered to have done something wrong, people – whether they were directly involved or not – tended to have an emotive reaction to it. This emotion is often a negative emotion – perhaps dislike, anger, hate, frustration. And it is that emotion which encourages the person to make a judgement on how the person who carried out the act should be dealt with. If people didn't respond to things emotively, every action would have a limited reaction, and perhaps nothing would be considered good or bad. This is what enabled the

Warren to get away with so much – because the humans living within it were not able to respond to their treatment in a normal emotive way. Which meant there was no reaction. Which meant nothing ever came of it.

Angus hated that he was suddenly plagued with a conscience. It had appeared that his brain had somehow rewired and was now processing things in a more – dare he think it – *human* way.

The word 'guilt' floated around in his head again for a couple of seconds, before he burst it with a single pin. *Stop this.*

The king's gruff voice brought Angus back to the present. "Son, anything to bring to the meeting today?" he asked, crossing his left leg over his right.

"Nothing." Angus shook his head, uninterested. He looked up to meet his father's eyes, lingering there for a split second before detaching. He never had anything to add to the meetings. This was because he really didn't care about the Warren. To him, the Warren was everything he despised.

"How's that new donor of yours?" the king asked. He shut his eyes, clicking his fingers in an attempt to jog his memory. Vampire's memories were excellent. It showed how little they thought of humans that they couldn't even remember their names.

Angus didn't want to remind his father of Ivy's name. He didn't want his mouth to utter the sound. He didn't want him to have anything to do with her.

"Ahhh!" He clapped his hands together. "Ivy, that's it, I've got it. How is she?"

"Well," Angus replied, lips tight.

Garrett was the one to speak next. "Quite an odd donor, would you not agree? Especially for *you,* no?" he asked Angus this with a slight smirk. God, he despised Garrett. He was a flighty thing, with no real loyalty except that of one to power.

"Are brunette's having more fun these days?" Fraser asked, dryly. "I must have missed the memorandum."

Angus ignored them, allowing them to all prattle along

without his input.

"If she *is* having more fun, she certainly knows how to hide it," Garrett scoffed, his face sour. "Miserable cow."

The vampires laughed. Angus stiffened.

"Maybe you should compel a bit of life into her, Prince. She's nearly as dead as your last donor! Or is that how you like them now?" The vampire whose name always eluded Angus's piped up, looking around the room to see if his joke had landed. The king chuckled, but then batted his hands in the air.

"Hush, hush now. My son isn't here to be a punching bag." There were a few snickers. "We are here to stick to the matters on the list. Garrett, remind me, would you?"

Garrett's back straightened and he took out a piece of paper. I doubted he needed it to recall the points, but he looked down to it nonetheless. "First point of call is blood donations."

"Go on," encouraged the king, nodding Garrett's way.

"It appears we have had a sudden drop in the amount of AB that is available," he continued, now looking up from the page, brow creasing. Angus's ears pricked with interest. This couldn't be good for him.

"Are not enough donations being made? Why aren't we encouraging more to come forward?" the king asked, and Angus bristled at the word 'encouraging'.

"That doesn't seem to be the issue," Garrett stated. "It appears that enough donations are being inputted, but a disproportionate amount are being outputted."

"As in..." the king probed.

"Well, obviously the demand for AB has been high in the hospital recently," Angus interrupted.

"I can't see how that would be possible. I don't believe human habits have changed, and no one has reported an increase in casualties. Surely something is amiss here," Fraser said, eyes keen as he searched the faces in the room.

"Nothing appears to be amiss on the records," Garrett replied, but spoke to the king more than to Fraser. *Arsehole.*

Angus was completely certain that his change in eating habits had caused this. He had thought that his compulsion had been concrete, but there was obviously some loophole he didn't consider. Had Callum told someone other than Sorcha? *Surely not.*

"Well, this is clearly something we need to keep an eye on," the king stated, and the council nodded in unison. None of them noticed that Angus did not nod himself.

"It appears someone is very thirsty at the moment," Fraser added, smirking slightly, obviously finding the idea humorous.

Yeah, I'm really fucking thirsty.

"Well, as true as that may be, it is completely unacceptable," spat Garrett, his eyes slits. "We have donors for Christ's sake. No need to be so greedy, I say."

The word *ripper* seemed to hang in the air even though it had not been uttered, and Angus felt incredibly uncomfortable. But he also knew that Garrett could probably do with having a blood bag now and again. He knew that he was an avid feeder, and his donor always looked incredibly drained – literally and figuratively.

Angus had never liked Garrett, but he had to admit it was more to do with his slimy politics rather than the way he treated his donors. Angus had never cared much about donor treatment. But today, at the council meeting, despite Warren politics being at the forefront of his attention, this was not why Garrett annoyed him. Angus knew that he didn't really have a leg to stand on when it came to donor etiquette, especially considering his track record over the last few months, and maybe it made him a complete hypocrite to think it, but he couldn't help but think Garrett an incredibly lowly creature. Angus, on reflection, never actually *wanted* to hurt anyone. Sometimes it was simply in his nature. A vampire was, at the end of the day, a predator. When breaking this down into its simplest form, it was kill or be killed, just like it was like in the entire animal kingdom. The only issue with vampires having this view of feeding was that the likelihood of anything other than another vampire actually being a threat was unlikely.

So perhaps it was just kill and be done with it.

However, though he definitely could have felt *more* remorse, Angus believed that he felt it a great deal more than Garrett did, and somehow that meant something. Perhaps it didn't mean *very much*, but *something* was better than *nothing*.

"Son?" The king turned towards him, eyebrows raised in questions.

"I agree with Garrett." The words felt stale in his mouth. "We must keep an eye on the supply. Obviously, if nothing goes amiss over the coming weeks, we can assume it was a blip."

"Agreed. Duncan?" *Ahh yes, that was his name.* "I place you in charge of this. Keep an eye on the donations and how and when they are being used. I want detailed records consistently for the next six weeks."

Duncan nodded, looking a little irritated that he had been handed such a boring and menial task. *Serves you right.*

Angus also felt very negatively about the entire thing. With a vampire in charge, there was no way he could get away with feeding only on blood bags. This meant that he had to find another means for sustenance. He could ask Sorcha if he could feed off her donor now and again, but that somehow felt dirty.

He *really* didn't want to think about the alternative.

He *really* didn't want to think about feeding on Ivy.

He thought how she would react, and it made him shiver. The image of her face flitted through his mind like he was watching a series of pictures all taken seconds apart, creating a stuttered movie. The anger, the fear, the resolution to be completely defiant. He'd seen them all before, and even *enjoyed them*, but this was different – because none of the pictures held the most cherished of components. A component he hadn't realised that he craved – her trust.

But he also knew that he really didn't have another option. If he were to continue as he was, he would easily be caught, and perhaps the boardroom would finally be used for one of those trials that were so rare.

He didn't put it past his father to put him on trial. The thing was, despite their blood tie, he and the king held no other bond. They certainly didn't have any loyalty between them. And this was mutually known, even if it was never spoken of. After all, despite what Garrett liked to believe, it was Angus who was the biggest threat to his father's reign. He was, at the end of the day, the rightful heir. And although a vampire death was unlikely, it wasn't impossible, and nor was an uprising.

Angus, therefore, had no doubt that if he had the opportunity, his father would seek to destroy him. And Angus simply couldn't have that. And so, sitting there in the boardroom while the other council members titillated over other topics, Angus became resolute in his decision.

I guess we're about to find out if my bonny brunette has a thing for fangs.

CHAPTER 16

Loop Holes

Ivy

"I've said it before," Sophie began, "and I'll say it again, friend, I don't think this is one of your wisest ideas."

"This is the first and only idea I have ever given you," I frowned, sitting on my bench in the courtyard. Sophie was always so blunt. I tried to remember it was refreshing.

"My point exactly," she replied, squinting off into the distance, her eyes sensitive to the light. It was unusually bright which likely meant that the sun was shining outside. We had both already voiced our joint disappointment at missing out on it. My skin had taken on a slight grey tinge, and I was concerned that I might need to start taking vitamin D supplements.

"She's just a shit person. Hence the lack of trust." She was speaking of Freyja, and my intention to tell her about compulsion.

"Yeah yeah, you've said it a million times already," I mumbled, rolling my eyes.

"And apparently you haven't listened even *once*," she snapped, her shoulders turning towards me, stiff. "I'd honestly be more comfortable with you telling a fanger."

"A what?!" I choked.

"A fanger," she replied, bringing her two index fingers up towards her mouth, pointing them downwards in line with her own canines. She made a hissing sound.

I laughed, amused by the charades. "Why does that sound so offensive for some reason?" I asked between chuckles.

"I think it's because it sounds like 'fucker'."

"Hmm, that's probably it." I nodded. "But seriously? You'd trust a vampire over Freyja?"

"Well, perhaps I'm over-exaggerating." She shrugged.

"Perhaps," I drawled. "At least Freyja won't bite you if you say something out of line."

"I wouldn't be so sure," Sophie said, her nose scrunching in distaste.

"What if I told you that we could make her forget if she wasn't... agreeable," I offered, treading lightly. I'd been thinking over the last few days about telling Sophie about Angus and our... understanding. Me and Sophie had become firm friends, and I genuinely trusted her. And weirdly, I even trusted Angus. I'd like to think that if I managed to get myself in a sticky situation with Freyja, he would pull me out of it. And Sophie too. Call it a hunch.

"Jesus Christ. If you tell me that you've been a vamp all along I'm going to swear off friends for life," she said, her eyes large, but slightly humorous.

"Hilarious, *friend.*" I mocked her use of the term of endearment. "But seriously, there is something I need to tell you."

"Oh my gosh!" She slapped her hand over her mouth in mock horror. "You're pregnant! Look, don't worry, we'll take care of it. I know a place." She ended her act with a smirk.

"God, this isn't Dirty Dancing." I rolled my eyes at her for what felt like the hundredth time in the conversation.

"Eugh, I wish it was." She tipped her head back so it was more in the mirrored sunlight. "Patrick Swaze was a real hottie. And pancreatic cancer is a real bitch."

"You're getting really side-tracked here. I'm trying to tell you something important."

"Yeah, I was deflecting. Surprised you couldn't tell. I wasn't being subtle about it."

"You're not subtle about anything."

"I've heard it's endearing."

"Who have you heard that from?"

"The mirror."

"Hilarious." She stuck her tongue out at me in response. "Okay, seriously stop with the deflection. I feel like a hockey puck." I shook my head, trying to re-centre myself. "I'm trying to tell you something important about Angus," I whispered.

"He's not the one that's pregnant, is he? Because I *don't* know a place for that."

I ignored her, trying to fend off her distractions. She had an issue with speaking seriously. "Angus knows," I blurted.

"You've lost me," she frowned.

"Did I ever *have you*?" I asked.

"Not gonna lie, I was mainly just trying to come up with funny replies in my head, so no, you didn't," she said, shrugging apologetically.

"Incorrigible," I muttered under my breath. "Angus knows that I can't be compelled."

Sophie's eyes squinted to slits at first, like she was trying to trap the words inside her head before they left, allowing adequate time to process them. Then her eyes popped open, realisation hitting like a freight train. "Explain," she said, her eyes normal now, will a frown line in between her dark eyebrows.

"He kind of found out a couple of months ago," I replied, shyly. I waited in anticipation. How would she respond? Would she be mad that I had lied? By omission, but still, most people saw that as lying.

"You're telling me that your master, the P*rince of the fricking Warren*, has known that you can't be compelled for *two fricking months*?!" She whisper-shouted, her eyes darting all around the courtyard in search of eavesdroppers. There didn't seem to be anyone around.

"I kinda am, yeah," I confirmed, guilt on my face.

"Well, I don't know what I was expecting, but I'm almost certain that it was *not* that." She looked away from me to turn towards the water. Her face, which was usually so full of animation (with me at least), was blanketed in a dulled mask, as if the nerves towards her facial muscles had just given up. I winced, letting her stew and take in the information for a few minutes, worried that if I said something wrong, she would spiral.

Sophie was many things. She was witty, highly intelligent, conversational and wonderfully sarcastic. But she was also at the edge of her mental capacity to cope. That's what years in the Warren will do to you. Which meant that I always veered on the side of caution with her, just in case something I said accidently pushed her past that edge.

"How did he find out?" she asked, still not looking towards me. "I don't mean to be rude to you friend, but I've been playing this game a lot longer than you have and I'm still under the radar. You're clearly the worst half of our group." She was joking, I knew it, but she was also entirely right.

"He found a map I had been drawing of the Warren and the security in each area."

"You made a *map?!*" she exclaimed, turning towards me. "Couldn't you have just stored that information in your head? I would have." Her face was marked with a combination of disgust and disappointment. It wasn't cruel, and I could tell she wasn't really judging, but it didn't stop me from feeling really stupid.

"Great, we adding 'photographic memory' to your repertoire now, smarty pants?" I said, trying to lighten the tone.

Sophie looked smug. "I'm a real catch. I've told you this before. The mirror does not lie." She rolled her shoulder back a few times and cricked her neck left and right as if she were preparing herself for something.

And she was – an interrogation.

"What'd he do when he found out?"

"Ummm..." I began, thinking of the best way to phrase it. "He was angry."

She nodded. "Annnddd...?"

"Annddd... I kinda kicked off at him and then he pinned me against a wall and–"

"Wait." She held her palm up to my face. It reminded me of Andy. "Pinned you against a wall?! Like, attacked you with a bite? Or pinned you against a wall in a sexy way?" Her eyes were glittering slightly.

"I'd say it was a bit of both." Sophie's mouth popped open. "Except without the biting. Angus hasn't actually ever... bit me." Her mouth opened more.

"Never?!" she asked, shocked.

"No. And before you ask, I don't know why he hasn't. I thought maybe it was because I'm AB negative and he thinks that's weird what with that old disease and all," I said, shrugging.

"Ha, trust me, if that was it was you would be long gone, pet." The Scottish term of endearment rang in the air. "No, it's got to be for another reason."

"He prefers blondes," I stated. I felt it was an important piece of information for some reason.

"Yeah, it's well known he's a blonde banger. You turning up as his donor certainly got the people talking."

"Blonde banger?! How do you even come up with these phrases?" I asked, mildly shocked.

"It's my weird brain. But no, seriously, him not biting you is really unusual. I doubt anyone else knows about that. If any of the vamps knew he was keeping you without using you for your sole purpose, I think there would be a problem." Before I could respond, she had already conjured up another question. "What about sex?" Her blunt delivery made me flinch.

"As in do I know what sex is?" I replied, obtusely. Two people could deflect in this friendship.

"You do look like a virgin, so yeah, let's start with that," she smirked, eyes backlit with mischief.

"I have you know that I am *not*. But I am a vamp virgin."

"Vamp virgin? I love that phrase. Did you coin that?

I'm gonna steal it." She snapped her fingers in the air, as if confirming her decision.

"No, actually it was my friend Andy. You two are very similar," I mused.

"He sounds like my kind of person. But stop sidetracking!"

"Oh, how the tables have turned wee one," I smirked. She waved her hands in front of my face to get my attention.

"Okay, so let's summarise. Your vampire prince knows you can't be compelled, he hasn't bitten you, and he hasn't slept with you. Am I right?"

"Correct," I nodded.

"Well, colour me pretty. We might just have ourselves an ally."

"I think that we just might. If we play our cards right," I replied, hopeful.

"And so, the resistance increases again. Now, let's go grab another member."

◆ ◆ ◆

We sat in the courtyard a little longer before Freyja turned up. We moved off the bench and sat under the tree where I had originally found her crying. She has insisted on it, saying that she didn't want to look like a 'wee cretin' sitting on a bench with 'uggos'. Sophie had instantly bristled at that, and I had had to stop her from lunging at Freyja in response. Perhaps not literally, but verbally, certainly.

The tree created a little shade, but I stayed out of it, trying my best to soak up as many mirrored rays as possible. The Scottish weather wasn't exactly notorious for consistent sun, so any I could get I would grab onto.

"Christ! Why are you sitting so far away from us you weirdo?" Freyja spat. "People may overhear us if we have to shout to one another, for God's sake."

I turned to her, my eyes narrowing in annoyance. "I'm trying to soak up the sun. Obviously."

Sophie nodded. "It *is* rather obvious."

"No one asked you, Miss Glassy Eyes."

"Original," Sophie muttered. The nickname was likely in response to the way Sophie had been before she had found out about me. Since then, she has appeared less depressed and 'glassy eyed'.

Sophie turned towards me. "Remind me again why we are doing this?"

"Trust me," I replied, turning towards Freyja with a frown. "Look, I know this is a hard concept for you to understand, what with your innate heinousness, but could you please just play nice for like, ten minutes?"

"What do I get out of it?" she snapped back, her eyes as unfriendly as ever.

"Sometimes it's okay to be nice without getting anything in return, you know," I said.

"That seems completely pointless," she snarled, turning away from me and staring off into the distance of the courtyard.

Sophie mouthed, *'See? Bitch,'* nodding towards Freyja. I rolled my eyes at her.

"Freyja, trust me when I say this, but you are really gonna want to be nice to us right now," I said, feeling like I was talking to a toddler who was having a tantrum.

"Why don't you tell me why you dragged me here and then I can decide if I can be nice."

Sophie's eyes were hard as she stared at me. I ignored her.

"Fine." I took a breath in, feeling it high in my chest. "You know when we spoke last time under this tree and you said you felt some things you did or thought couldn't be explained?" Freyja turned her attention back to me, her head cocking, before she nodded. "Well, there is a reason for that."

She shrugged. "You gonna tell me then?" Her voice was monotone and uninterested, but her eyes showed the opposite. It appeared that Freyja was suddenly engaged in the conversation, even if she refused to admit it.

"Well, the vampires are able to control the minds of

humans. It's something that they call 'compulsion'."

Sophie jumped in, ready to share. "Yeah. They can force you to do something, make you forget something or someone. They can change your personality traits. They can make you believe you enjoy something when you don't. They can control it all." Sophie looked pained, and I had an urge to squeeze her hand, but I was too far away.

Freyja's face screwed up. I could tell she was desperate to make a snarky comment, but something within her, probably a part of her which was usually less dominant, made her hold her tongue. "Compulsion?" she asked, frowning in confusion.

I nodded. "That's what they call it. It's a form of mind control. It's how they are able to make all this," I gestured around myself, "possible. The Warren is essentially a blood bank for vampires, and without mind control, they wouldn't run it with the ease that they do. People would revolt. People like you."

Freyja mulled over my words for a few beats, her lips twisting in thought. "How do they do it?" she asked, leaning inwards towards me slightly, intrigued.

Sophie scoffed. "How do they do any of the things they do? How do they survive off blood? How do they have immortality?"

"I think Freyja is asking what the vampires have to do to compel?" I guessed, and Freyja nodded that I was right. I continued. "I'm not sure entirely, but I've noticed that when a vampire is trying to compel me, they have this look in their eye. It's very intense. I can't describe it," I shrugged.

Sophie nodded, agreeing. "Yes, it's an intense look. Their eyes brighten."

Freyja's attention turned to Sophie, to me, and then back to Sophie, as if she was watching a rally in a tennis match. "Wait. How do you two know about this and no one else does? I smell bullshit." Her eyes squinted to nothing.

"Me and Sophie can't be compelled," I explained.

"How very convenient," Freyja muttered, rolling her eyes.

"If you think me having to be bitten and raped without compulsion is *convenient*, you need to think again," Sophie snarled. Her face had contorted into something feral, and I had to raise my hand to snap her out of it. But Freyja didn't need my intervention.

"Don't give me the sob story, Glassy Eyes. I'm perfectly aware of the rape and molestation. Baron does it to me all the damn time, you bitch," she spat.

Bingo.

I smiled widely. "I think we just found our loophole."

"What are you talking about, loser?" Freyja turned her venom on me now.

"Do you know what you just said?" I asked, still smiling.

"Of course, I do. I don't have short-term amnesia, you freak. And stop with the weird creepy smile, you're worse than Glassy Eyes."

"Seriously? The nickname is *so* old. Shut up," Sophie said, her voice dripping in irritation.

"Both of you need to shut up and listen. Freyja just openly admitted that Baron is a rapey bastard," I stated, waiting for things to click into place for the two women in front of me. I made a face which I hoped said *'get there faster'*.

Then Freyja did something I never thought I'd see her do. She smiled. A genuinely happy, face-splitting smile. It made me smile just as wide.

"Holy fucking shit you uggo's," she laughed, flying her head back. "I'm free." She clasped her hand over her mouth and screamed into them. Sophie laughed too, eyes twinkling. "I want to kill that blood sucker with everything in me. What a piece of shit! At least the other vamps seem to try and take the pain away. But he just enjoyed my pain. And I just couldn't *do anything* about it!"

"Well, you're on the other side of that now," I said.

"Ermmm..." Sophie raised a finger. "Not exactly. She still has to pretend that she doesn't know about this to Baron. And she isn't like you and me. She's still susceptible to compulsion."

"This is true. But realistically how often is Baron going

to compel Freyja? Surely, since she's been his donor for years now, she already possesses all the qualities that he requires. As long as she still acts like she's unaware, she should be okay."

"What?! You mean nothing changes? I just have to endure this shit exactly as I did before?" Her voice was shrill.

"Look, I'm sorry, but it's complicated. Ideally, we'd be able to get you away from Baron, but it's not that simple. We still don't know how to get Sophie out of this either. She's in a similar situation to you," I explained, sympathy on my face.

"Aren't you also in the same situation?" she asked.

"Not exactly," I admitted, lowering my eyes, feeling guilty.

Sophie looked at me with a grimace on her face. "You've got to tell her, Ivy. You can't go halfway with the truth." It almost felt like she was taking a dig at me for keeping the truth from her, but I wasn't sure.

I sighed, pulling back my shoulders for confidence. "Angus – the prince – he knows I can't be compelled. And he hasn't told anyone."

"Well, shit," Freyja scoffed, her head falling back in disbelief. "You're telling me that Mr 'I Kill Donor's Like It's Child's Play' is all cool with you just running around this place with a free mind?"

"Yeah, I am."

"What a fucking joke. What's so special about *you*, huh?" Suddenly, she was back to her old self, like she had simply just switched it back on again. *That was quick.*

"Nothing," I stated, looking her dead straight in the eye. "It's just timing. And my timing was better than yours."

"Yeah, if that's what you wanna believe," she snarled.

"Look, don't be a bitch again just because Ivy got the fittie with a decent heart and you didn't," Sophie said to her, her eyes sharp. There was silence for a while as we waited to see which version of Freyja we got next. We were in luck.

"Fine. But we've got to think of a plan to get me and G.E.

out of this shit, and fast."

"G.E?" I asked.

Freyja looked at me like I was the dumbest person in the world. "Yeah, duh. It's Glassy Eyes over there." She gestured to Sophie.

"For fuck's sake. Give me strength," Sophie said, putting her head in her hands.

We stayed under the shade of the tree for a few more minutes, the ongoing bickering between Sophie and Freyja a low-key undercurrent to the conversation.

We were so distracted that we missed the red-haired vampire who had been leisurely sitting on the grass, tucked under the shade of a tree, listening to our conversation the whole time.

◆ ◆ ◆

I walked away from the courtyard and headed back towards the quarters. On passing through a corridor, a hand snaked around my arm, and I flinched, trying to snatch it away.

"Easy, Miss Ivy. It's only me." Anthony's face was soft and warm but his hand was cool and firm. "Got somewhere to be?"

I looked down at his hand on my arm and then back up to his clear eyes. He noticed, and released me, but I could tell it was reluctantly. "Not exactly," I replied.

"Have you got a confession for me yet?" he asked, smiling smugly.

He began to walk closer to me and I backed up, not realising that's what he wanted me to do. I was now in a little separate corridor off the main one with poor lighting, the cool wall behind me.

"What are you? A priest?" I snapped. I didn't know why Anthony always made me irritable. I sounded like Freyja.

He chuckled softly, brushing a piece of hair out of my face with his long fingers. "There she is. Oh, how I've missed you, Lass." He then added, as an afterthought: "You smell delightful today. Did you do something differently?"

"Nothing."

"That must be it then." He nodded once, smirking, somehow managing to get more into my personal space. He also smelt good, but I resisted the urge to sniff him. Or tell him. "I'm off to the gym. Perhaps you could come and watch me in the boxing ring. I know how much you liked watching me last time." He winked, his smile now lopsided.

I stiffened in embarrassment, my cheeks heating.

My mind drifted to the first time I had met him, when he was what could only be described as *dancing* in the ring with a fellow vampire. He had been stunning. He was still stunning now.

"Ahhh, I knew you liked me," he said as he brushed the back of his knuckles against my red skin. "Finally, a confession. I like you, too," he whispered, his breath tickling my neck.

"Your ego is stifling," I commented, trying to take the attention off myself.

He laughed, heartily. "I think it's my best trait, no?"

I stayed silent.

His smile dropped and he began to focus on my face. His index finger traced my cheekbone, and I wondered what he had found there that was so interesting.

"You have the most subtle freckles right here." His finger continued its path along my skin. "I've noticed them before and I've always wanted to touch them – to see if they were real and not just a mirage. Sometimes I think I've made you up." He was muttering to himself more than to me, and I let him do it, staying stock still and silent. "The second I first saw you, I wondered what it would be like to lick your skin. It's why I did it at the ball. I just couldn't help myself." He leaned forward and ran his tongue along my cheek. His tongue was warm- the complete opposite to his fingers. His left hand slid behind me and gently clawed into my hair.

Suddenly, his tongue was back in his mouth once again, but his lips were resting right near my eye and he was breathing heavily.

"What are you doing?" I whispered.

"Exactly what I want to do," he replied. "Am I out of line?" he asked, pulling away from me.

"I don't know," I said, lost for words.

What he was doing was just so... erotic. And he had hardly even touched me.

And yet, despite all the gorgeous feelings Anthony was giving me, I couldn't help but think about another Scottish vampire, wishing that it was him that made me feel like this, rather than the one in front of me.

CHAPTER 17

First Bite

Angus

Angus was starving. His throat felt like it was constricting, as if the dryness there had caused chaffing and then inflammation.

Just like a human, when vampires were hungry, they became irritable. But irritable to a human was perhaps snapping at someone they loved when they hadn't really done anything wrong. Irritable to a vampire was snapping someone's *neck* who *certainly* hadn't done anything wrong. He felt one was more threatening that the other.

It had been four days since the council meeting, and two days prior to that was when Angus last ate. Or *drank*.

Six days.

He was in need of sustenance and knew that the conversation would have to be broached with his brunette donor sooner rather than later. He didn't want to tell her what he needed to do. But he really did *need* to do it. It wasn't only to cover his own back, but to cover hers, too. And he also wouldn't mind sating the hunger. But it was going to be difficult, and Angus had spent years successfully avoiding any real difficult situations or conversations.

He wasn't a big conversationalist – Sorcha could contest to that. And his conversation with Ivy had been lacking, even from the moment he had met her those months ago. They had managed to build up some sort of relationship and Angus was pleased, nay, *happy* with that. But although it did hold a degree of trust and some form of mutual respect, it did not hold much conversation.

No – Angus couldn't handle that.

He was currently boxing in the gym. The boxing bag thumped with each hit, swinging and creaking in protest. The bag in question was a vampire-friendly bag. A.K.A it was considerably heavier than the ones on the human side of the gym. He doubted even the most physically strong human could budge it.

On one of his more violent swings, the bag suddenly stopped, and Angus stuttered, his rhythm broken. Two hands held around the outside of the bag, clearly the reason for the halt in its movement. Anthony's face peered from around it, a sly smirk plastered on his face.

"Fancy a real fight?" he asked, waggling his eyebrows, goading.

"I think I'll pass," Angus replied sternly, his hands fisting even more than they had before.

"Och, naw! Don't be a feartie!" Anthony bellowed disappointingly, his Scottish drawl loud. "You scared of competition?" he mocked, smirking again. His smile was irritating, and Angus suddenly had the greatest desire to knock it right off his face.

"Fine, perhaps a bit of sparring would do me good." His mouth was so dry, and he was aware that his movements were slightly laboured, but one good hit to Anthony's smug face would make it all worth it.

Anthony had become an acquaintance of Angus's when they were both members for the Black Watch – a senior highland regiment within the British army. They had served together during the Crimean War in 1853. Vampire's made good soldiers. He didn't think he needed to explain why that was.

They had been friends, and Angus had even seen in him

the qualities of his late brother.

A memory began to spur within the vampire's brain – one that he rarely thought of – and he instinctively pushed it down to the depths where it couldn't bother him any longer.

Things were different now. They weren't in the highlands anymore. But that didn't mean they couldn't have a good old-fashioned brawl. In fact, Angus couldn't think of anything better than putting Anthony in his place – just like he used to do in the Army.

"Excellent, I'll see you in the ring, Prince."

Angus sighed, irritated by Anthony's consistent charisma and charm. He thought back to the sound Ivy had made when he had had the audacity to place his tongue on her neck, and bristled.

He made his way to the ring where Anthony stood, bouncing eagerly on the balls of his feet. He had taken off his training top, exposing his chest, and now just wore shorts only, his feet bare. Angus followed suit, toeing off his trainers and slipping off his socks. He removed his top.

A crowd had started to gather – the Warren loved a fight. There wasn't much else to do when it came to entertainment. Had Angus mentioned that it was boring? Yes, thought so.

He slipped into the ring, walking towards his opponent with sure, intentional steps. This was as close as he ever got to feeling like a predator again, and he relished in it, rolling his shoulders down his back and tilting his neck this way and that. He ignored the burning in his throat, swallowing.

Another vampire with dark skin and dark hair walked to the edge of the ring. "You guys want me to officiate?" he asked.

Angus shook his head. "That shouldn't be necessary," at the same time that Anthony replied, "Forget it Callum. We're gentlemen." The vampire that Anthony seemed to know nodded and walked away to find a spot where he could observe. Anthony turned his attention back to Angus.

"You ready?" he asked, still bouncing on his feet like an excitable puppy.

"Aye," nodded Angus in return.

Anthony made the first move, stepping forward with his left foot to get some power behind his right hook. But Angus had seen it coming, and artfully dodged it with ease. He then ducked under Anthony's arms, appearing behind him, before jamming him in the back with a punch. Anthony's back arched forward, and Angus took the opportunity to attempt another attack, but his opponent was quicker than that and easily evaded the blow, countering with a hit to Angus stomach and then right eye.

Angus's head snapped at the force, and he had to recentre himself before he could respond.

When his focus was back, he watched Anthony waiting patiently in front of him, dancing on his feet.

Damn. He's going easy on me, the swine.

Angus rushed towards him, jumping high into the air using his left foot, and came down over Anthony's head, knocking him square in the face. The vampire stumbled back, laughing and spitting blood onto the floor.

"Nicely done, Prince. I didn't see that coming."

Angus didn't waste his advantage, and instead delivered another punch to his jaw. He heard a crunch.

Anthony shook his head, eyes wide, before bringing his bloody hands up to his lower jaw, shoving it back into place with a jolt and a pop. He smiled, his bloody teeth on show as he sneered masochistically. It was almost off putting. "Watch it," he said, eyes glittering with humour. "This jaw is why the ladies like me so much." He then lunged gleefully towards Angus in a counterattack.

Anticipating the strike, Angus attempted to deflect with a straight shot, but Anthony saw it coming, and spun his body out of the way, clipping Angus behind the knee with his foot. Angus buckled to the floor.

They fought some more, Angus getting a couple more hits in, but he was flagging, and Anthony knew it. Multiple punches in the head later, and Angus was spent, bending over himself in the corner, while Anthony appeared only a little laboured.

"What?" Anthony spat on the floor – his spittle stained red. "That all you got, Little Prince? Surely not?" He wiped his hand over his mouth, smearing some of the blood away

"I'm finished," Angus spat back, heaving himself back off his knees.

"You look it." Anthony's posture changed, no longer on alert, and headed to Angus's side, patting his back. "I wasn't expecting that to be as easy as it was. What's wrong with you, pal?"

"It's been a few days since I've fed," he admitted, brushing Anthony's hand off him, making his way out the ring. The other vampire followed.

"A few days?!" exclaimed Anthony, frowning. He had picked up a towel from the side and was wiping away the now dried blood from his face. His face had almost completely healed. Angus's still felt very tender and swollen. "Is your donor sick? Is Ivy unwell?" Angus watched Anthony's face as it became etched with concern.

"My donor is fine," he replied, irritated. *Don't speak of her.* "I've just been busy." The lie slipped from his mouth.

"If I were in your position, I'd be making sure that I carved out a mountain of time to devour that specimen. Try harder." He slapped him on the back in a friendly manner and Angus had to force himself not to slap him away. "And do us all a favour. Feed. You look a mess. Not braw at all."

Anthony didn't wait for his reply, and Angus was left standing alone, with a swollen face and a deflated ego.

◆ ◆ ◆

Angus returned to his quarters, finding them empty. It was just after seven, and he assumed that Ivy was eating dinner.

He stepped into the shower, washing away the sweat and blood of his body from the fight. He found that as he ran his hands over his face and limbs, pain radiated through him and his muscles tightened.

Fuck.

He knew he couldn't carry on as he was. To not feed now would result in too many people asking questions. If people saw him with an unhealing face – no matter how subtle – he would be in trouble. And he didn't want trouble, as that often meant a meeting with his father, which was something that he avoided wherever possible.

So, it was decided. Tonight, he would feed off Ivy.

It wasn't long after he had gotten dressed that a knock came on the door. He knew who it was before he even opened it.

Sorcha stood, hands on hips, on the other side.

"What have I done now?" he asked, not even bothering to block her entry to his quarters, and instead moving away from the door to head towards his desk chair. He slumped down in it like he usually did and waited for the interrogation.

"So," she began, sitting on the opposite chair to his, across the desk, "I can't believe I'm about to tell ye this, but I know about yer donor."

Angus frowned, genuinely unsure of what Sorcha meant. He raised his eyebrows, as if to say *'what?'*, not bothering to actually respond. His face hurt, so minimal talking was a priority for him.

"I know Ivy can't be compelled. And I know that *you know* about that. And I know that you've done nothing aboot it."

Angus physically stiffened and he felt his bruised ribs protest. He couldn't believe what he was hearing. How could she possibly have known?!

As Angus was about to feign innocence, Sorcha raised her hand to stop him. "Don't bother denying it ye wee liar. I've heard it from the horse's mouth."

"Ivy told you?" Angus asked, disbelief flooding his words.

"Not exactly. I heard her speaking with a couple of donors in the courtyard. One was Garrett's donor and the other was that girl Freyja – the one who belongs to Baron."

"What was she saying?" he asked, curtly.

"She was explaining compulsion to Baron's donor. I think both Ivy and Garrett's donor are unaffected by mind control. The Freyja girl, I'm not so sure. She seems compellable and yet Ivy managed to get her to admit that Baron molesters her. It was as if she was able to find some sort of loophole."

Angus absorbed all the new information. He didn't know how to feel. "Ivy I knew about," he admitted. "The other's I did not. Ivy hasn't trusted me with such information." That annoyed him somehow. "Did anyone else hear?"

"No, I'm certain it was just me." He nodded, relieved. "Why are you protecting her?" Sorcha asked, a look of pain on her face.

"I do not know." And he really didn't.

"What do you think will come of this, Angus? Have you even thought it through?"

"I don't know," he repeated.

Sorcha scoffed, and turned away from him, shaking her head. He could sense disappointment. "What you are doing here – it's dangerous. If your father finds out that there are humans who are resistant to our mind control, he will kill them. And if he finds out that you have been knowingly protecting them, he will kill *you*, too. He hardly even needs that excuse, either!" Her eyes were pained, as if she was willing him to listen with all her might, and it was hurting her to do so.

"I'm perfectly aware of that, Sorcha," he snapped, his voice dripping with irritation. More at himself than at her.

"Ye need to *do something*," she willed, her face tortured. It upset him to see her that way – worried for him.

Her face suddenly changed, and he watched as her eyes focused and traced around his face. "What's wrong with ye? Have ye been fighting? Why haven't ye healed?" Her questions were like rounds from a firearm. Each one hitting its target with precise aim.

"I sparred a little with Anthony. He got in some good hits." He paused, watching her face. She wasn't satisfied, so he continued. "And I haven't fed in a few days."

"Why not?" she asked, her eyes wild.

"The council knows about someone taking more blood bags than usual. They are monitoring it. I can't afford to drink them anymore."

"What? Ivy's blood not up to scratch still?" she replied, her tone snarky. She was annoyed with him.

"Something like that."

"Oh, for God's sake, vamp up!" she said, biting the words out, standing. "You not feeding from her no longer just affects her. It affects *you*, too. You continue the way yer going and you and her will *both* die. I'll keep yer secret because I love ye, but if ye can't sort your shit oot, I can't protect ye from your father. Ye know that." She stalked to the door, turning at the last second. "I'm *begging* you. Feed. Start there, and then we can talk about the rest of the shit ye have managed to get yourself into."

"Stop swearing," Angus muttered, but she had already left. It was likely she still heard however, and Angus could picture her eyes rolling in response.

◆ ◆ ◆

Ivy returned back to the quarters not long after Sorcha had left. It didn't take her long to notice Angus's altered appearance, much to his annoyance.

"What happened to you?" she questioned, eyes wide, standing stock still ahead of where he was sitting at his desk.

"Me and Anthony boxed in the ring. It's nothing." He brushed off her question, standing and walking away from her as if he had something to do. She followed.

"I've seen Anthony box. He was bloody to start with, but his face was fully healed within minutes. Yours is a real show," she commented, her face a grimace.

"Thanks," he muttered, sarcastically. "It's because I haven't fed." He could sense her stiffen – *feel* it. It made him flinch also, and he turned back to face her.

"Maybe you should... well... eat something then."

She said it in a way that Angus assumed was meant to be helpful, but instead just came across as jittery and nervous, her eyes darting here and there, never truly landing on him. He found himself chasing them, willing that she give him attention. A man starved in more ways than one.

As he eyed her, he knew he looked stony and cold. He knew he looked frightening. "Maybe I should. It can be your punishment."

Ivy gasped, taking a slight step back. Her mouth set into a line and her eyes finally darted around his face as if she were looking for clues as to what he would do next. He remained resolved, keeping emotion off his face. "What did I do?" she asked, her voice a whisper.

"Hmmm…" Angus tapped his chin, goading her. "Perhaps not telling me you know about another donor who cannot be compelled? Perhaps telling another donor about compulsion? Perhaps letting another vampire *overhear* such conversations?!" With each example, his voice rose, and he watched as she shrank into herself.

"Who heard?" she whispered.

"Sorcha. My friend. You would have seen her at the ball. Red hair."

Her shoulders dropped. She was relieved.

She shouldn't have been.

"Why didn't you tell me?" he asked, eyes sharp.

"I was going to, I promise. I actually was." She said it as if she couldn't believe it herself. "If Freyja hadn't responded well, I was going to get you to compel her to forget the conversation. I would have trusted you." She was looking at Angus with large doe eyes.

"What about the other one? Garrett's donor?"

"Sophie? She's my friend. You can't hurt her."

Angus frowned. "I wasn't intending to hurt her, Ivy. But that doesn't mean other people won't."

"You're going to tell the vampires?!" Her voice was panicked, and she took a step towards him. When Angus's face became stern, she stopped.

"No," he cut.

"Then what?" she asked, her heart galloping across the room right into his ears.

"You're telling me there is a donor out there who cannot be compelled, and her master likely still feeds off her and uses her for his... sexual gratification. Don't you have a plan to get her out of that situation?" Ivy stared at him for what felt like forever. He stared back.

Suddenly, her face changed dramatically, taken over with the most gorgeous smile he had ever seen. He would bet his immortal life on it.

"Wait. Does this mean that if I had an idea, you would help me execute it?" Her eyes glittered, and he was almost sure he saw unshed teas. His heart hurt for some reason.

"I would try what I could, yes." He nodded once, face unchanging.

In the next moment, Ivy ran at him, and when she reached his still frame, wrapped her warm upper limbs around his torso and squeezed. Her scent engulfed his nostrils, and he allowed himself the rare pleasure of inhaling deeply, enabling it to burn his insides, and set him alight. He opened his own arms, wrapping them around her soft, small frame, encasing her to him, and returned the embrace. But it felt awkward to him, so he released her, and stepped back.

"I'll think of a plan to help Sophie and Freyja," she said. "And when I have one, I'll tell you." It was an olive branch of trust, and he accepted it.

"Good," he said. "But now I need to ask you a favour," he told her. He hated to break her good mood, but he didn't have a choice.

She frowned, stepping back a little so she could get a better look at his face. "What?"

"I need to feed off you tonight," he stated, bluntly. He didn't try and sugar coat it. She deserved better than that.

Her eyes became fearful, and he noted the ever-increasing rate of her heart and breath. Her chest filled with air, and he watched her breasts move. God, how he wanted to see her the way he had in the bathroom when he had tasted her. He wanted that and more.

Say something, Ivy.

"Why?" Her voice was but a whisper, and her eyes had been drained of their joy, replaced instead with a lacklustre coffee hue – the glittering obsidian a distant memory.

Angus's charred heart clenched like a vice. He hoped she didn't think that he only agreed to help her because he needed to feed. How low she would think he was if she believed that. In truth, he had wanted to help. No one should have to endure rape. No one. But the need to feed was unrelated to her dilemma, and he knew that it couldn't be helped. He was just frustrated at how her reaction seemed to affect his body. Why was his throat ever drier than before? And why did his eyes sting?

"Because the council knows someone has been stealing blood bags. And now they are keeping an eye on it, so I can't feed that way anymore," he told her, his tongue darting out to wet his dry lips. "And it's been nearly a week since I've fed. My injuries aren't healing, and I don't need the questions. It will attract attention to us, which is the last thing we need – especially now."

Ivy absorbed his words, and he watched her patiently, allowing her the time to process the information. This wasn't something he could push or force. It had to be her choice. She had to want to say yes.

Her spine straightened and she pushed her shoulders back. He had watched her do this countless times when she was looking for some confidence. And boy, would she need it now.

She met her brown eyes to his blue ones, not shrinking from his gaze. "Okay," she said, nothing more. Nothing more was needed.

Angus let out the breath he had been holding. "Okay."

"What do I have to do?" she asked, obviously apprehensive.

"Well, I have to explain some things before, if that's okay?" She swallowed and then nodded yes. He gestured for her to sit on her usual chair, and he walked to his own as if he was conducting some sort of interview. "I need to tell you about feeding."

"Isn't it just bite and go?" she asked, her words humorous, but her tone anything but. Angus almost smiled at her naivety, but his muscles couldn't quite allow him to do it, as if they knew it wasn't the right time.

"Not exactly, Brunette," Angus admitted, sighing loudly, the air in his lungs feeling stale. He didn't actually need the air – his lungs weren't able to oxygenate the small amounts of blood which grated through his parched vessels – and yet it was a habit which had seemed to have followed him from his human life into this other existence.

What he had to tell her felt cheap. He didn't want to have to explain it. It was ridiculous really, when he thought about it. He had been on this Earth for over four centuries, and yet it hadn't prepared him for this in the slightest. He felt cheated somehow, and he pleaded with himself – begged himself to make sure he said the right thing, and that she understood.

"In the Warren, we compel our donors because it removes complications, but in the real world, we don't often have to compel people to allow us to feed off them. The process can actually be... quite pleasurable for... both parties. The compulsion is something we need after the deed is over. It keeps our anonymity. Keeps our secret safe." Ivy frowned in confusion which encouraged him to continue. "When coupled with sexual desire, humans can find the process of feeding very enjoyable. It doesn't have to be this horrible, painful experience. It can be good. *Great,* even."

Ivy's eyebrows raised in shock. "Is that what you want to try with me?" Her voice wobbled slightly, and her eyes darted to his lips.

"Yes," he swallowed. He was hungry. For everything.

She nodded once. "Will you bite me?"

"I thought that's all it was? Bite and go?" He smirked at her, hoping she would at least enjoy his joke. He was rewarded with a little upturning of her lips, and yet he was still left wanting. "I don't have to bite you. Not if you don't want." Not that that was what *he* wanted. Every damned fibre of his being screamed. His skin felt tight, the muscles underneath coiling in anticipation. His mouth filled with saliva laced with venom – the venom which would leech into her blood and combine with her hormones in order to alight her pleasure. His fangs strained against his gums, begging to be released.

Oh God. How *desperately* he wanted to bite her. It was pathetic, really – how he couldn't control his primal nature after all this time. But he couldn't be selfish. Not about this.

"Will it be better?" she asked, her hands clutching fiercely in her lap. "Will it feel better if you bite me?"

Angus was shocked at the question. Firstly, because she was engaging him in conversation about the topic in the first place. Secondly, because her question alluded to the fact that she might *want* to gain pleasure from the experience, so much so that she wanted to know which option would provide her with the *most* pleasure. If it were possible, Angus might have gotten hot under the collar. A shame it was, however, that he was in fact dead, and couldn't induce such a cardiovascular response.

He thought about his answer carefully. He knew that it would feel better to *him* if he were to bite her. There was something about the bite as a means of starting a feed. It sated his predatory nature more than most things, and with Ivy, he knew that it would sate his possessive one also.

At least for now.

"Biting you will allow me to get more venom into your system. My venom combines with hormones in your blood like oestrogen, progesterone and dopamine, and this heightens your pleasure. It encourages them to work harder, and with that comes... more intense feelings."

"This feels like a science lesson," she mumbled.

"That is certainly *not* my intention, Brunette," Angus admitted, running his hands through his hair to give them a job to do. Because all he could think about was putting them on *her*. "But you need to know what to expect."

"You're hungry." Her words were fact.

Angus looked at her in what he assumed was apology. "I'm hungry."

"If you start feeding, will you be able to stop?" It was the question he hadn't wanted her to ask. It pained him to know that she was thinking about his previous (less animated), donors, and how he hadn't been able to control himself. But it was a smart question, and he mentally congratulated her on it. The girl had a solid head on her shoulders. He thought that that might have been a reason as to why he liked her a little.

Only a little. Just a little.

"Nothing comes without risk," Angus confessed, his face stern to convey the gravity of his words. "I am a vampire, after all." He wished he could evade the truth. He wished he could tell her that all would be fine, but he wasn't going to lie to her to get her to accept. It didn't sit well with him. "You haven't been exposed to a lot of vampirism since you have been here. I admit that I am partly to blame for that – I have found myself unusually repressing my nature in front of you. You haven't experienced feeding, and I have avoided parading you around this heinous place like a prize mare, despite what some may think of it." Her face contorted at his words. "You'd be surprised what some vampires like to do to show power," he told her. "I can only promise that I respect you – and myself – enough to use every ounce of self-restraint I own to control my hunger. I've had a long time to think about feeding off you. I've practically obsessed over it. I hope that will make me more prepared, if nothing else. And besides, we practiced that one time, didn't we? In the bathroom."

Ivy's face flushed, and it was enough to push Angus over the edge.

His fangs dropped.

He hadn't knowingly shown Ivy what he looked like when he wasn't masking his true nature. Whether or not she had seen it in the bathroom that time was not known to him, but when she jumped off out of her chair, her mouth agape, he knew that the sight she was seeing was a novel one. She didn't know that his pupils dilated to completely engulf the blue or his irises, or that his lids and skin under eyes became maroon in colour as blood pooled to heighten his sight even further. His lower face remained mostly the same, except for his fangs. They were an extension of his canines, and when they dropped, they almost felt like the roots were elongating in his gums. It was a pleasurable feeling, and he relished in it. The veins in his arms became more prominent. Everything was ready for the kill.

He stood himself, and locked his eyes with hers. She was like a statue, and didn't move as he approached her steadily.

When they were toe-to-toe, he tentatively brought his fingers up, stroking the side of her neck. She was warm, and it felt so pleasurable against his own skin. He brought his index finger to the dip at the base of her neck and watched as she swallowed.

Fuck.

"You don't look like how I imagined you would," she whispered as if she were telling him a secret. He watched her neck with unabashed interest, failing to drag his attention away from it.

"I could have said the same about you," he murmured, remembering her standing in the glass box when he had first met her. "I was furious."

"I'm sorry I'm not what you wanted."

"I wouldn't say something you don't understand, Brunette." He then brought his face down, placing the flat of his tongue against her pulse.

He couldn't believe it, but he could taste her through her skin, and his body buzzed greedily.

He could feel that she was looking up at him like a willing victim, and he felt pleasure roll up his body. He dipped his head again to her neck, his nose inhaling her scent greedily. "By all the Gods, you smell like the most amazing elixir," he whispered against her skin.

Ivy stiffened, but he was happy to note that it wasn't from fear. "You *like* the smell of my blood?" she asked, her voice also quiet, as if she didn't want to break the moment.

"Of course," he growled, licking her from the base of her throat up towards her jaw. "Since the second I smelt you, I've wanted you in my mouth." Ivy gasped, and he smiled at her response.

"I thought maybe AB negative blood grossed you out or something," she breathed.

"Not in the slightest, my wee bonny brunette. In fact, it does something quite a bit different." He dropped his hands and placed them underneath her jumper where he came into contact with her bare skin. He moaned at the sensation of her subtle curves under his cool hands. Her breath hitched, and he relished in it. He wished he could catch those breaths – place his mouth over hers just before she did it – possess them.

His hands continued their unrelenting pursuit up her sides, bringing her jumper with them and taking it off above her head. Underneath she wore a cropped top without any padding, and he marvelled at the visibility of her nipples through them. He felt cheated somehow – he'd been missing out on all of this?! He ran his fingertip just slightly under the edge of her top and watched in delight as she closed her eyes – them rolling back into her head – and arched her back up towards his touch.

"God, is this what you've been hiding from me?" he said, his voice gruff.

"I haven't been hiding anything, you arsehole," she smarted, eyes flying open.

He chucked low. "Easy, Tiger. You're in *my* territory now. Not yours." He grabbed both of her wrists and pinned them behind her back with one of his hands, *showing* her that he was in control. *"Behave."* Her snarky comments wouldn't get her anywhere here.

With his other hand he cradled the nape of her neck, tipping her head back so she had to look him in the eye. "What underwear are you wearing?" She told him that it was white lace, and he groaned. "How very virtuous of you, Brunette."

"Just do it," she said resolutely, clearly asking for the

bite, her voice all breathy and delicious.

"You don't have to ask me twice."

He lifted her up, gripping her under her thighs, and all but threw her onto the bed. Air escaped her lungs in a gust, and he cocooned himself with it, allowing it to push his instincts into overdrive.

He stripped her of her leggings and was rewarded with her little white lace knickers. He smiled wolfishly, running a finger along her apex to find that it came back damp.

Fucccckkk.

And then he sunk his teeth into her inner thigh.

CHAPTER 18

The Plan

Ivy

My back arched off the bed. The feeling of his teeth on the soft flesh of my thigh was sharp at first, but it had suddenly become immensely pleasurable, and I was struggling to keep still.

I wanted…*needed*… more. More of his mouth, more of his words, more of everything.

Although it wasn't my main focus, I could hear Angus's groans of pleasure as he fed off me, his lips vibrating against me. He clutched at my legs, pushing them apart so he could access me better. His hands were cool and firm, and they soothed my skin as it burned under his touch.

My eyes flung open suddenly at the cessation of pleasure, but he was already moving up, sucking and nipping gently up my torso, until he settled at my breasts.

The anticipation was almost too much, and I closed my eyes to protect myself from it.

"Can I keep going?" he pleaded, his voice husky. His lips were redder than I had ever seen them, but there were no smears of blood around his mouth. He hadn't wasted a drop. "You taste amazing," he scoffed in disbelief, "but I'm in control."

I watched his black eyes – they were engulfed by pleasure, but also by that animalistic part of him that I would likely never understand. They looked almost sunken as a result of the purple red shadowing which surrounded them, and his lips were parted, unable to close due to the length of his canines. It was fucked up to think, but in that moment, I had never been more attracted to him.

"Relax, *mo leannan.* I'm not gonna drain you dry," he told me, clearly thinking the expression on my face was fear rather than pure lust.

I nodded at him eagerly. "Keep going."

He watched my face for a beat before narrowing in on my breasts clad in my bralette. His fingers traced the lower outline, and when I didn't protest, he lifted it up and over my head. Cool air touched my skin at the exposure, and I resisted a shiver.

Angus's head cocked to the side, his eyes taking keen interest in the view. He pressed his tongue to the point of his left fang, and then whipped his gaze up to my face. "You're in so much fucking trouble," he growled, face ablaze.

Before I could even respond, his hand came out in a blur, his movements like liquid, to cover my mouth. He leaned into me, his face mere inches from mine. It was clearly threatening, but I couldn't help but clench in pleasure.

He was right. I *was* in trouble.

"You've been hiding these from me this whole fucking time?" he asked, running his left hand up the side of my torso before cupping the underside of my left breast.

I widened my eyes and mumbled nonsense into his palm.

"It was a rhetorical question, Brunette." He smirked at me, teeth glistening. "Now, you're gonna be a good girl and be quiet for me while I make up for lost time, aren't you?"

I nodded, breathing heavily through my nose as my body went into pleasure overload. Who knew I liked to be told what to do in bed.

Suddenly, he was dousing my breasts in slow, seductive kisses, placing the flat of his tongue right over my left nipple. I slapped a hand down on to the mattress next to me, clutching at the duvet. A wanton moan escaped into his palm.

He hummed at my response. "The sounds that come out of your mouth drive me crazy. They always have. And now I get to feel them as they come out of you. I get to catch them in my hand."

His lips moved over to my other breast, and he began to suckle on my nipple as I writhed and groaned in pleasure.

Don't stop.

He was relentless, to the point that it was almost painful. Almost. And then he bit me on the underside of my breast, and the breath left me in a rush, as if my damned soul had separated itself from my physical body.

Fucking hell.

He moaned, finally releasing my mouth and wrapping his hands on either side of my ribcage, bringing me closer to his mouth. My head lolled back against the bed, and I took in an audible gasp. I felt like a doll in his hands, but in a good way – as if I was the most treasured doll in his collection. The *only* doll.

After what seemed like not long enough, he detached from my breast, wiping his mouth greedily. His smile was beautiful, and I felt high staring at him.

His last bite was on my neck.

"You look, and taste, delicious." he confessed, eyes mischievous. Maybe he was high, too. I hoped so. "I've wanted to do that to you for so long. Do you have any idea?" I shook my head, unable to speak. "Of course, you don't," he chuckled.

"Are we done?" I managed to muster, feeling slightly… wanting. He laughed more, his head falling back.

"My greedy girl. Now she can't get enough." I blushed, turning my face to the side slightly, embarrassed. "But I've actually drunk quite a bit of your blood. You're looking pale. It's time to stop."

I frowned, disappointed. "I feel fine."

"You do *now*, but trust me, in another pint you wouldn't have been so happy. The moans would have turned to screams, and not the kind I chase after. The screams are good though; means I can't ever take things too far," he muttered. An afterthought.

I smiled. "Like a safe word?"

He chuckled again. *God, I could get used to this.* "Exactly. Although I'd rather you never had to use it." He got up off the bed and handed me my clothes that were on the floor. "How that was for you?"

I sat myself up, my body like jelly, and dressed myself. "It was...good. Really good," I mused.

"So, I can do that again?" he asked, hopeful.

"Yes." I nodded, shameless. Seems like I didn't know the meaning of *playing hard to get.* "But," I continued, "will you do the other stuff to me every time?"

"The sex stuff?" he asked, clearly amused by my question. I nodded. "Not necessarily. I usually like to feed every day, but I can understand how that might be a bit too frequent for you. Obviously, I wouldn't drink as much as I did tonight. I was just hungry."

"Could we say every other day? And perhaps without the sex stuff?" I offered.

"Was there something wrong with the sex stuff?"

"Not exactly." *Not at all.* "But I just think it could make things complicated. Don't you?"

"How so?" His face twisted into a frown.

"Sex complicates everything. And I think that's also relevant in human-vamp relationships, too," I admitted.

"But if you enjoy it, why does it matter?"

"It just does," I answered, defensive. The thing was, if Angus was to do that to me every other day, I didn't think I'd be able to see him clearly. I'd end up falling for him, no doubt. And that wasn't what I wanted. Because it would be one sided. To Angus, I was a human – below him in the social hierarchy. I'd only ever be an attractive blood source. We would never be equals, *not really.* Not like I would want us to be.

"Fine. As you wish, Brunette. But doesn't mean I won't

try and convince you otherwise now and again," he smirked.

I shrugged. "Try all you want, but no means no when I say it," I said, firmly.

He raised his hand up in defence. "Believe it or not, I'm not about breaking consent." His face was serious.

"I'm glad."

He stared at me in silence for a few beats, his eyes roaming around my face. Something passed in his eyes, but I wasn't able to identify what it was. It made me uneasy, and I turned away. "Get dressed. Go to dinner. You'll need the energy."

And we are back to cold, firm Angus. *Vamp* Angus. My least favourite version.

◆ ◆ ◆

I placed my tray on the table with my friends, Sophie sitting next to me, her eyes wide. It had been two days since the bite. Well... *bites*. Plural. I had put on a high polo neck before I left for dinner to make sure there was no evidence. The marks were like bruises, and I didn't want the questions. My body ached, but in a good way. I wondered if that was normal.

"Guys, this is Sophie." I nodded towards my friend, trying to keep things light. Sophie looked positively nauseated, and I resisted the urge to squeeze her hand. She wasn't big touchy-feely person. I had once tried to give her a hug and she had stiffened like a board and given me the weirdest look, before just closing her eyes and shaking her head no. *"It's a personal space thing,"* she had said.

To be honest, I did understand that in some ways. Personal space was a thing for me too, mainly before nine am.

I didn't like keeping Sophie from my other friends. It felt like cheating somehow – having lunch with her and then ignoring her at dinner. Getting her into the fold was the only solution, and she had agreed, albeit reluctantly. It seemed I was forcing Sophie to do a lot of things she wasn't too keen on recently.

Heather smiled broadly, and just like she had with me, spoke first. "Hi Sophie. I already know you, but it's amazing to see you."

Sophie nodded, tilting her mouth into a closed-mouth smile.

"Hi Sophie, I'm Duke."

"Yeah, hi. Andy." Andy stretched his arm out in front of me and offered his hand to her. She took it with a tight smile. "Ignore, Sass. She's being boring," he said, rolling his eyes, gesturing to Sass who sat opposite me.

I stared at her. She looked… well… awful. For lack of a better word. "What's wrong, Sass?" I asked. I could feel my face contort into a mask of sympathy. She really did look that bad.

"I'm just not well," she muttered.

Heather flung her eyes to Andy. "Why aren't you being more sympathetic to her? Isn't this your field?" she snapped.

Andy shrugged. "I'm not on the clock. She's not my patient."

"Woah. What the hell's up with you? Stick up your arse or something?" Duke asked, dropping the fork he held in his hand.

"If a stick was up my arse, I can assure you I would be in much better spirits," he joked, smirking. Sophie chuckled next to me, scoffing. Andy's face went back to neutral. "I'm just having a bad day. Sorry, Sass." He apologised to her, and she nodded thanks.

"Have you been to the doctor?" I asked.

"Nah," she shrugged. "It's probably just a head cold or whatever. It'll pass."

Heather gave her a side hug. "My poor wee friend. Let me know if you need anything, okay?" Sass smiled slightly, nodding again. She was lost for words, and it was so unlike her. It made me uncomfortable.

"So, Sophie," Duke started, "what's it like working with a princess?" He smiled broadly, winking at me, and I rolled my eyes at him.

"It's a real ball," she said, her eyes lightening slightly. "We make a good team."

I smiled broadly at her. *Cute.*

"What you guys cooking up in those labs for us healers in the Hospital?" Andy asked, mouth full of pie.

"Some new drug," I replied. "They haven't actually told us."

Andy shrugged, and the conversation came to an end rather quickly. Duke relayed his day to us, describing how some patient had come in and tried to stick their broken tooth in with super glue. He made it clear to all of us that that was a really bad idea. I felt disappointed in the human race that Duke actually had to clarify that.

Don't put super glue in your mouth, kids.

It was then that something caught my attention out of the corner of my eye. I turned towards it, finding Freyja waving at me from the other end of the canteen. She began to act out some sort of charade. I worked it out in my head.

I…need…to…talk…to…you.

Two… minutes. I replied back to her in charades also, finding it all ridiculous. I wanted to finish my food. Why couldn't she just come over and ask. Probably something about being seen with 'uggos'.

She nodded, pointing outside the door.

I finished my soup, and Sophie followed suit, noticing me rushing slightly.

"What's up?" she whispered.

"Freyja wants a chat."

"With me too?" she asked. I could tell she didn't want me to leave her with the group, so I nodded yes. "Sure."

We excused ourselves, blaming work and the need to do some out-of-hours research. No one seemed to mind or see it as unusual.

Freyja was waiting on the other side of the doors of the cafeteria. She had her hands on her hips and a sneer on her face. So, not different to normal, really. "That was *not* two minutes," she spat, eyes like slits.

"It's a turn of phrase," I replied.

"No, it's a specific temporal phrase," she retorted.

"Jesus, what book did you swallow?" asked Sophie, her eyebrows raised.

"I'm smart," Freyja snapped back. "Get over it G.E."

"I'm taking this nickname as a term of endearment, because otherwise I'm gonna end up punching you in the face."

"Whatever you need to do to make yourself feel better, Glassy Eyes," she said, then turned her attention back to me. "We need to talk."

"About what, exactly?" I asked.

"About the fact that we still don't have a plan that's meant to get me away from Baron."

"Saying Baron's name without some sort of insult ahead of it sounds wrong. I veto it," Sophie announced. Freyja glared at her, but didn't reply.

"It's not easy to think of a plan. We are hardly overflowing with options," I said, apologetically. But I was also kind of frustrated. Surely Freyja could also be trying to think of plans. I wasn't the only one with a brain here.

"Can you *try harder* then?" Freyja moaned. "I feel like I'm going crazy. And I'm *certain* that he's suspicious." She bristled when she spoke, her face as sour as ever. Her hair was on top of her head in a messy bun. She looked tired and ill kept, and Baron would certainly be clocking onto that.

Not good.

"Hey, you aren't the only one in this predicament." Sophie waved her hands in front of her face to gain attention. "Get your arse out of Freyja Land, you narcissist. I'm being abused too."

I raised my hands to stop the brewing cat fight. "Enough. I'm so damn tired of breaking up the fights between you two." I pointed my finger at each of them in accusation. "If you two would just *get along*, maybe the energy I use to split you two up could be used to help Little Miss Self-Centred over here."

Both of them looked at me, frowning, then to each other. Sophie shrugged first.

"Fine, I'll do it if she stops being such a shite bag."

"Seeeee!" Freyja exclaimed. "She starts it."

"She doesn't start it every time," I reminded her, scolding. "You are as bad as each other. In fact, I think that's why you don't get along. You are too similar."

"Oh, Christ! Don't say such things!" Sophie spluttered. "That's blasphemous!"

"Get a grip," I replied. "*Both* of you."

After a few more insults, they both settled down and we were able to negotiate moving towards the spa. We could have gone back to the courtyard, but we didn't want to risk being overheard. Angus had made it clear that that couldn't happen again. We were lucky it had only been Sorcha.

We went our separate ways, each getting our swimsuits from our rooms, before reconvening at the jacuzzi. I'd taken my hair down and tried to cover up the bite marks with makeup. It was pretty much invisible, and I hoped that the low light in the spa would make it even more so.

It was unusual to me that the jacuzzi always seemed to be empty. Back home, the jacuzzi at a gym was always rammed. It was almost as if people only paid the extortionate monthly fee for it alone. And maybe the sauna. But in the Warren, the humans didn't seem to seek much self-pleasure. I guessed that was not what they were there for. They were there to *provide* the pleasure, not experience it. And even if they carried out an activity that appeared pleasurable to them, say like getting a haircut, it was more likely at the request of their master or mistress, rather than a form of self-indulgence. Besides, who knew if they were even able to determine what real pleasure was anymore. Their pleasure was only what the vamps wanted it to be.

The way Heather spoke of sex with her donor made it seem like the most pleasurable experience of her life. And don't get me wrong, sex could be that pleasurable. But not in the way that you would never want to seek another pleasure – a different type of pleasure. Humans needed balance. And although Heather was the one who had introduced me to the spa in the first place, I didn't get the impression that she used it herself particularly often. It was only really to take me or Sophie when we were sad. I wondered if that was Heather's true self shining through the compulsion – her compassion. I smiled at that.

"So, what's the plan?" Freyja asked, settling herself on one of the side seats so her body was almost fully submerged under the bubbles. Her eyes closed slightly, as if she was about to allow herself a moment of complete peace, but then they snapped back open, suddenly aware where she was.

That was the problem with knowing the *true* Warren. You could never be at ease. Not really.

"Well, we ideally need to be able to get you a new master," I muttered, starting the cogs of thought in my mind.

"What?! Another vamp?!" Freyja's face was one of shock.

"I can't imagine it would be possible to allow you to not be paired at all. You can't just be a loose donor. I've not been here long but I'm almost certain that that's unheard of."

Sophie nodded her agreement. She was being quiet, trying her best not to get agitated by Freyja.

"But what if the same thing happens again?" Freyja whispered. She looked...*scared.* It was unusual to see her face soften and harden almost entirely at the same time. Scared Freyja wasn't nice to see.

"It can't, surely," Sophie uttered. "Gross Baron is another level of depraved. Garrett's a bastard, but I'd rather him than the alternative of a sadist any day." Sophie was being as blunt as ever.

"So, whose donor would I be then?" she asked, her eyes wide and watery. But it wasn't from the steam from the jacuzzi.

I'd been thinking about this, on and off. It had become apparent to me that the three of us couldn't handle the situation alone; that we needed an ally – one with sway. "That's where Angus comes in."

"Ahh yes. Your weird vampire prince who thinks you're

too ugly to drink from." Freyja's bitch face had snapped back into place, and I had the urge to rip if off with my bare hands.

"I never told you that," I said, alarm and question in my voice

"Yeah, but she did." Freyja nodded to Sophie, who was looking a little sheepish.

"Since when do you guys speak when I'm not around?!" I asked, shocked. I always assumed if they ever were alone in the same company, they would tear each other to shreds. And not figuratively.

"It happened, like, once. Calm down. Jealousy is a really ugly thing, P.I.," Freyja said, shrugging nonchalantly.

"Okay, I'll bite. What's P.I?"

"Your new nickname," she said blankly. "Like G.E over here."

"Okay... but what does it stand for?"

"Poison Ivy."

"That's awful," muttered Sophie, rolling her eyes.

"You got anything better G.E?" she roared, almost getting off her jacuzzi seat.

"Fine! Fine. I'm P.I. But then you need one too, Freyja."

"Like what?"

"B.F.," I replied, looking at her as blankly as she was looking at me.

"Awwh," she cooed sarcastically, placing her hands over her heart. "Like 'Best Friend'?"

"No. Like 'Bitch Freyja'."

Sophie spluttered, laughing hysterically. "Simple, yet effective," she said in between breaths. "Didn't think you had it in you, P.I."

Freyja simply shrugged. "I like it. Well done."

It wasn't like her to give out a compliment, so I accepted it gratefully, knowing it was unlikely to happen again any time soon.

"Okay, okay, enough with the side-tracking. I think I have an idea. We need to get BF a new master, correct?" They both nodded. "But we can't just request that obviously, because we are so low on the food chain that it hurts my soul." More nods. "And we also aren't meant to have the mind to even ask such things. But have you guys heard the story about how the king got his donor?"

"Didn't he steal him from another vampire?" Sophie asked, but it was more of a statement.

"Yes. He requested her. And because he was the king, her master at the time couldn't say no."

"Okay... but the king doesn't want Chesnut." Sophie was clearly making a reference to Freyja's hair.

"I veto Chesnut!"

"Shut it, BF. Keep going, friend," Sophie said to me.

"But Angus could."

"What?!" They both said at once.

"I could get Angus to request Freyja from Baron. He's the *prince* for God's sake. Baron couldn't say no."

"But then where would you go?" Sophie looked worried. "Not with Baron, surely." She didn't even say a mean word before Baron's name so she was *definitely* worried.

"No. We'd get Angus to tell Baron they were on the hunt for another donor for him. And it will just happen to take a very long time. Serves the arsehole right."

"But where would you go, Ivy?" Sophie repeated.

"I haven't got to that part," I said, head hanging slightly in disappointment.

"I could give ye a wee idea."

The voice shocked us all, and we turned towards it. Next to the jacuzzi stood the red-haired vampire I recognised as Angus's friend, Sorcha.

God, she's light-footed.

"Don't mind if I join youse, do ye?" she asked, not waiting for a reply before she hopped gracefully over the edge into the spare seat in the jacuzzi tub.

She was wearing an emerald green one-piece swim suit which was cut out around her waist, the neckline halter necked and plunging low, accentuating her ample breasts and broad shoulders. She was stunning. Her eyes were the clearest of icy blues and her hair the richest auburn I had ever seen. I thought about her at the ball and was unable to conjure up a clear image. In fact, a lot of the vampires that had passed me hadn't cemented into my mind. Likely the shock that the entire event delivered to my system.

The slight spattering of freckles on her nose and cheekbones were pixie-like and they contrasted her blunt features in such a way that was mesmerising. I could imagine that as a human she had been a sight to behold, but as a vampire, she was ethereal.

I thought about Skye and her more conventional and obvious beauty, and those thoughts soon became ones of sympathy for the blonde. Because although she too was stunning, she didn't command a room like Sorcha did. She didn't have the *thing* – the thing that made her otherworldly. Sometimes, there was such a thing as being a little too perfect; a little too pretty. Someone like me needed to remember that now and again.

But Sorcha's appearance wasn't what really made me stare. It was the openness of her face, the softness of her features. Her expression was welcoming, and for once, I didn't feel threatened by a vampire.

"I'm Sorcha," she announced, smiling widely. It made her look even more beautiful.

I noticed her eyes lingering on my neck slightly and a smirk take over her smile. It only lasted a second.

What was that?

"Hi, Sorcha," I said quietly, my voice almost a whisper. Freyja and Sophie said nothing.

Maybe I should go red...

"Hello, Ivy," she nodded to me. "Sophie. Freyja." She gave each of the other girls a reassuring smile.

"Hi," Sophie croaked.

"Well, since introductions are over, perhaps I could share with ye my wee idea?" she announced.

I nodded. I wanted to tell the girls that it was okay – that Sorcha knew about us. But I didn't know how.

"I believe you are acquainted with Anthony, yes?" she asked me. I nodded. "Are ye aware of his interest in ye?" She didn't give me time to reply. "Because I've been watching him, and I've never seen him so... preoccupied. I'd go as far as saying that I think he cares for you. And I have a wee hunch that he wouldn't tell anyone yer secret. He could be the one who took you if Freyja were to be given to Angus."

"Who's Anthony?" Sophie asked, tentatively.

I looked at her, reluctantly. It wasn't that I didn't want to tell Sophie about Anthony, exactly. I wasn't embarrassed or ashamed to. But he kind of did feel like my little secret. We had shared some really rather intimate moments, just me and him, and to say it all out loud almost took the magic away from them somehow.

"He's one of the vampires."

Freyja looked at me, rolling her eyes. "You are going to need to say more than that."

Sorcha watched me intently, and I could feel a blush running up my neck. The makeup I had applied to it began to feel really heavy and I had the most intense urge to scratch it all off.

"He's just...," I tried to think of the right words. "He just took a bit of a liking to me, is all."

Sorcha scoffed, but then covered her mouth with her hand to cover it up.

"Ugh, seriously! Another vamp fawning over you? This is really getting old, P.I.," Freyja said.

"How could I be sure he wouldn't tell anyone?" I asked Sorcha, trying to divert the attention to a more comfortable topic.

Sophie and Freyja's eyes both bored into me, clearly highly unsatisfied with my explanation. I would definitely have to fill them in on Anthony at another time.

"You can't. But do you have another option, wee one?"

I shook my head.

"So, what's the plan?" Freyja spoke up. She sounded mildly irritated, but also hopeful. It felt like we had taken a full circle in the conversation.

"Looks like we have to convince Angus to take you on," I said to her.

Sorcha turned to me once again. "And convince him to let *you* go."

♦ ♦ ♦

We all got out of the jacuzzi; Freyja was starting to complain that her skin was beginning to look like an 'old wrinkly hag's.'

Once the girls had both gotten acclimated to Sorcha being in the same vicinity as them, I had been able to explain why it was safe to speak to her. It hadn't really crossed my mind why it was that Sorcha was helping us. All I could really assume was that she was just genuinely nice, and that was enough for me.

I scrubbed the chlorine off my body – I could tell Angus hated the smell – and got dressed (polo neck securely in place), before meeting the girls and Sorcha outside the entrance to the spa.

"You ready, Ivy?" asked Socrha. Her hair was wild from the humidity, but she hadn't done anything with it.

"As ready as I'll ever be to ask my master to hand me over to another man," I muttered.

"Chin up, wee one. You'll be grand."

We made our way to mine and Angus's quarters, walking through the corridors. I reassured them that he would likely be in since he usually was when I came back from dinner.

"Don't worry. If he's not there, he'll get there quickly if he knows what's good for him." Sorcha winked at me, and I couldn't help but smile.

I felt Sophie nudge my side with her elbow. I turned to her, and she mouthed, *'I like her'*. I nodded my agreement. Yes, Sorcha seemed like one of the good ones.

"Don't think you've gotten away with your shite explanation of Anthony," she whispered. "I want to know *everything.*"

"I do, too," Freyja added. "He's fit. If you've tapped that I want to know."

"Seriously?! No one has been 'tapped'. We haven't even kissed. I mean, he's put his tongue on–"

"What the fuck?! Where?! Where did his tongue go?"

Sophie blurted.

"Jesus! Just on my neck. And once on my cheek."

"Your arse cheek?" Freyja asked.

"No! My face cheek!"

"I mean whatever floats your boat," Freyja said, putting her hands up in surrender.

"It wasn't like that! It was–" I stopped myself mid sentence, exhausted with the conversation. "Look, I'm not getting into this with you guys. Just forget it."

"This is not something I'm gonna be able to forget easily, friend," Sophie said, patting me apologetically on the arm.

Freyja nodded her agreement.

I scowled at them both.

We finally reached my room, and as I expected, Angus was sitting at his desk, pen in hand, brow brooding.

What are you thinking?

His eyes met mine first, and then darted next to Sophie, then Freyja, and finally, with a deeper frown, Sorcha.

"Am I in hell?" he asked, flippantly, directing his question at Sorcha.

"Probably," she stated, "but tough shite."

"Don't say shite," he muttered. She ignored him.

Yes, I definitely liked Sorcha.

"We are here to discuss a proposition with you. Actually, it's more your donor's proposition, isn't that right, Ivy?"

Angus raised his eyebrows at that, and turned his eyes towards mine, challenge sitting deep within them. It was as if he was saying, *'have at it, Brunette.'*

"I have an idea. An idea to help Freyja. With Baron."

"Trash Baron," Sophie muttered under her breath.

"And what exactly is this idea? And why do you need a female army to propose it?" His voice was smooth, and almost cocky.

"I propose that, like your father did with his current donor, you request Freyja from Baron." Angus's hand gripped into fists, but he let me continue. "And you give me to another master." He visibly shook and opened his mouth, desperate to protest, so I added, "For now."

"Is this your doing?!" Angus boomed, his wrath directed towards his red-haired friend. She remained impassive as ever.

"I couldn't possibly take credit, my lord." She was smirking fully, and the sarcasm was dripping from her words like treacle.

Angus turned towards me. "You are not safe with another vampire, Ivy. I won't allow it."

"You said you would do what you could to get my friends out of this. You said it," I pushed, sadness on my face.

"Well, I cannot do this. It is not *safe*."

"What if I was given to a vampire who wouldn't hurt me? Who would look after me? Treat me well?"

Angus's face filled with confusion. "What?! Sorcha?! That will never work! She's a known heterosexual for God's sake!" He was standing now.

"I didn't mean Sorcha," I said bluntly, locking my eyes onto his, trying to reel in his erratic behaviour.

"Then who the fuck did you mean?!"

"Anthony."

Angus's hands gripped the underside of his desk and flipped it over, the wood rattling in protest as it made contact with the floor. All but Sorcha on the other side jumped back in shock. Both Freyja and Sophie's eyes were wide, and I swore I almost saw Freyja's hand reach out for Sophie's. *Almost.*

"What the *fuck?!*" Angus almost howled, it was as if he was in pain. Maybe he was. "You *cannot* be serious, Brunette! Anthony?! Really?! I thought you said nothing was going on with him?!"

Sorcha stepped in then, clearly seeing that things were escalating in the wrong direction. "Easy, Angus. That bit was my idea, not hers," she admitted.

"Why would you suggest such a thing? Are we no longer friends?! Is this revenge for me turning you? Is that it?!" He was off the handle, his eye darkening just like they had before he had fed on me. He wasn't far off going full-on vamp.

"Do you ever think that not everything is about you, ye wee shite?" she asked, words sharp. "Yer donor's friend needs help out of the clutches of a sadist, and you have the ability to do that. Handing her over to Anthony doesn't mean you've lost her. It means you've helped her by helping her friend."

The word friend kept being flung about and I wondered how I felt about it. Was Freyja my friend? Yes, maybe she was, in the dysfunctional sense of the word. I couldn't deny that I cared for her, even if I did want to slap her sometimes. She was a bit like a sibling in that sense.

I thought about my real sister, and suddenly became very heavy hearted. I hoped she was okay. I hoped she wasn't worried. She did love to worry.

Angus was breathing heavily. It was unusual to see – his chest didn't normally move with breath. He slumped back into his chair, defeated, his head in his hands.

"Tell me more."

◆ ◆ ◆

Angus summoned Anthony – albeit reluctantly – to his quarters. The door swung open, and the lean vampire walked in, head high, a smirk plastered on his face.

The smirk faltered slightly when he noticed the other people in the room, and he gave Angus a questioning glance. "If this is for an orgy, I can't deny that I'm entirely confused by the line-up. But yes, I accept." His face was cocky. Handsome. He nodded towards the turned over desk. "Has the fun already begun? What did I miss?"

"Nothing, Anthony. Please be quiet," Angus spat, his head still in his hands. "This isn't a fucking orgy."

"Shame," Anthony muttered. "What less interesting event is happening then? And why have I been invited to it?"

"Perhaps you should sit down." Angus took his hands away from his face and stood, gesturing to the other chair in the room before placing his hands into the pockets of his trousers.

"I think I'll stand, Prince," replied Anthony, his voice cautious. He rolled back onto the heels of his feet. "Spit it out."

"I'm aware, as you have spoken to me about it, that you have an interest in my donor."

It wasn't a question, but Anthony replied as if it were. "Correct." He nodded.

Anthony had told Angus about being interested in me?! That was rather... brave.

"I am also aware that you notice something... different about her, yes?"

Anthony nodded again. "Yes." He turned towards me with a sly smile. "Although I cannot for the undead life of me figure out what it is."

I thought about what he had done to me in the corridor and willed my skin not to flush.

"Would you like to know?" he asked. His eyes were glassy, and I wondered what emotion they were harbouring.

"Of course I would. It drives me mad," he admitted, his eyes shimmering with anticipation.

"If I tell you this, you have to swear to your prince that you will not speak of it to anyone that doesn't already know. Do you understand?" Angus's voice was as sharp as a knife, and I flinched involuntarily.

Anthony frowned, then turned towards me again. His eyes searched my face, found what they were looking for, and then turned back towards Angus. "I understand. I won't tell anyone, as I'm sure that if I did, it would put her in danger. Am I correct?"

"You are correct."

"Then I shall not speak to anyone about it, unless they know also."

Wow, Sorcha had been right. Anthony *did* care for me.

Angus stood taller, demanding the attention of everyone in the room. Freyja seemed to take an unconscious step back from him, clearly intimidated by his presence.

His announcement was sharp and to the point. "Ivy cannot be compelled."

Anthony processed Angus's words for a moment before shaking his head, responding in a hollow voice. "That's not possible."

"It's true," I piped up. "It worked once, I think, when I was initially brought here, but I haven't been compellable since. And vampires have tried. *You* have tried." Anthony had turned towards me again, and his eyes squinted at my last words. I continued. "At the ball. You asked me to explain why my eyes looked more alert than other donors. And I replied that there was nothing to explain."

Anthony's face flashed with recognition, and then flattened again. "That did happen, yes."

"You were trying to compel me when you asked me that, but it didn't work. I could tell what you were doing, and it didn't do anything to me. My reply was my choice. It was from my own mind. You didn't force that reply from me."

"*Fascinating*." And that was all he could say.

"That's not all," I added. "Sophie over there, she can't be compelled either." Sophie waved meekly at him with a closed lip smile. "And Freyja is more resistant than others, although we aren't sure about the extent of her resistance. But she knows about the Warren. She knows about compulsion."

Anthony continued nodding.

"The thing is, Freyja's donor, Baron, is a sadist. He basically compels her to hate his company or perhaps, more accurately, doesn't compel her to like it, and enjoys… raping her." I watched Anthony's shoulders stiffen, but he still kept quiet. I also watched Freyja harden out of the corner of my eye. "So, we need to help her. We also need to help Sophie, but we've agreed Freyja's situation needs more immediate action."

"How do I fit into this?" Anthony asked. His face wasn't giving anything away, and I found myself wishing his lips would turn up into his signature cocky smile.

Weird.

"Well, we believe Angus has the power to request any donor he wants. We want him to request Freyja from Baron. He won't be able to refuse the prince."

"What, and you go to Baron?!" exclaimed Anthony. "Absolutely not!"

"No, no." I shook my head. "We want *you* to take me."

Anthony's eyebrows shot up into the air. "Seriously? And he's okay with this?" He nodded towards Angus, who looked like he was about to rip his own face off with how clenched his fists were.

"He understands why we need to do it," I replied. Angus bristled.

"And what happens to *my* donor?" he asked. "I don't want her going to Baron either if that's what he's like. Scummy bastard."

Relief washed over me. Anthony's words confirmed he was actually a good person.

"We don't intend to give anyone to Baron, trust me. I was thinking we could maybe give her to John? We can tell him that she is a surplus and then anyone who needs a donor can have her."

Sorcha's eyes shot up. She looked surprised at the idea. Her eyes met mine and they appeared to say, *'nicely done'*.

"Okay," Anthony nodded, chewing on all the information which had been given to him in the last few minutes. "I'll do it."

I let out the breath I was holding.

And then watched Anthony and Angus flinch.

What's with that?

"I have some rules," Angus said.

"What?" Me and Anthony both said at the same time.

"Oh, do you really think you're getting away with this that easily?" Angus directed this to Anthony and his response was the smile I'd been craving.

"Fine, what are your rules?" I asked.

"Ivy will still be my blood donor. I shall drink from her," he announced.

"Glad ye finally had the balls to do it, ye eejit." Sorcha said, smiling. She then turned to me, gesturing towards my polo covered neck. "Nice bite mark, by the way. It suits ye."

I could feel blood rush to my face. She must have seen it when we were in the jacuzzi.

Stupid vampire vision!

"Then who will I feed off?" Anthony threw his hands up in annoyance.

"Also, Ivy – if she allows it," Angus replied, his face stony.

"So, I'm doing the job of two donors now?!" I asked, shocked.

"It's your choice, Brunette. Trust me, I'm not exactly thrilled about it, either. I just thought since your friend has been through so much, we could give her a break from doing the duties of a donor."

I hung my head, nodding. *He's right.* I hadn't been doing the real role of a donor for months while poor Freyja was being subjected to God knows what. The least I could do was give her some time off from it all.

"But it's only with her permission, got it, *Smiles?*" Angus said to Anthony, who looked like a kid in a toy store.

"Of course, Prince. I'm aware of the word 'no'."

"Any other rules?" I asked, frowning at Angus.

"That we figure a way for you to be my donor again."

"Surely you could just ask Anthony for me back? Obviously, you'll have to give it some time otherwise it looks suspicious. But you could say you decided you prefer me to Freyja after all. And then Freyja can be Anthony's donor long term," I announced.

"Charming," Freyja muttered under her breath.

"Why couldn't Anthony just ask for Freyja outright? So we can skip all of this...stuff." Sophie's hands gestured around her, trying to articulate what 'stuff' was.

"He doesn't have the power to," Sorcha explained, her eyes trained on the vampire she was speaking of. "Baron wouldn't have to give her up because he is of an equivalent rank to Anthony. It just wouldn't work."

"Looks like it's still plan A then," I announced.

"Okay, so I'll get Ivy until Angus requests her back,

correct?" Anthony confirmed.

"Yes," Angus replied, tight lipped.

"And what if Miss Ivy prefers my company to yours after all this? I am *very* charming, you know."

Freyja snorted, and Anthony turned to the sound.

It was the first time that he had really looked at her. I watched as his eyes narrowed in on her face and the colour of her hair. His lips tipped up slightly – just the tiniest of movements – but it was gone before I got a chance to bank it.

"If that's the case, then I cannot deny her her free will. She will choose."

I knew it hurt Angus to say those words. I knew that he wanted with all of his being, to say 'tough shite, she's mine' – not because I thought her cared, but because he was possessive. But instead, he stood in front of a vampire that I knew he loathed, and told him that if *I* wanted it, he could have me.

A couple of months ago, this wouldn't have happened. Angus hadn't understood choice, not really. If he had wanted me to do something, he would have made me do it. And if I had pushed, he'd have pushed back, but harder. If a choice didn't match up to his ideals, I wasn't allowed to make it. But now, that version of Angus didn't seem to hold much weight, and I was suddenly enthralled with him – at how far he had come.

"So how do we go about this, then?" Anthony asked, a serious look on his face. He meant business.

"Angus will have to speak to the king about changing donors. I'm assuming Baron will then be summoned to confirm the deal, and then we can just iron out the other stuff with Anthony as it comes," I said.

"I say both Angus and Anthony will have to go. Angus can make the request but within that he has to say he wants Ivy to go to Anthony. It can be in his terms. Then mention Ivy's idea about putting your donor into *the collection*," Sorcha said, nodding to Anthony. "I also need to tell Callum," she added. "I can't keep this from him, Angus." She had turned to him, her eyes almost hurt.

"Whose Callum?" Sophie asked. "Don't mean to be rude, but I'm getting concerned about how many fangers are getting involved here." All eyes turned to her. She raised her hands in a surrender position. "Eeshh, sorry. It's just I'm not exactly wired to trust you guys. No offence."

"You know, for once, G.E, I actually agree with you," Freyja said, looking surprised at what she was admitting.

"Callum is my partner. We can trust him," Sorcha said, a determined frown on her face.

"I understand you may have concerns," Angus said, directing his words at my friends, "but it's either trust us, or stay as you are. And I don't think you want the latter."

Sophie scoffed and Freyja dropped her head back in defeat, huffing.

Well, that was that then.

CHAPTER 19

Our Lips Were Made for Talking

Angus

Angus really wanted to rip someone's throat out. Preferably Anthony's.

How had this happened? How had *his* Ivy managed to become *Anthony's* Ivy? Well, not quite yet, he supposed. But nearly. And he didn't really have a choice about it. Or maybe he did, but the choice was between giving her up temporarily or losing her completely – she would never forgive him if he didn't try and help her friend.

Ivy, he'd noticed, was a stickler for right and wrong. The fact made her morally pure, and he had to admit that he liked that about her. She was everything he wasn't. Except stubborn, perhaps. They were definitely *both* guilty of that.

But even though he knew it was *right*, there was a part of him (and it was a larger part that he would have wanted to admit), that desperately wanted to tell her it wasn't possible and keep her all to himself.

A few days prior, when he had finally been able to bite into her soft flesh, it had consolidated something – more so than simply tasting her blood like he had in the bathroom. It was as if her pleasure and his had entwined, linking them together in such a way that if she were to ever stray from him, it would somehow hurt on a visceral level. Which meant that her being with Anthony *hurt*, and he hated that it hurt. It was the solitary predator within him – he distinctly disliked feeling vulnerable.

He thought about Anthony sharing the same thing that he had with Ivy and flinched. He thought about Anthony's hand on her warm skin, his mouth on her neck, his lips on hers. But worse was the thought of Ivy's face – her face in the throngs of undeniable pleasure at the hands of anyone but him. It was... *horrifying.* He didn't want that. He really didn't.

A part of him worried that Ivy had in fact orchestrated this all in order to be with Anthony. Perhaps it was pleasure from him that she craved – that the pleasure he himself had given her was simply a placeholder for the true pleasure she desired. His ego was taking a real battering. He couldn't remember the last time he felt this... inferior.

He had always been the superior one. Even when he had been human. Angus had been – and still was – handsome. Even in comparison to other vampires, he was considered to be rather braw, and he knew it.

At the end of the day, vampire venom could only work with the foundation it was given, and although it could be said to work miracles, it couldn't work that sort of miracle. Believe it or not, there was such a thing as an unattractive vampire. The only way to produce a species of pure beauty would be to turn only the most beautiful, and Angus could confirm that this had not happened. Not in the slightest. Baron was a fine example of this.

But Angus was in fact, beautiful. He had been told by enough people to know it as gospel. He was also talented. He was fluent in seven languages, trained in three martial arts, and could play the cello with impeccable skill – a skill he had perfected while he attended the Royal Conservatoire of Scotland in the early 1900s, becoming the Head of Strings – and a skill that was easily transferrable to the bass guitar.

His bravery in battle was also commendable. There was a reason he had been a Master Sergeant within the Black Watch, and Anthony had only been a Corporal. He was intuitive, smart, decisive and forward thinking. And yet, he felt inadequate suddenly, as if none of those things mattered anymore. He was simply Angus. Angus without Ivy.

But despite all of that, he was still making his way to the boardroom to set that in stone. To make her *his. Anthony's.*

"This meeting better be entertaining," Fraser commented, an uninterested look in his immortal eyes. "I'm terribly bored of this place." He sat on a chair on the front row, very close to the throne.

"Fraser, enough with the dramatics," the king responded, frowning. "Let him address us. Son, speak." His father looked mildly irritated. It was likely that Angus's request for a council meeting had disrupted something. Most likely an event involving the king's donor's neck. His father was an avid feeder.

Like father, like son.

Angus winced at the thought. He never had wanted that to be, and certainly not now.

"I have a request," Angus announced, his face expressionless. He hated engaging with the council, and he tried to avoid it whenever he could. Even more so, he hated saying the next words. "I wish to swap my donor with another vampire's donor."

"I beg your pardon?" Garrett piped up, jumping up from his seat in protest. "That's the most ridiculous thing I've ever heard!"

The king's eyes turned to Garrett, still holding annoyance, and he faced his palm outward in a stop sign. "Silence," he snapped. "Continue." He nodded at his son, a degree of curiosity slanting in his cool eyes.

"I wish to have another's donor. The vampire in question is called Baron. His donor is Freyja. I wish her to be mine."

Fraser huffed, snickering. "Brunette *is* the flavour of the year, it seems."

"What is wrong with your current donor?" the king asked. He was sitting back in his throne, arms thrown over the arm rests in a casual fashion. Somehow, it still made him look threatening. His father had the uncanny ability to never quite look like he had his guard down. Knowing what Angus thought of him, it likely wasn't such a bad way to be.

"Nothing. I would just prefer another." The words stuck to his mouth like glue.

"Well tough shite, wee man. It doesn't work like that." Garrett's voice was brittle, like porcelain, but much less attractive.

"Enough, Garrett!" his father boomed, his voice bouncing off the walls. "My son is not a 'wee man'! He is the prince of this realm, and you *will* address him as such. You forget your place too often in this boardroom. Reign it in."

Garrett's demeanour changed markedly, and he seemed to shrink in to himself. Angus took that action with a pinch of salt. He was still a power-hungry swine, and Angus knew that submission wasn't in his making. His reaction was simply to please the king. It did exactly that, and Garrett knew it.

Bastard.

"Yes, my lord," he muttered.

"Son, I apologise but I must, once again, ask you to continue."

"I would like to take Baron's donor," he clarified, although he thought he had already made his intensions pretty clear.

"And what of your current donor? Are you telling me you have killed another lass?!" Disappointment and something else laced his father's words. Angus felt nothing in response to that. His father's opinion of him was inconsequential to him.

"My current donor is alive and well," Angus corrected.

"So, if you wish to have his current donor, you will hand your current one to Baron?"

Angus suppressed a growl. *Absolutely fucking not!*

"No. I have another vampire who will take my current donor. His name is Anthony." Angus turned his attention to the heavy-duty double doors at the entrance of the boardroom. They were such that they were soundproof, even to vampire ears. "He's on the other side of that door, waiting to be summoned."

Angus's father's eyebrows began to rise in what looked like surprise. "And Anthony's donor goes to Baron?"

Angus shook his head no, and he could see the king's eyes turn cooler than they had before. His father didn't like being out of the loop, looking in from the outside. It made him feel weak, out of control. Angus liked that he had caused him to feel like that. It was a small win. "Anthony wishes for his donor to placed back into the hands of the collectors. When another donor is needed, she can be part of that selection. I hear she is lovely."

"If she is so lovely, why is Anthony willing to give the lass up?" Fraser uttered.

Angus turned his attention fully to the old vampire for the first time since the meeting began. He was intrigued to find that he looked... *interested.* He was leaning forward, his posture oddly to attention, and his eyes held a quality that Angus had never seen within them before.

Fraser was an intriguing character. He was old- older than Angus and his father. The connection between them was not quite known, and Angus often found himself disappointed with Fraser for associating himself with the king. Angus thought that Fraser appeared better than that. But perhaps he was wrong.

"Maybe he thinks my donor is bonnier," Angus shrugged.

Garrett piped up. He had been sitting in silence, his eyes flickering to each person who spoke, his face getting more and more irate with each spoken word. "What is happening here?! Some sort of donor swapping club?! I object!"

His comment was ignored by all, and this only seemed to irritate him further. Angus realised then that he had never enjoyed a council meeting so much in his entire existence. A smirk began to take a hold of his cool, marble face. He simply couldn't help the emotion.

"And what will happen to Baron? Who will be his new donor?" asked Fraser, taking an active role in the conversation.

Angus shrugged, uncaring. "He can apply for another."

"What do you have against this Baron?" the king asked, suspicion laced within his words in the most intricate tapestry. Angus didn't miss it.

"Nothing," Angus said, bluntly. "Me and Anthony just agreed that neither my current donor nor his current donor would be suited to Baron's needs."

"How would you know of Baron's needs?! The donor preferences of clan members are *strictly confidential!*" Garrett again, his voice shrill.

"Correct, they are," Duncan announced proudly. Angus scowled at him, and he cowered slightly.

Again, Garrett's comment was ignored. Angus didn't think Duncan's response counted. To him, Duncan was the lowest of the low.

"I think it is right to say that a clan member should be able to decide what happens to their donor if they are no longer wanted. It seems like the ethical thing to do."

"Ethical?" his father repeated. He said the word as if he didn't know the meaning, or had never had to consider it.

Angus nodded, not wanting to elaborate.

The king held his gaze for a long time, and Angus began to think that maybe things wouldn't go his way, but then the king shrugged, and said, "As you wish, Son. Now summon this Anthony fella. I wish to confirm with him."

Angus nodded again and turned to the doors, opening them in a flourish. Air swept around him as he did so, and Anthony walked in, following it. Something in the room seemed to change. He couldn't remember the last time outsider vampires were allowed in the boardroom, except John, perhaps.

"Anthony, is it?" the king asked, still sitting on the throne in a laid-back fashion, all loose limbs and cavalier mannerisms.

"Correct, Your Majesty."

"Is it true you have agreed to some sort of arrangement with my son?" He waved his hands about in a gesture.

"Correct," Anthony repeated.

The king nodded. He was silent for a moment. To a human, perhaps it wouldn't have even seemed that any time had passed, but time did pass, and Angus waited patiently.

"I agree to your proposal, Son," the king announced. "However, with some caveats."

Angus stiffened.

"I don't like the idea of donor's just… floating around… free. I therefore propose an idea." The room waited in anticipation. "I'm sure there are some clan members who are in need of new donors soon or perhaps are getting bored with their current ones, as you have, Son. I therefore propose a sort of…" He turned his head up slightly, tapping his finger on his chin. "… donor auction."

"Go on," Fraser encouraged, leaning even further forward in his seat. It almost looked like he was about to stand completely, as if doing so would get him the information he wanted more swiftly.

"Any clan member who wishes to exchange a donor can put them forward into a sort of… ballot. Those donors will be presented to the other clan members who have also put their donors forward, and they have a form of auction to decide who gets them."

Angus listened. But it was Anthony who interrupted.

"So, I have to win the auction to get his donor?" he asked, nodding towards the prince.

"No, no. You two have agreed on something and I respect my son enough that I will honour that. Angus's donor's participation will simply be for show, as will Baron's. You will both get who you desire. A kindness I give you both."

Angus didn't like that. The king was trying to make Angus owe him something, and Angus couldn't think of anything worse than being indebted to his father. But he couldn't protest it, and he knew it.

"This is rather... interesting, Your Majesty," Fraser announced. "Can anyone put their donor forward?"

The king shrugged nonchalantly. "I dunnae see why not." Angus hadn't missed how many colloquial Scottish phrases his father had dropped in the last twenty minutes.

Fraser clapped his hands together in delight. Angus was almost shocked. The movement on Fraser just didn't seem to fit with his normal behaviour. It seemed everyone was acting a little out of character.

"Well then," Fraser beamed. "I shall be putting my donor up. You are quite right, Your Majesty, I am one of the clan who is getting rather bored of mine. Why not mix up the status quo."

"I didn't realise you were an advocate for disrupting the norm, Fraser," Angus commented.

"I'm not usually. But as I said when the meeting came into session – I'm terribly bored. The yearly balls we hold are predictable and I'm quite fed up of them. This new... *donor auction*, as you say my lord, is exactly the kind of entertainment I've been craving. A fantastic idea, if I may say, Your Majesty."

Angus was shocked into silence. He didn't think he had ever heard Fraser say so many words at once, and for a second, he just stared at him, bemused.

"Baron will attend the auction," the king said. "He will also have a pick of the litter. But, Anthony, I will make sure he is not given your current donor. I, again, will respect your wishes."

Anthony nodded. "Thank you, my lord." His face was grim, set with a straight lipped grimace. Seemed Anthony didn't like owing the king, either. And that was twice now.

"Duncan, you shall create the announcement and spread it throughout the Warren. I want this event to be lavish, so please make sure it reaches all clan members of all genders. This isn't just an auction for female donors." Angus could tell that Duncan wanted to complain, but then he seemed to think better of it, and nodded instead. He realised that his father always seemed to give Duncan the menial tasks, and he almost liked him for it for a second.

"Perhaps it would be best if we hold a dinner?" the king announced, his eyebrows raised and eyes searching.

"A dinner?" asked Duncan.

"Yes, dinner. I will hold it in my quarters. You are all invited. As are your donors. And your prospective donors. This includes Baron and his current donor – the one you want as your own, Son."

Angus thought that the word 'donor' was beginning to sound very strange indeed.

"Okay, Father," Angus said, nodding once.

The king sat up straighter in his throne and brushed his hands once, twice, down his thighs, as if he was ridding himself of something. "Right. Now Anthony, I must ask you to leave. I have other issues to discuss with my council members and they do not concern you," the king told him, his face bored, yet stern.

Anthony nodded, then bowed, before taking his leave out the double doors.

Angus became uncomfortable. This meeting wasn't scheduled before he himself had requested it. What more possibly needed to be said?

"Duncan, give me an update on the AB blood bags. Do we still have a wee problem there?" A frown was carved into the king's smooth face.

"No issues since it was brought at the last meeting, Your Majesty. We have managed to bring the AB blood bags back up to a suitable level and it's been assured by both Callum and myself – I never trust anyone to do a job alone – that the blood bags are no longer being...raided."

Raided?! Angus thought that was a little bit extreme. He hadn't been *raiding* the stores... had he?

"Fantastic. But it's only been a few days, so I still want this monitored long term. Duncan, you are still in charge of monitoring, but I will accept less thorough investigations from now on out."

Duncan nodded, grunting slightly.

Angus's shoulders sagged in relief. He'd managed to

get away with it. He hadn't fed on Ivy in over seventy-two hours. He knew he needed to do it again, but unlike last time, the thought thrilled him.

"Garrett, how about you update us on the labs while we're all here," the king continued, snapping his fingers in the direction of the dark-haired vampire.

"The labs, Your Highness?" Garrett looked confused and it wiped all the frustration which had been on his face off completely.

"Yes, yes. The samples we are making in the labs," he replied, impatient.

Angus's ears twitched. He hadn't heard of this before. Or perhaps he had, but hadn't really listened. It was the fact that he knew Ivy now worked in said labs that made this information relevant.

"All well. The samples are doing as we expected to human DNA. They look promising. I assume we can get them into circulation soon. Obviously it's a risk, but we can trial it and just hope none of them die." Garrett chuffed smugly, looking around to see if anyone was laughing at his 'joke'.

No one was.

It appeared Garrett wasn't in tune with the crowd that evening.

"Sorry, but what's this?" Angus piped up.

"The compliance serum, Son," his father said, irritated.

"No, sorry. I'm still unsure of what you mean."

"Angus, what have I told you about listening in council meetings." Sternness marked the king's face. Angus suddenly felt like a child again.

"I'm listening now," he snapped, clutching the arms on his chair. He had to restrain himself, feeling the material bowing under the pressure.

The king's icy eyes widened, but then softened slightly, as if he had decided the argument wasn't worth the energy. "Clan members over the last couple of years have noticed a slight drop in compliance in humans. Our compulsion is still sound, but some have said they just have to work a little harder to get the compliance we require in the Warren. The serum we are developing in the labs – or should I say that the humans are unsuspectingly developing – is one that overcomes this small hurdle, Son. No more compelling twice."

Angus visibly flinched. He knew it was visible because all of the council members were suddenly watching him with narrowed, curious eyes. It suddenly became apparent that Ivy would be one of the unsuspecting humans who was doing this work. He felt... empty. What if Ivy was injected with the serum and she became just like any other donor? God, that made his heart hurt. He didn't even know that was possible, but there it was, right in the depths of his chest, right underneath the left side of his sternum, around his third or fourth rib. He felt it.

"I can't say I've noticed anything myself," Angus deflected. "Perhaps the issue is with the vampires in question, rather than the donors."

"What are you suggesting?" Fraser asked, his smooth, pale skin etched with a deep frown.

"Perhaps it is our compulsion that is the issue, not the humans," Angus stated.

"Nonsense!" Garrett exclaimed, nearly standing up from his seat again.

"What an interesting and sceptic thing to say," his father said, tilting his head to the side, studying Angus with new eyes. He watched as the king pressed the tip of his tongue onto his front tooth in distaste. "How... unpatriotic."

"I'm just offering another angle."

"I've never been a fan of playing devil's advocate," the king replied, still studying Angus with an odd expression on his face. "It's a wicked game. Someone always seems to get hurt, and it never seems to be the bad guy." It wasn't said in that way, but Angus knew a threat when he heard one. He remained silent and his father continued to stare, as if weighing something up. He met the same eyes he saw himself in the mirror, and it made him sick to the stomach.

And then suddenly his father's eyes were no longer locked on his, and he snapped his head up.

"Right! To this dinner then? When shall we meet?"

"Two days from now," Fraser announced, his tone taking on its usual monotone boredom.

"Very well. Within that time, I expect you will let Baron know of your intention to take his donor before you invite him to this evening event, Son. I do so hate people being blindsided."

◆ ◆ ◆

"You want my donor?" Baron questioned.

Angus had summoned him, and they were within his quarters. Ivy was away eating dinner.

"Yes, Baron. And you can't protest. The king has already agreed to this."

"I don't see what's so special about her. She's a pain in the hole if you ask me. Take her." Baron rolled his shoulders a couple of times, uninterested.

"You will get another donor. A donor auction has been decided. More will be explained at the dinner you have been requested to attend on Friday evening," Angus explained, trying to encourage Baron out of his presence.

Baron shrugged. "As you wish, my lord." He stood from the chair he was sitting in and wiped his hands through his thinning hair before doing the same over his face. Angus could see the slight unevenness of his skin from his seat across the room. He wondered how cratered it had been when he had been human if it were still noticeable as a vampire.

"I shall see you on Friday."

Baron nodded before walking through the threshold of the front door. On the way out, he passed Ivy, who was returning from dinner, and his eyes dragged over her body in such a way that made Angus grind his teeth together in fury. He growled slightly under his breath, but loud enough for Baron to hear him.

Ivy didn't notice.

"Did you tell him?" she asked. Her eyes were unusually bright, and he suspected that they were laced with hope.

It flattered her features completely. Ivy was beautiful. Perhaps not conventionally – her nose was a little too wide and her eyes slightly too close together – and yet it was these un-conventionalities which made her all the more stunning.

He wondered if she knew. He wondered if she knew what she did to him. He wondered if she knew that she had him – all that he had, it was hers. He doubted it, considering he had only just come to terms with it himself.

"I told him," Angus replied. "He was surprisingly unphased by the idea." Somehow that managed to make him think even less of Baron, if that were even possible.

"That's great!" she beamed. "I mean, I'm sure if he hadn't been happy, you would have just told him to shove it and get over it. But it makes it easier I guess if he's not bothered by the idea." She sighed heavily at the end of her sentence as if she were letting something go; something that needed to be released. As she did it, she raised her arms upwards, catching the gorgeous mass of her dark hair into both her hands, before pulling it upwards as if she were about to put it into a ponytail. However, she didn't do that. Instead, she lolled her head back, sighed again, and then released it all at the end of her exhale.

Angus stared, mesmerised. Her movements weren't as smooth as a vampire's. They jolted slightly – a product of her having less finite control over her muscles – and Angus watched each stutter in awe.

"God, you're stunning," he muttered. It was involuntary. He hadn't meant to say it out loud. But he couldn't not.

"What?!" she gasped, her eyes snapping to his.

"You're stunning, Ivy. I could watch you all day. Just you going about any menial tasks. I'd buy a front row seat to that show."

Her face flushed, but she kept eye contact, silent. Her breath had increased, and Angus allowed the sound to overwhelm his senses.

He paced towards her purposefully and she backed up

towards the wall until her back was flush against it, next to the door.

He didn't know why, but he needed her. He needed her body, her soul. After everything that had happened in the last couple of days, he just needed to know that she could be his, even for a little bit longer. It was entirely selfish. But he just really *needed* it.

Her scent was maddening, and he couldn't help himself. He picked up some of her hair, ran it through his fingers and then raised it to his nose and inhaled deeply.

"Fuuuckkk...," he hummed. "You smell fucking amazing."

She was still silent.

"Turn around," he demanded.

Her eyes popped open, but he ignored her. He didn't want her sarcastic comments tonight. No. Tonight she had to do what he said.

His face was obviously stern because she didn't say anything and did as he said.

That's a first.

With her face towards the wall, he ran his hands through her hair. It was as soft as it looked, and his fingertips relished the sensation, greedy for more.

He gathered her hair up into a high ponytail. "Hand me the hair tie on your wrist," he whispered in her ear. She always had one to hand.

She did as he asked. Again.

He began to wrap the hair tie around her hair, being careful not to snag at her scalp. When he was done, she stepped back a foot to admire his handiwork. Her hair fell down her back in waves. "Perfect," he breathed under his breath.

He then stepped closer again, grabbing her hair with a little more force, tilting her head to the right so he could access her ear better. "This polo neck you're wearing is exactly the kind of thing I would normally want you to wear. But right now, it's getting in my way, Brunette. Remove it."

He let go of her hair so that she could peel the top over

her stomach and breasts. He watched over her shoulder as her skin became more visible. "Better," he hummed in approval. "Now take off the leggings."

She did.

"Ohhhh, God," he growled, his head throwing back slightly in pleasure. "You in a thong. Fuck. Just for me, Brunette?" He licked her neck and revelled in the little sounds which escaped her full lips as he did it.

His fingers began to run up the front of her thighs. He felt the tiny, fine hairs on her legs standing to attention, her flesh covered in goose-bumps. When he found the seam of her underwear, he waited for a protest, but it never came.

His foot forced itself in between her now bare ones, opening her legs up slightly, exposing her. "Open your legs wide for me, Brunette. Wider... wider... Stop." The wider her legs went, the more she had to tip forward for balance, and the more her arse had to stick out into his crotch.

His dick throbbed.

He'd stared at her arse on many occasions: when she wore her gym leggings, when she bent over to pick things up off the floor, when she was taking off her clothes for the day and changing into her pyjamas.

But this was different. And he loved it.

He shifted her thong to the side, exposing her, and her head fell back onto his shoulder. He ran his nose up and down her neck, following the throb of her carotid artery. He used all the self-restraint he had and started touching her clit, circling with his finger, spreading the moisture she had created between her folds.

She rocked rhythmically into him.

"Angus...?" she whispered, her voice filled with lust.

"Yes, Brunette. What do you want?"

"I want you to bite me," she whispered, and the words nearly made him cum right there.

"My pleasure...," he said, his lips sucking her neck first, before he delicately bit into her.

She moaned deliciously, and he let go of her hair to support her head better, still circling her clit, her pelvis bucking into his hands greedily.

Her blood swelled into his mouth, and he felt like a man who had been left in a desert, taking the first sip of water he had had in days. He lapped at her neck, holding it as close to his lips as he could. He just wanted her…closer. He just wanted *more.*

Once he'd had the fill of her neck, he ran his tongue over the wound to stem the bleeding.

Her disappointment radiated off her in waves. "Don't stop. Why did you stop?" He'd taken his hand out of her underwear too, but he didn't think that was what she was talking about.

He turned her around so he could look at her face. Her skin had a sheen of sweat and it was flushed, with eyes that looked almost drowsy with pleasure, but alert at the same time.

She looked glorious. God, how he wanted to sink his dick into her while he drank from her neck.

"I'm not stopping, Brunette. I'm just moving," he said as he picked her up, grasping her arse in both his hands, her legs wrapping around his hips. He placed her on the edge of his desk, and she placed her hands behind her back on top of the surface for balance. The position made her breasts lift and Angus stared. "I can't decide what I like best," he muttered. "You're arse or your tits."

"What about my personality?" she asked sternly, a mocking look on her face.

He chuckled. "I hate it. Don't mention it again," he mocked in return, and she smiled, although it may have faltered at the end.

He stared at her neck where he had bitten her. A wave of something came over him, but he couldn't place it. It wasn't pleasant, so he ignored it.

"Take off your thong. Open your legs," he demanded.

She frowned. "You're being very demanding. Where has this all come from?"

"And you're taking too long," he snapped. "Take off your thong, or I'll do it for you. With my teeth." He smiled wickedly. "And I bite."

She hesitated only for a second before shimmying the thong down her legs. His eyes started at her apex the entire time.

"Open your legs, Ivy," he pressed when they remained closed.

She scrunched up her face slightly before releasing a big breath.

A big breath right into his face.

Angus growled, the scent of her breath completely encasing him, and the animal within him pounced so it was now just under the surface. Her breath had always been a weak spot for him. It was why he always asked her to do it away from him. It was just the most gorgeous scent, and it just about drove him crazy. It just made him want her – always.

He placed his hands on each of her knees and spread her legs wide. She gasped, but didn't resist – she wanted this as much as he did.

He knelt in front of her – as if she was a shrine and he was the most devout theist – and inhaled deeply, the smell of her almost burning his nostrils. "I want to taste this part of you more than I want anything in my existence," he admitted, his voice gravelly.

He didn't wait for her reply and instead pressed his tongue right up against her. He licked from her opening and up to her clit, and he did that again and again, so much that she began tugging on his hair with one of her hands.

"Ahhh... Angus." His name was like a benediction, and he relished it. This was like a religious experience to him.

He then, when he knew she was ready, inserted his middle finger into her and began to pump, his index finger following not long after. She clenched around his fingers tightly, and he knew that she was close.

He continued licking and pumping, and just before he knew she was about to cum, with vampire speed, he lifted her, took her to the bed they shared together, and flung her on to it, face down. He grabbed the front of her thighs from behind and hiked her arse in the air and bit her on her left cheek, pressing onto her clit with one of his fingers. She screamed and screamed, her body convulsing as she came in his arms, and he sucked on her arse until he was full.

And it was only at the end of her come down that he realised that during that entire session, they never once touched lips.

In fact, they hadn't kissed since the first time when he thought he had compelled her. And for some unknown reason, he thought that if he were to kiss her now, something between them would be consolidated – something that he wasn't sure he could face. Not yet.

He was so focused on that detail that he completely forgot the mention of a compliance serum in the council meeting.

Which meant he never told Ivy that she was contributing to a disaster.

Which meant no-one had the chance to do anything about it.

CHAPTER 20

Mind Games

Ivy

Angus wiped his mouth, looking fulfilled, and yet there was a frown on his face – one that soured the last twenty minutes, making me feel self-conscious.

I was all too familiar with this – the male's ability to scratch an itch. Their ability to brush people aside when they had had their fill of them.

I was suddenly sixteen again, being told by the guy I liked that he didn't want to see me anymore, right after I'd put out. The same guy who was then able to move onto one of my friends almost instantly.

I thought about that guy and how, even now, I still didn't think I could look him directly in the eye if we were to ever meet again. He'd made me a loser of a game that I hadn't even realised I had been playing. And God, had I felt the loss.

Was that what was happening? It almost made me want to reject Angus first – to distance myself from him – so I could be the one to win the game, not him. And yet, I couldn't. Instead, pathetically, I simply hoped that the game hadn't begun yet, or that it never would.

"Why are you frowning?" I was on my back now, the duvet covering my body. This was a power thing for me – controlling what parts of me he could see, and when – made me feel less ashamed.

"No reason," he replied, bluntly. His eyes didn't quite meet mine.

"Are we done?" I asked.

His eyes flicked, now holding mine. "Done?"

"Yes. I mean… with the drinking and… stuff." God, why was I embarrassed? Why couldn't I be one of those women who could just talk freely and unashamedly about sex?

"You finished, did you not?" It was almost a snap.

"Yes, but–"

"Then we're done."

I reared back slightly at his words, shocked at how he had become so cold.

"Why are *you* frowning, Brunette? Most women would be thrilled at the idea of only taking and not having to give." He still stood over the bed, his presence intimidating and powerful.

"So, am I supposed to thank you?" I asked, shocked. My eyebrows were raised to what felt like near my hairline.

"It wouldn't hurt," he replied. I noticed how his right hand was clenched into a tight fist, the skin covering the bones around his knuckles straining at the immense tension.

"You can be a real dick, you know that?"

"Yeah, Ivy. I know that."

"Ever thought about reformation?" I asked, sarcastically.

"Every day," he whispered.

I rolled my eyes, not in the mood for his pity party. "Well, when you get there, let me know. Because only then will you be able to do any of that shit with me again." I was fuming, waves of anger pulsing and tangible on my skin. I wanted to punch something. Something that had Angus's face on it.

He took a sharp intake of breath, his eyes squinted slightly, and his right fist tightened even more, before letting go. "Is that what it is to you? Shit?" He looked deeply offended.

Welcome to my world, arsehole.

"I'm not in the mood to stroke your already inflated ego, Angus."

"That's not why I'm asking." Both fists clenched now.

"Then why are you asking?"

He inhaled again, audibly, before turning silently to walk to his desk where he gracefully sat in the chair which faced it. He placed his head in his hands for a second, before running them both over it and then through his hair.

"I taunted you when I said that things I say bother you. But I'm coming to realise that it is actually *you* that bothers *me*." He looked at the wall rather than at me. "Perhaps I am asking because what I feel is profoundly more than you will understand."

"I'm all ears."

"Unfortunately, I've not the words you wish to hear, Brunette," he said, his voice distant. And he then reached for the drawer on his right, taking out the little book I had almost forgotten about, and scribbled there.

I frowned at him in frustration. "What do you write in that book?" I asked.

Angus didn't lift his head and instead let the pen run along the page with perfect precision. I had never seen his writing, but I could imagine that it was likely beautiful cursive. He didn't give me the impression that he had chicken scrawl.

"Just thoughts," he muttered, still not looking at me.

I sat up straighter in the bed, pulling the duvet up to my chin, and then thought it best to put some pyjamas on. I stood, grabbing them from under the pillow I was resting against and put them on. It was late, and I looked at the wall clock to confirm it was after ten.

"So, it's a diary?"

Angus looked up then, his eyes pinning mine in that stern way they often did.

"Something like that," he said, putting the pen down

and closing the notebook. "Why are you interested?"

I thought about that question. I really did. Why *was* I so interested?

"I don't know," I admitted.

"Could it possibly be that you are as interested in me as I am with you?" His eyes were cool, but heating up by the second.

I listened to his words, surprised by them. Was he admitting to being interested in me? Or was he goading me? I could never tell with Angus.

When I failed to reply, he stood and walked over to the bed. He toed off his shoes (he hadn't taken off any of his clothes while he had been seducing me), and sat on his side of the bed, not facing me.

"The book is what I used to unscramble my thoughts. Vampire minds process things very quickly, which is a benefit, but it can also be terribly overwhelming. I find writing it down just gives my thoughts a little bit of structure, so I can at least try and understand them." He continued to stare at the opposite wall.

"What are you thinking now?"

Angus huffed, clasping his hands together. "That's exactly what I was trying to figure out." He paused before continuing. "I'm struggling with my emotions. It's new for me. I'm not used to it."

I let the silence stretch between us, using the time to unscramble my own thoughts.

When it was apparent that he had nothing more to add, I went to the bathroom to brush my teeth and wash my face. When I returned, Angus had removed his clothes and was sitting in bed, his chest bare, scars exposed, holding a book. He flipped through the pages quickly, as if he were simply skimming the words rather than actually reading with care. His hand came up to his head, and he ran his fingers through his hair. He then brought his index finger to his mouth, slipping his tongue between his lips, and touched his fingertip to it.

He frowned and then looked down at his right hand, humming deep in the back of his throat, before smiling secretly to himself. It was then that I realised that not long ago, that exact finger had been inside me, and he hadn't washed his hands since.

I could feel my skin heating up, and so could Angus.

"Don't be embarrassed," he muttered, not looking up from his book. "You taste incredible."

"I think you should wash your hands."

"But I don't want to," he replied. "Instead, I'll continue to use this finger to flip each page of this book, and I'll bring it to my mouth each time, just so I can taste you again."

And he did exactly that, until he had finished the entire novel.

◆ ◆ ◆

I was getting ready for the king's dinner. Angus had mentioned it last night as we lay in bed. He'd been staring at my face in an intense way – a way that made me want to shake his head until all the thoughts came tumbling out.

He didn't touch me once.

I understood why we needed to go to the dinner. The king wanted to be in control of the changeover. He wanted to make sure he was completely involved. I imagined that having members of your clan doing things behind your back made a leader feel... unsettled. Especially when the clan member happened to be the son who hated your guts.

"It's going to be like the ball," Angus started, "but more... personal. It's only a handful of people who are invited. That means you won't be able to get away with anything. No sarcastic comments. No side glances to your friends. No eye rolling. No... being yourself."

I thought about the way he described me, and realised I was actually rarely like that with my friends. There was always someone who was able to out-eyeroll me or be more sarcastic.

I tugged on my hair, trying to make it look presentable. Angus was leaning on the door frame, watching me in the mirror above the sink.

"Don't worry, I'll be on my best behaviour," I replied, spraying some hairspray over my head in an attempt to smooth off flyaways. "And Sophie isn't exactly new to being the dutiful donor, so she's also nothing to worry about. It's Freyja that's the liability. She's not been playing the game for very long."

"I could just compel her," Angus blurted. He frowned after the words came from his mouth but said nothing more.

"You wouldn't dare, Angus! That goes against *everything* we are trying to do here!" I exclaimed, spinning around to face him fully rather than talking to his reflection. "Compelling her, even if it's just to make sure she doesn't slip up, is *still compelling her*. It's all the same. It's all wrong."

"Yes, yes," Angus snapped. "I know how you feel about it, Ivy." His eyes were sharp. "But you have to admit, it does have its place in the Warren."

"I disagree."

"Of course, you do," he said, walking away from me to now slump into his desk chair. He placed his elbows on the table and steepled his hands. He was stressed.

I sat in the chair opposite him. I still had my makeup to do but this seemed more important to address. "You enlightening me in the…" I stopped, fidgeting in my chair, embarrassed about what I wanted to say. "…In the pleasure of feeding has made me realise that compulsion is even more ridiculous than I originally thought. I'm sure there would be people who would be more than happy to be seduced by gorgeous creatures and be fed on if it caused them that much pleasure. You could have built a community based on mutual trust, respect and pleasure. But you just took the easy way out."

"You're making out that I'm the one who created the rules. I did not."

"But you're part of the problem." I snapped in reply.

"Oh, am I really, Brunette? Am I not doing all of this to help you?" Angus's face was angry, and he flung his arms in the air in frustration.

I winced. He was right. After all, if Angus hadn't allowed the donor swapping idea, it wouldn't be happening. But he had. He was the reason this was possible. And for that, I had to give him some credit.

I placed my head in my hands, tugging on my hair strands slightly, trying to allow some sort of release. My hair wasn't playing ball anyway, what did it matter if I messed it up?

"What's wrong?" Angus's voice had softened markedly, and his voice was closer than it had been just seconds before. I lifted my head to find that he was now standing, his weight leaning on the desk edge, legs crossed at the ankles.

He was wearing plain black jeans that were fitted, but not ridiculously so, and a white t-shirt. The shirt should have stood out next to his skin, but it didn't. In fact, they almost blended slightly. His arms were crossed at his chest, causing his bicep muscles to contract in such a way that made my blood sizzle. I studied the veins which were visible just under his near-translucent skin, remembering how they became more prominent when he fed.

Perhaps the vamps are rubbing off on me...

It was then that I realised that I felt safe with Angus. Those arms were protective, not predatory. It was the kind of safety you perhaps felt with a large dog around a baby – you knew deep down they wouldn't do anything, and yet you were constantly on edge, just in case.

That was Angus – an Alsatian with a baby. And I was the baby.

"I'm scared," I admitted, whispering. My eyes reached his, and I thought I might have seen some reminisce of fear there, too.

"What are you scared of?"

"Everything. I'm worried we'll get caught. I'm worried someone is going to get hurt. I'm worried that I can't trust Anthony–"

Angus interjected with force. "I'll be keeping tabs on Anthony. He won't step out of line if he knows what's good for him. And, if I'm being honest, and trust me when I say I don't like to admit this, I think we can trust him. His feelings for you are almost unmatched." Angus crouched in front of me, his hands gently resting on my knees, although I knew it wasn't for balance. "I won't let anyone hurt you," he promised, his eyes demanding my attention. They were the softest I had ever seen them. It even appeared as if his jaw had softened. He brought his fingers up towards my cheeks and traced them. His fingertips were smooth and cool, and they glided over the planes of my face with new fascination, as if they had never felt the skin on another before, and I closed my eyes, feeling – for what felt like the first time – completely and utterly cherished.

It was a shame that that wasn't the case.

"I don't think it's really me I'm scared for," I whispered. "I'm scared for everyone else. I feel if something were to happen, it would be my fault."

Angus didn't reply. Instead, he swept me up into his arms, cradling me and taking me to his chair. He sat with me in his arms, rocking me slightly and occasionally pressing his lips into my hair. And I just let the tears roll down my face, realising that this was in fact the first time since entering the Warren that I had let myself cry. I did so without restraint, the moisture relentless, like a tap that had been left on, crying silently into the arms of the vampire I realised I loved.

Into the arms of the vampire who didn't love me back.

◆ ◆ ◆

I entered the king's quarters with my arm linked in Angus's – just as we had for the ball.

I was in a plain cool-red dress with spaghetti straps and a square neckline. It was mid-length and hit below the knees with a slit in the back. Angus had picked it out from my wardrobe. I was surprised at how many cocktail dresses were in it, and wondered how often I would be expected to dress up for some form of event or the other.

I had done the simplest makeup I could muster without

looking lazy – a small liquid eyeliner wing with mascara and a red lip to match the dress.

The quarters were magnificent. The ceilings were high as we entered into a wide hallway. A sideboard with flowers lined the walls and large, stately art hung decoratively above it. The lighting was dim and intimate, but I couldn't help but find it slightly threatening and ominous.

"Your heart rate is really high, *mo leannan*." The gaelic term flitted over my ears lightly. He'd used that a couple of times before and I still had no idea what it meant, but I was too scared to ask given the situation, so I just let it linger in the air, dissipating like cigarette smoke.

I looked up at his face, trying to extend my breath and allow my heart rate to slow.

"Good," Angus murmured. "Keep doing that."

I nodded, and we continued walking further into the quarters, down a corridor which seemed to split off at the end – one part leading to the left and the other to the right. We took the left turn and entered an open plan dining room and living area. Off this room appeared to be further rooms. It almost appeared endless. We stayed put though, as the dining room was full of our fellow guests.

Garrett sat on one of the lavish sofas, his hair as slick as ever, eyes sharp like an owl. Sophie stood next to him, her eyes wide, and she locked hers with mine for a single second, before dropping them to the floor modestly.

A vampire who appeared older than Garrett also sat on the sofa, his body into the corner nook near the arm, his upper limb draped over the back of the couch and his left knee bent, ankle resting on his right knee. He had an air of boredom on his face, and his eyes seemed ever so slightly glazed over, as if he was unable to find anything in the room to grab his attention.

"Garrett," Angus nodded. "Fraser."

"Prince," Garrett sneered, his face becoming almost reptilian in nature. "So gentlemanly, the way you support your donor's arm." Garrett nodded to our linked forearms, and I did everything in my power to resist pulling it away.

"Nothing wrong with showing a little courtesy, Garrett." Angus almost snarled. "Perhaps if you let your donor sit down for once, she might like you a little more."

"I don't have to be nice to her to get her to like me, Prince." Garrett chuckled.

"Hmmm…" This was Fraser. "Didn't know you were into BDSM, Garrett."

Garrett's face paled – if that were even possible – and his eyes widened to their utmost width. "Don't be so ridiculous, Fraser!"

"I didn't know Fraser even knew what BDSM was." The king slunk into the open room, his beautiful donor behind him. "Son, glad you could make it," he smiled, but his eyes remained vigilant and untrusting.

"I didn't think I had a choice," Angus replied and I gently squeezed his arm.

Easy…

"Ahhh, Son! You always have a choice in my realm." The king replied, arms open in a giving gesture.

"Of course, Father," Angus nodded, bowing his head slightly. "A slip of the tongue."

"You must, of course, sit!" the king announced. "We have only a few more to arrive. Baron and his donor are not long away and, of course, Anthony. Be comfortable while you wait for them."

Angus directed me towards a love seat and when we sat, he continued to keep his arm linked with mine.

"I thought you weren't happy with your donor," Garrett probed. "Seems you are rather cosy tonight, no?"

I winced, but again resisted the urge to release Angus's arm. A compelled donor wouldn't do that.

"Happy is a strong word," Angus muttered. "To say I am not happy seems realistic considering the circumstances of our living situation, would you not agree?"

I flinched internally. What was Angus doing?! This almost seemed like…treason. Him voicing his distaste with the Warren didn't seem smart on the best of days, let alone at a dinner hosted by the king of the Warren – the god damn founder!

"I would not agree, Prince," Garrett replied, firm. "Is the Warren not good enough for you?"

"Oh, come on now," Fraser said, languidly. "Don't be putting words into the prince's mouth. You're like a wee dog snapping at his heels tonight. Leave him alone and haud yer wheesht." Fraser butted in, his eyes slightly more animated. "I couldnae care less about how Angus over here feels about his donor. He's given me the first thing to look forward to in decades. Good on him, I say."

"Your slang is unbecoming, Fraser," Garrett said, lip curling up into a sneer.

"Your entire personality is unbecoming, Garrett."

Angus huffed, chuckling at the comment. It was obvious that the vampire was not his favourite.

It was then that Anthony and his donor entered. He locked with my eyes first, smirking in that way that he did, before addressing the room.

"Gentlemen, an honour to see you all again. This is my donor, Lisa." He gestured towards the woman next to him. They did not touch.

I briefly remembered her from the ball. She was beautiful in every way that I was plain. It became incomprehensible to me that this was what he *wanted*, and not just something he was forced to do.

"Your donor is bonny," Garrett said, bluntly. "More so than that one." He nodded to me.

I didn't like Garrett. In fact, he was one of my least favourite vampires in the Warren, second to Baron, and yet, his comment on my lack of beauty struck me right in the chest. It annoyed me that I was wired that way – that I wanted to be desired, even if the desire wasn't even remotely reciprocated.

Stupid, shitty upbringing.

"Yours is also bonny. Although she'd look better if she were comfortable." Another comment about Sophie standing, and another brush off by Garrett.

"She's fine," he snapped. Sophie twitched.

Baron and Freyja were next to enter the room. Freyja was dressed in a skin-tight bodycon dress with a deep v at the front. It was black. She looked uncomfortable in it, but her eyes remained resilient, her lips tightly pressed into a thin line.

Anthony turned to look at her, and his eyebrows raised slightly. It was a subtle change in his facial expression, but I noted it with interest.

"Ahhh," Fraser rose from his feet. "Baron, you have brought the donor which has caused all this fuss. Perhaps it is *her* I have to thank." He walked over to her, and in a motion I was more than familiar with, he leaned into her neck and kissed her on each side. She didn't flinch and her eyes remained forward facing. I thought I caught them, but then she blinked once, twice, and I knew that she wasn't looking at me at all – she was outside her body, like she most likely had to be with Baron.

"Yes. Beyond me, I have to say," Baron started. "But who am I to judge the preferences of a prince?"

"Indeed," Angus muttered. "Baron, good to see you again," he added, more clearly this time.

"She's got a lovely colour to her hair." Anthony stated, looking at Freyja again. "I can see what the prince sees in her."

"Ha, but nothing behind the eyes!" barked Garrett.

"I'm sure that has absolutely nothing to do with the donor, and everything to do with the master. Isn't that right, Baron?" Angus baited, and Baron stiffened slightly, taking on a degree of defensiveness.

"Some things cannot be overcome by compulsion, my lord."

"Of course not, Baron," Angus nodded, but there was a tightness to his facial features which suggested he wanted to say more about it.

I watched the vampires bicker and felt oddly nostalgic. It was like watching my parents fight in the passive aggressive way that they used to. It was all very...human.

The king re-entered the room and clapped his hands together, grabbing the attention of his guests.

"Everyone is here, finally. Come over to the dining table. I have a lovely bottle of 2004 AB negative waiting, and believe me when I say, she's been preserved beautifully."

I schooled my features, trying not to react to the mention of someone's blood that had been decantated into a bottle, spoken as if it were a bottle of wine. There was a slight hum as the people in the room made their way to the table. It was set in an old fashion manner, with large candlestick holders and foliage in the centre. To me, it just looked like a fire hazard, but to a more trained eye it was probably beautiful. Shame that I didn't have an artistic bone in my body.

There were name cards at each seat. The king was located at the head of the table, with Angus to his right and his donor to his left. I sat in my seat, on the right of Angus. Anthony sat next to me, his donor next to him and Fraser was at the end – he hadn't brought his donor with him, stating she was resting. I found that to be rather kind of him, and I hoped that he meant what he said, and wasn't trying to cover something up.

Opposite me sat Baron, and next to him was Freyja, who was facing towards Anthony. Garrett sat next and finally Sophie.

An unknown human entered the room, dressed in a black and white serving suit. He began to pour out a liquid into the glasses of the vampires – this must have been the 2004 AB negative the king had raved about. The donors were all given water.

How generous.

"To our immortality!" the king announced, raising his goblet with a flourish. "May it always be!"

"Our immortality." The remaining vampires joined in the toast. All donors remained stock-still.

I reached out for my glass, taking a tentative sip of the water within it. I watched as Sophie then did the same, then Freyja, and relaxed my shoulders. I tried to channel some positive thoughts and strength to my friends. *Come on girls, let's get this shit over and done with.*

Some bread was placed on the plates in front of the donors, and we each took turns with the butter, politely handing it around the table, while the vampires got down to business.

"So, the donor auction. Does everyone understand the premise?" The king asked, opening up the conversation.

"Your Majesty, I have to say I'm a little unfamiliar with the concept," Baron admitted.

"Yes, yes, Baron you are the odd one out, I apologise." The king flapped his hand in the air. "The donor auction is how we are to address my son's desire to have your donor. We shall invite any vampire – of any gender – who desires to place their donor into the auction, to do so. That donor is then fair game to the other clan members who also wish to put their donor up. We then auction the donors to the highest bidder."

"What's the currency?"

"Rank," replied the king.

"Rank?" asked Anthony.

"Yes. All clan members who wish to have a new donor from this scheme will be ranked by the council and higher ranks will have more play. For example, I of course, as king, have the highest rank and if I ever wanted to swap my donor, I would win the auction and a lower rank clan member would lose against me. The next rank is indeed by beloved son," Angus stiffened next to me at the word 'beloved', "and then so on and so on."

"So, no one can beat Angus's desire to have my donor?" Baron inquired.

"No. But you knew that, Baron," the king said flippantly.

"And what will determine one's rank?" Anthony asked, his elbows on the table, leaning forward in interest.

"For the council to worry about, Anthony. Don't trouble your wee head about it. And besides, we have that arrangement I so generously proposed, so no need for you to concern yourself."

Anthony sat back defeated, and nodded. What arrangement? And why did Anthony look less than happy about it?

"Surely it should be me that is ranked next?" Garrett said, frowning. "After the prince, of course."

"Most likely, Garrett," the king admitted. "Does this

change your stance on the idea?"

Garrett shrugged. "Perhaps. My donor is hardly the sunniest, no matter what I do with her!" he huffed, taking a slug from his goblet and wiping his mouth crudely. My stomach flipped.

"It might be good for you to mix it up a wee bit. Nothing worse than a sunless donor. But that's only if you think you're up to it, Garrett," Angus said, bluntness cutting his words. "I know you're normally a stickler for the rules. But that just seems a little... rigid. I've heard rigidity is bad for the soul – even a damned one. To be regal is better, surely. And there is something quite regal at being considered the third ranked member of the clan, behind only a king and a prince! Be regal, not rigid, Garrett."

Angus was playing right into Garrett's weak spot, I could tell. I watched as he processed the words – his eyes narrowing, and his lips twisting as if he had just tasted something foul.

And then he took a massive bite out of the bait.

"I am *not* rigid. And I never said I didn't like the idea." Fraser scoffed at that. "I was just trying to offer another perspective."

"My father hates people who play devil's advocate. You know that, Garrett." Angus said, snarling slightly with his face.

"Which is why I'm putting my donor into the auction," Garrett announced, determinedness in his eyes.

Sophie's eyes widened, but this time it was not out of fear. In fact, Sophie looked almost... hopeful.

"Oh, now that is fantastic Garrett!" the king exclaimed, his eyes unusually bright, rather than icy. Garrett sparkled in the light of the praise, like a flower in the sunshine.

But the question was, who would get Sophie?

CHAPTER 21

Revelations

Ivy

It was the evening before the donor auction.

Angus had summoned to his quarters all of those 'in the know'. This included: Angus, me, Sophie, Freyja, Anthony, Sorcha and also Sorcha's partner, Callum.

Callum was as tall as Sorcha, if not an inch taller, but didn't quite meet the height of Anthony or Angus. He was broad but not obviously so, with dark hair and dark skin. His eyes were light, and they contrasted his skin in such an abrupt way that it had made me do a double take. They were keen eyes. The kind of eyes that seemed to see everything, and his manner was one of quiet observation. He was all watching, no talking – the complete opposite of Sorcha, I thought. But as the old proverb stated: opposites attract.

He stood next to his partner, or perhaps just slightly behind her, his right shoulder butting against the back of Sorcha's left, and his hand was open next to her side, as if we were always in anticipation of her touch. Occasionally, he would glance over at the red-haired vampire and his lips would twitch ever so slightly. When she smiled, he smiled too, almost absentmindedly.

They were, in my opinion, a subtle and yet delightful couple to watch. The type of couple which made you yearn for such a connection – a connection so innate. Because really, that's all we ever really want – a connection. Someone who knows you, *all* of you, and thinks, *'yes, this person is for me'*. Someone to be in *awe* of you. Someone to *choose* you. Someone to *crave* you. But not just crave you physically – someone to crave your soul.

I wondered if anyone else in the room felt their energy. And I wondered if it made them feel as empty as I felt at that moment.

"Callum, welcome." Angus stood forward, shaking the vampire's hand.

That was the first time I'd ever seen Angus do that. Angus never shook anyone's hand. He clearly respected the man in front of him.

"Pleasure, Angus." *First name basis with the prince? Definitely some history with these two.*

"I hear that Sorcha has gotten you up to speed?"

"Aye," Callum nodded, cowering from the attention.

"You've certainly taken the news better than me, pal," Anthony injected. "My heid was gone."

Callum shrugged.

"Angus, why don't you just tell us why we're here?" Sorcha asked.

"I thought we could all do with a debrief before tomorrow."

There were nods and muttered sounds of agreement.

Angus went through the pairings for the auction and explained that the king had said he would ensure that Angus was given Freyja, and I was given to Anthony. That gave me a sense of reassurance but also some sort of dread that I couldn't place.

"Who's going to pair up with Sophie?" Freyja asked.

Now, this was the question I wanted answers to.

The room fell a little silent, and everyone's eyes darted around, not really staying in one place long enough to allow any form of eye contact. Well, apart from Callum.

"I have an idea," he said. When no one replied, he

continued. "I have a friend. He's called James."

"Christ, another vamp?!" Freyja exclaimed. When everyone turned to look at her, she looked embarrassed, warmth flowing into her face. "Sorry," she muttered.

Anthony chuckled.

"He *is* a vampire," Callum nodded. "But he's got a very kind heart. I trust him inexplicably. And his donor is old and tired – he's due another. It wouldn't draw attention, which is what we all need, isn't it?"

People nodded.

"Do we have to tell him that I can't be compelled?" Sophie asked.

"That's up to you." Callum spoke to her like she was a small animal. "I believe James has the discretion to be told, but I understand your reservations. Trusting vampires has never come innately to humans."

"Perhaps that's because we are your food," Sophie deadpanned. "Trust of cheetahs hasn't come naturally to the gazelles, either. It's called self-preservation."

"You're right. Which is why it is up to you. James isn't big on the intimate parts of donor relationships, and he's pretty well versed on consent," Callum replied informatively.

Freyja snorted. "Rarity in the male population," she muttered under her breath.

"How about we say that you don't have to tell him, Sophie. As you get to know him, maybe you could get there?" I said.

She nodded. "Okay."

"So, are we settled with everything?" I asked.

"Seems like it," Sorcha nodded.

"Well then, you're all free to go," Angus announced, turning his back and walking towards his desk.

He seemed to use that desk as some sort of safe space – as if being there meant he couldn't be touched by anything negative.

The combination of vampires and humans began to file out of the door. Anthony was the last to cross the threshold, but before he did, he turned.

"May I speak with your donor, Prince?" he asked, a smirk playing on his lips once more. "In private."

Angus stiffened marginally. "Up to her, *Ant*."

Anthony bristled at the nickname, then turned to me. "Miss Ivy?"

I was conflicted. One part of me was thrilled at the prospect of being in the company of the charm that Anthony always seemed to exude. The other part of me was untrusting.

The thrill won.

Great restraint, girl.

"Okay," I said, giving my permission.

Anthony beamed. "We won't be long, Prince. I'll bring her back. Unless she doesn't want me to." He winked, then beckoned me towards him, and I left out the door that the others had done just moments before.

When I was sure we would be out of Angus's ear shot, I spoke.

"Where are we going?"

"To *my* quarters," he announced. "I thought we could have a change of scenery."

We walked beside each other in comfortable silence. His arms swung softly, disrupting the air around us. He stopped outside a large door not dissimilar to the one that opened into Angus's quarters. He used his key to open the door, and the flicked a switch to his left.

His room was very different to Angus's. Where Angus's was regimented, minimalistic and tidy, Anthony's was rather chaotic. Not messy by any means, just more... busy. His walls weren't walls – they were bookshelves; each one filled with books of all sizes. They all looked well loved. His floor was hard wood but in the centre was a large fluffy rug the colour of milky coffee. His bed was made with crisp white sheets with blue and forest green throw pillows. It was cosy. And it was nothing like what I expected it to be.

"You seem surprised," Anthony said, his face playful.

"I am," I admitted.

"I'm mysterious, aren't I?" he said, proudly.

"Weirdly... yes."

"I love to see your face like this, all baffled. It's cute," he chuckled.

"Why did you bring me here?"

"Change of scenery," he retorted.

"And the real reason?"

"You got me." He smiled, his mouth crooked. "I wanted to speak to you about some things that have been playing on my mind."

I raised my eyebrows as if to say, *'let's have it then.'*

"When I'm your master–" He stopped abruptly to swallow. "What can I do with you?" he asked, looking almost timid. This was new for Anthony.

"I don't understand," I replied.

"How about I just tell you the things I *want* to do, and you can tell me if I'm allowed to?"

I nodded, my mouth too dry to reply. I was standing with my back to the door, and he was standing about five feet away, facing me, with his hands in his pockets.

"I want to bite you, obviously. I want to touch you in whatever way I need to in order to hear you catch your breath in that amazing way that you do. I want to press my lips to yours and slide my tongue in between them so that it touches yours as well. I want that kiss to be so good that you moan, and I want that moan to be felt in my mouth. I want to pick you up off the floor and wrap your legs around my waist so that your breasts are in my eye line. I want to kiss them. I want to have sex with you. I just want *you*. *You*, to *me*, are just divinely and inspiringly perfect."

My breath hitched.

He chuckled. "Maybe I don't even need to touch you to hear that sound after all. But that doesn't mean I don't want to." He was only a foot or so away from me now. I hadn't moved. "Say something," he whispered, his cool breath brushing against my overheated skin.

I tried to say something. I tried with everything I had, but I couldn't. Nothing was arising in my brain which was worthy of a response – not after *that.*

I had a sudden wash of emotion that I couldn't place. Here was a man – a *beautiful, charming, sexy* man – telling me all the dirty, unspeakable things he wanted to do to me, as well as also managing to say something entirely sweet, and instead of it invoking heat – that heat between your thighs and in your chest – it invoked close to nothing.

In fact, it *upset* me.

It upset me because the other sexy man in my life couldn't conjure up something even nearly as romantic or emotional. He couldn't tell me that he wanted to kiss me, because he had had many opportunities to do so, and had only ever done so once. And that certainly couldn't count. He couldn't tell me I was perfect, because he genuinely didn't think I was. It was just feeding and sex. That was all it was. And that really hurt. That hurt entirely.

Anthony was still waiting, his eyes wide and lazy at the same time.

"I'm sorry," I whispered. "I have to go."

I turned abruptly, opened the door and ran down the hall as fast as I could until the burning in my chest became normal, and it all just didn't hurt as much anymore.

◆ ◆ ◆

Angus was pacing the room when I returned.

I had gone to the courtyard to calm down, tears running down my face like a fresh-water stream, unable to face anyone. It seemed that after months of my body not shedding a tear, it was now ready to cry at the drop of the hat. Apparently, I had broken the seal on crying.

Great.

"Where have you been?!" Angus's face was filled with anger, but there was something else there as well which I couldn't quite place – it was in the set of his eyes and the clench of jaw. Was it... worry?

"Anthony took me to his room and–"

"He *WHAT?!*" He stopped still, his body shaking with something, and then stomped his way towards me. It was the first time I'd ever seen him move in a ungraceful way, and it unsettled me.

He reached me before I really even had time to react,

and cupped my face in his cool hands. He tilted it this way and that, inspecting me for what I assumed would be bite marks. His frantic eyes then settled on my eyes, and his softened slightly, before hardening up again.

"Have you been *crying?*" he asked, shocked. "Did he do something that you didn't like? I'm going to *kill* that fucking arrogant prick."

"I wasn't crying because of Anthony. Not really." I explained.

"Then why?" he asked, his face scrunched in confusion.

"Because of *you*." I pushed my way out of his hands, wanting the space away from him, and walked over to the other side of the room.

"Me?" he asked, shocked. "What in the hell have I done? I'm not the one walking out of here with another option!"

"That's not what *I* was doing!" I defended. "He *asked* me for a chat, so I went for a chat. And *nothing happened*." I stopped, and then checked myself, raising a finger. "Actually, even if anything *had* happened, you have no fucking right to be angry about it. You and me – we aren't together."

Angus came up short, eyes wide. He looked almost… *hurt*. No, that couldn't be right. This was just him not having control, and not being used to it.

"We aren't. But we sleep together," he said, bluntly.

"We haven't actually slept together, Angus," I corrected.

"Oh, fucking hell! Technicalities, Ivy." He threw his hands up in frustration. "What? I've got to put my dick in you to make this something, have I?"

"That's grotesque and entirely problematic!" I exclaimed, eyes wide in horror.

"Then what am I missing here, Brunette?!"

"That we aren't a couple. That you can't be angry if I had done something with Anthony. Not that I did, but it's the principle."

"Fine. But this doesn't explain why in some way I've managed to make you cry."

Admitting to Angus that he made me cry because he didn't love me, or show me affection, seemed pathetic. And yet, I thought that I owed it to myself to be honest. This was for sixteen-year-old me.

"You're just hot and cold," I admitted. "Sometimes you show me affection, and then immediately after you yell or dismiss me. You get incredibly jealous at the thought of me being with someone else, and yet when you have me, you don't treat me as if you are bothered in the slightest. You say you want to feed off me, but that's *all* you want to do. The thing is, you want donor Ivy, not human Ivy. You don't actually want *me*."

Angus listened shrewdly, and when I was finished, gave himself a moment before speaking. "And that upsets you?"

"Yes," I nodded.

"And that's what you really think?"

"You've never told me or shown anything that would suggest you felt differently."

"Are you blind?" he asked, firmly. My mouth fell open, shocked at his sternness. "I didn't feed off you *once,* not until you gave me permission, even though it *killed* me not to. I didn't report you when I found out you couldn't be compelled. I've let you have your free will, despite how much it can irritate me sometimes. I've tried to protect your friends, not because they are any consequence to me, but because they are of consequence to *you*. I've let Anthony flirt with you right underneath my nose, and I've watched you *enjoy it* – God how that hurt – without refusing you! I've tried to respect your body, avoiding any sexual cravings I have unless I need to feed. I've even held back from having sex with you. Do you think that's because I don't *want* to put my dick in you?! Because I can assure you that I certainly *do*. I've even fucking watched you sleep, for God's sake!"

He had started pacing again, and I watched, mute.

"All of that – all those things that go against everything that I am – I have done because I am entirely in love with you." He stopped then, his body turning to face mine, still across the other side of the room. "Can't you see what you are doing to me? I'm hot and cold because this is completely novel to me. I'm not used to caring about someone who is so vulnerable. My entire being wants to ban you from leaving this room so I know that you are safe. But imagine! Imagine if I ever asked such a thing of you! How you would react! You're so set on having your freedom that I couldn't even possibly ask that of you. You would be miserable. And if it were me that had caused that misery, I couldn't live with myself. And you would hate me, and it would mean I wouldn't be able to get at you. The *real you.* And that's all I ever really wanted. All I've ever wanted is to get *you.*

"You are entirely frustrating and exacerbating, and yet charming and intriguing in your mannerisms. Like the way you blow stray hairs out of your face because you don't have the energy to brush them away, or when you bite your lip when you are nervous, or frustrated, or trying to come up with an answer to something which puzzles you. You frown *constantly* – always appearing dissatisfied with people's answers – and somehow, you have made me see a complete and amazing beauty within brunette hair. Hair that I used to see as rather plain and shadowed, now holds a completely different image in my mind. For years, spun gold is all I have ever wanted. But no! Now I must have the shine of your hair running through my fingers! Who knew dark hair reflected so much light?! Who knew it could also be so like the sun, or perhaps is it the moon which it so replicates? Whichever, I do not care, because I am a slave to it.

"I am in awe of your physical beauty. I want to trace your face with my fingers, to remember it forever. If I were a painter, I would use your face as a muse. It's sickening, actually, how infected my brain has become with you – how it responds to your presence, to your laugh or even simply to your breath.

"Your eyes see everything, and from the first moment they had touched mine, I was almost certain you had seen straight into my soul – past the thick muscles, the flexible cartilage and the brittle bone; past the heart, past all that is physical about me. And perhaps, even as early as that moment, I knew you were mine, even if I could not be yours.

"You have consumed my entire existence for the last six months. Your smell, your face, your facial expressions – all of it. If I had let myself do and say all that I had wanted, I would have been afraid that I would scare you away. Humans do not feel as strongly as vampires do, and I wanted to respect that and give you time. Because I *do* respect you, even if you think I do not. I respect your mind, and I respect your body. I respect everything you are. I would do anything for you. I would sacrifice my own happiness for yours. It is something I have been doing for weeks now.

"But," he said, moving a little closer towards me, "if nothing I have said in the last few minutes even mildly resonates with the feelings of your own heart, then I am sorry, for I am perfectly aware that I am not holding anything back and I am likely to be coming across entirely obsessed. But I am afraid that is what I am – I am obsessed with you, body and soul."

I didn't think I had ever heard anyone speak for that long in my entire life, especially about me, and I found myself feeling lightheaded. Without saying a word, I lowered myself to the floor, and placed my head in between my knees, breathing deeply in and out through my nose.

"Ivy?" Angus asked tentatively. "Are you okay?"

I nodded limply. "Yes, I just feel a little faint."

"Have you eaten today?"

"Yes, I've eaten. I'm just a little…overwhelmed," I admitted, still refusing to look at him.

He was crouched next to me now, his cool hand resting on my back and running soothing up and down it.

"I'm sorry. That must have been… a lot, *mo leannan*," he muttered. *That phrase* again.

"What does that mean?" I asked.

"What?"

I repeated the gaelic term he had used before back to him, and when he didn't instantly reply, I lifted my head up out from between my knees and looked at him. He appeared slightly embarrassed.

He cleared his throat. "It means *my sweetheart*, or *my love*."

My mind flitted back to the first time I had heard him say it. It had been just before he had tasted my blood for the first time, when I had been sitting on the sink and he was trying to convince me not to let him taste it.

"You called me that for the first time only a few days after the ball," I said, frowning. That had been at least three months ago.

He reached up and brushed his fingertip gently over the flesh between my eyebrows, and I released the tension there.

"I think I loved you then, you know," he admitted, sitting next to me on the floor, both our backs resting against the wall, faces looking out into the room. "Watching you dance with Anthony was horrible. His hands were all over your skin and you kept blushing. I wanted to be the one to make you do that. The *only* one. And then you were dancing with me and *my* hands were able to explore you. And you just looked simply delightful. And then you were about to blow your breath in my face, and I had to stop you because I knew if you did it, I would have needed to feed on you. I would have dragged you back to our room and bitten you so hard. And I was so angry with myself that I felt that way – that my desires were so close to putting you in danger – because I realised that I really couldn't put you in danger. You were too important."

"But you were all snappy and angry with me after that!" I exclaimed, shocked at all the revelations which were coming my way.

"It wasn't because I was annoyed at you. I was annoyed at myself. Like I told you, something had changed."

"This is crazy," I said finally, head dropping back to gently rest against the wall.

"Yeah. It is," he nodded.

I turned to face him, us both still sitting on the floor.

"You love me?" I asked.

"Yes, Ivy. I love you."

Our eyes were locked, and it was as if we were in some

sort of void. I was completely tunnel visioned. All I could see was him. And then my face spread into the biggest smile I think I had ever given. "I love you, too," I said proudly.

He smiled back, eyes glittering. "I think I better kiss you then, before your smile splits your face in two and you become horrible to look at."

I laughed, but it wasn't able to fully erupt, because his lips were on mine.

He locked his hands around my head, unrelenting, and pursued me like a predator, but I didn't mind. This version of a predator was more than welcome. His tongue snaked out, opening up my lips, and when he could, he slipped it entirely into my mouth, his hands lightly running down the sides of my neck, tickling me slightly. I felt the hairs on my skin stand to attention, demanding more.

His tongue drew back, and his mouth began to give and take from me what they wanted from mine. Occasionally, his tongue would delve back in, and he even nibbled a little on my bottom lip, but was gentle enough not to draw blood.

It dawned on me that I was only a little disappointed by that fact.

His hands travelled down my body and settled on my waist before lifting me up off the floor and into his lap, our lips not separating once. Instinctively, I unravelled my legs and wrapped them around his waist, settling myself on his thighs. He drew in a deep breath and then deepened the kiss even further, really exploring my mouth with his wet tongue. I moaned directly into him, and he drew back slightly for air I knew he didn't need.

"Jesus christ..." he muttered, before attaching back to my mouth again. "The sounds you make make me so hard, Ivy."

I threaded my hands into his hair, and tugged slightly, pulling his mouth up closer to mine. He growled, deep in his throat, his hands now travelling up towards my breasts. He took off my top, and I was glad how fast he was able to do it, because I didn't like when our mouths weren't together. He palmed my breasts over the bralette I wore and made satisfied groans as he did so, muttering about how great I felt under his touch. I rocked on his lap, needing the friction between my thighs, feeling his erection underneath me.

"God, why do you even feel so fucking good between all these layers, Brunette? You're gonna be the death of me."

"Stop complaining," I grumbled, suckling on his neck.

"What are you doing?" he breathed, head lolling back. He looked so vulnerable like this, and it thrilled me knowing how it was because of me and how I was making him feel.

"Kissing your neck," I murmured between each nip on his flesh.

"Fuck," he hummed. The vibrations tickled my lips, making them tingle. "I–, I love it when you use teeth. No one has ever done that to me before…it's usually my job. Keep going."

I continued, watching him as I pursued his neck with my mouth, his eyes closed and mouth open, breathing heavily despite his lack of need for air. He looked completely human all of a sudden.

And then his fangs dropped down.

His hands tightened around my hips, before travelling lower to my arse.

"This arse is the most distracting thing I've ever seen. It should be illegal," he said smiling at me, eyes drowsy. He then lifted me up before flipping me slightly so I was on my back on the floor, and he was hovering on top of me. He stopped moving for a moment, and stared at my face, his eyes tracing every feature. "I think you are beautiful," he whispered.

I blushed.

He laughed, giving me a full show of his elongated canines. "I will forever chase this," he said, touching my skin. "I'll chase the feeling I get whenever I make you blush. I'll chase it for my entire immortal existence." And then he was kissing me again, passionately and yet delicately.

But he didn't stay delicate for long.

"I don't think I can take this much longer. Please tell me I can rip all your clothes off now," he said, his voice gravelly as he dragged his tongue up the collum of my throat.

I smirked up at him. "You can rip them off."

"Thank fuck," he growled. His hands grabbed the middle of my bralette and tugged hard, before going to my leggings and doing the same.

His face was animalistic and set at the task, and with each bit of skin that he revealed, he became more determined, his face taking on more of the vampire traits that I still wasn't used to seeing. His eyes darkened, and his skin around them became bruised looking. The veins in his neck rippled.

"God, I'd worship this body forever if you'd let me." He slunk down my body and grabbed my knickers in his teeth, his eyes meeting mine, a smirk playing around his mouth, and then his head jerked fast and hard, and the elastic snapped, exposing me entirely. I bent my legs, opening them slightly to allow better access.

"Good girl," he murmured against me, before running his tongue all the way up my apex. I cried out, and I could feel his smile. "You're so wet. My dick's gonna fit inside you perfectly, I know it. You're going to take me so fucking well."

He continued his pursuit of me, his tongue being relentless, and I came in a massive wave, my body shaking with the intensity. I squeezed my eyes shut, trying to absorb the sensation, and when I opened them again, Angus's face was hovering over mine, a sly, smug mask sitting there.

"You're welcome," he said, kissing me chastely on the lips.

I smiled, this time my eyes showing a playful edge. "My turn."

His eyebrows rose upwards. "I'm all yours, *mo leannan*."

I ordered him to stand up against the wall and he did so without questioning me, but I could tell he wasn't used to taking orders. I knelt in front of him, my knee burning slightly against the carpet, but I ignored it, my mind on other, more pleasurable things. I demanded him to strip, and he chuckled before taking off his clothes, piece by piece. I looked at his erection in awe. He was large, but not intimidatingly so. I leaned forward, and ran my tongue over the tip, tasting him. I watched in my periphery as his hands clenched into fists, a sharp hiss escaping his teeth.

"Fuuuucckkkk." I heard his head hit the wall, like he'd flung it back in pleasure.

I opened my mouth and took him in entirely, right to the hilt. Another bang made me jolt, and when I opened my eyes, I saw a slight indentation in the wall next to Angus's fist.

I smiled around his dick.

I took him over and over, and he made sounds like I'd never heard. Not loud sounds, but enthusiastic none the less. It only spurred me on more.

At one point, he placed my head in his hands and pulled my mouth away from him. I looked up at him in confusion.

"Stop frowning, Brunette," he chuckled. "I'm stopping you because I want to get inside you, and that won't happen if you keep doing that."

He bent down to lift me and watched my face as I winced slightly. My knees hurt.

"My poor Brunette. She works so hard. On her knees for me and everything," he chuckled. "Let's make you feel good."

He sunk me into the mattress, pushing my legs open and then angled towards my opening, before pushing in an inch or so.

I squirmed. "Keep going," I said, pleadingly. He nodded, pushing himself all the way. I winced again, but it was pleasurable more than painful, and I knew I'd get used to it.

"How you doing, *mo lennan*? Please say you're okay because I'm dying to move inside you." He dipped his head to my neck and breathed in deeply. "I've been waiting to fuck you for what feels like a fucking eternity."

"Please," I moaned.

"You want me to move?" he asked, his face alight with something.

I nodded, and he began to slide out, thrusting slowly at first, before increasing his pace. His muscles rippled, and I watched his body work over me with intent interest.

He put me into positions, moving me this way and that, until we had both come vocally.

He slipped out of me and rolled onto his back.

"Fucking hell, that was religious," he announced.

"Yeah," I agreed, breathless, not able to conjure up anything more articulate.

He smiled over at me, and as I looked at his teeth, I realised he hadn't bit me once, and my heart soared like a bird into the sky.

CHAPTER 22

Disguised Goodbyes

Ivy

"I just don't understand why he would do it," Heather said, her chin dipped towards her chest and her face sad.

We were at breakfast on the morning of the donor auction, and she had just told us that her master had put her forward for it. Needless to say, she was heartbreakingly devastated.

Sass, who was feeling much better since she had had her 'head cold', had eyes big in her face, and was looking at her friend with sadness. "Maybe he's just scared of his feelings for you, and needs a break," she reassured.

I felt my face scrunch up. Why did girls always do this? Spin ridiculous lies which are entirely implausible to soften blows. All it ever did was provide false hope. I could never understand it. I mean, I wasn't an advocate for being blunt and harsh, but I also wasn't keen on the idea of outright lying – it didn't seem fair.

"Or maybe," I added, "your feelings towards him were just more than the feelings he was able to give you back. I mean, he's a vampire after all. What can we expect from them, really?"

Heather's puffy eyes reached mine. "No, I think Sass is right. It's because his feelings are too strong, surely." She was nodding to herself. "Yes, that's what it is."

I gave a stern look to Sass, who grimaced at me and shrugged, as if to say, '*sorry, I didn't know what else to say.*' I hoped my face in return said, '*perhaps* anything *else?!*'

"Well, whatever the reason is, what's done is done, H," Andy said, mouth full of hash brown.

Nice, I mouthed at him, rolling my eyes in disappointment.

"What?!" he exclaimed. "Look at the bright side, Blondey! You're gonna snag yourself a new hottie, I can feel it. Look at you for Christ's sake! You're a snack!"

"Yeah!" said Sophie, a little too enthusiastically, considering she hadn't actually said anything since we had sat down.

Sass smiled at her, giggling slightly.

"I don't want just anybody," she replied, sadly. "I want Alistair."

God, why did all Scottish men have names beginning with 'A'?

"I bet you they make this a yearly thing," Duke stated, waving his spoon. "He may want you back then, Heather."

"That's a year away!" she wailed, throwing her head into her hands.

"Esssh," Andy said, wincing at Heather's high-pitched tone.

The breakfast continued much the same, with us trying to bring Heather back from the edge, and being unsuccessful. It was as if her mind just couldn't reason.

Sophie remained rather quiet, but she did chat a little with Sass, and they always seemed to be laughing at something or other, so I let them be. It was nice to see Sophie a little more comfortable. I had even heard her make some witty, sarcastic comments, and Sass had lapped them up.

Duke and Andy were very much engrossed in their breakfasts, pretty chuffed that neither of their mistresses/ masters had put them up for auction. Thankfully, they were both smart enough not to rub it in Heather's face. Sass had also been spared from the auction, although she didn't seem bothered either way.

I tried to reassure Heather – after all, me and Sophie would be there on the stage too – but nothing seemed to give her any comfort.

We all left the canteen, saying goodbye to each other as we did.

"Heather is going to have a breakdown," Sophie said when it was just me and her walking alone in the corridor.

"You think?" I asked, worry etched on my face.

"I mean, she's already knee deep into one, friend, so I'd say she's plus plus likely to continue to have said breakdown."

"Plus plus?"

"It's key to help you understand how likely it is."

"Of course," I nodded, smiling at her weirdness.

"How are you feeling about it?" she asked.

I turned to her slightly as we walked. "Honestly?"

"It's the best policy," she said, nodding.

"Shitting it to be honest, friend."

"Yeah, me too."

We looked at each other a little longer, and then I reached forward, grabbing her hands in mine and squeezing them slightly. "We'll do great, I know it."

"Yeah, of course we will," she said, smiling meekly. "And if we don't, it doesn't really matter, does it? I mean, we'll probably be killed, but it'd be a good story, wouldn't it?"

"Yeah," I nodded, smiling slightly. "The best."

◆ ◆ ◆

As the time for the auction approached, even Angus was showing signs of nerves. I watched him as he stood in front of the vanity in our bathroom, tidying up his stubble, no shirt on. It fascinated me that his hair still grew, and I asked him about it.

"There is a misconception that vampires are dead," he stated, sliding the razor under his neck. "We aren't. If we were, we physically wouldn't be able to be destroyed. But we can be, although it's not an easy feat." He smirked, before continuing. "Think of us like an old oak tree. We can live forever, generally unchanging, as long as we are provided with what we need to survive. For the oak tree, it is sunlight, water, and obviously safety – meaning as long as it isn't cut down or set alight, it shall live on and on and on. For us, it's blood, and obviously the lack of being harmed."

"Like having your heart ripped out." It wasn't a question.

He stopped his shaving, and instead of looking at me in the mirror, turned to face me directly.

"How did you know that?" he asked.

"Sophie told me. She says it's very surprising what you can learn from people who don't think you can listen."

He nodded, tight lipped. "I imagine she is right, yes." He blinked a couple of times, before going back to what he had been doing before. "Things like my hair still grow – think of them like the leaves of the oak tree."

I nodded. It was a good metaphor, and I had never thought of it quite like that.

"What about going to the toilet and such," I asked, timidly.

He laughed. "Vampire waste is different to human waste because our diet is different. Our body still filters out part of the blood which we cannot use and that is expelled in urine. But it's only urine and it's not as frequent as humans."

"Hmm," I replied. "Where are your scars from?" I asked, after a pause. I had always meant to ask, and for some reason, I had a feeling that I wouldn't be able to ask these sorts of questions soon.

"Battles. Wars and the like."

"What battles and wars?"

"Some battles in the Americas in the seventeen hundreds and then Belgium and the Crimean war in the eighteen hundreds. There were gaps between each time I could join, obviously. The lack of ageing would have made people suspicious, obviously. It's how I know Anthony, actually. We fought together in the eighteen hundreds. We were in the Black Watch."

"But you were a vampire then? Surely your wounds should have healed?"

"Most wounds when they are here and there can be healed easily, obviously. But wounds like these can never be fully healed. The fact that I'm here to tell the tale shows you the magic that is vampire venom. It was able to keep me 'alive', but it wasn't able to keep me unscathed." He shrugged, looking down at his marked body. "Our moto was *'nemo me impune lacessit'*. It's latin for 'No One Provokes Me with Impunity'. Needless to say, I've been tortured a few times. But we fight back, just like a thistle."

There were so many questions I wanted to ask. Who were the Black Watch?

"Couldn't you have just compelled them to stop?"

"It's a little hard to compel when you are injured in such a way and have no access to blood."

"That seems fair." I nodded. "How do you make another vampire?"

"Christ, *mo lennan,* you're asking a lot of questions today."

"I'm in a curious mood."

He chuckled, and I savoured the sound. "You don't say!"

I waited in silence, expectantly.

He shook his head. "It's a little complicated."

"Try me."

"The person has to have vampire blood in their system. And then they have to die. But they can only die in a certain way."

"Like what?" I asked, inching closer to the bathroom door frame, intrigued.

"They have to have enough blood in their system when they die so that the venom in the vampire blood can be spread to all parts of the body. You couldn't give someone vampire blood and then slit their throat and expect them to become a vampire. The venom would just pour out with their blood. That also means a vampire can't be made by draining the human of their blood during feeding."

"Is there anything else?"

"A person cannot have an injury which causes uncontrollable blood loss. So, if someone was injured and there was blood everywhere, you couldn't save them by giving them vampire blood and killing them. As before, the venom would leach out." Angus was frowning, looking off distantly with glassy eyes, as if he were remembering something. He continued without looking at me. "In those cases, if you were totally desperate, you would have to find a way to stop their bleeding before attempting to transition them, like sewing them up in some way."

He shuddered.

"Have you done that?" I asked, cautiously.

He nodded, clearing his throat. "Sorcha."

"I see," I whispered, not wanting to probe much more.

"Best way to ensure success is using a healthy, happy human. Which seems a total waste, doesn't it?"

I shrugged, not wanting to comment.

"Should I help you get ready?" he asked, wiping his face up with his towel, finished with his shave.

I nodded. I had chosen a black silk dress. It seemed appropriate. For some reason I felt like I was going to someone's funeral. It had an open v-neckline with spaghetti straps and a skirt that fell to the floor.

Angus brushed my hair for me, whispering about how much he loved the feel of it between his fingers, the colour as it reflected the light, and the smell as it moved around my face. Occasionally, he would bend down to kiss the spot between my neck and my shoulder, muttering that no matter what happened, he would always love me.

I shut my eyes and just enjoyed everything he was giving me.

I put my hair up into a high ponytail and smoothed makeup over my face.

"Lovely," Angus smiled. "You'll be snapping up all the suitors, I'm sure." He was trying to be light-hearted, but it all just fell a little flat, and we both knew it.

Angus put on his kilt and I helped him with his bow

tie, even though he certainly didn't need the help – his dexterity was a hundred times what mine was – but it felt right, and intimate, and it brought me some comfort and normalcy.

When we were both sure we were ready, he reached his hands up and held my head in them, caressing me. "We can do this. It will all be okay. Before you know it, you'll be back here, in my arms again. But for now, you can just know in your heart that you will always be, to me, the bonniest of brunettes I've ever known."

I nodded, a tear running down my face, and he caught it with a cool fingertip, placing it to his lips, before taking my arm in his, and walking us out to the corridor towards the room where the auction would commence.

CHAPTER 23

To the Highest Bidder

Ivy

I was hustled into a room by some unknown vampires wearing wires, separating me from Angus. They encouraged me to the 'backstage' area.

The room we had been brought to was called the 'boardroom'. I remembered Angus mentioning it at the summer ball, when he had been explaining where the king's throne chair was usually kept.

Gosh, that seemed like ages ago.

Also behind the stage was Sophie, Freyja and Heather as well as some men and other donors. I noticed Freyja was talking to a girl who I recognised as one of the group she associated with. Freyja looked irritated by what the girl was saying to her, and her lips were pursed.

Heather looked miserable, as expected. I walked up to her and gave her arm what I hoped was a reassuring squeeze.

"I can't believe he's actually gone through with it," she cried. "I thought that when I spoke to him after breakfast, he would see what a ridiculous decision this is! But no! He just told me to stop talking about it to him, and after that I just couldn't say another word about it. It was so frustrating!"

"I'm sorry, Heather," I said softly. "You look beautiful, though." And she really did. Her hair was in a lovely, intricate bun, and she wore a long red dress which complimented her figure perfectly.

"You know, I don't even care what I look like," she whispered, as if she were afraid of what she was saying. "If I can't be with Alistair, I don't want to be with anyone." Tears pooled in her eyes.

Freyja walked up to us then, nudging me in the back, and with a low voice, asked, "Why's Blondie crying?"

I rolled my eyes at her. *Really?*

"My donor has put me up for a god damn auction! That's why you snidey bitch!" Heather's voice was so curt that I was taken aback. She wasn't one for outbursts, and often was the one scolding others for their dire language.

Sophie had been right. She was having a breakdown.

"Hey, Heather, it's going to be okay. Your next master might be better than Alistair."

She continued crying more, her head shaking back and forth. "He won't, he just won't! I know it!"

"What's going on here?" A vampire had approached us, one clearly in charge of the smooth running of the auction. She watched Heather as she cried, showing absolutely no emotion towards it, and then grabbed her head in her hands, and locked her into a steely gaze.

"Stop crying and pull yourself together!" she snapped. And Heather did, almost immediately.

Great. Compulsion: the cure for human emotion.

"Oh, and what do you know, she's all better!" Freyja said to the vampire, a hint of sarcasm in her voice. "It must have been your soothing demeanour."

My mouth opened in shock, and the vampire gave her a stern look before storming away.

"What the *hell* was that?!" I whisper-yelled.

"Just giving my heart-felt thanks to Miss Compassion over there," she said, irritated.

"You aren't exactly known for your compassion, Freyja. We call you B.F for a reason," I said, my eyes narrowed.

"Yeah, yeah, I know. But for fuck's sake, the poor girl's crying her eyes out. A nice word couldn't have hurt."

"Look," I snapped, turning to face her. "Now is *not* the time to start some sort of rebellion. We are already in the king's spotlight, and he's probably watching everything we do. I mean, the reason this whole thing is happening is because of me and you! Snappy, sarcastic comments will get you killed, Freyja. This isn't a joke."

Her blue eyes were wide. She nodded, fear lacing her face. "Fuck, yeah, sorry," she said.

"Why did you look so miserable talking to your friend?" I asked.

Freyja turned to face the girl she had been talking to earlier. "Because she's a real self-obsessed cow, that's why."

"Hmmm, who does that remind me of?" I muttered.

"Oh, come off it," Freyja brushed off my comment, rolling her eyes. "I'm not that bad." She turned to me, and reading my face, added, "Anymore."

Sophie came over to us then, giving me a sideways hug and rubbing Heather's arm, who now just looked a little shell-shocked, rather than sad. She nodded to Frejya, which I accepted to be better than nothing.

"We ready for this?" she asked.

"As ready as we'll ever be," I shrugged.

"Should we all put our hands in the centre and call out 'go team' or something?" Freyja asked, rolling her eyes again.

"Arsehole," Sophie muttered under her breath, but we all heard it, and she knew it.

We were then all addressed by the same vampire who had just compelled Heather and were told the order of the evening. The male auction was to go first, with any clan member who wished for a new male donor to make bids. After that, the female donors would be auctioned off in the same manner.

This was also announced to the vampire crowds who were taking their seats in front of the stage, but with more detail. They were told that anyone could bid, but if anyone who was considered of higher rank also bid, this was them being 'outbidded'. They were told that rank was predetermined and could not be changed or challenged. Also, if two people of equal rank won the auction of a donor, the winner would be determined by a fight, or by one of the bidders conceding.

Once the rules were all confirmed, the men were called forward onto the stage. There was around forty of them, so we knew we were going to be waiting a while, allowing the time to pass with idle chit chat.

When the male auction was over (it had gone rather smoothly, with only one tie, of which had ended with one bidder conceding to the other), the women were brought onto the stage. I was placed between Heather and Freyja, with Sophie behind us. Freyja was first, then me and then Heather, followed by Sophie.

The speaker began the second round of introductions.

"Members of the MacGregor clan, settle once again please for our second and final auction – the women!"

A round of applause erupted in the room, and a chill ran down my spine at the noise.

"As we did with the men, I invite any members who are interested in the women to please come to the stage in an orderly manner to have a closer inspection of these lovely specimens. After that, the bidding shall commence."

The king sat on his throne, looking mighty and statuesque and incredibly entertained. He caught my eye, and I watched as his lips tipped up into what could only be described as a wild smile. My stomach bottomed out, and I caught a glimpse of the red pin on the lapels of his jacket, still as red as it was the first time I'd seen it.

The red primrose.

There was some bustle as members of the Warren arose from their tables to approach the stage. They peered at each of us, some even leaning in towards the neck of the donor they were inspecting, smelling them. A few vampires approached me, smiling into my face in a predatory manner, dipping their noses towards me. I tried to stay as still as possible, my body screaming for me to move away from them.

Angus and Anthony didn't come up to the stage, but instead observed from their tables. The tables were not full, and I noticed that some of the men from backstage were now sitting on them next to what I assumed would be the vampire who bid for them and won.

When all the vampires had sat down, the speaker spoke once again. "Now that you have all had a chance to enjoy some of these lovely women, it is time to commence! We shall start with donor number one, who stands at the end of stage right!"

More applause.

"This lovely donor is called Freyja. She's twenty-six and was a marine biologist in her life outside the Warren".

I turned towards Freyja. *Marine biologist?!* I mouthed, shocked. She just shrugged and replied quietly: "I told you I was smart."

"Her previous master says she is quite the compliant little miss! All her blood specifications can be found on the cards in front of you. Mull these over, and then I shall start the bidding!"

Many paddles were raised when the bidding started, and I swear I saw Freyja's skin pink slightly.

Obviously, as planned, Angus won the bid. He came to the stage to collect her, giving me a tight-lipped smile as he did.

"Oh, hard luck!" said the speaker. "But no one can out rank the prince except for the king! It was always going to be a losing situation for the rest of you! But never mind, there are still many beautiful donors to choose from, so don't be disheartened.

"Next up we have the lovely Ivy! She was a lab scientist before joining the Warren and is twenty-four years of age! Her previous master describes her as...like nothing he had ever imagined. Well, take that as you may, people! Read over her specs and then let's get bidding."

Bidding paddles flew up, but of course, Anthony won.

He walked up to the stage, hands in his pockets, a smirk on his face. The king nodded to the vampire, a knowing look leeching off him.

When Anthony reached me, he held out his hand, which I took, and then he leaned into my neck to kiss me there. He took me to his table, where I sat next to him in the empty chair, before turning to face the stage again. We were close to the front, and I could see the girl's faces clearly.

"Next up we have Heather! A twenty-two-year-old hairstylist out and inside the Warren. Her old master says Heather is rather skilful with her mouth! Wow, ladies and gentlemen, what a treat!"

I watched as Heather's face visibly fell. Her fists balled together, and her jaw clenched.

Fucking hell, Allistair.

Heather was won by a vampire I did not recognise. He seemed nice enough, but Heather was visibly unhappy, and she wasn't even trying to hide it. My mind turned to worry, but I stuffed it deep down. Unfortunately, Heather's wellbeing was something which would have to wait.

Sophie was next, and she looked nervous, her eyes darting everywhere.

"That's James over there, Callum's friend," Anthony whispered in my ear. I looked over at the vampire on a table a few over from us. He seemed normal enough. I could only hope that Callum had a good judgement of character. For a reason I couldn't quite understand, I didn't doubt it.

"Sophie is next!" announced the speaker, still entertaining the crowd. "A lab scientist. Oh wow! We do have some smart women in the line-up tonight!"

His surprise annoyed me. *Misogynistic arsehole.*

"She's twenty-eight and her old master says–" He stopped, looking over his cue card. "Oh, it appears her old master didn't provide us with anything. My apologies."

That actually worked in our favour, because the lack of a 'reference' from Garrett meant not as many vampires put their paddles up for Sophie. And that meant that Callum's friend James won her without any conflict.

She left the stage, and I nodded at her as she passed so that she knew the plan had worked. The slight inclination of her head was her response.

I couldn't believe it. We'd actually managed to pull it off.

I watched on as the auction continued, again without any real mishaps. The rank system seemed to work well, and no one ended up fighting for a donor. Even Baron appeared happy with his choice of donor, who happened to be Freyja's old 'friend'.

When it was over, the spokesman congratulated the audience on a successful evening, and then a toast was made for the king, who was credited for the idea in the first place. It was confirmed by the king himself that this would indeed be an annual event, which caused a buzz in the room. It was also announced that an after event would be held in the canteen, and we were all asked to convene there, leaving the boardroom.

Me and Anthony made our way up, our arms linked just as mine and Angus's had been earlier in the evening.

In the canteen, tables were set for a meal and a dancefloor, just like the summer ball. I excused myself from Anthony, telling him that I needed to use the toilet.

He nodded, before saying, "You look absolutely stunning tonight, by the way."

I smiled back at him, trying to be polite, before leaving out the double doors towards the bathroom. But instead of going into them, I turned down the opposite corridor and rested my back up against the wall, allowing it to take my weight. It was then when I finally allowed myself to breathe. It was over. The people I cared about were safe. It was all going to be okay.

I rested my hands on my thighs, lowering my head below my heart slightly.

It was then when I heard his voice.

"Well, don't you look all weak and vulnerable."

My head whipped up to the sound, and to the left of me, up the corridor, stood Baron. Behind him was clear, and I looked to the right. No one was there either. We were alone.

I stood up to my full height. I didn't want to give the impression that I was as he had described. "Not at all,"

I announced. "Crowds just... overwhelm me now and again."

"Is that right?" he drawled, slinking down the corridor closer to where I was standing. The way be moved was reptilian, the bones under his skin moving like they were all joined together on a string, being dragged along in unison. "Then you'll enjoy it being just me and you then, won't you, Lassie?"

"I do not know you, so I can't say I agree with that statement."

"You'll agree with it, trust me." He was advancing still. But the worst part was that I wasn't retreating. It was like my legs didn't know what to do – like they were not connecting to the rest of me anymore. "You look so scared, Petal," he cooed, licking his lips. His tongue was unusually pale, like the colour of a cyanotic creature.

I was scared. I was really fucking scared.

Could I scream? Or was that not what a compelled donor would do? No, a compelled donor wouldn't really be scared. Not night now. But if he touched me, I vowed to scream. I had to. And knowing Baron's tastes, he probably wouldn't compel me not to.

"I'm not scared. I would just rather I was alone. A *gentleman* would leave me to my own thoughts."

"I've never been much a fan of acting like a gentleman. I think it's much overrated."

"A shame, no, for the people who have to endure your company?" I almost spat the words.

"It's only the pleasure *I gain* from company that I'm bothered about."

I winced.

"Well, I must be heading back. My master will wonder where I am." I turned on my heel, ready to walk away, but Baron had managed to reach me within the second, and had a tight grip on my upper arm, spinning me back towards him.

"I'm surprised he even let you out of his sight in the first place. That's unwise. It makes you bait."

He shoved me then, right in the chest, and I tripped

backwards, landing on my back, my heels providing no balance whatsoever. He then picked me up off the floor using my hair that was still in its ponytail, and I wailed at the pain of it, unable to help myself as my feet hovered off the floor like I was hanging from a noose.

Pain radiated through my scalp as he thrashed me about like a wild cat that was holding its prey in its teeth. His behaviour reminded me of that of an orca, in how they liked to play with their food before they feasted. I was the seal being drowned by the pack.

He clamped his hand over my mouth, quelling any more screams, and forced me back up against the wall with a thump, my head knocking into the plaster, stars swimming in my vision. I tried to kick and even bite, but nothing worked. His body was insanely strong, and I could tell that any efforts from me to try and escape were only causing my body more harm. From the view of an outside, I bet it looked like I wasn't even trying at all.

God, I was going to die.

His head flung back, his neck looking like it had almost detached from the spine with the force of it.

It was then that I believed I genuinely saw the monstrosity of the vampire for the first time. Of course, I saw vampires every day. I'd even seen the physical changes that happened to Angus when his true nature was unleashed. But I'd never seen this. No. This was the nightmare – the vampire you thought of when you imagined death.

Baron's canines elongated to an absurdly long length, his yellowed teeth exposed as his upper lip curled back, his nose scrunching up in an animalistic mask, and his eyes became incredibly dark, as if his iris and his pupil had been having a battle, and the pupil had won out-right. His skin became ruddy, but also almost green in colour, and he looked all but rotten, his flesh being eaten from the inside out.

I tried again to scream with everything I had, but nothing escaped me. Nothing at all.

His bite came next, onto the top of my left breast. The

pain was like nothing I had ever experienced. The physical pain, the emotional pain – it was almost unbearable.

I whimpered, hating myself for being so weak. Hating myself for letting him do this. Hating everything.

I hardly noticed him being ripped from my chest. My body, not having had any of its leg muscles contracted, slumped to the floor.

I blinked, trying to concentrate on the scene around me. Freyja was to my left, her hands over her mouth, her eyes glassy with tears. Anthony was pushing her back, but his eyes were locked on mine in fear. To my right, Angus was holding Baron by the throat... by his teeth.

The prince growled in the most horrific manner. He was pulling at the other vampire's limbs, causing cracking and crunching sounds to engulf the corridor, the smell of decayed skin burning my nostrils.

Baron was yelling.

Angus released his neck and spat what looked like gristle onto the floor next to him. His voice was positively murderous.

"YOU FUCKER! I'M GOING TO RIP YOU LIMB FROM LIMB! YOU FUCKING SON OF A BITCH! HOW DARE YOU EVEN LOOK AT HER! YOU! FUCKING! CUNT!"

He was punching him now, over and over. So much so, that a large snap erupted, and Baron's head went limp.

That was when Anthony intervened, trying to drag Angus away. Angus spun to him, baring his teeth and crouching, his eyes not really seeing what or who was in front of him. Perhaps this was what people meant when they say they 'saw red'.

"Angus, you've broken his neck!" Anthony yelled. "You have to stop! He can't even fight back now!"

Angus blinked several times, and I watched how the hazy rage in front of him seemed to clear somewhat. He turned back to look at the unconscious vampire on the floor, before turning towards me.

He was next to me in a blink.

"Oh my God, *mo lennan.* Are you okay?" He was brushing his bloody hands over my face, and I shrunk away from him.

"What is going on here?!" the king exclaimed, standing now behind Freyja, observing with keen, angry eyes.

Anthony was the one to speak first. "Baron attacked Ivy." He spoke bleakly, like he knew that something bad was still to come.

I really hoped that wasn't the case. I felt awful, and I just really wanted to sleep. I could feel my eyes slowly drooping.

"Someone take her to the hospital! No, no. Not you, Son, for fuck's sake. I need to speak with you. I'll get a guard."

I was suddenly consumed by the feeling of weightlessness, and it allowed me the blessed ability to close my eyes and just sleep.

◆ ◆ ◆

Freyja

Freyja stood just behind Anthony, and watched as her friend, who was pretty much unconscious, got picked up by one of the vampire guards and taken to the hospital.

She wanted to go with her. She wanted to make sure that she was okay. Because, although she would never ever say it to her face, Ivy *was* Freyja's friend, and in some odd way, Freyja had come to love her dearly.

Again, she would NEVER tell her that.

But no matter how much she protested, they wouldn't let her go with her, so she just stood there, staring at the pool of Ivy's blood next to the wall, and the limp and lifeless body of Baron behind it.

"Son, can you please tell me what the living *fuck* is going on?"

Angus stood from his crouching position next to Ivy's blood and wiped his mouth with the back of his hand. Some of Baron's blood managed to get onto the cuff of his white dress shirt, and it stood out in stark contrast. He looked a little bit like James Bond – handsome and surrounded by chaos.

"I saw Baron attacking a donor. So I intervened." His face was stony and expressionless. It was haunting next to the chaotic scene which surrounded them. You could have heard a pin drop.

"I can see that. But *what* could have possibly occurred for you to intervene in such a manner?!" The king's voice boomed, and Freyja shrunk away from it slightly, towards Anthony. The vampire placed his hand on her back in comfort, his cool palm felt through the satin of her dress. Perhaps if they were not where they were – and not having to endure the traumatic event that they were currently having to – Freyja might have even thought it pleasant.

"I was protecting my friend's honour," Angus pointed towards Anthony, shrugging.

The king's mouth twisted in distrust. "Is that right, Anthony?" he asked.

"It could be," Anthony said.

The king was not satisfied with that answer. Not at all.

"Angus, there is nothing I can imagine that could have gone on in this corridor tonight which could condone what you have done to a fellow clan member. Friend or not, Anthony can fight his own battles. I know for a fact he is brilliant at boxing. I'm sure something like this could have easily been addressed in the ring. You reaction simply doesn't align with this. Unless..." the king paused, eyeing Anthony. "He is perhaps more than a friend."

Freyja watched Angus stiffen, a look passing between himself and Anthony that she couldn't read.

"He's a fucking sadist!" Angus snarled, flying his hands in the air. A drop of blood flung in Freyja's direction and landed on her face. Any other time and she would have kicked up a real fuss, but she couldn't move. She was stock still. She hardly felt Anthony's fingertip brush against her cheek to remove it. "How can *we* as a clan condone *his* behaviour? Fucking raping scared donors, attacking them. He's a disgrace to the MacGregor name! I demand a trial!"

"A *what?*" the king asked.

Freyja didn't know what he was on about either.

"A trial. In the boardroom. It can be used for that, no?"

The king was frowning but listening intently. "You wish to put Baron to trial over... what exactly?"

"Sexually assaulting and raping donors," Angus stated bluntly.

The king's eyebrows raised into his salt and pepper hairline. It was silent in the corridor, and all Freyja could hear was her breathing and her pulse in her ears.

"You are aware that this is unprecedented? Nothing of the sort has ever come to notion in my realm," he said, reaching up to touch the red pin on his jacket.

Angus nodded that he knew.

The king didn't reply instantly, and instead, he walked over to where Baron lay, nudging his limp hand with the toe of his shoe. He then crouched, dipping his finger into Ivy's blood, and brought it to his mouth. If Freyja hadn't known how the prince felt about her friend, she wouldn't have noticed the pain on his face when he watched his father do it.

"Very well, Son," the king said resolutely, standing back to his full height. "A trial it shall be. But *you too* will be on trial. If Baron is deemed to be as you say, he shall be sentenced to execution, but if he is not, it would appear your attack on him was unwarranted, and it will in fact be *you* who will be sentenced to death."

The air was heavy.

Nobody spoke for what felt like eons.

"As you wish, Your Majesty," Angus said finally, bowing his head slightly.

Freyja looked up to Anthony who had only fear etched into the lines of his face.

Her eyes asked, 'W*hat's happening?*'
And his replied, 'S*omething terrible.*'

CHAPTER 24

Premature Celebrations

Angus

Angus didn't have the heart to tell Ivy what he had done, and what it had meant. Freyja had been the one to tell her. He didn't know how she had reacted. He hadn't seen her since. He'd been selfish, just like he had been with Sorcha all those years ago. He had thought he had been putting Ivy first, but if he really had been, he wouldn't have attacked Baron like that.

Although it wasn't illegal, it wasn't warranted to attack another clan member without cause, and especially in such a brutal way. Baron would recover, maybe only with the odd scar – Angus hadn't ripped out his heart – but by attacking him so brutally, a line had been crossed. And now he had to face the consequences of his actions. And those consequences could easily put Ivy in danger.

He was a complete and utter shite bag, and he knew it. And he had somehow managed to wrangle himself into a trial – a trial which would likely not go in his favour. His father finally had the opportunity to rid himself of his main and only real competition for the throne. Angus knew him well enough, and knew enough about his loyalties (or the lack of them), to know that he would delight in taking Angus out of the equation. After all, he had been given the opportunity on a gleaming, spotless, silver platter. In fact, Angus had been the one to hand it to him himself, hand clad with a butler's glove, bow in tow.

Ivy was about to have his heart, figuratively and literally.

He walked down to the long corridors and down the steps towards the boardroom. It had been two days since it had all happened, and Angus could still smell vampire blood in his nose. As he entered, the members of the council all locked eyes on him. Garrett looked smug, and he wanted to pulverise his face, just as he had done Baron. Fraser nodded at him, bored as always.

A 'jury' was on the right, to his father's left. They were a random mixture of vampires from all aspects of the Warren, and he recognised none of them personally. He assumed they were also not friendly with Baron, although he wouldn't put it past Garrett – or his father for that matter – to make the jury biased against him.

"Nice of you to make it," Garrett sneered.

"Garrett." Angus nodded. "Always a pleasure." Sarcasm dripped off his tongue like Baron's stale blood.

He took his seat in the centre of the Boardroom, opposite Baron who looked... a little worse for wear. Perhaps his attack was a little more aggressive than he remembered.

Nay bother. You deserved it, you bastard.

As he sat there, he listened around him, and a fluttering heart caught his attention. He would recognise that rhythm anywhere. He looked upwards towards the sound, and there were her dark eyes, sitting in a frightened face, her hair flowing in a thick mass around her.

Ivy.

Wait, what the fuck is she doing here? She couldn't be here when – *if* – he was executed.

He was about to say something, but then she shook her head at him. Her lips were moving, and he watched carefully, not wanting to miss anything she was saying.

Don't make a scene. I'm staying, and I love you.

Anthony was sitting next to her, and he nodded once. It was like he was saying, 'd*on't worry, I've got your back'*.

Although so much had happened between him and Anthony, Angus knew that the man was loyal to him. It was just the way things were. Some things couldn't be changed.

It was in their blood.

Didn't mean he wanted his girl to be with him, though.

He calmed himself, knowing that whatever happened, someone, even if it was Anthony, would look after her. At least Anthony cared about her, he knew that, even if it did hurt. But he had to push his ego down, and put her first, and Anthony caring for her was much better for her than if he didn't care at all.

"We are here for the trial of Baron MacIver, and Angus MacGregor," announced the king, standing from his throne. Angus shivered at the use of his surname. It was, after all, the thing which had caused all the trouble in the first place. All the way back to the seventeenth century.

"After tonight, one of these two clan members will be executed for their crimes. It is up to the jury to decide who this will be. You must discern, jury, whether the attack on clan member MacIver was warranted due to his sadistic tendencies and accused sexual harassment and rape of donors, or whether these allegations are false, and that the attack was illegal."

There was no fucking justice in the world if Baron was able to get away with what he had done, Angus thought.

Angus was first told to stand and give his recollection of the evening, up to the point when he attacked Baron. He spoke of what he had seen, and how Ivy was being held by her hair, up against the wall, terrified. He spoke of the pleasure on Baron's face. To think of it was nauseating, and he would give his heart to never have to see his brunette like that ever again.

Baron spoke next, speaking of how he had found Ivy in the corridor looking ill and had asked her if she had needed assistance. He said she had refused aggressively, and that he had insisted on helping but that this had ended up in a tryst.

That fucker.

Angus vowed that he would kill Baron today, regardless of the outcome of the trial.

Angus then spoke again, this time of Baron's character. He spoke of how rumours were circulating about Baron's particular tastes, when Garrett interrupted him.

"But you haven't ever seen these tastes with you own eyes, have you, Prince?"

"I saw then two nights ago, in that corridor," Angus snarled, all but ready to snap another neck.

"Yes, as you say. But *before* that? Any witnesses to this?"

"Not me personally," he replied. "But his old donor has a lot to say about it, I'm sure."

Baron visibly stiffened in his chair and Angus eyed him like prey.

"Humans are poor eyewitnesses. They can be so readily manipulated, their brains like a sieve," Garrett told the jury.

"Not if you compel her to tell the truth. Or remove the compulsion she has which is linked to Baron," Angus said. He could feel Ivy tense in the crowd.

Trust me, mo leannan.

"I think this is where we should probably call upon this donor, Garrett, wouldn't you say?" Garrett nodded reluctantly at the king's request. "Remove any compulsion from her specific to her relationship with Baron, if you please." He snapped his fingers.

Freyja came from her seat – Angus hadn't noticed her before – and was told that she must tell the truth with regards to questions about her previous master. Her compulsion regarding Baron was removed. Not that it needed to be, but they didn't know that.

She sat on an empty seat, away from Baron.

"What is your name?" asked Garrett.

"Jane Prenton. But I'm known in the Warren as Freyja."

Interesting.

"And how long have you been this clansman's donor, prior to the auction two days ago?"

"Five years."

"And how did he treat you?"

Freyja jolted visibly.

She spoke of his abuse with a calm and monotone voice, staring off into the distance, unable to give anything her true attention. She spoke of countless rapes, attacks, physical and emotional abuse. How he enjoyed her physical and emotional pain and turmoil. She spoke of how he liked to see her in such a way and how the thought of him near her made her skin crawl. She said, if she could have, she would have killed him to rid herself of him, or even killed herself. But she said something had stopped her.

She was very smart with her wording, as to not give herself away, and Angus was entirely impressed at her strength and resilience. Ivy seemed to surround herself with strong women, and that made him feel slightly better about potentially having to leave her.

Freyja was dismissed, and to Angus's surprise, Ivy was brought to the 'stand' in the seat Freyja had just occupied. Garrett again 'compelled' her to tell the truth.

"What is your name?" Garrett asked again, all about protocol.

"Ivy Crest."

Crest? Yes, he remembered that now. He'd read it in her file all those months ago.

"And can you please describe, in your own words, what occurred between you and Clansman MacIver two nights ago?"

Ivy told her truth, and Garrett nodded, dismissing her. Baron was becoming visibly agitated, shuffling in his chair like a human. He was scared, and Angus knew it.

It then went on to some character witnesses for Baron, who all obviously sang his praises, claiming him to be a caring, moral and valuable member of the clan. But after the indisputable account from the 'compelled' humans, they didn't really stand, and everyone in the room knew it.

Baron was on thin ice.

The jury was left to deliberate, and the prince and Baron

were taken to separate rooms, unable to speak to anyone. When the jury was done, they were called back through, taking their designated seats once more. The king sat on his throne looking like a puppeteer, and Angus's heart dropped. One of the jury members stood, and the verdict was called in relation to Baron.

The words 'guilty' rang in the room, and Angus had to check that he had heard it right. He looked up to Ivy, and her sat with a grin on her face, and salty tears running down her cheeks.

So he hadn't misheard then? He was going to live? Then why did his father look the way he did?

Angus buried his scepticism and instead looked directly at Baron, smiling right at him, knowing he'd won, and knowing justice had been served.

Baron was dragged to the centre of the board room on his knees, Garrett holding him by one arm, and Fraser on the other.

The king rose from his throne, and advanced towards him with regal grace.

"Baron, you have disappointed me greatly." And then he turned to the rest of the room. "Remember this day, as this is the first day in Warren history that a vampire had been seen as guilty for a crime, and the first day in which one of our own will be executed."

He then turned back to Baron, placing a hand on his shoulder. "May your immortal soul find peace."

"Please, Your Highness, don't–"

But Baron was unable to finish his final words, as the king had plunged his first into the vampire's chest, and on its return out of the cavity, held his heart.

The heartless vampire collapsed forwards, no longer being supported by Garrett or Fraser, his blood spilling onto the white floor.

Angus felt relief. He stood from his chair, and looked up at the woman he loved, beaming.

That was until something sharp stung his neck. He spun towards the stimulus with wide eyes.

What the fuck was that?!

And then his head felt woozy – a feeling he had not felt in his vampire life.

And he collapsed.

◆ ◆ ◆

Ivy

Angus had been injected with something – I had seen it. Some sort of blue liquid. It was a colour I recognised, but didn't know why.

The room erupted, and all members were asked to leave.

"Anthony, what's happening?" I asked, my voice laced with worry.

"I don't know," he admitted.

Anthony held my hand, and we walked down to where Angus was now lying on the floor. I wanted so desperately to run to him – to ask him if he was okay – but that wouldn't have been appropriate, so, although it killed me, I stayed tight to Anthony's side.

Freyja flanked me.

"What was that? Why is he passed out? What did you do?" Anthony asked the king. His voice was a little irate. I was surprised considering that Anthony and Angus's relationship seemed strained at the best of times.

"I've injected our prince with a little bit of our compliance serum," the king said, wiping his hands with a white cloth to remove the blood which stained them.

"Compliance serum?" I asked. I couldn't help it. I needed to know what was going on.

"Don't you recognise the colour of the liquid, Little Donor?" the king asked. He looked so smug, his face pleased with a job well done.

My eyes focused on the remanence of the fluorescent blue in the vial that had one been in the hands of the king, but was now on the floor of the boardroom, cracked slightly. And then my mind made the connection. It brought a picture into my mind's eye, my hand in view as I pipetted the liquid in vials, as I purified it, as I *made it*.

It was the serum we were testing in the labs.

Oh my God.

The king's face took on a delight that was unmatched, as if he has finally been able to reveal his master plan, and watch his victims realise they had lost.

I could feel Anthony's eyes on mine as my face visibly fell.

"I feel I cannot trust him; he seems…off to me." The king's eyes lingered on me for a little too long as he spoke, and I turned my eyes away from his in what I hoped he thought was modesty.

"What does that mean?" Antony pressed.

"Let's just say he'll be a little bit more inclined to listen to his old man now he's had it," the king smiled cruelly.

"How long does it last?" Anthony, again.

"Indefinitely," he replied, turning his back to us as he did.

Angus began to stir, and his eyes flung open.

Relief washed over me.

Oh thank God, he's okay.

He jumped up to his feet, like a cat, and me and Freyja stepped back in surprise. Even Anthony edged away from him a little.

The king spun around, watching his son. "Ahh, lovely! What a response! To be honest, we haven't properly tested it on vampire DNA. I wasn't entirely sure he was going to wake up." His words were so nonchalant, not as if he were speaking of possibly killing his own son.

He walked up to Angus and locked his gaze. I recognised the change in the king's eyes – how they somehow became brighter and more concentrated. I'd recognise that change anywhere. The king was preparing himself to compel Angus.

"Now, I want the old Angus back, you understand? The one who was a little mean, a little vicious, but not with my clansmen. Kill another donor for all I care, but no more inter-vampiric violence where it is not deemed suitable. A ripper is better than a rebel. I see you want a rebellion. I see you want to give donors more control. I've seen the subtle change in your morals and your ethics. You want to make this a vampire and human haven. It isn't going to happen. Donors are there for sustenance. They aren't there to provide emotional value. They are designed for our pleasure. Their pleasure is without consequence. You'll stop this madness and sympathy for the humans, and whatever you feel for her," the king nodded to me, "you'll stop. *Snap out of it!*"

Angus blinked several times, as if he was allowing the words to sink in properly. He then nodded once, before turning to look at me, his eyes boring into mine.

"Do you always stare this much, Donor?" he snapped. I shook my head, silent. "Then I suggest you don't start. It's highly unattractive, and I wouldn't want you to ruin that face of yours." He grabbed me by the chin, roughly, tilting it to each side, inspecting. "Hmm, you'll do." And then his eyes widened, and he snapped his fingers in front of us. "Oh no! I got it wrong! I didn't want you anymore, did I?" he laughed, right in my face. He pointed at Freyja. "It's her I chose." He flicked his eyes between us both, frowning, and something flashed in his eyes, but then it went.

I watched him, shocked. His eyes weren't right, and although it *was* him, it didn't *look* like him. And then it hit me; this wasn't the Angus I knew, this was the Angus that the king *wanted* him to be.

And that meant that *this* Angus didn't love me.

And that meant that this Angus was dangerous.

For updates, including the release of book two in the Warren Vampire Series, sign up to email updates on my website : www.daisyveden.com or follow me on Instagram @daisy.v.eden

ACKNOWLEDGEMENTS

I wish to thank my family for being so supportive during this venture of mine. Thanks to my sister, who's talent always shocks and surprises me, thanks to my mum for her support and emotional cheerleading, and thanks to my dad for his subtle love and knowledge of Scottish slang. Without you, the dialogue just wouldn't have been authentic.

I would also like to thank my partner. You are my favourite person, and I know for a fact that I wouldn't be where I am today without you.

Thanks to Charlie and Loz, who this is also dedicated to. You don't know it, but your early support for this is one of the main reasons this is out there for other people to read. I hope you enjoy reading it for a second time. Things are a little different... I hope you don't mind.

To Holly, for being the best work colleague I could have asked for. Thanks for entertaining me on boring days with chats about books. I miss working with you. And thanks for hyping this one up. You're the best.

Sophie, thank you for not kicking me out of your life even though you are the most introverted person I know. I love you, friend.

Claire, thank you for your undying love for books. Our daily chats make mundane life more interesting, and you inspire me to be more fantastical!

Thank you to Jonathan. If you hadn't spoken to me about how there is 'nothing to lose', this never would have happened.

And finally, thank you, reader, for purchasing this book. I hope that you loved reading it as much as I enjoyed writing it.

Love, Daisy.

THE WARREN VAMPIRES SERIES

The Primrose That Poisoned Ivy

The Hidden Thistle Amongst Thornes

The next installment of Ivy and Angus's story. Release TBC

Printed in Great Britain
by Amazon